Readers and Reviewers Cherish *Kasey Michaels'* Dazzling Stories of Love

The Untamed

"Ms. Michaels writes with humor and poignancy in this spin-off of *The Homecoming*. . . . Another keeper from this heartwarming author."

—Joan Hammond, *Romantic Times*

The Homecoming

"A tale of love and passion . . . A fast-paced plot and the history of the Lenape tribe, told with poignancy and sensitivity . . . splendid and worth the read."

—*Rendezvous*

"Intriguing . . . Michaels provides vivid description and authentic historical detail . . . This colonial romance with a dash of English elegance and a touch of Irish sass is an uncommon mix. . . ."

—*Library Journal*

"Kasey Michaels' obvious adoration for Pennsylvania's history glows within the pages of *The Homecoming*. Readers will be fascinated by the colorful details, marvelous characters, and the exciting adventure and passion. . . ."

—Kathe Robin, *Romantic Times*

The Passion of an Angel

"This utterly charming, exhilarating romance is just what Kasey Michaels' fans adore from this master of the Regency romance. *The Passion of an Angel* is brimming over with lush, colorful detail and intelligent banter. Sit back, relax, and indulge yourself in this love-and-laughter gem."

—Kathe Robin, *Romantic Times*

"Tantalizing, delightful, and entertaining. . . . *The Passion of an Angel* keeps the audience on their toes . . . a page turner—I couldn't put it down."

—*Rendezvous*

The Secrets of the Heart

A *Publishers Weekly* Romance Pick of the Year

"Refreshing . . . a Regency romp with a writing style, voice and sense of humor perfectly suited to the era and the genre. . . . Michaels delivers what promises to be one of the best-loved books of the year."

—*Publishers Weekly*

The Illusions of Love

"*The Illusions of Love* is a fantastic Regency romance that only someone of the caliber of Kasey Michaels could have written. . . . Regency romance fans will love this novel."

—Harriet Klausner, *Affaire de Coeur*

A Masquerade in the Moonlight

"A *Masquerade in the Moonlight* is what Kasey Michaels fans have come to expect from a master storyteller. She doesn't disappoint as she leads you down a winding path of intrigue, danger, and dark passion. . . ."

—Kathe Robin, *Romantic Times*

The Bride of the Unicorn

"With great skill and a master's touch, Kasey Michaels crafts a mesmerizing love story filled with passion and suspense . . . a Cinderella tale with Kasey Michaels' unique touch—a not-to-be-missed romance."

—Kathe Robin, *Romantic Times*

The Legacy of the Rose

". . . will move you to tears and to joy. . . . It's heady and gutsy and altogether wonderful."

—Catherine Coulter

Books by Kasey Michaels

The Passion of an Angel
The Secrets of the Heart
The Illusions of Love
A Masquerade in the Moonlight
The Bride of the Unicorn
The Legacy of the Rose
The Homecoming
The Untamed
The Promise

Published by POCKET BOOKS

Kasey Michaels

The Promise

POCKET BOOKS
New York London Toronto Sydney Tokyo Singapore

This book is a work of fiction. Names, characters, places and incidents are products of the author's imagination or are used fictitiously. Any resemblance to actual events or locales or persons, living or dead, is entirely coincidental.

An *Original* Publication of POCKET BOOKS

A Pocket Star Book published by
POCKET BOOKS, a division of Simon & Schuster Inc.
1230 Avenue of the Americas, New York, NY 10020

ISBN: 0-671-50114-3

First Pocket Books printing June 1997

10 9 8 7 6 5 4 3 2 1

POCKET STAR BOOKS and colophon are registered trademarks of Simon & Schuster Inc.

Front cover illustration by Lina Levy

Printed in the U.S.A.

To my daughter Megan,
who insisted.
Happy now?
I love you, sweetheart.

Long ago, the ancient Lenape
came to the evergreen land . . .

The Wallam Olum, (Red Record)
Oral history of the Lenni Lenape

prologue
1793

the promise

Even God cannot change the past.

AGATHON

Thus I live in the world rather as a spectator of mankind than as one of the species.

JOSEPH ADDISON

prologue

When Daniel Cassidy Crown entered a ballroom, invariably conversation stopped then began again quickly, almost nervously, as he stood in the doorway and employed that easy smile which only rarely reached his heavy-lidded, stormswept dark eyes.

He was tall, Daniel Crown was, taller than most, with broad shoulders and a narrow waist above long, straight legs. And he was dark. Dark eyes, dark hair, dark past. Mysteriously dark. Arrogantly dark. Intriguingly dark. And handsome as sin. A living, breathing invitation to sin, that was Daniel Crown. A good-looking, marvelously titillating, mouth-watering, definitely dangerous invitation to sin.

All sorts of sin.

Females, young impressionable debutantes as well as dashing matrons, believed there was a secret torment burning in his soul and longed to explore the depths of his unknown passions. To a woman, they all ached to be that one very special woman who might someday unleash those passions, touch his heart.

Men, especially young, rather jealous men, were intrigued in a much different way than their female counterparts. They sensed the leashed power in Daniel Crown, the darkness in him, and feared his intensity even as they envied his rapier wit, his physical abilities, his cool self-assurance. They courted him because it would be fruitless to oppose him. They called him their friend, yet, as with the women of London, they were aware that they did not really know him.

No one dared.

It wasn't enough to show the world a handsome appearance, a rapier wit, a hint of mystery, a dollop of hidden sadness; and Daniel Crown—who was totally unaware of his effect on his fellow creatures—had not consciously done anything to create his quite provocative reputation among the members of the *ton.* Not consciously. However, one vision of his banked fires bursting into flame early in his first season, when a supercilious young leader of society dared to insult Daniel's "heathen" Lenni Lenape father and was promptly knocked down and challenged to a duel, had proved to be enough to keep a smart enemy well hidden behind a smiling face.

For society had learned quickly that there was no winning against Daniel Crown. There was no victory to be found in verbal sparring, no thrill in whispered insults, no reward in sly jokes about the dark, savage Crown, the half-breed, adopted son of the marquess of Playden. No, there was only the fear of discovery, and swift, total annihilation—all of which were feared even more than an almost sure death on the dueling ground.

After the disgrace and removal of that one supposedly all-powerful enemy three years ago, there were none in the *ton* who had ever again openly risked a similar fate. After all, hadn't Addison Bainbridge's disgrace been lesson enough for them? And where was Bainbridge, society's once acknowledged leader, now? In America, that's where—probably still figuratively nursing his wounds and wondering what had happened to him.

Yes, it was much easier, and safer, to be Daniel Crown's friend. A man could enjoy him as they played at cards, rode hell-bent for leather across country, drank themselves beneath the table in low dives, or talked the night away, discussing the merits of a good wine, a loose woman, or the poetry of John Milton.

So that was Daniel Crown. Adopted half-breed son of a marquess. Privy to one of the finest fortunes in all England. Handsome. Intelligent. Boon companion. Welcomed into society. The envy of many, the dream of more. All in all, Daniel Crown's reputation, his physical perfection, his connection to the marquess of Playden, would seem enough to make any young man happy.

All of which did nothing to explain his dark scowl when his younger adoptive brother, Michael Crown, ran him down in the card room of Lady Cornwallis's town house, pulling on his arm, begging him for a few minutes alone.

Daniel gently removed the young man's hands from his finely tailored sky blue jacket. "There you go again, Michael, creasing my satins with your clutching paws. And why so serious? What is it?" he then asked as he steered the younger man out onto the balcony, away from interested ears, for he had a fairly good idea what was bothering his brother. "You haven't outrun your allowance, have you?"

Michael colored beneath his liberally powdered hair. "Don't tease, brother. I've never been so foolish, and you well know it. Leave that to our idiot sibling, Joseph, who has discovered the myriad joys and pitfalls of cockfighting this past week. He'll be rusticating well before June, hiding from duns back in Sussex, if he keeps it up. No, this is not about me. This is about *you.* Mama tells me you're sailing to America next week on one of Uncle Dominick's ships. Why? And why now, before the season is even officially underway? Say it isn't so, Daniel!

And, if it is—say I can go with you. Mama will listen to you. She always does."

Daniel looked at his brother, younger than he by less than two years, but so very much younger in experience. Michael had been little more than a baby when Brighid and Philip Crown had packed up and left New Eden, departing from their sprawling estate of Enolowin in the Pennsylvania colony before the rebellion could reach them, returning to the safety of Playden Court and to the title of marquess that awaited Philip upon the death of his miserable, unloved, and unloving father.

"How old were you, Michael, when we left New Eden? Not quite six?" Daniel asked now, keeping his hand on the younger man's elbow as they went down the steps and into Lady Cornwallis's garden. "What do you remember of Enolowin?"

"Less than I should, I imagine," Michael said, frowning. "I remember a large stone house, a multitude of tall trees, and an old Indian woman who talked gibberish as she bounced me on her knee—God, she didn't have any teeth, did she? And there was a man. Another Indian. Old and gray. Lokwelend, wasn't it? But he was yours, as I recall, not mine. Joseph remembers even less. I asked him one time, and all he could tell me about was the trip home and that storm we encountered. Poor Mama, being pregnant with Johanna and all. It wasn't a good crossing. I suppose you remember more? Tell me."

Daniel sighed, shaking his head. How could he explain to Michael, explain what even he did not understand? Daniel's memories of Enolowin were still clear, etched into his brain. He remembered every room of that wonderful house, every path he had walked with the old Lenape, Lokwelend, the man he had called Grandfather. And yet, there were times when he felt as if he had forgotten everything of real importance.

He looked at his brother. "You have no real urge to return then, do you, halfling?"

Michael colored again. "Don't call me that, Daniel.

I'm not that much younger than you, for all you've been walking around looking as if you wear the worries of the world on your shoulders these past few years, ever since you reached your majority, now that I think on it. And, no, I'll admit that I see no reason to visit the place, except to accompany you. America's probably going to side with the French in this mess, you know. Rebels are rebels, I suppose. And I also suppose they both think they have good reasons for what they did, what they're doing. But that don't make me like them any the better. You'd best be careful, brother. What's to say the Americans won't set up their own guillotine and slice off the heads of any Indians they might find wandering about."

"They taught you this drivel at school, Michael? Now, why do I doubt that?" Daniel stopped on the path and looked up into the night sky. Lokwelend had taught him about the sky, the clouds, the positions of the stars. "I suggest a closed carriage if you're doing any more carousing after this deadly dull party. We'll have rain before morning."

"Devil take the weather! And devil take all this talk about you leaving us. You know that Mama has been crying most of the day, don't you—and Papa was locked in his study when I left, fiddling with estate work, he says, but I know better. I believe neither of them thinks we'll ever see you again." He turned and grabbed onto Daniel's sleeve with both hands. "Don't go, Daniel, please. There's nothing for you there. We're your family. We've always been your family. You're our brother in everything but blood."

"I'm sorry, Michael. I really am. But I have to do this." Daniel stepped back and, with a wave of his arm, indicted all of London. "This is a vacuum, Michael. I cannot exist here. I can't *breathe* here. Powdered, bewigged, rigged out in satins and jewels. Spending the day waiting for the evening and the evening searching for amusement. Playden Court is yours, Michael, not mine. Enolowin could be mine. Papa has made me a bargain. If

I live there for a year, work the land, the estate is mine. If I live out that year and want to come back to England, he'll sell Enolowin to Uncle Dominick and use the proceeds to buy me my own land in Sussex. I am a Crown by name, little brother, not by birth. I am not entitled to take anything from you and Joseph and Johanna. I need to make my own way."

And I need to know who I am. What I am. What I will become. But he did not say these words, for Michael couldn't understand. Not when he himself did not understand. All Daniel knew was that he was not happy. He wasn't settled. He didn't belong; trapped in England, trapped inside his stylishly clad half-breed body whose mind told him he was a civilized white man—but whose tortured soul cried out for the more earthy yet mystical life of the Lenni Lenape. His father's people.

"I've got to go, Michael," he said at last, turning back toward the well-lit house and the sound of violin music being sawed out by an energetic if not talented lot of musicians. "If you can risk a bit of poetic nonsense—I believe I have to find out who I am."

"But you'll come back to us," Michael pleaded. "You *will* come back to us, Daniel."

Daniel smiled, giving his brother's shoulders a quick squeeze. "Of course I'll visit, Daniel. I'm not going out of your life forever."

"No? Then where *do* you think you're going?"

The smile that had not quite reached Daniel's eyes slipped away, to be replaced by the dark look that obscured his deep-running emotions. "I don't know, Michael. Could I possibly be going home?"

book one

the paradox

How happy those whose walls already rise.

VIRGIL

Bliss was it in that dawn to be alive,
But to be young was very heaven!

WILLIAM WORDSWORTH

chapter one

New Eden, Commonwealth of Pennsylvania, U.S.A., 1793

There was a smell to late spring that was unequaled by any other season. The smell of rich, turned fields; the soft breeze that carried the perfume of wildflowers. The clean fragrance of growing things. And in the morning, with the dew still wet on the grass—ah, then it was most wonderful of all!

Especially when one was racing that summer breeze; cutting through it on the strong back of Freedom's Lady, Brianna Cassidy Crown's huge bay mare. The horse's long mane and tail both flew in that part natural, part speed-generated breeze, as did Brianna Crown's own long chestnut curls. Riding with her knees lightly controlling, her hands loose, yet steady on the reins, her head bowed low over the mare's ears, Brianna watched the ground flying by beneath her, yet kept one emerald green eye on the horizon that rapidly approached, the fence that would fall away beneath Freedom's Lady's hooves and take them both onto Enolowin land.

Her land. Or so she had always seen it. Until last night.

Brianna's hands tightened on the reins as she glowered into the distance, remembering her father's words of the previous evening, when he had taken her into his private study to "discuss" something with her.

She dreaded these "discussions," for they never boded well for her. *Lectures* was a better word for those uncomfortable interviews during which her papa would talk and she would listen. Quietly. Respectfully. Agreeably. And then escape the study to go do exactly what she pleased!

Her papa knew this, knew he was talking to a pleasant, smiling young woman whose iron will, if not exceeding that of her mother's, certainly matched it. But they both kept up the pretense, both played the small game that seemed to satisfy her mother, who had long ago learned that attempting to personally reason with Brianna was about as fruitful an exercise as trying to hold back the wind.

But her mama would order a "conference," and her papa would obey. Brianna would trail into the study, dutifully listen to every word, every suggestion, every warning—and everyone would be happy again.

Her older brothers, all four of them, had seen their own share of "discussions" in their youth but, Brianna was sure, if they had counted them all up and totaled them, they would not come within a mile of the talks she had been forced to endure. Not even if her sister Felicia's trips to Papa's study were added into the figure.

Of course, Felicia had been a dream of a child; quiet, biddable, never a bother—and since she was long married and living in Virginia with her gentleman farmer husband, that left only Brianna to suffer the tender mercies of her mother's notion of the correct behavior of a proper young lady.

Being the youngest of a family was simply not fair, that's what it was, Brianna had long since decided. And, with all four of her brothers gone to sea for the summer, and Felicia nowhere to be found, her parents seemed to have nothing better to do with their time than to fill it by doing their best to bring their youngest, their *baby,* up to snuff.

Which explained Brianna's most recent trip to Dominick Crown's oak-lined study. Which explained his lecture on the folly of wearing her brother's cast-off breeches and riding Freedom's Lady neck-or-nothing all over the countryside. Which explained why she had been told, in no uncertain terms, that—now that her cousin Daniel Cassidy Crown was about to arrive to tend to the Enolowin estate—she was no longer to race helter-skelter all over the fallow fields as if that land were her own property.

Which, alas, also explained why Brianna Crown, after listening to this latest lecture and agreeing with her papa's every word, was out and about early, clad in her brother Rory's old white shirt and fawn breeches, riding astride Freedom's Lady as the mare took the five-bar fence with ease and began racing across the newly planted fields on her way to visit Winifred and Otto Bing, who were caretakers for the long-abandoned property.

The chimneys of Enolowin appeared above the treetops as she slowed Freedom's Lady to a walk before entering the tree line that separated the fields from the more private grounds, and she smiled as she caught the aroma of baking bread. Winifred always baked on a Friday. She did her wash on Monday, her ironing on Tuesday, her cleaning on the following days—Wednesday "up" and Thursday "down"—and her baking on Friday. Potato bread. Small white loaves stuffed with raisins or currants. Lovely fat buns drizzled with sweet white icing. And, if Brianna was very lucky, a wet-bottomed shoofly pie with buttery crumbs on top for her very own.

Her mouth already watering, for she had run off before breakfast, before her mother could espy her in Rory's breeches and send her back to her room to change, Brianna guided Freedom's Lady through the stand of trees and out onto the sweeping, well-scythed lawns—to see three smart traveling coaches lined up in the circular drive.

"Well, would you look at that mass of grandeur, Lady," she muttered under her breath as her heart sank to her toes, knowing that her cousin had arrived. And he had arrived in some style, she was forced to acknowledge, watching as a half-dozen servants she didn't recognize busied themselves unloading the three coaches and carrying box after box inside the house. "So, he's here. Cousin Daniel. Sweet Heaven protect us, Lady. I'll wager he wears red-heeled shoes . . . and minces."

Deciding to investigate, and uncaring that her mother would be mortified to see her daughter approaching Enolowin looking more like a stable boy than a well-bred young lady of means, Brianna urged her mount forward, riding straight up the drive, fully intending to be polite, and welcoming—and then wheedle permission to ride Enolowin's fields out of the English dandy before he could summon up a way to deny her.

She had kicked her feet free of the stirrups and was just levering her right leg over Lady's head—for she dismounted Lenape style, gracefully jumping to the ground—when a pure white stallion came galloping around the corner of the house.

After that, things happened quickly. Freedom's Lady, always an amorous sort, lifted her head, aware of the stallion's presence, and seemingly forgetful of her mistress's momentarily precarious presence on her back. The stallion was pulled to a plunging, dancing halt by its rider. Freedom's Lady swiveled in place, then lifted her front legs and pawed at the air.

And Brianna Cassidy Crown, who above all things prided herself on her horsemanship, landed bottom down in the gravel drive, her legs sprawled out in front of her and her wind gone, knocked straight out of her. She sat there, dazed.

"You—boy! Are you all right?"

The voice was deep, and cultured, and definitely British. And definitely laced with humor at Brianna's expense. And, if she could only catch her breath—and stop those silly blue stars from circling around her head—she'd give the man a piece of her mind! "Boy," indeed! It was one thing that the rider had no brains. Did the man also have no eyes in his head?

But all she could do was sit there, feeling foolish, trying to make her mind order her body to *breathe,* for heaven's sake, and stare up at the man who, she decided with a fatalistic sinking of her heart, just had to be her adopted cousin.

Lord, but he was a handsome specimen! Tall—she could see this clearly, as he had dismounted to stand in front of her—with thick black hair casually tied back at his nape, a pair of devil dark eyes, and a distinctive, hawkish face that shone with intelligence and humor. The humor, of course, was all directed at her and her predicament, a circumstance that precluded Brianna from lingering long on her cousin's attributes and urged her to center on the fact that she didn't want the man here, probably would not like him very much, and wished he would go away and leave her alone to suffocate.

"Good God, you're no boy, are you?" Daniel Cassidy Crown exclaimed, bending over and putting out a hand to her, offering his assistance. "Here, let me haul you up on your feet. Your breath will come back soon enough. Don't fight it."

"I'm . . . not . . . *fighting* . . . it," Brianna gasped out, the stars circling her skull gratefully fading as she swayed on her feet and took a few short, painful breaths. "But . . . I'd like . . . to see . . . your horse gelded."

"Never blame the horseflesh for your own inabilities, young lady," Daniel responded, dusting her off with more energy than concern for her possibly broken bones, Brianna thought nastily, knowing her anger came from her embarrassment at having been unseated like a raw novice. His blithe condemnation of her expertise only doubled that anger.

"But I will apologize for riding on my own land, if that soothes your ruffled feathers at all," he went on, obviously not noticing, or caring, that she was not merely chagrined but mad as fire. "Leaving us with one question, I suppose. Delighted as I am to make your acquaintance, what are *you* doing on my father's land?"

Brianna wrinkled her nose, already anticipating the tongue-lashing she was bound to receive from her mother when she returned to Pleasant Hill. "Then you are him, aren't you?" she asked dully, doing her best not to be overly impressed by her cousin's handsome, fairly exotic face. "Daniel Cassidy Crown? Cousin Philip and Brighid's adopted son?"

"Cousin Philip?" Daniel looked blank for a moment, then smiled broadly. "My God, you must be Brianna! The unexpected jewel in the Crown family, I believe your mother called you when she found out she was increasing again. I don't believe it! I helped deliver you, you know, no more than a month before we left for England. Uncle Dominick was away playing at rebel politician, and Mama and I were the only family handy when you decided to come into the world at midnight in the midst of a terrible thunderstorm, as I recall. I was very young, and your arrival made quite an impression, you understand. A few pains, a bit of bother, and then there you were—all red-faced, clench-fisted, and squalling."

He paused a moment, then added, still smiling: "And,

by the look of things, seventeen years haven't served to change you much."

"How very droll, I'm sure. I, of course, have no recollection of the matter," Brianna answered tightly, turning to mount her mare before her cousin could see the blood rushing into her cheeks at his description of her birth—and his joke at her expense. On Freedom's Lady's back once more, she looked down at Daniel Crown—not very far down, for he was extremely tall—and counted to ten, attempting to control her temper.

She smiled politely and summoned up all the training her mother had instilled in her, saying, "It has been a delight, truly, to see you again, cousin. But I fear I must leave now to return to Pleasant Hill and inform my parents of your arrival. You will drive over for dinner this evening, I assume? We dine at six. Otto Bing, your caretaker, can be counted upon to give you our direction. My parents doubtless will be delighted to see you."

Daniel reached out and took hold of Freedom's Lady's bridle. "Yes, I imagine they will, as I'll be pleased to see them again. Tell me—do they allow you at table? Or are you still in the nursery?"

The man was deliberately goading her, as if he knew just where to stick his pins in order to prick her temper beyond its limits. Brianna's tongue would soon bleed, in fact, if she had to bite it any harder. "La," she fairly trilled, hating herself, "I'm less than a month away from becoming eighteen, cousin, with my nursery days far behind me. So, yes, I will be at table tonight. Why, I may recall how to use the silver and even refrain from spitting in my soup. You might, in fact, be surprised at my accomplishments since last you saw me."

He looked her up and down as she sat astride the horse, and for the first time in her life she felt uncomfortable under a man's gaze; uncomfortably aware of the tightness of her breeches, the way they hugged her thighs, her calves. "I am already surprised, Brianna. And fairly impressed. Until this evening, then?"

Her mouth was so dry she couldn't speak, and so she only nodded her agreement. Then, digging her heels into Freedom's Lady's flanks as she pulled on the reins, she and the mare wheeled about smartly and broke into an immediate gallop, heading away from Enolowin, from that great white stallion, from Daniel Cassidy Crown—just as fast as the horse could move.

Which was fairly self-defeating for them both, Brianna concluded nervously, as she and the mare, it seemed, were both almost painfully aware that they were suddenly and most foolishly looking forward to the dance and whirl of the mating season.

Daniel was still looking in the direction Brianna had gone, his expression thoughtful and not a little troubled, when his attention was caught by the approach of Finn, his valet.

"We've got most everything inside now, sir, no thanks to Skelton, that bloody scalpeen, who says he's a horse trainer, not a servant, salvation seize his soul. Horse trainer, is it? A bloody groom he was back in Sussex—and still is, I say. All the world would not make a racehorse of a jackass, don't you know. Getting more uppity by the day, Skelton is, and oughta be taken down a peg or two, which I'd do m'self, if it weren't for this leg o'mine," Finn groused long-windedly as he came to stand beside Daniel, pulling up his breeches as he dragged his stiff left leg along with him. He sniffed, testing the air, then pronounced, "A fine, fine bit o'heaven yer gots here, sir. Mighty fine. We're riding on the pig's back now, as my sainted mother used to say."

"Indeed, yes," Daniel said, taking one last admiring look toward the tree line and Brianna's departing figure. "And climbing closer to paradise by the moment," he added, draping an arm around the much smaller man's thin shoulders and turning him toward the front steps. "Do you think you can find time to press my bottle green frock coat? I feel a sudden need to impress my relatives with some fine English elegance."

The one-time jockey sniffed again. Rather a snort, actually. "Jaybird naked, you'd impress them straight out of their stockin's, sir, and no doubt. They only be Americans, after all."

"And my adopted kin, Finn," Daniel reminded him as they walked into the foyer, to stand beneath the large chandelier that looked very much like the grand piece in the entrance hall at Playden Court, which was what his adoptive father had intended when he'd built Enolowin so long ago. "They, more than anyone, know who I really am, how I came to be here at all. I'm a halfbreed, Finn, if you'll remember. But, for tonight at least, I plan to be as English as the king."

"Weren't he German, sir?" Finn inquired cheekily, hoisting his breeches yet again. He had been laid low with a fierce bout of seasickness for their entire crossing, and had lost valuable pounds from his already thin frame. "Aren't the lot of those fat Georgie-porgies German? I'm Irish to me toes and yet still closer ta English than that sauerkraut-stinkin' bunch, don't you know."

"You're a brave man, Finn, making those statements only a scant three thousand miles away from anyone who'd take umbrage hearing them."

"Afraid of a bunch o'Bugs, sir? Me? Hardly!"

"Obviously, or you wouldn't dare to call my fellow countrymen by such a name. Although I can think of a few who deserve it." Daniel looked to his right and the entrance to the drawing room, then reconsidered attempting to wade through the white cotton shrouds that covered every stick of furniture and, instead, followed his nose to the back of the house through the door that led to the servant area and the kitchens, Finn in his wake.

"Hello—Mrs. Bing?" He called out, treading carefully, for Brighid Crown had taught her adopted son that even the master of the house would be wise to tread carefully in the housekeeper's domain. "Would it be possible to have a bite of whatever is responsible for that wonderful aroma?"

A woman with a most prodigious derriere, quite possibly the size of a modest barn door, turned away from the dry sink and smiled a welcome as she ran a hand through the iron gray hair she wore scraped back into a small, tight bun. Winifred Bing was as round as she was tall, with rosy cheeks and twinkling brown eyes that told of a good humor, just as her white apron-girdled girth boasted of the superiority of her cooking.

"Ach, now, Mr. Crown," she said, her German accent thick as newly churned butter, and her voice moving up and down the scale, turning her words into more of a lilting song than just simple speech. "I'll be happy to serve you anything you like, seeing as how that's what I've been waiting these nearly twenty years to do. Feeding my Otto just ain't the joy it was our first thirty years together. His leg's as hollow as it's skinny, and he'd eat dirt if my bread was all. Come, at the table sit, and I'll slice you a bit of my funeral pie—not that the church bell has rung for a single soul in New Eden this past year. You, too, Mr. Finn. Ei-yi-yi! You look like you need some fattening up or else a good pair of suspenders to keep those breeches offen the floor and my eyes in my head."

"I wouldn't mind it, you know, if you were to slide the kettle on for a bit of tea? And the name's Finn, Mrs. Bing," the valet grumbled, first pulling out a chair for his employer, and then sitting down himself. "No *mister* about me. None at all. Just Finn."

"Ach! You're a touchy one, aren't you?" Mrs. Bing said, smiling as she put huge slices of pie in front of both men. Or at least that's what she called whatever it was she was serving. Daniel looked at the triangular-shaped wedge of pastry filled with plump brown raisins—a battalion of raisins swimming in dark molasses—and eyed Finn, watching to see if he dared to take a taste.

Finn did. He scooped up some of the pie with the spoon Mrs. Bing gave him and, taking a deep breath, shoveled it into his mouth. He closed his lips around the mouthful, shifted the stuff around in his mouth, then swallowed. And then he smiled. "Oh, sir, I think it's in love I am. Truly! Beats kidney pie all hollow, I swear. Now I understand the name, sir. Looks like hell, tastes like heaven."

Finn was right. By the time Daniel was finished with his second slice of the sweet pie, washed down with a large tumbler of cold, fresh milk, he, too, was halfway in love with Mrs. Bing, a woman who stood on no formality, had no notion of how he had been treated in England as the son of a rich, titled gentleman, and seemed to harbor not a single reservation about his Lenni Lenape blood.

In fact, Mrs. Bing possessed no guile at all. And, certainly, no secrets. By the time he and Finn had quit the kitchens, they had learned that Winifred and Otto Bing, childless—"but not by choice or lack of trying, mind you"—had been expressly retained by Mr. Dominick Crown to take care of Enolowin in the absence of its owner; and they had spent the past eighteen years doing just that. Winifred minded the house, and Otto minded the acreage. "Or what he can see of it from that rocker on the side porch," Mrs. Bing had explained with a wink directed at Finn. "Lazy as a hound in the August heat, Otto is, but a good man for all that. And a passable lover," she added, and the Irishman had choked so on his tea that some of it shot out his pointed nose.

"Yes, sir, it's liking it here I'm goin' to be," Finn said confidently as he stood on the front porch once more and patted his stomach. "And we're having a joint of beef big as Mrs. Bing's tender heart for dinner. With potatoes cooked in their own brown skin. She told me so herself."

He took a deep breath of fresh air, snorting it up his nostrils the way another man would take snuff. "If my lovin' mama could see me now she'd think her only son has died and gone to live with the angels, that's what."

Daniel deliberately hid his smile. "And what would that lovely lady think if she could see you standing over an iron hot from the stove, pressing the lace ruffles on my shirt? On *all* my shirts?"

Finn screwed up his face, wincing. "You're a hard man, Mr. Crown. A hard man. I'll be toddlin' off now, I suppose."

"I suppose," Daniel answered with a grin as he walked down the few steps to the gravel drive, then looked to his left—to the sight of the cliff that loomed in the distance. Lenape Cliff. The cliff was an uninspiring, looming mass of dark gray, jagged limestone. But part of the cliff face had broken away in a storm long ago, revealing the harsh, craggy features of a proud, hawk-nosed Indian who looked out over the valley, over Enolowin, guarding it. Just as Enolowin, in the language of the Lenni Lenape, meant "on guard."

Pematalli was buried in the rocky hillside that crested Lenape Cliff. Pematalli, Lokwelend's only son, who had perished in the last Lenape raid on New Eden a good thirty years ago. His grave was unmarked, as Lokwelend had wanted it. Pematalli translated to mean "always there," and Lokwelend had said that his son needed no monument to be remembered, that—because of Pematalli—the Lenape presence in New Eden would never be forgotten by the White Man who had displaced his people.

The storm that had come to New Eden shortly after Pematalli's burial—the lightning strike that had blasted the limestone, revealing Pematalli's face—had seemed to justify Lokwelend's belief in his son's place in the memory of generations to come, his somber image a lingering nudge to their consciousness, reminding them of another time, of another proud race that had once walked this land.

Pematalli had certainly seemed alive to Daniel when he had been a young boy, sitting across a campfire from Lokwelend a lifetime ago, listening to the story of how Philip Crown, Daniel's adoptive father, had been the one to give Pematalli a warrior's death, then be adopted as Lokwelend's new son. It had all sounded so right, almost romantic, poetic and heroic, until Daniel had run to Philip and asked him to tell him more, tell him how the brave young Indian had died. That had been Daniel's first lesson in the futility of war. His second lesson had been one in hatred, as Philip had explained that Lokwelend had not marked his son's grave because there were still those in New Eden who would then dig it up and desecrate Pematalli's body.

And now Lokwelend rested near his son. Lokwelend, and also Lapawin, Daniel's grandmother—the wonderful old crone Michael had remembered, yet forgotten. Only Kolachuisen remained. Kolachuisen, Lokwelend's daughter, who now called herself Cora, and who had married Lucas Deems, Uncle Dominick's butler.

Would Cora remember him? She had called him "little brother" when he had lived at Enolowin, when he had visited Pleasant Hill to play with the Crown children. It seemed all so long ago—when he had been young, and unimpressed with the complexities of life, the tangled history of love and hate and tragedy that had led to his own presence in this world.

No one was as they seemed. Dominick Crown was really Lord Dominick, and Philip's half-uncle—a man who had turned his back on England, on his own title, and fought against his native country in the rebellion that had split the family for nearly a decade.

Bryna Crown, Dominick's wife and Brighid's cousin, had stubbornly persisted in writing letters to England after the war ended, begging her husband and Philip to put aside their political differences and remember that they were family, that they loved each other and would always love each other. With Brighid's help, Bryna had finally arranged for the men to meet in Sussex. Had it been during that wonderful visit, with memories of Pleasant Hill and Enolowin brought home to him by Dominick and Bryna's presence, that Daniel had felt the initial hint of uneasiness, his first longings to return to Pennsylvania, to visit the grave of his mentor, Lokwelend?

For Lokwelend had been his grandfather in everything but blood. He had taken the young Daniel into the woods, taught him the ways of the Lenape, told him marvelous stories about the travels his people had made, their illustrious history, his own heritage.

Daniel had spent his days in a deer skin loinclout, his skin made brown as a berry by both his father's blood and the summer sun, racing through the dense woods, communing with the spirits of his ancestors, and his evenings at table with his adoptive family, buttoned and buckled and starched, listening to the arguments against the colonies breaking away from English rule, English protection.

His adoptive family. Philip Crown, marquess of Playden, had come to New Eden as a young man to broaden his horizons. What he found was a home and a wife—and a new life he always knew could only be a temporary respite from his true duties in England. Brighid Cassidy Crown, her family killed in the first Lenape massacre, had been a captive of the Indians for five long years. She had risked everything, even her own hope of happiness, to protect the half-breed infant boy, Tasukamend, entrusted to her care by the dying Johanna Gerlach, her fellow captive.

Tasukamend. That had been Daniel's Lenape name. The Blameless One. The son of Johanna Gerlach and her Lenape husband, Wulapen. A child born to a dead father and a dying mother and left in the care of a young white woman and an old Indian widow. Until he had been taken to New Eden along with Brighid and Lapawin after the Lenapes' treaty with the English. Until he had traveled to Sussex before Philip could be branded a Tory scum by the residents of New Eden, who had once welcomed him as their friend. Until he had been placed in the care of an English tutor, sent to English schools, taken his place in English society.

Until the call of his homeland could no longer be denied.

Daniel blinked away unexpected tears as he continued to stare at the image of the Indian in the cliff face. The face of Pematalli—always there, standing guard over Enolowin. Looking down on Daniel now, in hope, in question—in censure?

Tomorrow, Daniel promised silently. Tomorrow he would take his horse and travel the well-remembered path that led to the top of the cliff, to Lokwelend's and Lapawin's well-marked graves, to Pematalli's eternal home.

Tomorrow, he would begin to ask the questions that had brought him here. Brought him home, if this truly was to be his home.

But, for tonight, he would be Daniel Cassidy Crown, Englishman. And he would dine at Pleasant Hill in all his English finery, seated across the table from the hauntingly beautiful Brianna Cassidy Crown, who was his sacrosanct, untouchable cousin—yet not of his blood.

Such a strange family.

Don't go with your fingers in your mouth.

IRISH SAYING

chapter two

"Still don't see the reason behind all these ditch dull fabrics and colors, sir, and that's a fact," Finn said, giving a final brush to the shoulders of Daniel's bottle green frock coat as his master stood in front of the mirror in the main bedchamber of Enolowin, inspecting himself for flaws. "I mean, look at you—not that you don't look as if you've been melted into this here coat and all. But there's no flash, no dash, don't you know. Why you left your lovely satins behind in London for those two babies to fight over is beyond me."

"Michael and Joseph will need wigs and satins if they're to go to balls put on by old-fashioned hostesses like Lady Cornwallis," Daniel said, tugging on the cuffs of his jacket, wishing he wasn't wondering what one Miss Brianna Crown would think when she saw him. "The French have gone somber in their revolution, and I imagine the Americans have done so as well. It wouldn't do to march into Pleasant Hill like some damned peacock, Finn, showing off my jewels, wearing red heels and yards of lace, not when I remember my Uncle

Dominick's politics. Besides, to tell you the God's honest truth, I've learned to much prefer the comfort of trousers and jackboots."

Finn snorted. "At least your cravat and waistcoat will dazzle them all hollow. I can't have you lookin' shabby, for it would shame m'mother somethin' terrible if her son should be less than the top valet from here to County Kerry."

Daniel hid a smile as he bent his head and tucked a slim gold watch into his pocket. When it came to valets, Finn made a wonderful jockey, but the man did try hard. The Irishman had been up on one of Daniel's mounts, exercising him, when he'd been thrown, permanently injuring his leg. Daniel had felt it his duty and, later, his great good fortune, to have found alternative employment for the man. Now, after five years together, Daniel often found it difficult to remember who was the servant and who was the master. So he had settled on allowing Finn to be his friend. And it felt good to have a true friend.

"Your boots good enough?" Finn asked as he stepped back, taking one last long assessing look at the man who would shortly be riding to Pleasant Hill to break bread with his American relatives. "Spit on 'em until my mouth ran dry as a Methodist's wine cellars, I did, and rubbed so hard my elbow nearly dropped off."

"And I thank you from the bottom of my heart for your sacrifice, Finn. God knows, I'm lucky to have you," Daniel said, knowing it was expected of him. He then took the hat and gloves the valet offered him, took a deep breath, and turned to leave the room. "Don't wait up, my friend. I hope to be very late."

"Miss Brianna, either you be putting a stop to rutsching around like a weary child in a church pew, or I'll never get these buttons lined up right."

"I'm sorry, Wanda. I'll stop." Brianna pressed her lips

together between her teeth—the better to bring some color into them—then leaned forward to peer into the three-quarter length mirror. "Oh, would you look at this rat's nest on my head! I can't go downstairs like this."

Wanda, a woman of nearly forty who had bounced the infant Brianna on her knee, gave a sharp tug to the fabric of the gown, pulling her squirming, wriggling charge upright once more. *"Maacks nix aus,* missy," she said reasonably. "Makes no difference. You're the prettiest thing from here all the way to Philly-delphia, no matter what. Now that I have these buttons done, no thanks to you, I'll just dip my fingers in the washbowl and spritz some water over that strubbly hair and set it to curling already. You'll see."

"Mama says I'm not to say strubbly," Brianna told Wanda as she dutifully sat on the small velvet-topped bench in front of her vanity table. "Not strubbly, nor spritz, nor even rutsch." She turned her head just as Wanda took hold of a fistful of long, burnished curls, yelping at the tug of the roots against her scalp. "But I like those words. I like the way you sing them. You do sing when you talk, Wanda. Just like the Bings. Do you know that?"

"Ei-yi-yi, how the girl goes on," Wanda trilled, dipping her fingers into the cold water in the basin, then flicking them so that water droplets showered straight into Brianna's face. "Winifred and Otto Bing came here from the Palatine, I do think, while my mother, rest her soul, took ship from Holland and my father, curse his, was German through and through. Now we're all just Pennsylvania Dutch, like we're one big lump. The Germans, the Swiss, the Alsatians—all of us living together and slowly taking a half-dozen languages and mashing them into one. That's why Benjamin Franklin hated us, you know."

Brianna rolled her eyes heavenward, for Wanda's was

an old story and an old argument. "Mr. Franklin did not *hate* you, Wanda. He just didn't want all of Philadelphia speaking German instead of English—"

"And, like I tell you and tell you, he never could make a go of his German newspaper, like he did with that there *Almanac* of his. Couldn't stand it! So he crossed the ocean to put a bug in old Georgie's ear and made sure the English put a tax on German printing. That tax made it cost us dear to read or do business, and then that Franklin fellow made sure we all got talked into moving out of the city, to places like New Eden, saying farmers should farm. So don't you sass me, Missy. My mother told me the whole of it, and a liar she wasn't. Said she would have been married to a nice Swiss clockmaker in Philadelphia if it hadn't been for that sneaking Franklin and his talk of fertile farms. She never would have come to New Eden with her parents, never have met my father, never would have watched him drink himself to death."

"And you never would have been born," Brianna pointed out, as she always did, knowing Wanda could be counted upon to rail on at length on the subject if she didn't stop her with a thick application of good old Irish codding, as her mother called flattery laid on with a liberal hand. "Which would have made me quite sad, as you're one of my favorite people, Wanda," she added mournfully. "One of the dearest, most favorite people whose presence ever blessed this whole wide world. I say so all the time."

The maid blushed to the roots of her thick crop of ditch water blond hair. "Ach, you go on with you now. I ain't not. But, while you're busy flinging the truth around, tell me why it's so important that you look your best tonight. It's only some English cousin coming to dinner, or so that's how I hear the gossip in the kitchen."

It was Brianna's turn to blush, and she did so prettily, hot color running into her cheeks, her emerald green eyes sparkling with mischief and excitement. "You wouldn't ask that if you could see him, Wanda. Oh, he's a fine-looking man. Tall as a tree, and with the most interesting face. He's half Lenape, you know. And then there's how he was born, how he came to be a Crown. It's all so exotic, don't you think? And mysterious."

"And not none of your business, missy," Wanda scolded as she set down the silver-backed brush with a loud thump against the cherry wood vanity. "The man's English raised, and he's kin. Besides, a girl shouldn't be thinking of marriage until she can sew a man's shirt and roll out a nice round pie crust. That's what my mother told me. And, seeing as how I wasn't about to so much as darn a hole in any man's Sunday coat, I stayed as far from the altar as I could get."

"But I *can* sew, Wanda," Brianna reminded the maid, leaning toward the mirror on the vanity and pinching her cheeks until they turned pink again. "And even Mrs. Bing has vowed that I make the best, lightest pie crust in all of New Eden, thanks to her tutoring. I can do anything I put my mind to, and you know it. In fact, you've said so yourself."

Wanda looked at the young girl's reflection, wincing when she saw the determined look on her face. "Ach, there's trouble coming now, just as plain as the rain comes when my bunions set in to throbbing! You're going to go after this poor Englishman the way you go after anything you set your mind to, aren't you? Don't lie, for I see it in your eyes. You've got it in your head to get him, and get him you will."

"Oh, I will, will I? Well, thank you kindly, Wanda," Brianna said, rising and dropping a kiss on the woman's plump cheek. "I appreciate your confidence in me."

"Getting is one thing, missy," Wanda called after Brianna as the young woman swept out of the room in her pale yellow gown. "It's what you're going to *do* with him once you get him that will have my hair turning gray overnight!"

* * *

Daniel let Lenape Traveler set his own pace along the hard-packed dirt road that wound between Enolowin and Pleasant Hill, the white stallion meandering lazily, then breaking into a smooth trot for a space, the two of them taking in their surroundings, getting accustomed to the scenery as they mounted each new, low hill.

The landscape reminded Daniel very much of Sussex; with a velvety haze hanging over the entire large valley, softening the bright red of a barn in the distance, dusting the green of the growing wheat, turning the wandering, tree-covered mountains in the distance a grand, smoky blue.

From the crest of one particular hill Daniel could see a rolling patchwork quilt of fields planted with wheat and barley and corn, and admired the still new and bright greenery on the trees that divided the quilt into individual plots. The air smelled of honeysuckle growing wild by the roadside, of tender crops, wild roses, ripening cherries, and strawberries. Above him, circling the trees in preparation of nesting for the night that would not come for hours, he saw scarlet tanagers, robins, wood thrushes and wrens, their joyful noise cheering him as much as did his easy remembrance of these particular birds, their particular names.

The day was warm, even as it climbed toward twilight, and he could hear the soft tinkle of cowbells below him in the meadow, clutches of fat milk cows slowly meandering toward one of the large red bank barns at Pleasant Hill and their ritual evening milking.

It was as if he were in England, but an England built on a much larger scale. For England was an island. Here in America there were valleys large enough to swallow up all of Sussex and still leave room for half of Surrey or Kent.

A smile curved Daniel's lips as a bobwhite flew by, its whistle sending Lenape Traveler to dancing, and he nudged the stallion's sleek flanks, urging him forward once more—feeling happy, feeling safe, feeling very much at home, with the soot and chimney pots and confinement of London far away.

He looked to his left, to the forest that edged the wide fields, looked into the dense stand of towering oaks, shaggy hickories, portly maples, slender hemlocks, and shadowy chestnuts and black walnuts that turned the ground beneath their branches to night even in the middle of day. He'd read somewhere that a Lenape brave had proudly reported that it once would have been possible for a squirrel to jump from limb to limb through this great forest, from the shores of the Atlantic and nearly all the way to the wide river to the west of Pennsylvania, with its feet never touching the ground. Until the *Yankwis* had come, of course, until the fields had been cleared and planted. Until the Lenni Lenape had been pushed westward, ever westward, forced to abandon the homeland of their grandfathers.

Still, the scattered drifts of lacy white dogwoods and the more fragile green of smaller trees, the tulip, the sassafras, the sumac, could not successfully lighten the dark impenetrability of this particular wide swath of still virgin forest where a much younger Daniel and his mentor, Lokwelend, had spent so many wonderful, carefree hours.

Daniel's smile faded as he stared into the trees and the memories rushed into his mind, memories of stories he'd heard, an existence he could only imagine—leaving him feeling empty, alone, somehow lost. Leaving his blood burning, his muscles bunched, eager for a barefooted, lung-bursting run through the dense trees.

If he just cut to his left, leaving Lenape Traveler behind so that he traveled on foot, he could probably still make his way through this dense tangle, over the fallen tree trunks and haphazardly scattered, huge gray boulders. He could run all the way to the thin sliver of bubbling creek, where he would turn to his right and circle behind Pleasant Hill itself, standing high and proud on a rise in the distance, following the meandering path that eventually led to wider water, and Lokwelend's log cabin that perched beside its banks.

Was it still there?

Pematalli was Always There. But Pematalli's father, Lokwelend, was The Traveler. Had his spirit stayed here in the log cabin that had been his home or hovering over the cliff where his mortal body lay—or had Lokwelend's soul taken to traveling once again, shepherding the remaining Lenape, guiding them with his strong spirit, counseling them with his deep wisdom?

Or, perhaps, was he waiting, still waiting, for the young Tasukamend who had left him so very long ago?

"I have returned, Grandfather," Daniel called out loudly, startling the wrens who perched on the tree limbs overhanging the path. "Years too late and still a child, still full of foolish questions, Tasukamend has returned."

"He's coming! Mama, Papa—he's coming!"

Brianna let the sheer white curtains fall back into place as she quickly stepped away from the drawing room window facing out over the massive, well-scythed, sloping lawns and curved, oak-lined lane that led to the imposing red front door of Pleasant Hill. It wouldn't do to have Daniel Crown see her peeping out at him like some child yearning for a treat.

She smoothed the skirts of her gown, then peeked into the gilt-edged mirror hanging above a small cherry wood table, not because she was especially vain but because she was female enough to want to reassure herself that she was looking her best. *"Mama!* Did you hear me?"

Bryna Cassidy Crown swept into the drawing room in a swish of dark blue taffeta and silk underslips. She was similarly petite as her youngest daughter, but with her long, silver-streaked copper hair pulled into a soft, upswept style, and with small, featherlight laugh lines giving her once breathtakingly lovely face a look of maturity, serenity, and ageless beauty.

"I imagine, Brianna," she pronounced in a lilting, cultured voice that had never completely lost its faint trace of Ireland, "that Cora and Lucas have heard you in Philadelphia, and your brothers—far out in the middle of the ocean—have just now run to the rail of their ships, expecting to see you coming up alongside in a rowboat. Your cousin Mary Kate has lifted her head from prayer at her convent in County Clare to cock an ear toward America. Your sister Felicia is shaking her head in Virginia, mumbling something to the effect that her dearest Brianna still has much to learn of deportment, and your father has doubtless just sliced his own chin as he shaves in preparation for Daniel's arrival. So, yes, my pet," she ended with a quick wink and an indulgent smile, "I heard you. We *all* heard you."

Brianna rolled her eyes, wishing her mother would, just this one time, treat her as an adult, if not precisely as her equal. Would she and her father always persist in lecturing her with every second breath—kindly lectures or nay? Would she always be seen as the youngest child, the baby, even when she was dandling her own infants on her knee? She sighed, believing she already knew the answer to that question.

"Forgive me, Mama," she said quietly, trying to keep her eyes downcast so that her mother couldn't see the expectant twinkle that could not be hidden if she had looked at the woman head-on. Then she sobered, her head jerking up. "Papa isn't ready? Oh, don't say so! It's Daniel's first night here! He'll think us shabby and provincial if we've invited him here to supper just to have Papa come late to table because he was grubbing about in the fields."

"Your father does not *grub about,* Brianna," Bryna said, walking over to the window and tilting her head ever so slightly in order to get a quick glimpse of her cousin's adopted son as he dismounted and handed over a fine-looking mount to a boy who had come out from the stables. "My, he is tall, isn't he? Even taller than your father. But, then, the Lenape are not by and large a short race, like the English. Lokwelend had a most impressive stature, even in his old age."

"Uh-huh." Brianna nervously sliced her gaze around the room as the knocker went, attempting to quickly decide where she should be standing when Daniel was presented by Whittle, the butler who was newly arrived from London, taking Lucas Deems's place since that man and his Lenape wife had retired to Philadelphia, where their son had opened a draper's shop.

She frowned, furious with nerves. To be standing here—just *standing* here when Daniel was announced? Was that really such a good idea? Wouldn't that make her look just a smidgen too eager to greet him? Lord, yes! She should have remained upstairs, then made an entrance of sorts down the long staircase, one hand sliding lightly over the deeply carved mahogany railing, her skirts raised just slightly as she daintily sought out each step—and gifted her relative with a small, tantalizing glimpse of ankle. That's how these things were done in London. She was sure of it.

"Well, and now's a fine time to think of *that,* Brianna!" she scolded herself, knowing she didn't have time to race across the foyer and up the stairs without Daniel seeing her. "I should just sit down," she mused further, walking first to the rose satin settee, starting to lower herself toward the cushions, then rising and glaring at the cream-and-white striped chair near the fireplace. "Yes. I'll sit down. But where?"

"On your sweet rump, pet, as my shameless father would have said," Bryna quipped, pinning a wide smile on her face and walking toward the doorway, her arms outstretched in greeting. "Daniel! Oh, my, but you've grown. How could you have done that when we just saw you not five years ago? Come here, and let me give you a kiss."

"Aunt Bryna! I would have known you anywhere," Daniel said, bending over so that the woman could sling her arms up and around his neck, then straightening, holding her at the waist and whirling her about in a circle as if she were no heavier than a feather—which she wasn't, Brianna thought proudly. Her mother was the most beautiful creature in creation and always had been. Just as her father was the most handsome gentleman ever to walk God's green earth.

"Daniel!" that handsome gentleman said now, coming into the room just as his flushed and giggling wife was gently set back down on her feet. He transferred his cane to his left hand and stuck out his right, grinning as Daniel took it in his own and heartily pumped it up and down. "My God, you're all grown-up. The last I saw you at Playden Court, you were all arms and legs and ears—none of them fitting quite right, as I recall. How old were you then? Seventeen? Eighteen?"

"About that, sir," Daniel said, his voice sounding rather thick, husky, as if the moment of reunion had brought more emotion with it than he had anticipated. "I have letters for you both from Mother and Father. Letters, a few bolts of material and ribbons and such Mother insisted I bring, and some seeds. Flower seeds, I believe, and possibly some others garnered from Mother's vegetable garden. Oh—and a fine new pipe, sir." He turned to look at Brianna. "And a doll of some sort for you, I'm afraid," he said, smiling. "Obviously my mother still pictures you as a child, which you most definitely are not. May I say that you look quite recovered from your spill this afternoon."

"Spill?" Bryna was instantly all clucking brood hen, worried over her smallest chick. "Dominick, I keep telling you Freedom's Lady is simply too much horse for the child. And, Brianna, how many times have I warned you not to dare that fence at Enolowin?"

"Oh, but it wasn't at the—"

Brianna shot Daniel a fairly nasty look, warning him into silence. Thankfully, he seemed to understand, and his words ended in a small, polite cough. "Yes, Mama," she said quickly. "I promise to be more careful in future. Too headstrong by half, that's me. I'm so sorry. But it was only my pride that was injured, as a tumble from my horse was no way to introduce myself to my cousin, was it?"

Bryna shot her daughter a quick look, then slid her gaze toward Daniel, who was still coughing into his fist. Bryna's expressive left eyebrow rose ever so slightly, so that Brianna, who could read her mother much more easily than she could please her, felt another lecture coming on—and not a dressing-down on the subject of Freedom's Lady. Oh, no. Not by a long chalk. And she was right, for her mother only said quietly, "I believe I'm beginning to understand. We'll talk, pet, you and I. Later."

Dominick walked to the drinks table, asking Daniel his pleasure, and the subject of his daughter's previously undisclosed adventure at Enolowin was dropped as wine was poured for three, lemonade for one—another reminder to Brianna that her parents simply refused to face the fact that their daughter was a young lady of nearly eighteen now.

But that didn't matter to her for more than a moment, as she sat down on the settee and Daniel sat down beside her, throwing her yet another friendly smile. Her stomach performed a small flip as she returned his smile, and she felt as if they had already formed some sort of small bond between them, having fibbed together, as it were.

"How is the family, Daniel?" Bryna asked after taking a small sip of wine, then placing her glass on the table beside her. "You must fill me in on all the particulars. I haven't had a letter in ages and ages."

"Yes, three days at the very least, when Philip told us of your imminent arrival, Daniel," Dominick put in cheerfully, taking up his wife's hand and lifting it to his lips. "She's going to get me back aboard ship before the fall storms, heading for Playden Court, this time with Brianna coming along as well, now that she's out of the nursery. I'm convinced of that. We'd be leaving sooner, if it weren't for your arrival, which has served to soothe her somewhat. Was Enolowin properly prepared? Mrs. Bing is a prodigious housekeeper, so I doubt you stumbled into a mess, even on such short notice."

"The Bings have been outstanding stewards, Uncle," Daniel said. "And Mrs. Bing is a most excellent cook. She served me this most unusual, delicious dish this afternoon . . ."

Brianna allowed the conversation to float over her head as she watched Daniel. Watched the way his well-formed mouth moved when he spoke, the way his dark eyes twinkled, yet seemed to hide exactly what he was thinking, the way his hand held the wineglass, his long fingers seemingly caressing the fine crystal. She could smell him, her nostrils teased by some dark, sharp, intriguing fragrance that suited him much more than the cloying smell of musk many of the local young farmers seemed to favor.

From the way he held his dark head tipped slightly to show his interest in whatever her father was saying to the way he crossed his legs at the knee, everything about Daniel Crown fascinated Brianna. Intrigued her. Excited her. Made her dream of what it would be like to have those eyes on her, that mouth on her, those hands on her . . .

"Brianna? Your face is looking quite flushed. Are you feeling all right?"

Brianna swallowed hard and forced herself back to attention, looking at her mother blankly for a moment, then feeling even more betraying color racing into her cheeks. Why couldn't she have favored her father, as Felicia did, with dark hair and more olive-toned skin that didn't send up warning flags signaling her every change of emotion? "I'm fine, Mama," she said quickly, adding, "although I admit to being extremely hungry. Will supper be served soon?"

As if to rescue her from herself, Whittle obligingly appeared in the doorway, announcing that dinner was ready to be served in the dining room. Brianna all but leaped to her feet, then flinched as Daniel put a hand on her elbow, clearly intending to escort her to the dining room—as if she couldn't find her way there on her own. Which she probably couldn't, not when her head was so filled with the quick Hail Mary she was reciting in the hope of knocking at least a day off the time her poor soul would be spending in purgatory for the thoughts she'd been having about Daniel Crown.

"Will it be too dark after dinner for a quick walk to Lokwelend's cabin, do you think, Cousin?" Daniel whispered in her ear as they followed her parents into the dining room. "Or should I be patient and wait until tomorrow?"

Brianna thought she would swallow her tongue, but she managed to answer. "I think there would be time this evening. It won't be dark for some while. Can you find the path on your own, or would you like me to come with you?"

His smile threatened to melt her knees, even as his eyes remained unreadable. "Your company would make the trip twice as pleasant, cousin. Thank you."

She lifted her chin, and her left eyebrow—daring him, flirting with him—determined to let him know that if he wished her company this evening, it would not be two relatives taking a stroll but two people—a man and a woman—going off alone into the darkness. "I'm not really your cousin, you know. Not, that is, in any way that matters."

"Oh, it matters, Brianna," he said, his dark eyes becoming even more shuttered. "But, as you're still very much the precocious child, I doubt that either your parents or I shall concern ourselves overmuch on that head."

She opened her mouth, longing to say something bright and witty and viciously cutting, then shut it again, knowing that anything she said to rebut him would only dig the pit deeper around her ridiculous notion that Daniel Crown would take one look at her in her pretty yellow gown and tumble head over heels in love with her. He was just showing her that she had a battle on her hands. And wasn't that what she wanted? After all, what great joy was there in gaining a victory without any hint of challenge?

If Daniel Crown wanted a woman, she'd give him a woman. More woman than he'd ever encountered before! "So," she murmured at last, leaning against him every so slightly, unaffectedly brushing against his arm, "tell me more about this doll Aunt Brighid has sent me. Will I want to tuck it up in bed with me tonight as I snuggle beneath the covers, do you suppose?"

"Only if you eat all your porridge first," Daniel countered cheerfully, although she noticed that the muscles in his cheek had grown taut. "That is what they feed infants, isn't it?" And then he removed his hand from her elbow and allowed Whittle to pull out her chair for her as he took his seat on the other side of the table at her father's right hand. Thinking himself clever, no doubt. And safe.

You'll pay for that, Brianna thought as she laid her napkin in her lap, caught between embarrassment and an increased longing to see this man at her feet, professing his deep, abiding affection for her, his unquenchable love. Because she had decided to win him, just as she had decided to be the best seamstress in New Eden, the best pie maker Mrs. Bing could make her, the best at singing, the best at dancing, the best at harp playing, the best at horsemanship. Because victory always came to Brianna Crown, and she never so much as considered the prospect of defeat. Only boredom stopped her, turned her away from her latest conquest, her newest achievement, once her end was so effortlessly achieved.

She smiled up at Whittle, thanking him kindly as he ladled soup into the bowl in front of her. *Oh, yes. This has just begun, Daniel Crown—not ended. One battle does not win the war.*

Women are like tricks by slight of hand,
Which, to admire, we should not understand.

William Congreve

chapter three

The men retired to Dominick's private study after dinner to enjoy brandy and cigars, leaving the women to sit together in the drawing room. Daniel was grateful for what he could only consider a lucky escape—as he had found himself looking, much too often to be considered cousinly, in the direction of the laughing, enchanting face of Brianna Crown.

Daniel could remember being in this exceedingly masculine room, located at the back of the house, overlooking his Aunt Bryna's extensive gardens. He had come here with his adopted father, to curl up in the corner of the soft leather couch as Dominick and Philip had discussed farming and debated politics, while his aunt and adopted mother visited in the drawing room or walked the paths of the gardens, stopping to stoop over and remove a weed that had dared to poke its head up next to a painted daisy or a thick knot of parsley.

There had been happy times here and sad times. More sad times, as the division between Dominick Crown's politics and that of his nephew had caused more than one evening to end with Daniel being scooped up into Brighid's arms as she followed her frustrated husband out the front door to their carriage.

Lokwelend had explained it all to Daniel and told him that "no man can serve two masters, my son, and serve them both well." Dominick, the old Indian had patiently explained, had committed himself, his family, and his future, to this new land that had once been the Lenapes', and Philip had his loyalty buried deep in the soil of Sussex and in service to his king. It had been inevitable that uncle and nephew should clash when it became apparent that the colonies would defy King George and dare to strike for independence.

"But these two good men love each other, Tasukamend," Lokwelend had told Daniel when he had run away from Enolowin, a few shirts and other belongings tied up in a blanket, determined to live with Lokwelend and not return to England with his parents. "Your mother loves her cousin and always will. It is men's laws that divide them, not their hearts. They will be together again someday, just as your heart will lead you back here to your home. It is your destiny."

"Will—will you still be here, Grandfather, waiting for me?" Daniel remembered asking the old man, fearful that, once he was in England, he would never see Lokwelend again.

"I will be here, Tasukamend," the old Indian had promised. "Look for me in the trees, in the bird soaring in the sky. In the hills, in the turkey running in the forest, in the fish swimming in the water, in the corn growing tall in the fields. I will be here."

Daniel rubbed a hand across his closed eyes, sighing as he saw Lokwelend as he had last seen him, standing tall and strong and silent, his hand lifted in farewell as Philip Crown's carriage drove off from Enolowin. *He had known,* Daniel thought now. *Lokwelend had known I'd never see him again.*

He looked to his uncle, who was gingerly lowering

himself into the large leather chair behind his desk. "Your wound is giving you trouble, isn't it? You weren't using a cane when you visited us."

"I wouldn't use it now," Dominick said with a grin, "except that your aunt has promised to club me over the head and shoulders with the damned thing if I don't. And, much as I hate to admit any such thing within her hearing, she's right. The pain is less when I use it. My one blessing is that I'm still wonderfully comfortable on horseback."

"You were injured shortly after the winter the Colonial Army spent at Valley Forge, as I recall. I-I've read something about that winter, about George Washington's remarkable control of his troops. Was it as bad as they say—what with the lack of provisions and all?"

"Was it bad, Daniel? You mean, how miserable could it have been to be cold and dirty and hungry while the British were warm and well fed in Philadelphia, holding balls and practicing their drills in the city streets?" Dominick shook his head. "Let's just say that I never want to see any of my sons caught up in similar circumstances. War is never easy, and it was made harder knowing that I was fighting against my own countrymen. I lived in fear that I might meet your father on the battlefield."

Daniel cleared his throat, then took another long pull on the cigar Dominick had offered him. "It wasn't a good time, was it? By the time I was old enough to fully appreciate what was happening, it was over, thank God." He smiled at his uncle. "And now your sons are spreading their wings, taking over the reins of the truly impressive empire you've carved out here, Uncle. I congratulate you, sincerely. And I thank you for your careful caretaking of my father's estate. I only hope I can do half so well for him."

Dominick looked at him—curiously, Daniel thought—then took a sip of brandy. "How long will you be at Enolowin, Daniel? Philip's letter was disturbingly vague on that head."

Daniel stood up and walked over to the windows to look out at the rapidly darkening gardens. They had lingered long over dinner, so that it was already too late to take the path to Lokwelend's tonight. But there was still tomorrow. Many, many tomorrows. "I'm to manage the estate for a year," he explained, feeling a nearly overwhelming longing to be on with his business, to take up the reins his father had offered. "If at the end of that time I wish to remain at Enolowin, Father has agreed to deed the land to me in return for my services. If I choose to return to England, he will purchase a similar estate for me there, probably in Sussex near Playden Court. Either way, I intend to repay his generosity out of my profits, not that he knows that, of course."

He turned away from the window and looked levelly at his uncle. "Already, just in these few short hours, I cannot imagine going back, to tell you the God's honest truth, much as I know such news will pain my family. I can't understand why I waited so long to return."

Dominick nodded. "I see. Smart man, my nephew," he said quietly. "Philip's making sure to leave your options open to you. You'd be wise to do the same, Daniel. Make no decisions until you've been here awhile." Then he smiled. "And, since you say you will be with us at least for a year, I think perhaps you ought to know a few things that might make your stay more, shall I say, *comfortable.*"

"Sir?"

"I'm talking about Brianna, Daniel. One of the brightest lights of my life, the terror and joy of my old age—and the most determined young woman you'll ever meet. Or haven't you noticed that she has already taken it into her pretty young head to make a conquest of you?"

Daniel shook his head. "I remember that Lokwelend told me you were a quiet man, but that you saw everything. He was right, as he always was right. But don't worry, sir. I think I can manage one romantic young girl."

"Young *woman,* Daniel," Dominick reminded him. "She's nearly eighteen now, which is why we're planning to take her to England. It's time she found herself a suitable husband, and Philip told us he already has somebody in mind. Felicia was easily and happily settled, but Brianna presents more of a challenge. And she *is* challenging, Daniel. I believe you may also have already discovered that?"

"Oh, yes, sir," Daniel said, remembering the way Brianna had deliberately brushed up against him on their way in to dinner, proving without doubt that she was far from a child. "She is that. Her mother's daughter all the way down to the ground, I believe my own mother would say."

"And Brighid would be right. Impatient, wonderfully affectionate, intelligent, headstrong, fearless—and with a temper and determination that would put many a man to shame. Brianna's greatest failing is that she so seldom does fail. Everything she attempts she masters and with lamentable ease. And then, sadly, she loses interest and abandons each new accomplishment. Except for her horses. I will say that about her. In her horses she has found something that continues to challenge her. Which is why, I must also tell you, she has been making Enolowin her second home. With most of the fields allowed to lie fallow, it presents the perfect place for her to run Freedom's Lady and her other mounts. I fear she considers you not only a challenge, Daniel, but an intruder. I thought you ought to know that."

Daniel reached up a hand and scratched at his cheek. "You've had your hands full, haven't you sir?"

Dominick leaned back in his chair, chuckling. "Yes, son, I have. And now, Lord love you, so do you."

"I won't do anything you wouldn't want, sir," Daniel promised solemnly. "I know I am not a blood relative, but I am family, even if I am not yet quite sure who I really am, where I truly belong. And until I do, the last thing I need in my life is the complication of a young woman's romantic notions of conquest."

"Such a complication may be the last thing you need, but I'm afraid Brianna hasn't thought to give you a choice in the matter. And, I warn you, she's fairly irresistible. I can't think of anyone at Pleasant Hill, in all of New Eden, who doesn't dote on the child."

Dominick rose and motioned for the younger man to precede him out of the study. "Ah, well, I'll rely on your good judgment, Daniel, and your promise not to hurt her. She is as you've said, her mother's daughter, full of fire and courage. And with a tender heart that is more easily bruised than she will ever want you to know. So I'll hold you to your word. If the time ever comes when your circumstances change—well, we'll discuss that if and when that time arrives, all right?"

Daniel crushed his cigar in the glass dish on the desk, then walked to the door, his hands closed into fists at his side, believing his uncle was skirting the issue of his Lenape blood and the obvious unsuitability of mixing it with the pure Crown blood of his beloved daughter. A part of Daniel called himself a fool for thinking Dominick Crown capable of such a judgment, but the man had seemed to feel it necessary to share the information that he intended to take his daughter to England, hadn't he? To England, where he could match her with some thin-blooded, blue-blooded aristocrat's son?

Daniel needed to get away, be alone. Think. "Could you make my apologies to the ladies, sir?" he asked as they walked down the hallway and stopped outside the closed doors to the drawing room. "I find I've suddenly realized how tired I am after my journey, as we were up before dawn to make the last few miles to Enolowin. And, if you'll give your permission, I'll return tomorrow morning to keep Brianna to her promise to take me to Lokwelend's cabin."

Dominick grinned. "Can't stand the thought of facing her again just yet, I imagine? I don't blame you. A tired adversary is soon bested." He put out his hand and Daniel placed his in it. "Good night to you, son. I can't tell you how much I look forward to having you close by, at least for the next year."

"Thank you, sir," Daniel said, taking his hat and riding gloves from Whittle. "I'll do my best to please both you and my father." Then, pushing his hat down onto his head, he walked through the doorway as Whittle stood at attention, holding the door, and then down the steps, signaling to the waiting groom that he was ready for his horse.

As he waited, slapping his gloves against his palm, he raised his eyes to the full moon hanging over New Eden and wondered just who he had meant when he referred to his father. Philip Crown, the man who had raised him? Or Wulapen, the Lenni Lenape warrior who had died before his son was born, fighting in defense of all he knew, all he hoped to preserve?

And then, as the night wind sang through the tree branches high above his head, Daniel heard again Lokwelend's voice: *"No man can serve two masters, my son, and serve them both well."*

With a last look toward the brightly lit house he had just left, Daniel mounted Lenape Traveler and headed out into the night.

Brianna watched from behind the sheer summer draperies as Daniel stood on the gravel drive, looking up at the sky. She worried her bottom lip between her teeth as he pressed a coin into Billy Baxter's paw and then, with a strangely sad look toward the house, toward her, mounted his fine stallion and rode off into the night, the horse's white rump and long, full tail visible in the moonlight until the large oaks blocked her vision.

She had been angry at first, realizing that Daniel was not going to come back into the drawing room, to sit beside her, to let her watch him, observe him, measure his strengths, gauge his vulnerabilities—*learn* him, so that she could discover the best, quickest way to conquer him.

But as she had watched him during dinner, she had realized that there was something deeper about Daniel Crown than the handsomeness of his outside, the brilliant flash of his smile, or the intriguing mystery in his dark, unreadable eyes. He wasn't just a challenge. He was a man. A man she could not even begin to understand in a few short hours, yet alone master with the ease with which she had mastered watercolor painting, or tatting, or Wilhelm Schmidt's fiddle.

Daniel had seemed so sad as he had stood outside Pleasant Hill, although his shoulders had been very straight, his head unbowed. Sad. Alone. Lonely. Not at all the laughing young English gentleman who had made their dinner such an enjoyable interlude, filling it with tales of her cousins in England, the gossip of polite society, even silly stories about his valet, Finn, and that man's earnest vow that Irishmen were not born to go to sea, uttered as the poor man hugged the rail for most of the nearly six-week-long crossing.

All of which made Daniel Crown even more appealing to her romantic heart.

"You're nothing but a silly, shallow child, Brianna Crown," she whispered to herself as she stared out into the night and saw her own reflection on the windowpane. "Do you really plan to go to all the trouble of attracting the man simply because he laughed at you when you landed rump down in the dirt in front of him? Because he mistook you for a boy and then called you a child? For that—and just to prove that you can do it?"

"Did you say something, Brianna?" her mother asked, looking up from her knitting. Bryna Crown had taken up knitting when Dominick had gone off to align himself with the Colonial forces, and the mindless exercise meant to fill her lonely hours had become one of her greatest prides. "Oh, Dominick, you're here," she continued, looking toward the doors that had just opened. "Where's Daniel?"

Dominick sat down beside his wife. "He asked me to convey his apologies, as he was tired, and begged to be excused. I wonder if I should have sent a groom along with him to help guide him back to Enolowin in the dark."

Bryna patted his hand. "Daniel is not a child, sweetheart, and can find his way home well enough on his own."

"Yes," Dominick said, speaking quietly, as if to himself. "I believe that's what he hopes."

Brianna came over to the settee and sat down on the carpet in front of her parents, her skirts billowing around her. "Tell me the story again, Papa," she asked, resting her cheek against the side of his knee. "Tell me about Daniel and Brighid and Philip."

"It has always been your favorite fairy tale, hasn't it, pet?" With his hand on his daughter's bright curls, Dominick told her the story once more, and Brianna closed her eyes, imagining herself a young girl, alone, frightened, torn from the bosom of her family and thrust into a new life with the Lenape.

Brighid Cassidy and her younger sister, Mary Catherine, had been the only ones to survive a Lenape raid on their parents' farm, located no more than a mile from Pleasant Hill. Her younger brothers, Michael and Joseph, and her parents, Daniel and Eileen, had all been killed, hacked to death as Brighid watched, and little Mary Catherine, hidden under her parents' bed, had spent months unable to speak, a captive of her fear. Dominick had taken Mary Catherine in and she had lived with him and Bryna until she had gone off to fulfill her heart's dream, that of becoming a Holy Sister back in Ireland.

But it had been Brighid's story that had captured and held Brianna's fascination: the sixteen-year-old Brighid who had been carried off, then sold to a kindly old Lenape woman, Lapawin. The old woman had also bought Johanna Gerlach, who had been traveling with Brighid as their captors raced across the colony, moving westward to avoid capture.

Five years had passed by the time the English had forced a treaty on the Lenape, and Johanna and Lapawin's son, Wulapen, had started their family, with Brighid as their beloved sister. With Wulapen dead in some far-off battle, with Johanna and two of her children dying soon after of smallpox, Brighid, now a woman grown, was left with no other choice than to be returned to Fort Pitt with the other white captives the Lenape were forced to hand over to the English.

But she did not come back to New Eden willingly, and she did not return alone. She had brought Lapawin with her and Johanna's last surviving child—the infant boy, Tasukamend.

"Cousin Philip went to Fort Pitt along with Lokwelend and escorted her home, didn't he?" Brianna asked, already knowing the answer. "He brought her back to Pleasant Hill and then fell madly, desperately in love with her."

"That he did, pet, even though it took some time, and some heartache, before they could find their way to that love," Dominick said, affectionately ruffling her hair. "But they all lived happily ever after. Although, in truth, I believe your mother and I would be content to forget most of that strange summer."

Brianna sighed even as she smiled. "I want a love like that, Papa. Like yours. A love so real, so deep, that nothing and nobody can destroy it."

"And someday you'll have it, pet. Now, don't you think it's time you were off to bed? Daniel told me he hopes you'll join him tomorrow as he goes to visit Lokwelend's cabin. From the look in his eyes, I'd say he'll be here before breakfast, so you'd better get some sleep."

Brianna lifted her head to look up into her father's face. "He's still coming here tomorrow? I thought—" She broke off, lowering her eyes.

"You thought you might have frightened him away?" Bryna asked, shaking her head. "Oh, Brianna, you're not ready for a man like Daniel Crown, and I doubt that he is ready for you or for any romantic involvement. Please don't make me fear that your father and I will be having another summer to forget!"

Brianna got to her feet and smoothed down the skirts of her gown. "Mama," she teased, winking. "How could you even think such a thing? After all, Daniel is my cousin." She bent down, kissed both her parents on the cheek. Then she skipped off to her bed, already forgetting her earlier misgivings, planning the next skirmish in her war to best Daniel Crown—and completely convinced that Daniel Crown might be a challenge to her mind, but never to her heart.

Daniel picked up the candle that waited for him on the table in the foyer, lit it from the small candelabra, then walked within its small yellow circle of light as he climbed to the main bedchamber, remembering that his adopted father had once told him he'd hung a thick bunch of fresh, fragrant grasses from the ceiling of that room, Lenape fashion, in an effort to make his new bride feel more at home.

For five long years, his adopted mother had slept on blankets arranged on the floor of Lapawin's longhouse or simply beneath the stars, breathing in the clean night air, the heavens as her roof. It had taken Brighid long months to reaccustom herself to a soft feather bed, all the forgotten comforts of "civilization" that she had found so stifling, so confining.

It was difficult to believe these things now, knowing that his mother was one of the premier hostesses of any London season, that she was the chatelaine of Playden Court and four other Crown estates scattered through

England, that she moved with a grace that seemed regal, spoke with a gentleness that charmed all who knew her. But Brighid Cassidy Crown had once been Nipawi Gischuch, the Night Fire, and she had once dressed in deerskins, had once carried her adopted son on a cradleboard lashed to her back, had once nearly scalped a man.

Once inside the bedchamber, Daniel touched his candle to others he found there, then smiled as he saw that Finn had certainly been busy in his absence. All of Daniel's personal belongings had been unpacked, the heavy packing crates removed. Even his silver-backed brushes were neatly lined up on the high dressing table, his collection of small portraits of his family arranged on tables on either side of the wide, high bed.

He sat on the edge of his bed, crossing one knee over the other in preparation of removing his boots, when his eye was caught by the miniature portrait of his adopted aunt, Lady Lilith Crown. The portrait had been a gift, and it pictured Philip Crown's older sister as she had looked when she was about the same age as Brianna Crown.

Picking up the portrait that sat inside its heavy, gilded frame, Daniel leaned back against the pillows and crossed his booted feet on the coverlet. He took a deep breath, then sighed. "Ah, Lilith," he said. "You know how I feel, don't you? How I have always felt since I was old enough to realize that I am different from the rest? You, more than anyone."

He traced his finger along the outline of Lilith's painted cheek, seeing the dark, exotic beauty that had certainly faded now that the woman was in her fiftieth year, but a beauty that age could never totally erase. For her youth was in her dark, flashing eyes, the knowing curve of her smile, the hint of mischief in that uniquely rakish tilt of her head.

"You're my favorite, you know," she'd told him more than once when he had visited her in her town house in Half Moon Street—a gift from one of the last "protectors" she had taken over the years. "We're the mongrels, you see, our blood mixed in a way that makes us outcasts. But that does not mean we cannot enjoy life. No, indeed! In fact, it gives us an excuse to be as outrageous as we wish, with no one to tell us otherwise. Ah, yes, Daniel. It is a different life, but delicious."

Daniel hadn't understood what she meant. Not at first. After all, the woman was Lady Lilith, daughter of a marquess, sister to his own adopted father, who was accepted everywhere. Her blood was also Philip's blood. Wasn't it?

One day, as Lilith had sat with him in her elaborately decorated drawing room and poured the twelve-year-old his first glass of unwatered wine, she had at last explained her words to him. Explained a society that arbitrarily picked and chose those who were acceptable and shunned those they deemed unworthy.

"Philip has money, you see, and the title. Also, he is, above everything else, a man. Our Jewess mother could not completely taint him, not as I am considered tainted. To be frank, my little savage, Philip has no womb—only money. Why seeds are less tainted than eggs, I cannot say, but society does seem to believe it so."

"Ma'am?" Daniel had asked, gulping down half the contents of his glass, his eyes having grown wide as saucers, he recalled now.

"Call me Lilith, my love, but not when your sweet mother is around or she'd box both our ears, for she is raising you to be a proper young gentleman—probably believing that she can somehow keep from losing you, poor thing. But here, here in the lap of the luxury my lax morals have bought me, we can be friends. It will be our secret. But, to continue today's lesson? Philip has money, yes, but he also has his father's blond good looks, while I am my mother's child—dark hair, dark eyes, looking more like Ruth than the vaunted Mary, my love, if you have read your Bible enough to understand that. No fitting repository for good English seed, although I've had my fair share of deposits, mind you," she ended, winking at him.

She had drained her glass of wine as she laid back against the deep red cushions of her chaise, looked into Daniel's confusion-clouded eyes, then dropped her head back and laughed out loud. "Oh, Philip would have my liver on a spit if he could hear me, wouldn't he? Dear, dear Philip. The apple of our moneylender grandfather's eye—and the sole beneficiary of the old bastard's great fortune. To be fair, he probably would have left me a penny or two as well, if I hadn't already been tipping my heels to the ceiling with any randy gentleman with a title and the good sense to drape my Jewess throat with diamonds, all just for the giggle of it."

"Yes, ma'am," Daniel remembered saying, part of him wanting to bolt from the room, part of him seeing beyond his aunt's rakish banter all the way to the pain she tried so hard to hide. "I am half Lenni Lenape, you know," he had gone on, hoping to change the subject and praying his speech didn't sound as slurred as he thought it did. Why, his teeth had already gone numb, and he was having a most difficult time trying not to yawn. "I had to bloody a boy's nose last week for calling me a savage. That's why I'm here in London and not at school. Got sent down for the whole term." Daniel grinned now, as he had done then. "But it was worth it, ma'am. It truly was worth it."

"We all have our way of getting some of our own back, Daniel," Lilith had told him, toying with the long string of pearls that hung low on her bosom. Then she giggled. "I just happened to discover mine was by *being* on my back! And, Daniel, little friend, what did you call me? Not ma'am, surely!"

Daniel had looked at his aunt, unable to understand her joke. "I'm sorry—Lilith," was all he had said, then asked: "I can't ever be like Michael and Joseph and Johanna, can I? I'll always be different."

Lilith had let out a small, pained cry and then sat up,

slid her feet to the floor, and held out her arms so that Daniel could be drawn into her soft, fragrant embrace. "Oh, Little Savage, of course you will always be different. You will be Daniel. And there can only ever be one of you. You just have to know who *you* are. It doesn't matter what anyone else thinks, what anyone else believes. *You* are the one who has to believe in yourself. Do you understand?"

"Yes, ma'am. Yes, Lilith," Daniel had promised, although he hadn't understood. He hadn't understood at all.

He still didn't. Because he still did not know who Daniel Crown really was.

He smiled now, sadly, and replaced Lilith's portrait on the table. He and his aunt had become fast friends that long-ago day in London, and she had shocked the family by taking him everywhere with her. She had shown him areas of London no young boy should ever have seen, had sat him down in small, shabby drawing rooms so that he could listen to poets and writers and men and women with a far different idea of the world than that of polite society. She had held his hand as they rode the Hi-Low at the Bartholomew Fair, had shared greasy meat pies with him in Tothill Fields, had slipped him into dark pubs that served throat-searing Blue Ruin for a halfpenny a glass.

She had been his mentor, his teacher, his friend. She had shown him *life* in all its forms, all its variety, and minus the disguises of class and birth. She had opened his eyes to the world, made him wish to reach beyond his grasp, taught him that there was more than one way, more than one path.

And she had told him just this past year that it was time he left England and discovered even more of the world and found his place in it.

"You're as good as anyone else, Little Savage," she had whispered to him as she hugged him good-bye the night before he took ship to Philadelphia, "and you are better than most. At the bottom of it, I am bitter. I've always been bitter and done my best to shock the world into noticing me. I've had a good run at it, too, and yet somehow managed to keep your parents' love, which is my greatest treasure—and if you tell that particular truth to either Philip or Brighid, I will have your ears! But now it is your turn to show the world what a mongrel can do, what a mongrel can accomplish. Don't disappoint me, Little Savage. Don't wallow in the bitterness or let it color your happiness. Reach out to life with both hands. Grab it tightly and clutch it to your heart. Be better than me, my love. Be better than me and, perhaps, a little worse."

Daniel looked at the portrait for a long time, until the smaller candles had guttered in their holders. "I'll do my best, Lilith. I'll do my best," he promised quietly, then slowly began to undress.

After all, he would be seeing Brianna Crown in the morning. He'd need to be fully awake and with his wits about him. For although there was little shared blood between them, Brianna Crown had Lilith's same promise of youthful passion in her flashing emerald eyes, the same knowing curve at the edges of her smile, the same bewitching hint of mischief in the uniquely rakish tilt of her head.

Yes, he would need his wits about him in the morning.

A sweet thing, for whatever time, to revisit in dreams the dear dead we have lost.

EURIPIDES

chapter four

Brianna was at the window—curled up on the soft cushions of the wide window seat, her bare toes tucked up under the hem of her white cotton nightrail—a good full half hour before the first soft light of morning rose above the blue mountains in the distance.

She had spent a confused, dream-filled night, a night full of Daniel Crown and his pitch-black eyes, his bright smile that lit those dark eyes, but revealed none of their secrets.

His full head of ebony hair was thick, looked somewhat coarse, and in her dreams she had touched it, run her fingers through its night-dark depths.

His wide, slashing mouth, so intriguing when he spoke, had been hard, yet soft, as she had lifted her lips to his.

His hands, those well-formed, long-fingered hands, had held all the strength in the world and all of its tenderness as they had drawn her close, fully into his embrace.

Puffin, Brianna's coal black cat—an animal her mother swore weighed more than most dogs—hopped up onto the window seat and Brianna nearly cried out, startled from her unnerving recollection of her dream.

"Naughty Puffin," she scolded, putting her hands under the cat's solid belly and pulling him up onto her chest, rubbing her cheek against his short, thick fur. "You're not supposed to frighten me like that. Not when I am thinking things no well-bred young lady should even *imagine.*"

The cat pressed its bewhiskered face into Brianna's neck and began to purr as he licked her skin, so that she giggled as a shiver of reaction ran down her spine. "Yes, yes, Puffin, you're my one and only love. I swear it, you big baby." She held the cat away from her so that it curled its fat tail up and under furry back legs. "But if you're thinking of attacking Daniel Crown the way you sneaked up on poor Henry Merritt that day in the gardens when he dared to hold my hand and pounce on *his* neck with all your claws digging into him—well, you'd best reconsider the matter. I don't believe Cousin Daniel will make quite the same easy target."

Brianna's smile faded as the echo of her last words rang inside her head. Was she warning Puffin or herself? Because it was true. Daniel Crown was no Henry Merritt, who worshiped the very ground she walked on—so very boring!—nor was he Peter Haskins or Charlie O'Donnell or James Trinkle or any of the young men of her acquaintance.

He was Daniel Crown. Part Englishman. Part Lenni Lenape. A rare mix of a man, and all man, from the top of his well-formed head to the soles of his shiny black boots.

And he thought she was a child. A precocious child, no doubt, but a child after all. He didn't see her as a woman. Probably refused to do so. Although he had certainly been unable to ignore her last night at dinner—and he had run off afterward as if afraid to face her back in the drawing room.

So maybe he did know that she was planning to snare his interest, his affections. Why, he would have had to be a complete dolt *not* to know it.

She had warned him in both subtle and obvious ways, which might not have been a good idea, now that she'd had time to sleep on her plans for the capture and taming of Daniel Crown.

And, worst of all, she didn't even know why she wanted him. But she did. She wanted him very much. On his knees. Prostrate before her. Begging for the touch of her hand, a smile meant just for him.

Just to prove she could do it.

Just as she had proven she could do everything else, everything she did so well, so effortlessly.

Although conquering Daniel Crown, she already knew, would not be accomplished without effort.

Considerable effort.

Brianna rubbed her face into the purring cat's warm fur. "But there's more, Puffin," she said, closing her eyes against the dawn. "There's something else. Something about Daniel Crown that I can't explain and don't understand. Something in his eyes that turns my stomach into mush. A look to him that makes me nervous and intrigued . . . and a little bit frightened. Are you ever frightened, Puffin? Well, of course you are. You're just a big, old scaredy-cat, aren't you?"

She laid Puffin on the soft cushion and stood up, eager to bathe and dress and be waiting outside for Daniel when he arrived, taking him off to Lokwelend's before her mother or father could invite him in to breakfast.

Because, more than anything else, she wanted to be alone with him. Wanted to observe him as he moved through the woods, along the narrow path leading to Lokwelend's cabin. Wanted to see how he reacted, watch where he looked, hear what he said.

If only she knew why . . .

* * *

Daniel wore his white, full-sleeved shirt open at the collar beneath a chocolate brown, serviceable vest and atop a pair of deep brown trousers that looped under his instep and were partially hidden by his nearly knee-high riding boots. He wore his long, unpowdered hair tied back with a thin, black taffeta ribbon and had left his hat and riding gloves behind, untouched, on the foyer table.

He had done all of this over the impassioned protests of a still sleepy-eyed Finn—who had asked his employer, more than once, what the wicked, wicked world was coming to. He had then departed Enolowin on Lenape Traveler's back before the smell of cinnamon coming from the kitchens could lure him into staying for the undoubtedly delicious breakfast the early-rising Mrs. Bing was preparing for everyone.

Daniel had wanted to wear the deerskins and moccasins Brighid Crown had given him before he took ship, but he was convinced Brianna would take one look at him and laugh. So he'd left them in the mahogany wardrobe, still wrapped in a large square of deerskin. He continued to be amazed by his mother's farewell gift and Philip's explanation of how he had obeyed his wife's plea that he "harvest" the needed deer for her project from the home woods. She had then spent long hours tanning the hides in the Lenape way, cutting and sewing them into two pairs of leggings and two loose-fitting, fringed jackets. She had even sewn dyed seeds onto the jacket for decoration and woven him a long, colorful sash to tie around his waist.

And she had done all this last winter, long before Daniel had gone to his parents and told them he wished to visit Enolowin. When Daniel had questioned her about it, she had only smiled and squeezed his hand and said that Lokwelend had told her long ago that one must not only put their trust in fate but always be prepared for it as well.

Daniel guided Lenape Traveler along the trail, circling

around to the place where a grassy hill made it possible to climb to the top of Lenape Cliff, then tied the stallion's reins to a young sapling. He looked up at the hill, beyond the tall, waving grasses sprinkled with blue periwinkle on long, woody stems, sighed, and began climbing, the package in his jacket pocket hitting against his thigh as he walked.

Inside the packet he carried smaller packages of cornmeal, and sunflower seeds, and two wee blue, cork-topped bottles of Mrs. Bing's molasses—gifts for Lapawin and Lokwelend. In his other pocket was a fine hunting knife, which he would bury near the edge of the cliff, where Pematalli's spirit could find it. And Daniel did not feel in the least bit foolish, because he and Lokwelend had always brought gifts to Pematalli. Now he would bring gifts to his "grandparents" as well.

His long strides made short work of the steep incline, and as the sun slanted over the cliff top, shining off the shiny new leaves of the smaller trees, he walked to the edge of the precipice and looked out over the valley, down on Enolowin, his heart bursting with pride and pain and a love whose intensity frightened him. Tears filled his eyes, and he let them fall, sliding unashamedly down his cheeks.

He took the knife from his pocket and sank it into the ground, the blade disappearing all the way to its hilt. The soil was soft, yielding, accepting of his gift.

Daniel's throat muscles worked painfully as he attempted to swallow the emotion that rose in him as he closed his eyes, acknowledging what he had always known—what Philip must always have known and Brighid had probably always feared—yet a knowledge Daniel had never before allowed himself to believe.

England was small and stifling, and London was suffocating. He had never felt alive there but had merely existed. He knew that now, as his adoptive parents must have always known it. *This* was his land, his home, his heritage. The virgin forests, the sweeping green hills, the clear, bubbling streams, the low blue mountains where the beaver had once run free, the smell of freedom all around him. Wulapen's blood sang in his veins; Lokwelend's memory, Lapawin's spirit, lived in his heart.

Daniel turned, looking at the painted wooden pole markers that marked the place where Lapawin slept, where Lokwelend's body rested. He went down on his knees beside each simple monument, then offered his gifts. He pressed his palms against the sun-warmed grass and felt Lokwelend's spirit rise inside him.

For years Daniel had fought his destiny. For years he had done his best to forget. For years he had tried to be someone he could never, ever be.

But not now.

Now, at last, Tasukamend was really home.

If the land and the people would accept him.

Seventeen years, and Lokwelend's log cabin was still as Daniel remembered it. Oh, it was smaller than it had been when seen through the eyes of an eight-year-old boy, and there was a big black iron padlock on the door and sturdy boards nailed across its single window. But it was still Daniel's special place, where he had sat across the outdoor fire from his grandfather, listening to fine tales and stories told for the first, fifth, tenth time, until they were embedded in his brain, his memory.

The path between Pleasant Hill and Lokwelend's home had narrowed but still existed very much as it had in Daniel's memories, twisting and turning through the dense woods, opening onto the small clearing that had always seemed to emerge miraculously from the dark depths of the trees.

The stream still ran past the log house, singing as it bubbled over the rocks, dragging at the long, fragile branches of the willows that wept into the clear water.

Deer still came to the water to drink, as a doe and her young did now, standing on the far bank, looking at Daniel and Brianna, gauging the danger their presence might mean to them, then bending their heads to drink once more.

Brianna pulled a large key from the pocket of her simple rose-colored gown and walked toward the door. "Mama told me that Papa put on the lock himself the day after he buried Lokwelend, and he personally keeps up the repairs, filling in the chinks between the logs when the weather opens new holes. Cora would come here once in a while, but nobody else. Now that Cora and Lucas and their children have all moved to Philadelphia—well, I've visited a time or two in her place, I guess, keeping up her vigil until she or one of her children returns as she says they will. It's so quiet here, you understand. So very peaceful."

"It wasn't always peaceful," Daniel said, pushing the toe of his boot against one of the rocks that circled the campfire. "I did many a dance around this campfire. Your brothers, Roarke and Nicholas, would join me—the three of us clad only in loinclouts and painted faces—leaping and howling and making Lapawin laugh so hard her cheeks would nearly split in two. We danced for rain and for a good harvest and, once, in the hopes your mother and mine wouldn't learn that we'd used their petticoats for fishnets and then lost both of the things to a strong current."

Brianna laughed, her green eyes sparkling. "Roarke and Nicholas? Oh, I would have loved to have seen that! They're two such solemn stick-in-the-muds now, creeping toward thirty and acting as if they are ninety—and never seeing the joke in anything. As if it was *my* fault that my last three nannies fell in love with the pair of them. Them, and Sean and Damon as well. It's a true trial, I keep telling Mama, that I should have been cursed with four older brothers—and two matched sets of them, at that. Why, it is all I can do to say hello to a boy in the village without the four of them growling and glaring at the poor soul."

"My sympathies, Brianna. But *three* nannies?" Daniel asked, raising an eyebrow as he looked at her, watching her cheeks flame. "You must have been quite a handful."

"I had six, actually, or at least six that I can remember," she answered, walking toward the cabin and mounting the three steps that led to the door. She fitted the key into the lock, then looked over her shoulder at Daniel. "And they all loved me dearly. I just seemed to, well, wear out a few of them, I suppose you could say. The others either fell in love with any one of my four handsome, bachelor brothers or decided that living in the back of beyond was simply too tedious to be borne."

The key turned in the lock and the large padlock snapped open. She grinned at him in triumph. "There! Shall we go inside and see what wonders we can discover?"

Daniel followed her in, shaking his head at her youthful exuberance, her eagerness for a bit of adventure. She had been standing outside when he had ridden up to Pleasant Hill, laughing out loud, tossing chunks of bread to a crowd of chirping birds who seemed so totally unafraid of her that he wouldn't have been surprised if they had eaten out of her hand.

The sun had been glinting off her deep copper curls as they hung loose halfway down her back, looking as warm as a mother's touch, as bright as a spring morning. Her trim figure, her waist so small, the swell of her breast so almost painfully perfect, the tilt of her head so naturally enchanting—all had combined to send warning bells clanging in Daniel's head. *Stay away. Stay away,* the bells had cried. *This one is not for you. This one could hurt you.*

But her greeting had been cheerful, unaffected, and genuinely voiced, as if the greatest pleasure she might find in this particular day was his presence in it, and he hadn't been able to resist smiling back at her. If she treated everyone she met in this same open, warm manner, well, it was not difficult for Daniel to understand why Brianna Crown was universally loved.

And so he had followed her as she led him to the back of Pleasant Hill, down through the acres-wide gardens made up of neat squares of flowers, vegetables, and fruit trees, and into the tree line. He had stopped behind her, waiting patiently as she gathered a few wildflowers, exclaiming over their beauty, breathing in their scent—and then tucking a single pink blossom into her hair, above her left ear. He had put out a hand as she navigated a fat, moss-covered tree trunk that had fallen across the path and had continued to hold her hand until they had at last come out into the clearing in front of Lokwelend's cabin.

Now here he was again, like an eager puppy, once more following where she led, bending his head as he negotiated the low lintel that had once seemed so high, and stepping into the musky darkness inside the cabin.

"Here," Brianna said, her form only faintly visible in the dim light as she dug into the pockets of her gown, "I've brought two candle stubs from the kitchens, one for each of us. Help me strike a light?"

The golden glow from the two candles, added to the sunlight pouring in through the opened door, lit the interior of the small cabin, all except for its darkest corners, which were also closer to the center of the single room than Daniel remembered. Had he grown so tall, or had the cabin grown smaller?

Lokwelend's rope-strung cot still leaned against one wall, and the crates and boxes that had served as his only storage lined another. A patterned blanket hung drunkenly from the wall over the bed, as did an old bow and a quiver of arrows. Brianna gave out a small squeak of alarm as a small brown mouse scurried across the dusty floor.

"Let's see what's in the boxes, shall we?" she asked, then knelt in front of one of them before Daniel could say anything. "Oh, look!" she exclaimed a moment later, holding the candle stub close to the box as she wiped her hand across the lid. "This one has your name on it."

Daniel dropped to his knees beside her, his heart pounding. "Here, let me do that," he said as Brianna struggled to untie the knot in the coarse brown string holding the box shut. He stuck out his leg, reached into the wide cuff of his boot, and extracted a knife that sat in the sewn-in sheath that reached nearly to his ankle. Its sharp blade glinted in the candlelight.

"Oh, my," Brianna said, chuckling. "A knife in your boot. Who would have thought it? How very fierce you are, cousin."

"Not all the wild bears are in America," was all he said as he slid the knife blade under the twine and sliced it neatly in two. A moment later, the wooden lid was lying on the rough floor and Daniel had extracted a square of deerskin tied up with another length of twine. Holding the package to him, he offered his free hand to Brianna, and the two of them rose and walked out of the cabin back into the sunshine.

Daniel longed to open the package, but he wasn't sure of his reaction to the unknown contents, although he was quite positive that whatever that reaction might be, he didn't want Brianna to witness it. Which was, he realized a moment later, as fruitless a wish as hoping for the stream next to him to turn into a river of molten gold.

"What are you waiting for?" Brianna asked, fairly dancing with excitement. "How can you just stand there? I mean, Lokwelend left this to you. It's his legacy, his fortune, his—well, it's his *something!* All these years, just sitting here, waiting for you. This is like seeing my presents at the breakfast table on Christmas morning, and then having to wait until everyone is seated before I can so much as touch one. Damon would always be late, just to tease me. Oh, hurry, Daniel! I don't think I can wait another moment!"

He shook his head. "You're such a child, Brianna," he

told her, trying not to smile. But her anticipation was infectious, and he walked over to the old fire circle and the wide, flat rocks that served as seats, waited until Brianna had sat down, her skirts spread around her, and then joined her. This time he didn't use his knife on the twine, not wanting to destroy a single thing Lokwelend had left him, a single thing the wise Grandfather had touched.

The deerskin was old and stiff and impossible to completely unfold, and Daniel's mouth was dry with suppressed excitement, with nervousness, as he carefully peeled back the layers.

"What is it?" Brianna asked, leaning forward, doing her best to see beneath the last corner of the deerskin. "Why, it's books! Of all the things that could be in the package, I never would have thought of books."

Daniel lifted the three well-worn volumes, paging through them one after the other, his vision clouded with unexpected tears. "Euripides," he said, smiling as he held the first book out to Brianna. "How could I have forgotten? Lokwelend greatly admired the man and quoted him often. He considered him to be a great and wise chief."

Brianna took the book and laid it in her lap, lightly stroking the worn leather cover with her fingertips. "And the others?"

"A prayer book, given to him by the Moravian missionaries from Bethlehem. And," he hesitated for a moment, then continued, "and Lokwelend's private journal." He slipped the journal into the pocket of his jacket without showing it to Brianna, then handed her the prayer book. "There's more," he said, searching inside the folds of deerskin and coming out with Lokwelend's wire-rimmed spectacles. "I guess he didn't think he'd need them anymore, once he was welcomed to the warrior's table. I'd like to think he was right."

Now Brianna reached into the packet, searching its corners with her fingertips and coming up empty. "I guess that's everything. No! Wait! There's something else." She pulled out her prize and held it up for Daniel to see. "What on earth . . . ?"

Daniel stared at the loop of wolf's teeth, tied together by a thin leather strip that had been threaded through holes bored into each separate tooth. "My God, he saved that?" He reached out his hand and took the string from Brianna, squeezing it in his hand, feeling the dull, worn teeth press into the skin of his palm. "Lokwelend made this for me when I was still an infant, not that I remember. But he showed it to me many times as I grew older."

"And? Don't tease, Daniel," Brianna pleaded. "What *is* it?"

He handed it to her. "Those are wolf's teeth. I used to chew on them to ease the pain in my gums when I was cutting my own teeth. They were meant to make me strong like the wolf."

Brianna stared at the string, then touched a few of the teeth with the tip of her finger. "That's fascinating, Daniel," she told him, looking at him in something that seemed close to awe. "I chewed on a silver cup Papa brought home from one of his trips to Philadelphia. I imagine the metal felt cold and soothing on my gums. I still have that cup—all dented with tiny teeth marks. How different customs are, but how universal the pains of growing up."

Avoiding her eyes and the eagerness he could see in them, Daniel took the string from her and replaced it in the deerskin, along with the books and Lokwelend's spectacles. "Yes, Brianna, we are very different. Whole worlds apart, I'd say, for all that we both live in this same supposedly civilized world."

She chased after him when he rose and began walking back toward the cabin, her skirts hitched a good six inches off the ground so that she could keep up with his long strides. "I know what you're saying, Daniel Crown, and I have to tell you that I very much resent being warned away in such a fashion. You're no more the savage than I am, no matter what the circumstances of your birth."

He turned around quickly, so quickly that she nearly barreled into his chest, and he had to put his hands on her shoulders to support her. "You're right, Brianna. I'm not a savage, noble or otherwise. I'm a man. No more, no less. But you see me as some sort of exotic creature, don't you? And in your foolish, juvenile mind I have, overnight, become a challenge to you. But I'm too old to play at your games, Brianna, and you're much too young and innocent to play at mine."

He watched the hurt cloud her eyes and he wanted to kick himself, but he couldn't let her know that she—in her very openness, her willingly offered friendship—had the power to bother him, to touch him. "Brianna, do you understand what I'm saying to you?"

Brianna's chin lifted and the skin over her cheekbones grew taut even as the color drained out of her face. "I don't have the faintest idea what you're talking about, cousin, although I do believe you most likely have a mighty high opinion of yourself," she said, her voice not wavering in the slightest as she stared straight at him, her eyes wide and guileless. *Oh, she's a handful,* Daniel thought. *And someday she's going to lead some poor fellow a merry dance. But not this man. Oh, no. Not this man.*

He let her win because it was easier. "In that case, Brianna, I offer you my most profound apologies. Now, if you'll just give me the key, I'll secure the cabin and we can return to Pleasant Hill so that I can retrieve Lenape Traveler and be on my way back to Enolowin. I have more to do today than visit old memories."

"Yes, of course you do," Brianna said, giving him the key. "Why, I suppose you have to scalp at least three babies before luncheon." And she smartly turned on her heels and walked away from him at a fairly furious stomp.

He admired her departure, the soft swing anger lent her hips, until she disappeared into the trees. A smile played about his mouth even as he warned himself that the precocious infant was, in fact, no child at all, but a lovely, frustrating, tormenting thorn in his side—and one that showed no signs of giving him any sort of peace for some time to come. He hefted the heavy key in his hand, then locked the door, and slipped the cold metal into his pocket.

Skelton was standing outside the stables when Daniel got back to Enolowin, his back turned to his employer, his arms akimbo as he stared up at Lenape Cliff.

"It's the damnedest thing, sir," he told Daniel as he hurried to hold Lenape Traveler's head as Daniel dismounted. "I keep looking and looking at that hulking mass of rock, and I could swear it's looking back at me.

Daniel laughed, rubbing the older man's mostly bald head, so that the fringe of lank, shoulder-length brown hair—that started just above his ears and fitted the back of his shiny head like a skirt—was set to swaying. "It is looking back at you, Skelton," he told him. "That's Pematalli, Lokwelend's son. He lives in that cliff, reminding everyone that this is his land. Always was, always will be."

"Lokwelend's son? Go on with you, sir. That there stallion of yours ain't even been put to stud yet. Oh—wait a minute! You mean that old Indian fella you told me and Finn about whilst we was aboard that bloody ship. The one you named the Arabian after, right?"

"Right, Skelton," Daniel said, pulling the blanket off the stallion's back after Skelton had removed the saddle. "Remember? Lenape stands for the Lenni Lenape, the Indians who once lived here. And, in English words, Lokwelend means 'The Traveler.'"

Skelton crunched up his features, his fat button nose nearly disappearing into his chubby cheeks. "Lokwelend, the traveler. Thought I had it right. M'sainted mother would have called that poetical, sir," he said, hefting the saddle onto his shoulder and heading for the stable. "I'll just put this down, then walk that traveling Indian of yours awhile before putting him to his vittles. Have you given any more thought to letting him serve that fine mare I saw here yesterday? They'd make a fine match, I say. The stallion's speed, and the mare's size and muscle. Good foals there, sir."

"You're in a hurry to get started, aren't you, Skelton? The horses we bought in Philadelphia will be here soon enough." Daniel remarked, watching as the short, portly man passed the saddle over to a freckle-faced young lad he didn't recognize. "Who's that?"

Skelton looked over his shoulder at the boy, as if he needed a second look to remember his name. "Him? That's Toby. Met him in town this morning at the smithy's shop. I liked the way he talked to my horse, soothing him, and hired him on the spot. You got a problem with that?"

Daniel shook his head, trying not to smile. He didn't know why and didn't plan to investigate the matter; but, although he was respected, even somewhat feared in his own circle, he seemed to have a talent for attracting the most insubordinate servants imaginable. Finn, Skelton—and probably the Bings as well, who had thus far seen no reason to put their employer on a pedestal. "These are your stables, Skelton," he said, touching the book in his pocket, remembering that he was in a hurry to go someplace private and begin reading its contents. "What is it Finn says—I don't keep a dog and bark myself? Yes, that's it. You're the best horse trainer in all of England and now all of America, my friend. I wouldn't think to nay-say your decisions."

He turned away, planning to head for the porch and the pair of rockers he remembered seeing there yesterday. "Oh," he said, turning back for a moment, "how much am I paying this Toby? I do hope I'm not a miserly employer."

Skelton grinned. "No worry on that head, sir. You're generous to a fault. Did I tell you that Toby's ma is a widow woman? And pretty as a picture, I swear. Round and merry, and my hostess for dinner this very night. Oh, you're a fine, open-handed employer to young Toby, sir. Just fine."

Still shaking his head, Daniel walked across the lawns to the house and climbed the steps to the large, wraparound porch. Taking one of the rockers, pulling it closer to the porch rail so that, once seated, he could rest his booted heels on the railing, he opened Lokwelend's journal, carefully turning to the first age-dry page, and began to read, admiring the man's clear, legible script.

So, Tasukamend, you have returned. This is good. You are a man now; tall and strong like your father. Lenape, like your father. Decent, like both your fathers. Blessed among men to have so many choices. Troubled because of those choices.

I have left you the white man's God to teach you to be kind, and gentle, and loving. I have given you the wise chief, Euripides, to guide you. I leave you my words to remind you. For you are Tasukamend, the Blameless One. You are the promise, the hope, the future.

I miss your parents. Tauwún, my son, who you know as Philip. Your mother, Brighid, who is Nipawi Gischuch, the Night Fire. But they live in my heart, as they live in yours. They love you well, Tasukamend. I know this because they have sent you back to Enolowin, even though it pains them.

I pray that Crown is still with us, that his wife, the Bright Fire, is still with us. Listen well to my friend Crown, for he, like Euripides, is a wise chief. Allow the Bright Fire to love you, for her strong will cannot be bent in any other direction, no matter how hard you might try.

You have met Wapa-Kwelik, the Dawn Sky, have you

not? She is the Bright Fire born again. The new beginning. She visited me in a dream long ago. I was there, waiting, when she was born. Her small fingers closed tight around mine, and she looked at me with her mother's eyes. Her will also is strong and cannot be bent.

You have much to look forward to, Tasukamend, and much to fear. But remember, my son, what the wise chief Euripides said. "The nobly born must nobly meet his fate."

Put this book away now, Tasukamend, and live your life. It will be here, waiting for you, as I will be waiting for you, when you have need of us again.

Daniel closed the journal and looked out over the sweeping lawns of Enolowin, amazed at Lokwelend's words, at his great love for the child he had taught so long ago.

And he thought of Brianna Crown, and her strong, unbendable will.

Advice is seldom welcome; and those who want it the most always like it the least.

EARL OF CHESTERFIELD

chapter five

Brianna sat on the floor in the middle of her bedchamber, surrounded by every gown in her not inconsiderable wardrobe, her chin in her hands, and glaring at each separate piece of clothing in turn. "Too yellow, too short, too babyish, too old-fashioned, too much lace, too—well, just *too.*"

"Ei-yi-yi!" Wanda exclaimed, coming into the room, her arms full of freshly laundered underclothing. "Would you look at this mess! And when I work so hard to keep things just so."

Brianna winced, acknowledging the jumble of clothes, but not to be deterred. "I'm sorry, Wanda, but it's hopeless. I have nothing to wear."

"Really?" the maid said, setting her load down on the bed. "And how many bodies would you have that you need more clothing? As my ma said to me many a time, make do or do without. So, make do, young lady, for doing without would keep you locked up here all the day long in your dressing gown."

Bryna set her chin stubbornly, not ready to give up her

bad mood even though the older woman's words made her want to giggle. "I'm serious, Wanda. Three of these gowns were Felicia's, for goodness' sake, and I've had that blue one forever and ever. You yourself have taken out the seams and hem twice. I must look completely provincial compared to the ladies of London. Rustic. Bucolic." She sighed, deeply. *"Young."*

"Ach, now we have it!" Wanda bent down and began gathering up the offending gowns, rehanging them in the cherry wood wardrobe. "You think your cousin would look more if you had a few new gowns. Ones with the neck cut down to the waist, no doubt. Well, your mama will have none of that, I'm sure. And neither will I. Just you remember, missy, whistling girls and crowing hens come to a bad end."

Brianna looked up, frowning. "And what on earth does that mean?"

Another gown was put back into the wardrobe. "I have no idea, child, but my mama said it any time I thought to try something she didn't want me to try."

Handing another gown to Wanda, Brianna thought about the thing for a few more moments, then said, "I know! Your mama didn't want you whistling like boys or crowing like men. Your mama wanted you to be a polite, malleable young miss—just the sort of young lady Mama despairs of me ever becoming, I suppose. Well, what would a few new gowns have to do with that, Wanda?"

Wanda averted her head, mumbling under her breath, "Ach, I grow too soon old and too late smart." Then she turned to Brianna with a bright smile. "Didn't your mother say you were to get a whole new wardrobe when we go off to London in the fall?"

Brianna wrinkled up her nose. "That will be too late, Wanda." She picked up the yellow gown and eyed the bodice assessingly. "If we could just snip off some of this lace—"

The maid grabbed the gown out of Brianna's hands.

"Not with my scissors, we won't! Next you'll be wanting me to put up your hair."

"As a matter of fact, Wanda," Brianna said, struggling to her feet, "as Papa is already off to Enolowin, inviting Cousin Daniel to dinner this evening, I *was* thinking of doing something different with—Mama! I didn't hear you come in."

Bryna Crown swept into the center of the room, looked at the clutter of gowns and other clothing, and looked apologetically at Wanda. "You can go, Wanda. I believe the one who made the mess should have the cleaning of it, don't you?"

"Yes, ma'am," Wanda said, shooting Brianna a fairly triumphant look, then scurrying out, unable to hide her relief at making this unexpected lucky escape.

"You have an explanation, I'm sure," Bryna said as Brianna hastened to remove a pink-and-white striped gown from the brocade chaise longue so that her mother could sit down. "One that, from what little I've overheard, has little to do with fashion and much to do with Cousin Daniel?"

"I'm eighteen, Mama. Or I will be in three weeks," Brianna said, telling the truth only because she was unable to summon up a quick lie. "And Daniel is not a blood relative. Is there any harm in wanting to look nice for him?"

"None that I can think of, pet," her mother answered, arranging her skirts about her after reaching beneath her and extracting a silver-topped comb—the one Brianna had been experimenting with earlier, then flung across the room in a temper when it had failed to hold her heavy mass of burnished curls on top of her head. "But I do have a question, if I might?"

Brianna nodded, her tongue suddenly stuck to the roof of her mouth. Her mother was never mean, never condescending—but she had this most annoying habit of finding her target with a single, incisive shaft. There was no fooling her, no hiding behind a fib, no self-protection to be found in evasion. Sooner or later, mostly sooner, her mother found out every little thing Brianna did wrong, every little thought she might have, every big and small problem she might be facing—and any mischief she might be considering. In the end, it was simply easier to tell the woman the truth, and then together the two of them could deal with what had to be done next.

"What is it, Mama?" Brianna asked now, feeling the first drops of the cold rain of reality about to descend on her daydreaming head.

"You are, my love, a brilliant, talented child, if a somewhat mischievous and even trying one. You get that touch of disobedience from me, by the by, for we are both cursed with a headstrong nature. But I have learned, as I have had to, that wanting something is not the same as getting that something. There are, I'm afraid, limits to our reach, our grasp. Even limits to what we *should* have."

"Yes, Mama," Brianna said, sitting down on the edge of the bed. Her mother was taking the long road leading to her "question," and she might as well make herself comfortable.

"Do you remember insisting, at the age of about seven, I believe, that you should be taught how to play the harp?"

"Yes, Mama," Brianna mumbled again, squirming a little on the bed, knowing where this line of questioning was heading. "I begged and I begged until Papa sent all the way to Easton for a teacher."

"And you play beautifully, not that you go within ten paces of that harp more than once a month and haven't for years. The same is true for your singing, your passion for gardening, your insistence upon learning to tat. All challenges, all met and exceeded, and all nearly abandoned the moment you mastered them."

"I like a challenge, Mama," Brianna protested, although only weakly, for her mother was right. "But once something becomes easy for me, I do lose some of my earlier interest. It's a failing, I know."

"Exactly. You've also conquered half the boys in New Eden, although I will say that you never set your cap at any of them. They just took one look at you one fine day a few years ago and the next thing your father and I knew, Pleasant Hill was knee-deep in sighing, fawning young men. Young men you most happily ignored, being content with your horses."

"Can I help it if Peter and Charlie O'Donnell and even James Trinkle insist upon riding out here and making calf's eyes at me? I never asked them to, you know. And, yes, Mama, they do bore me to flinders. But I adore my horses and have for years. They continue to challenge me, I suppose. I could never give up my horses."

Bryna stood and walked over to her daughter, putting a hand on her cheek. "And what of Daniel, pet? Unlike the young men in the village, he doesn't come here and make calf's eyes over you. Which makes him a challenge to you, yes? And so, Brianna, my questions to you are these—if you see Daniel as a challenge, and you conquer that challenge, will he then end up like your harp, your abandoned tatting, your gardening? Or will he continue to challenge you? And if he does, are you prepared to deal with the consequences? Because Daniel Crown is not one of those silly young boys from the village. He's a man, my love. He's very much a man and unlike any man you have ever met."

Brianna looked up at her mother, her lips suddenly tight, so that she had to moisten them with the tip of her tongue before answering. "Are you warning me, Mama? You are, aren't you? Is it because Daniel is a half-breed? Because I don't care about his blood. I'm just happy we don't really share any."

Bryna's lovely face went stern, so that her daughter immediately knew she had said precisely the wrong thing. "Daniel has a proud heritage, and your father and I would be honored to have him join our family as more than Brighid and Philip's adopted son. But you're our little girl, Brianna, our baby. We don't want to see you hurt. Daniel is here because he is unsure of who he is, of what he wants. You can only complicate the questions he is asking himself. You can only be hurt if the answers he finds do not include you. Or if they do, and you cast him away, bored with yet another easy conquest, then *he* will be hurt. I adore you, pet, but I also owe it to Philip and Brighid to watch over their son, as they would watch over you. Do you understand now?"

Brianna turned away, avoiding her mother's eyes. "Yes. Yes, I do. You think I'm a spoiled, willful child. And I suppose I am." She swiveled back to her mother. "But this is different, Mama. I took one look at him—just a single look—and I knew. I *knew* that he was the one." She reached out, impulsively taking hold of her mother's hands. "Did you feel that way when you first saw Papa?"

Bryna laughed, her memories giving her the appearance of a young girl. "Good heavens, no! I wanted to rip out his guts and use them for garters. Only later, much later, did I realize that the reason I hated him so much was because I loved him so much." She bent down and kissed her daughter on both cheeks. "We'll see about a few new gowns, pet, but this conversation will remain a secret between the two of us. Your papa would probably feel honor bound to warn Daniel and, as in any war, there are advantages to be found in secrecy."

Brianna sprang up from the bed and hugged her mother close. "I love you, Mama," she said sincerely, tears stinging her eyes.

Bryna patted her daughter on the back. "As I love you, pet." Then she laughed. "I believe you are growing up, although it is not going to be a painless experience for you. And I also believe this is going to be another long, long summer for all of us."

* * *

Dominick Crown was waiting when Daniel got back from putting Lenape Traveler through his paces, riding him neck-or-nothing over the still fallow fields, taking the five-bar fence Brianna and her mare must have taken to get onto Enolowin land.

Pulling the stallion to a plunging halt and then dismounting in one easy movement—Toby running forward to take the horse's reins and begin walking him around the paddock—Daniel strode over to Dominick, took off his glove, and shook the man's hand. "Good morning, sir. It's good to see you."

Dominick returned the greeting, shaking his head. "Brianna would probably give up her hope of heaven to ride that beauty," he said as the two men fell into step, walking back toward the house. "Or has she already been over here, begging for your permission? No, I take that back. Not that she wouldn't ride over here, for she would in a heartbeat, but she'd be challenging you to a race. Freedom's Lady is quite a horse, you know, although I'm not sure she could best that stallion of yours over the long course, not with its Arabian blood."

"Then I'll have to arrange for a shorter race, where her mare's quick speed will help to even the odds," Daniel said, passing his gaze out over the lawns in front of the house—his house—smiling, as he always did when he felt his heart tighten at the beauty that surrounded him.

"Do and she'll hate you," Dominick warned him as the two men climbed the steps and entered the foyer. "Ah, it's good to see the furniture out of dust covers. Do the Bings suit you? They've been here so long on their own that I imagine they are a bit proprietorial about the place. Just remember, Daniel, that you're the one in charge."

As they made their way to the study at the back of the house, Daniel laughed aloud at this suggestion. "Me tell Mrs. Bing what to do? I'd rather wrestle a wounded bear. And Otto has taught me a lot in these past few days as we've spent the evenings sitting on the side porch, rocking and watching the stars rise. He's a good manager, as he told me himself. What was it he said to me last night? Oh yes—a fat wife and a fat barn don't hurt any man. And Mrs. Bing fairly beamed at him when he said it, believe that or not."

Dominick chuckled as he sat down, then thanked Daniel for the glass of wine he'd handed him. "Otto is full of strange wisdoms and superstitions, I'm afraid, and some of them don't make much sense. For instance, he is convinced that planting beans during an ascending moon will make them climb their poles more easily, just as planting onions at the same time will make it impossible for them to stay in the ground."

"I've walked through Mrs. Bing's kitchen garden, sir. The beans are already high, and the onions are still in the ground, their green tops growing nicely." Daniel took a full swallow of wine, his throat dry from his long ride. "So, as long as Otto doesn't expect me to harvest hay at midnight, or some such thing, I imagine I'll let him keep doing what he's doing."

"Just don't tell him to begin the hay harvest on a Friday," Dominick warned. "That's bad luck." He shook his head. "I only wish he'd told me that five years ago, when I began the haying at Pleasant Hill on a Friday, only to have a clear blue sky turn black by noon, followed by three days of drenching rain."

Mrs. Bing knocked on the already opened door and stuck her head inside without waiting for an invitation. "Ach, it's company! Hullo, Mr. Crown, sir. Would you be wanting something for your stomach? The apple tart is all, but there's blueberry yet. I'll fetch you both a slice and some nice cold milk. Oh, and some chowchow to take home to the missus, seeing as how she fair dotes on my recipe. Ain't seen Miss Brianna here in days, or I woulda given it to her to carry home over to Pleasant Hill. Just go on talking. I'll be back in a minute."

Daniel grinned at Dominick. "We're, ah, rather *infor-*

mal here at Enolowin, sir," he explained. "And I rather enjoy it, actually."

"We're a long way from England, Daniel, and every one of us feels confident that we are the other's equal," the older man said, nodding. "That being the case, I'd rather you called me Dominick. Hearing a man of five and twenty constantly addressing me so formally is, well, *aging.* So, Brianna hasn't come visiting? I find that difficult to believe."

Mrs. Bing reentered the room, carrying a heavy wooden tray, which Daniel relieved her of, holding it as she set out plates of pie, two heavy, homely kitchen forks, and a pair of fine lead glass goblets filled to the brim with milk on the desktop. She took the two large linen napkins and handed one to Dominick before waving the other one in Daniel's face. "Put this on your lap if you're neat, or tuck it up under your chin if you're anything like my Otto. Ach—the scrubbing it takes to outten blueberry stains from a good white shirt! Well, go eat now. I'm back to the kitchen. Otto brought me from the hen house a fine fat chicken for dinner."

"I'm sorry, Dominick," Daniel said, fighting a grin after Mrs. Bing bustled out of the room. "You were saying?"

Dominick reached out and picked up the plate and fork meant for him, then sat back, eyeing the blueberry confection with approval. "Bryna has sent me to invite you to dinner tonight. Will this be the first time you've seen Brianna since she left you at Lokwelend's, hoping you'd get lost in the woods and never find your way home?"

Sobering, Daniel nodded. "She was right to be angry with me. I wasn't as subtle as I could have been, I'm afraid. But I have enough on my plate right now without the romantic notions of a young girl to complicate matters further, if you'll forgive me for being blunt."

With a wave of his fork, Dominick seemed to dismiss

both Daniel's admission and his apology. "You found the box Lokwelend left for you?"

"I did." Daniel wasn't ready to share any more information with his uncle, and the man didn't press him. "I want to thank you for preserving his cabin so well. I only wish Lokwelend could have been there to greet me. Although," he continued quietly, "in a way, he was. What an extraordinary man."

"I've never had a better friend, save Philip," Dominick said, looking toward the window, toward the past, Daniel thought.

"Lokwelend left a journal behind for me. In it he told me to rely on you, for you are a great chief," Daniel told him. "My father said much the same."

"You'll be fine, Daniel," Dominick said, putting down his empty plate and retrieving his cane as he stood up. "But I will be here if you ever need me. And you will still come to dinner tonight, won't you? Good! We're having other guests as well, or so Bryna informed me this morning. Our neighbors, the Paytons, and their daughter Corliss and her young man, some English gentleman she met in Philadelphia. I think you'll enjoy John Payton. He's quite the individual."

Daniel walked back through the foyer beside Dominick, the two of them stopping at the front door. "I'm sure it will be a pleasant evening," he said, realizing that with the number of guests, he would automatically be paired with Brianna. "Until tonight?"

Dominick put out a hand, laying it on Daniel's sleeve. "About Brianna, Daniel," he said, sounding suddenly serious. "I thought over our discussion of the other evening, and I'm afraid I might have given you a few wrong impressions."

"Sir?"

"Don't be polite, Daniel," Dominick cautioned him. "So, just to make myself clear, I want to tell you that I'd be happy to have you as a son-in-law, not that you have any such leap into a dizzying abyss planned, of course," he ended, smiling again. "Just remember that Brianna is not the child you think her or still the infant in arms her mother and I wish her to be. And with that said, I can only wish you luck and patience. If I know my younger daughter at all, I'm afraid you're going to need both."

Daniel raised a hand to his forehead, spanning it so that he could rub at his temples with thumb and index finger. "Marriage is far from uppermost on my mind right now, Dominick. Even marriage to your very beautiful daughter." He dropped his arm to his side, grinning. "As a matter of fact, I'd have to say that marriage to your daughter is quite the *last* thing on my mind."

"Yes, you probably think so," Dominick said, descending the few steps, then paused, turning to look up at his adopted nephew. "We'll be expecting you at six—and in full protective armor, I imagine." And then he took the reins of his horse as Toby offered them, still chuckling as he mounted and rode off.

Brianna and her childhood friend, Corliss Payton, walked arm in arm through the gardens at Pleasant Hill, catching up on all the news since their last meeting, before the Paytons had left to visit cousins in Philadelphia.

"Tell me all about him, Corliss," Brianna pleaded, remembering the tall, handsome Mr. Addison Bainbridge, who was at that moment sipping wine in her father's study with Dominick and Mr. Payton. "When did you meet him? Have you danced with him? Has he kissed you? Is he going to ask for your hand?"

Corliss, a pretty girl almost a year Brianna's senior, blessed with pale blond hair and blue eyes, and cursed—in her opinion—with a dimple in the left cheek of her round face, bent her head, concentrating on giving another kick to the pebble she had been nudging along in front of them as they walked. "We met at my cousin's house, Brianna, at a small party that, yes, did include dancing. And, no, he hasn't approached Papa yet, although I believe he will."

"And? Did he kiss you?"

"Brianna Crown, you're incorrigible! Of course he hasn't kissed me. Oh, he has kissed my *hand*—but that doesn't really count, does it?"

Brianna was thoughtful for a moment, then shook her head. "No. I don't believe it does. I know I have a much different picture of passion. And you've known him for a whole month? What's the matter with him? Is he a slow-top?"

Corliss giggled, laying her head on Brianna's shoulder. "Oh, how happy I am to listen to your nonsense, Brianna. Everyone in Philadelphia is so very proper and solemn." She raised her head, stiffening slightly, so that Brianna immediately looked to her left, where Corliss was now staring.

"Now, who is that?" Brianna asked, seeing a tall, dark-haired man clad in a sober brown suit. He was walking along the perimeter of the gardens, an open sketchbook in one hand, a piece of charcoal in the other. As she watched, he halted in front of one of her mama's favorite rosebushes and began to sketch.

Corliss started walking again, pulling the curious Brianna along with her. "That's Marcus," she explained, strain visible in her voice. "He's Addison's slave."

Brianna dug in her heels as Corliss gave her arm another tug, turning her head and straining to get another look at the man her friend had identified as Marcus. "His *slave?* But he doesn't look like a slave. He's—why, he's nearly more light skinned than Papa, albeit Papa is always darkly tanned from being in the fields."

"Marcus is nearly white," Corliss said, her voice sounding rather sad. "Only his great-grandmother was brought from Africa, I believe, and he is the grandson and son of white plantation owners. He is a talented artist and wonderfully educated, thanks to his last owner, who was also his cousin, if you can believe that, although he certainly wasn't recognized as such. She had promised to free him, but then died before that was possible. So he is still a slave."

"You've spoken with him?" Brianna asked, curious. "You seem to know a lot about him."

Corliss bit her bottom lip. "Addison told me," she said. "He bought Marcus when he was in the South and uses him as his personal attendant. He says Marcus's presence lends him a certain *cachet.* Now come along, Brianna. I wouldn't want Marcus to think we're talking about him."

Brianna blew out her cheeks as she exhaled a small portion of quickly built-up rage. "Well, I'm afraid I don't like your Addison Bainbridge quite so much anymore, Corliss, no matter how handsome he is. To own a man so that he might lend him *cachet?* What foolishness! Papa won't like this when he hears about it. He won't like it above half. No person should be able to own another. And if the opportunity presents itself, I shall tell your Mr. Bainbridge exactly that!"

Corliss sighed. "Oh, Brianna, how I wish I had your fire, your courage. It must be so comforting to a person to always be so sure of herself."

"Yes. I used to think so," Brianna said, immediately thinking of Daniel Crown, who had probably joined her father and the other men in the study by now, with dinner to be served precisely at six. "Now, Corliss," she rushed on, hoping to change the subject, "tell me what it feels like to be in love. Do you find it impossible not to think about Mr. Bainbridge every waking moment? Does your stomach get all fluttery when he looks at you? Do you think your name never sounded prettier than when it is on his lips?"

Corliss laughed out loud, squeezing Brianna's arm. "Oh, my dear, good friend, how I have missed you!"

* * *

Daniel followed Whittle down the hallway toward Dominick's study, his step light, his mood good, his heart fairly carefree. It had been a good day, a comfortable day, and he was looking forward to a pleasant evening. He was even, Lord help him, looking forward to seeing Brianna again, verbally sparring with her, perhaps even walking with her in the garden as dusk fell and the full moon rose.

So it was unpleasant to be surprised by the presence of Addison Bainbridge, sitting on the arm of the leather couch in the corner, a wineglass dangling from his long, narrow fingers, his handsome head tipped to one side as he listened to Dominick explaining that, yes, it was possible to maintain a decent wine cellar this far from "civilization."

"Daniel!" Dominick exclaimed, rising from the chair behind his desk as his adopted nephew stood just inside the door, Whittle disappearing once more down the hallway. "Come in, come in. I want to introduce you to my friend, Mr. John Payton, and his houseguest, Mr. Addison Bainbridge. Gentlemen—my nephew, Daniel Crown. Mr. Bainbridge has been in America for a few years, Daniel, but he has spent considerable time in London as well. Perhaps you are acquainted?"

"We are acquainted, yes, as we traveled in the same small social circles," Daniel said, taking John Payton's offered hand, and then acknowledging Addison Bainbridge with a small nod of his head. "Bainbridge."

"Crown," Addison said, remaining where he was, rudely not rising as was expected in polite society. "I had wondered at the similarity of surnames, but I was thrown off when I saw that Mr. Crown is totally English. But then you were adopted, or discovered amongst the bulrushes, or some such thing, am I right?"

Mr. Payton, a short man nearly as round as he was tall, and not known for his mental profundity as much as he was his good humor, bubbled into speech. "What? What? You know each other? Well, if that isn't above all things wonderful. The world gets smaller every day, I say. You say that, Dominick? I do. Well, come, come, Daniel, my boy. Sit down, have a glass of wine before we go surprise the ladies with our news." He beamed at the three men in turn, obviously oblivious to any undercurrent of tension in the room. "Isn't this jolly?"

*Those who are believed to be most abject
and humble are usually most ambitious and envious.*

SPINOZA

chapter six

"You don't like him, do you?" Brianna asked as she and Daniel walked along the main garden path, a good dozen paces behind Corliss Payton and Addison Bainbridge.

Daniel looked down at her in surprise, for he'd thought he'd handled himself very well during dinner, neither ignoring Bainbridge nor contradicting the man each time he opened his mouth to say something obliquely cutting about one of their mutual acquaintances in London.

"Well? You don't, do you?" Brianna persisted, looking quite lovely in a pink-and-white striped gown, her burnished curls artlessly piled on top of her head, a few tantalizing ringlets tumbled onto her shoulders, caressing her neck. His fingertips itched to reach out and touch one of those fragile curls. "As a matter of fact," she went on brightly, "I think you'd probably like to have his liver skewered on a spit, not that anyone else at the table noticed. Except, perhaps, Papa. He notices everything."

"As do you, Brianna," Daniel remarked, looking at Bainbridge's erect spine, his well-tailored clothes, his polite way of bending his head just so, as if concentrating on every word spoken by the shy, fairly pretty Corliss Payton. Fairly pretty, but not nearly the sort Bainbridge had sought out in society, and with a father not half so deep in the pocket as many of the young debutantes he had led down the dance in the ballrooms of London. Not half so wealthy as, for instance, Dominick Crown, who also had a daughter of marriageable age.

"Oh? Then I'm right, aren't I? You don't like the man. I don't, either, although it is probably for a reason completely different from yours. Here," she continued, pulling him down one of the side paths, and toward a bench set into the flower beds, "let's sit down and you can tell me your reason, then I'll tell you mine."

Daniel smiled at Brianna, shaking his head at her enterprising spirit, then sat down beside her. "Quid pro quo, Brianna?" he asked teasingly, delighting in her artless enthusiasm for gossip. "You'll trade me something for something?"

Her green eyes sparkled with mischief. "It seems only fair," she answered. "You go first. And, just so that you don't think I'm merely being nosy, Corliss is my very dear friend, and I don't wish to see her hurt."

"She's in love with him?" Daniel asked, realizing that it was rather pleasant sitting here, with Brianna beside him, sharing confidences. He had made it a rule to keep his own counsel, leave his opinions unvoiced, and to act when he felt it necessary—without consultation with anyone else. Wasn't that what he'd done when Bainbridge became a nuisance in London?

"In love with him?" Brianna tapped a finger against her chin, as if considering the question. "I can't be sure. He hasn't yet kissed her, and she doesn't seem very put out about that. You'd think she'd be insulted. After all, they've known each other for nearly a month, and he *has* come back to New Eden with her, although many people do try to leave Philadelphia as summer approaches. It's so hot, you understand, and sometimes there is disease, so perhaps Mr. Bainbridge has invited himself to New Eden. On the other hand, Corliss is quiet and rather shy, but she does know what she wants, if you understand my meaning, and can be surprisingly stubborn when she has made her mind up to some course of action. She may have invited him, hoping he'd offer for her. Perhaps I'm worrying for no good reason."

Daniel attempted, and failed, to hold back another smile as he sorted through all that Brianna had said, then concentrated on what had interested him most. "Insulted? Because Bainbridge hasn't yet attempted to steal a kiss? Don't you have that backwards, Brianna? Corliss should expect him to behave as a gentleman."

"Oh, no! I would think restraint very ungentlemanly in a man professing to be in love. After all, he should be consumed by passion, unable to keep his hands off her, made nearly mad for wanting her. Lucretia, who was our cook years ago, told me how Papa threw Mama over his shoulder when she had infuriated him enough and carried her off to be married. That's the sort of love I want. Mad. Passionate. Daring." She turned to look at him inquiringly. "That's the only sort of love that's worth anything, don't you think?"

Dominick raised his eyebrows, considering her words, and purposely ignoring how very beautiful she looked, how very appealing. "Dominick flung your mother over his shoulder and carried her off? I should have liked to have seen that," he said, smiling yet again. For a man who did not smile easily or often, he was finding himself constantly surprised by how often he felt a lighthearted grin tickling his lips when he was in Brianna's company. Surprised and not necessarily sure he should be pleased. "But we're getting away from the subject," he added, refusing to answer her question as to his opinion on what constituted a love worth having—a question that had unexpectedly tied a knot in the pit of his stomach. "We were, I believe, discussing Addison Bainbridge."

"Oh, yes. Yes, of course we were." Brianna turned

slightly sideways on the bench, taking one of Daniel's hands between hers. She was always touching him, always open in her shows of affection, hugging and kissing her parents, Corliss, the Paytons—where he had always shied away from personal contact. And yet he allowed her to keep his hand captured, oddly pleased by this unaffected gesture of friendship. "Now, please tell me. Is he a fortune hunter? A card sharper? Perhaps even a thief?"

"None of those, Brianna, but something as satisfyingly titillating, I suppose," Daniel said, wondering, even as he spoke, why he felt safe confiding in her, sure that she would not betray his confidence. Not that he would tell her everything, of course. Just enough to be sure she would go to Corliss and warn the girl away. "Bainbridge merely insulted the wrong man, insulted his entire family, and then took ship for America rather than face him on the dueling field. The man is a coward, Brianna, pure and simple. And more than faintly malicious, although he hides it well beneath that ingratiating manner we witnessed at table."

Brianna, who had seemed to be enjoying their little gossip, sobered immediately and Daniel watched, secretly amazed, believing he could actually hear the gears turning inside her head as she raced to form a conclusion to his abbreviated story. "Oh dear. He was forced to leave England under a cloud then, wasn't he? Then he has probably been disowned by his horrified family and has now run low on funds and sees marriage to Corliss to be his only salvation."

"You read novels, don't you, Brianna? The marble-backed ones, full of dashing knights, beleaguered ladies, and sadistic ogres?" Daniel asked, chuckling, which earned him a sharp slap on the back of his hand.

"Don't tease, Daniel. And, it's true, Addison Bainbridge *is* an ogre of sorts. He keeps a slave to lend himself cachet. I saw the poor fellow earlier in the gardens, and Corliss told me about him. His name is

Marcus, and Corliss vows he's a talented artist." Her eyes shone with righteous indignation. "I'm going to ask Papa to buy Marcus and then set him free. If Mr. Bainbridge is penny-pinched, as I suspect, he'll probably leap at the offer."

"Bainbridge keeps a slave?" Daniel felt the muscles in his jaw grow tight with disgust. "Yes, that sounds just like him—building himself up by standing on another man's shoulders." He helped Brianna to her feet, and they walked back toward the main path. "I'd wait a while on going to your father, however. If Bainbridge thinks freeing Marcus would please anyone else, he'll refuse to sell him."

"But I—oh, all right, if you say so," Brianna said, sighing and clearly frustrated. "Oh dear. Here they come now. Much as it will pain me, I'll try to be pleasant." And then, as Daniel began to relax, feeling his private interlude with her had, by and large, gone fairly smoothly, she asked quickly, "So, Daniel. What horrid thing did Bainbridge say about your family that had you calling him out? Never mind trying to dissemble, because I don't have to know right now. You can tell me another time."

The words "incorrigible minx" sprang to Daniel's lips, but he didn't say them, as Bainbridge and Corliss were already within earshot. "Enjoy your stroll?" he asked, smiling at the young woman, who appeared strangely tense, almost tearful.

"The mosquitoes were gathering at the bottom of the garden, where there are still puddles from last night's rain," she explained quietly. "And I'm a bit chilled as well. Brianna? Would you please accompany me back to the house? The gentlemen can join us later in the drawing room. Addison?" she then asked, looking up at him even as she withdrew her arm from his. "You don't mind, do you?"

He lifted her hand to his lips, barely touching his mouth to her skin before releasing her. "As I've already said, I'm sure you could do with a bit of combing and primping after our walk, my dear, and I am, of course, loath to detain you, as I know you must be feeling anxious to improve your appearance. I imagine Crown and I can find our way to the drawing room without your kind assistance."

Daniel felt Brianna stiffen beside him, and he squeezed her hand, warning her not to leap to her friend's defense, as he could see that Corliss was already near tears over Bainbridge's veiled insult. He then bowed in Corliss's direction, saying, "I cannot imagine any lady more dazzling than you appear at this moment, Miss Payton, but Bainbridge and I, with regret, will release you and Miss Crown and attempt to stumble along out here on our own. Bainbridge? Would you care to have a look at my uncle's fine stables?"

"Th-thank you, Mr. Crown," Corliss said, her cheeks flushing an attractive pink as she looked to Brianna.

Bainbridge merely shrugged. "I suppose that would serve to pass the time," he said, then, as Brianna quickly took Corliss's hand and directed her back up the path, motioned for Daniel to lead the way. "You will excuse me if I don't turn my back to you?"

"Having done it once, complete with your tail tucked between your legs," Daniel answered smoothly, "I don't imagine a second time would make any difference. How long has it been, Bainbridge? Two years? Three?"

"Too long. Not long enough," Addison answered shortly, coming abreast of Daniel as they left the gardens behind and walked along the gravel path leading to the stables. "I suppose you're fairly champing at the bit to run to Payton and tell him what a rotter I am?"

"Not that the idea doesn't hold a certain appeal—but, no. I'll not say anything. Our seconds and the doctor and myself had a pleasant enough breakfast at a local inn when it became obvious that you weren't going to appear. Your voluntary banishment from England these past years seems sufficient punishment for your insult.

Although," Daniel added, "if you were to repeat any of the things you said about my family, I probably would find myself compelled to immediately take my whip to you. After all, I wouldn't wish to be left standing in yet another field at dawn, awaiting your pleasure."

"I don't have any notion of the two of us crying friends, for that would be absurd, but I also suppose an apology would be useless at this late date?" Addison asked, nearly running to keep up with Daniel's quick, long strides.

"Quite."

"But you'll keep your silence?"

"If you are seriously in love with Miss Payton, yes. Who knows. You may have improved over the years. Until and unless you prove otherwise, I am content to give you the benefit of the doubt. Grudges, my wise grandfather taught me, are for small minds. In truth, I haven't thought of you a single time these past years. Oh dear. I do hope I haven't offended you."

"You're an arrogant bastard, aren't you, Crown?" Addison bit out, stopping dead on the path. "Just as if you actually *were* somebody and not just some mongrel nobody the Marquess picked up from the gutter. I'm going back to the house. You can go muck about in the stables if you wish, but you'll do it alone."

Daniel merely shrugged, honestly indifferent to the man, his anger, and his insults. "Less of a stink that way," he remarked placidly, then watched Bainbridge stomp off, clearly in a high temper.

But when Daniel returned to the drawing room a good half hour later, it was to see Addison Bainbridge sitting beside Corliss on one of the couches, listening with every sign of rapt attention as she explained a sampler she had sewn for her mother last Christmas.

Brianna rose from her chair beside the cold fireplace and walked over to greet him. "I don't know what you did, but Mr. Bainbridge hasn't left Corliss's side since his return to the house. I only hope he makes her happy."

"Even if he has yet to draw her into his arms and kiss her? Madly? Passionately?"

Brianna didn't blush, didn't flinch, showed no signs of embarrassment. "Unlike Mr. Bainbridge, who is doubtless thinking his own thoughts while Corliss natters on and on about her sampler, *you,* Daniel Crown, have the most annoying way of listening to and remembering every foolish, girlish bit of nonsense a person might say in the heat of the moment. I'll have to remember that."

Daniel smiled. "And you are the most original flirt I have ever encountered, Brianna," he told her honestly. "You know full well that I have committed everything you've said to me to memory. And to my imagination as well," he added, to be rewarded by the quick rush of color that at last betrayed her nervousness, and her awareness of the outrageous unsuitability of their conversation.

"Ride with me tomorrow?" she asked, looking up at him unblinkingly, behaving as though unaware that her mother was staring at her from across the room, a concerned expression on her face. "Freedom's Lady needs a good run. I can be at Enolowin an hour past dawn."

"It would be my pleasure," Daniel said, then quickly excused himself to join Dominick and John Payton as they discussed the merits of the new bull the latter had bought on his trip to Philadelphia, wondering why he did not feel as if he'd had another lucky escape from the beautiful, incorrigible, nearly irresistible Miss Brianna Crown.

Daniel sat on Otto Bing's rocking chair, his moccasin-clad feet crossed at the ankle and resting on the porch railing, Lokwelend's journal open and lying on his lap. He had arisen early and donned his deerskins for the first time, marveling in the comfort of them, feeling very much at home in them. Tying the multicolored sash tightly at his waist, he had then gone to the kitchens, cut himself a fat slice from the rye loaf he found in a cabinet, and headed for the porch just as dawn slid over the low, blue mountains, smudging the low-hanging clouds with crimson, dusting them with gold.

Wapa-Kwelik. The Dawn Sky. The name Lokwelend had given to Brianna Crown. Daniel rubbed a hand across his forehead, mumbling a curse, erasing the unexpected thought.

He didn't know why he had picked up Lokwelend's journal again or what he was looking for. But the old Indian had said that the book would be there when he needed it, and Daniel found need of it now. For he was still feeling restless, and not because of Addison Bainbridge's unexpected arrival, nor because of his confused feelings for Brianna Crown—not for any easily identified reason at all.

But he felt the need to read more of Lokwelend's words, feed on his grandfather's great wisdom, although he couldn't be looking for answers. As yet, he had no definite questions.

He had simply allowed the journal to fall open at random, feeling this was what Lokwelend had intended, and began reading:

I have told you, Tasukamend, the story of how the Lenni Lenape came to be in this place, how they found their home—coming across the cold country, passing by the place of ice and storms, the land that was hot and dry, going beyond the wide river. Ours is a long history, and sacred, passed down from son to son and kept close to our hearts.

The good Moravians have told me their own story, and it is much like ours. Hardship, a great flood, the need to move on, to find a better land. Dominick Crown has lent me books. Many books, full of many stories similar to the Lenni Lenape, to the Moravians. The Greeks, the Romans, the Norsemen, the Chinese. All have a great story of creation, a retelling of the birth of their gods, their world, their people.

But only in the Moravian story, in the Christian story, is guilt to be found, Tasukamend. Only in your Bible, in the story of your Adam and Eve, is there mention of shame. Do you not find that intriguing?

The whites carry their shame, their guilt, and they do not like it. The two make for a heavy burden, and they long to put these soul-searing afflictions down. They want to be blameless in all things, guiltless in all things, but their guilt follows them. Their shame will not release them. So they were when they came across the water in their strange ships. We welcomed them, but they did not want to see us, did not want us to be here. We made them feel guilty, we shamed them with our presence.

You are asking, "Why, Grandfather? Why were they shamed by us?" And the answer is simple, my son. The white man came here, came to the new Promised Land, ready to take possession of it, to claim it as their own. But we were already here, standing on the shore. This land is our Promised Land, our history, our story of Creation and travel to a new world. Their New Eden was ours, and we were seen as the snakes in the new paradise.

So we had to be beaten down, vanquished. Our language, our culture, our history. Denied. Destroyed. Erased. Forgotten. We were called savages, made to forswear our past, made to forsake our own religion so that the white man could say, "These people are nothing! This land is mine! This has always been mine! This will always be mine!" To erase us was to erase their guilt. But in killing the "snake" they realized that they were once again left to face the shame of their actions. So they had to keep on killing, denying their guilt, removing the source of their shame.

Pematalli knew this, as I know this. My son chose to remain, to be the reminder that the Lenape were here first, that the white man only took what we allowed them to take, what they killed to own. I feel his spirit every day, as do you. He is Always There. He is the white man's guilt here in this place they call America; he is the white man's shame.

And now the Lenape are gone, scattered to the four winds, retracing their long-ago steps that led them here. Back across the wide river, back across the dry, hot land. Over the mountains, to where the sun sets on the great water.

But Pematalli is still here. You, Tasukamend, are here. What will you do, Tasukamend? How will you stand? As Tasukamend or as Philip Crown's adopted son? Or as your own man. Much time has passed since you left me. Time has become my burden, but it must not become yours. Think, Tasukamend! Walk your land. Take its good soil in your hand and hold it tight. Smell the sweet air. Dream your dreams, seek your accomplishments. Pray and study and decide where you have been, where you are going, who you are. Then, Tasukamend, time is nothing, even as it is all. And for you, guilt and shame are banished.

Daniel closed the journal, resting a hand on its leather cover, and looked out toward Lenape Cliff to the last resting place of his grandparents, of Pematalli, and shook his head. As always, Lokwelend had been there for him. For he couldn't be a Lenni Lenape brave, just as he couldn't be solely Philip's son. For good or ill, he was the sum product of his background. Half-breed Lenape by birth, Englishman by adoption, American—if he so wished it—by choice. But there was still the shame, the guilt. Because he didn't know who he was, where he fit. Not yet. In spite of Lokwelend's words or because of them, he was still unsure.

And Pematalli still watched him, waiting.

Somewhere, beyond the mountains, beyond Fort Pitt, the Lenni Lenape were even now struggling to maintain their lands, their freedom. Somewhere, to the north, to the west, into the Ohio, Lenape braves were painting their faces, preparing their sacrifices, and heading off to war against the constantly encroaching white man. Knowing they were outnumbered, knowing they were doomed, the many tribes were gathering together, forming alliances, planning battles, daring for victories.

"You'd have me ride with them, wouldn't you?" he asked, looking up at the face visible in the outcrops of stone, the blank, staring eyes of Pematalli. "You'd have me declare the white man my enemies and take up arms against them. It was not just your father who had dreams, Pematalli, for I have had them also. I still have them. Dreams filled with blood and screams and crying children. My dreams haunt me. *You* haunt me."

He shook his head. "*N'dellennówi*—I am a man. *Lennápe n'hackey*—I am of the Lenni Lenape. Oh, yes, I remember the words, the words you spoke to your father before you ran out to sacrifice yourself on the sharp blade of Philip Crown's knife. Is this what you want from me? What my grandfather wants from me, although he would never ask? Or am I to stay here at Enolowin and keep this one small plot of land for the Lenape?" He dropped his head into his hands. "Who am I, Pematalli? Where do I belong?"

Brianna took the longer route to Enolowin, bypassing the shortcut across the fields and the five-barred gate, keeping Freedom's Lady to a leisurely walk so that the mare could conserve her energy for the race she fully intended to suggest once she and Daniel were in the west pasture.

She was clad in her brother's breeches and white shirt, as she had been the first day she'd met her new neighbor, for comfort, for ease in riding astride, and because she had liked the way Daniel had looked at her legs. And if that made her a hoyden, well, surely there were worse things. For one, she could have been a stick-in-the-mud like dear Corliss. Although she loved the girl dearly, her friend hadn't a bit of adventure in her and never would think to do anything the least bit daring.

Brianna had dreamt about Daniel again last night, as she had done every night since he had arrived at Enolowin to turn her formerly predictable world upside down. Once so very sure of herself, she now questioned everything she said, everything she thought, every notion she'd ever had about the world and her place in it.

Mostly, she couldn't stop thinking about what it would be like to be important to his happiness, as he was rapidly becoming indispensable to hers. Which puzzled her, as she really knew nothing, less than nothing, about the man.

But she wanted to. She wanted to learn all about him; how he thought, what made him happy, the things that angered him, what made him sad. She wanted to *know* him, inside and out, and learn if he lived up to her silly, romantic imaginings, if he fulfilled the increasingly disturbing dreams that filled her nights, that had her waking with her cheeks flushed, unable to meet Wanda's eyes when that woman came into the room, bearing a cup of hot chocolate for her mistress.

"Good morning!" she called out brightly now as she rode up the circular gravel drive of Enolowin, waving her gloved hand in greeting. She watched as Daniel uncoiled his long, lean body and rose from the rocking chair, and quietly marveled at how much the Lenape he looked clad in deerskins. How much the proud savage, how handsome, how threatening to her peace of mind. "Are you ready? If we ride down to the stream, we might see some deer drinking at the bank."

He walked down the length of the side porch to the steps, then took hold of one of the carved wooden posts and swung down to the ground in one graceful leap. "The stream, Brianna?" he asked, untying his white stallion's reins from the ring through the mouth of the black, cast-iron horse's head stuck on top of the hitching post.

There were a pair of these decorative hitching posts at each entrance to Enolowin, and as a young child, Brianna had named them all, pretending that at night, during a full moon, the metal horses pulled themselves up out of the ground to gallop across the fields on magically appearing feet. Daniel's mount, she thought, biting her lip to restrain a giggle, had been tied up to Guinevere, with Lancelot, her faithful companion, standing guard at the other end of the steps. What a fanciful child she had been. What different fancies she had now, now that she was grown.

"Yes, the stream," she answered once Daniel was mounted. He hadn't bothered with the stirrup, she noticed, but only rested his hand on his mount's mane, then leaped into the saddle in one remarkably strong, graceful, fluid move. "A-hem, yes," she went on, realizing that he was waiting for her to speak again. "However, as our ride to the stream will take us across the fields Otto Bing has put aside to lay fallow this season, I thought—um, I thought . . . what *are* you grinning about, Daniel Crown? Do I have a smut on my nose or something?"

"You're wearing breeches, Brianna," he answered, motioning for Freedom's Lady to precede his mount back down the circular drive. "Somehow I'd think that the possibility of a smut on your nose would be your least pressing question. Now—tell me about this competition we're about to have, as I'm convinced there is one in the offing."

Brianna waited until Daniel's mount had come abreast of hers, then grinned at the man, finding it impossible to be angry with him for having guessed her intentions. "Freedom's Lady has won every race she's ever run," she told him, unable to keep the pride from her voice. "Her bloodlines are true, if obscure, and I've raised her from a foal, along with a half-dozen others in my father's stables."

"And done a fine job of it, obviously," Daniel said, measuring the sturdy mare with his gaze. "Now Lenape Traveler is here, and you see him as an interloper. A flashy, delicately boned, too high-strung showpiece that most definitely needs to be put in his place. Am I right?"

Brianna avoided Daniel's eyes, for he had struck right to the heart of the matter, damn him. "I would never think to be so boorish," she protested, knowing her tone didn't quite ring true. She turned to him once more, grinning. "However, now that you've issued the challenge?" She employed her chin, using it to point in the direction of the tree line in the distance, across the field they had just entered. "To the large oak in the center of that line, all right? At the count of three?"

She tightened the muscles of her legs, then leaned low over the front of the mare. "One . . . two . . ."

"And the stakes?" Daniel asked just as she was about to dig her heels into Freedom's Lady's flanks.

Brianna sat back in her saddle, looking at him blankly. It had never occurred to her that Daniel might want to make a wager on the outcome of their contest. "Stakes? I hadn't considered stakes. I race for the thrill of it. Don't you?"

He looked at her, straight-faced. "Lenape Traveler would be insulted if there were no stakes," he said, then waited for her response.

She looked at him owlishly. "Your *horse* would be insulted? Really?" A smile played about the corners of her mouth as she tried to remain serious. "All right, then. So that your *horse* won't be insulted—if I win, you will agree to pose for me later, as my fingers are itching to sketch you this afternoon. Just as you look now—in your deerskins, standing in front of Lokwelend's cabin."

"Agreed," he said promptly. "And if I win?"

Brianna looked at Lenape Traveler again, taking in the

apparent fragility of the stallion's fetlocks, the delicate bones of its dish-shaped head. She gave in to an imp of mischief, the one that rarely ever resided too far beneath the surface. "If you win, you can name your own prize," she said daringly, then quickly counted to three again, and spurred Freedom's Lady into an immediate gallop.

And Freedom's Lady was flawless in the gallop. With her inside foreleg leading, the mare stretched out her steps, lengthened her stride until each hoof kissed the ground, one after the other, followed by that supreme moment of freedom when all four hooves were off the ground and horse and rider floated through the air.

Brianna held her body even further forward, her body just clear of the saddle, her ankles and knees absorbing the shock of each new contact with the ground and giving the strong mare complete freedom in her back, her loins.

The ground whisked by below them, clods of fresh earth being flung out behind the impact of the sharp hooves. Her eyes on the rapidly approaching horizon of tall, old trees, Brianna had no time to indulge in a look backward to see where her opponent was at the moment.

And, as it turned out, she had no need to turn her head, for suddenly, to her right there was a flash of white, and Lenape Traveler dashed past the mare in a near blur.

"Damn it!" Brianna gritted out, leaning further forward, urging Freedom's Lady on. "Damn it, damn it, damn it!"

And then she gave in to the inevitable and eased back on her heels. She coaxed the mare slowly back down to a canter, to a trot, to a jerky, fairly impatient walk as she watched in silent admiration the perfect blending of horse and rider. There was a beauty to be found in such a union of man and beast, and Brianna's heart squeezed in her chest at the magnificence of the sight.

Daniel Crown rode as if he had been born to the saddle, moving as one with his horse and not fighting him; fluid, light, their progress a sort of poetry, a painting come to life, a beautiful, flawless song. Man and nature become one.

"There you go again, Brianna, being fanciful," she warned herself as she watched Daniel ease back in the saddle, calling off the swift, forward plunge of tendon and muscle, allowing the sleek, delicate animal to find its own comfortable gait before halting at the tree line so that he could kick free of the stirrups and, in one unbroken motion, swing his front leg up and over the stallion's head and drop lightly to the ground.

"Come on," she told the mare, guiding the horse to the place where Daniel stood, waiting. "Let's get this over with. And I do hope, Lady, that you enjoy the taste of crow more than I."

Daniel walked to meet her, taking hold of Freedom's Lady's bridle and then reaching out a hand to Brianna, offering to assist her in dismounting. "You'll have to forgive Lenape Traveler, Brianna. He's a bit of a show-off."

"And I don't need to wonder where the blasted horse learned that," Brianna grumbled as she kicked both feet free of the stirrups and deliberately fell forward into Daniel's arms, so that he had no choice but to catch her up against his chest. He lowered her slowly to the ground but did not step away from her. "I'm sorry," she said quietly, looking up into his dark, unreadable eyes. How could a man smile so openly and still hide his feelings behind those impenetrable eyes? "I was being petty, and it was entirely uncalled for. Obviously, the better horse won. Congratulations. Oh, yes, and you may name your forfeit."

His hands tightened on her waist. "You already know the forfeit, Brianna," he told her, his full mouth unsmiling, and unnervingly close. "You hoped for it deep in your heart. You may even have planned for it, although you're right. Lenape Traveler is the better horse."

Brianna swallowed down hard over the sudden lump

in her throat. "I don't know what you're talking about," she protested, belatedly realizing that her hands were holding tight to Daniel's shoulders.

His smile was mocking, strangely frightening. "You're a remarkably talented tease, little one, but a total failure as a liar. I warned you, but you refused to believe me, didn't you?" His head moved closer to hers, blocking out the sun that slanted through the trees behind them. "You're too young to play at my games, Brianna Crown. Years too young. And eons too innocent. You're a complication I hadn't looked for and a problem I don't need."

"Then let me go," Brianna said bravely, knowing that if he did, she would crumple, boneless, to the ground at his feet. "Let me go back to my dolls and my silly dreams and my damning innocence. Well? What are you waiting for, Daniel?"

"Yes, Brianna. What am I waiting for?" He lifted a hand to her face, tracing across one eyebrow with his fingertips, then as her eyes closed, skimming his fingers down the side of her face, over her cheekbone, touching her lips—dragging against them so that her bottom lip came forward in a pout—then cupped her chin in his palm. "God. I'll be damned if I know."

She opened her mouth to curse him for touching her, to curse him for *not* touching her more. But she didn't have time to say anything because his lips were suddenly slanted against hers, hot and hard and demanding. As his hands were demanding, moving to roughly cup the back of her head as he held her to him, abruptly pulling her closer against his solid length, the physical evidence of his arousal.

This was no childish kiss. Not the nervous fumblings of the local youths who had dared to steal an embrace at the church picnic or after the Harvest Dance. This was a man's kiss, a man's emotions, a man's needs—blatantly male, insistent. Frightening. Awakening.

Daniel's teeth nipped at her tender skin, his tongue

plundered her mouth until she was reeling from the assault, her blood singing, her heart racing, her mind a merciful blank. She forgot how to breathe, didn't need to breathe, for he was introducing her to a whole new life with a whole new set of requirements.

And then she was standing there alone, her eyes still closed, her hands outstretched, holding nothing but emptiness, and listening to Daniel grind out a string of low curses that had her turning her head away, flinching.

"Go home," he said at last, when she had opened her eyes, looking at him through her tears, humiliation coloring her vision. "Go home, little girl, and play with your dolls. For your sake, for mine—just go home."

Brianna struggled to control the trembling of her lower lip, fought to keep her chin raised in defiance, steeled herself as if preparing for another physical assault. "You did that on purpose. You thought to frighten me, didn't you? Make me go away and leave you in peace? Why? Have I disturbed *your* peace, Daniel Crown? Have I clouded your future with yet another uncertainty? And just who is frightened now, Daniel—me or *you?"*

He ran a hand through his hair, looking distracted, confused, and vaguely sad. "I don't know what you're talking about, and neither do you."

She took a single step forward, filled with a sudden courage that might, she knew, have found its birth in desperation. "Oh yes, I do. I heard my parents talking about you. About how unhappy you were in England. About how you came here to decide who you are, where you belong. How absurd! You can't find yourself in England or here. You have to look *inside* yourself to do that. And, maybe, just maybe, you have to look at *me."*

"Are you quite finished with your childish romantic notions?" Daniel asked coldly.

She shook her head. "No. No, I'm not. You may not know what you want, but I know what *I* want. And you can't frighten me away with your dark eyes or your punishing kisses. You will not sway me with anger or indifference or cruel words. I'm here. I'm everywhere you look, and I'm not going anywhere! Now, you just think about that, Daniel Crown, or Tasukamend—or whatever and whoever you think you are."

She turned away from him, trembling with nerves, took up Freedom's Lady's reins, and lifted her foot into the stirrup. She mounted the horse in one swift movement, her motions dictated by memory, for she was suddenly too nervous to think, and turned to look down at Daniel as the mare danced beneath her, more than ready for another run. "*Now* I am going home. And you, Daniel—well, you can just go straight to hell. Only I warn you, I'll be there, too, waiting for you!" With a quick prod of her heels against the mare's flanks, she was off, racing across the field, her tears blinding her, grateful that Freedom's Lady knew the way back to Pleasant Hill.

indifference or cruel words. I'm here. I'm everywhere you ask, and I'm not going anywhere! Now, you just think about that, Daniel Crowell, or Teddy—or whatever else you-whoever you think you are."

She turned away from him, trembling with nerves [illegible]

book two

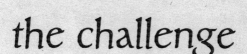

the challenge

THEY BOTH FOUGHT,
THEY BOTH DID WRONG,
THEY BOTH HAD NO PEACE.

THE WALLAM OLUM, (RED RECORD)
ORAL HISTORY OF THE LENNI LENAPE

A person who gets all wrapped up in himself makes a mighty small package.

PENNSYLVANIA DUTCH SAYING

chapter seven

Daniel spent the next two weeks steeping himself in the land, riding across it, walking it, learning it. With Dominick Crown beside him, he traveled into New Eden and met a few of his neighbors. With Otto Bing leading the way, he inspected the barns, the outbuildings, the stock. With both Skelton and Finn by his side, he watched the new horses being settled into the stables. And, on his own, he spent long hours visiting the woods and the secret places he remembered from his youth.

He did not, however, visit Pleasant Hill during this time, and he did not receive any visits from Brianna Crown.

Oh, she had ridden over to visit with Mrs. Bing, but she had never done so when Daniel was at home. Whether by chance or because she and Freedom's Lady waited at the edge of the woods until she saw him leave for the day, he hadn't been in her company for a long fourteen days.

This did not mean that he didn't think about her or that he didn't hear about her. As she had warned him, he could not move in any direction without hearing about her, thinking about her, knowing that she was near.

Over their evening meal, Mrs. Bing related each of Brianna's visits, extolling the "dear child" for her kindness in stopping by to show her one of the latest batch of Pleasant Hill kittens, or relating the events of the afternoon Brianna had spent helping the housekeeper wash the prisms that decorated the large chandelier in the foyer, singing nonsense songs the whole time, which had sent Mrs. Bing into gales of hysterics—and still had that effect a good four hours after the fact.

Why, Brianna—the "little darling"—had even dropped by just yesterday afternoon, it being Tuesday and all and Mrs. Bing's day to iron sheets and "make up all the beds fresh," and politely volunteered to do the job herself.

Which, Daniel thought now, as he walked up the steep hill that led to the top of Lenape Cliff, explained why he had slid his feet beneath the covers last night, only to find that his top sheet had been folded in half and brought up to the head of the bed again, so that he had not so much as crawled into bed, a weary man, as he had slipped himself inside a short, wide envelope.

As punishments went, and he was quite sure he was being punished, this one had not been overly onerous. He had spent the next half hour quietly searching the house for a second sheet—as he had refused to wake Mrs. Bing and let her know how he had been tricked—and then making up his own bed so that the housekeeper wouldn't notice the lack of a top sheet in the morning. In fact, by the time he had slung the bedspread back onto the mattress, he had found himself laughing rather heartily at Brianna's joke—and missing her, damn it. Missing her.

He missed her almost as much as he missed himself, because he had still not discovered so much as a glimmer as to who he really was, where he belonged. He slept on fine linen sheets and wore deerskins with an ease that still amazed him. He lived in a huge house—a mansion, really—and yet was at home in the woods, all of Lokwelend's lessons coming back to him with an ease, and a pleasure, that astounded him.

And, still, he felt the hunger inside himself. He simply did not know how to feed it.

Was he trying to reconcile the Lenape blood in him with the man he had been in England? Or was he just another restless young man looking for the boy, the youth, that had escaped him? Could he stay here, communing with his shadowy ancestors, or was his life in England with his adopted family, the mother who had risked all for him, the father who had accepted him without questions, the brothers and sister who had wept as they saw him off at the dock?

Did he have the right to go searching after some nebulous dream when he owed so much to so many?

"Itah!"

Itah. Good be to you. Lokwelend had taught him the stiff, eloquently simple yet formal Lenape language, and Brighid had kept up the lessons so that he would never forget. *Were his ancestors speaking to him now?* Daniel lifted his head, his head tipped, to listen to the slight breeze that ruffled the trees above his head, the long grasses at his feet, then shook his head. He was getting fanciful, hearing things.

"Careless boy," the disembodied voice continued, still speaking in guttural Lenape. "Do not think harm cannot come to you on your own land. It came to us before, it can come to you now. You'd be dead now, careless boy, had I wanted your hair."

Daniel had whirled around in a full circle as the disembodied voice came to him through the trees, his searching gaze finally dropping lower to where a bundle of filthy deerskins and brightly colored rags made a blot against the ground. His hand still on the hilt of his knife as it waited, at the ready, tucked into the sash around his waist, he approached the tree line and peered into the darkness that hid at the base of the mossy trunks, the sun blocked by the density of trees and the canopy of leaves.

"Itah, grandfather," he said as he made out the figure of the old Lenape Indian who sat cross-legged on the damp dirt, his fingers and face shiny with grease from the turkey leg he was gnawing on with what appeared to be more desperate need than mere hunger, although he hid his appetite well, as a Lenape brave would never show hunger, even if he were dying from it. "What brings you to this place to honor me with your presence? What, in short, Grandfather, do you do here?"

The Indian used his amazingly white teeth to rip at the drumstick, chewing lustily for a minute before shifting the meat to one cheek and answering in guttural Lenape. *"N'mamitzi.* I say, I am eating, if your mind cannot stretch to remember the language of your people, the original people, the true people. You are standing still. The birds are resting. And time is passing. Open your eyes and see it go, and weep with me."

Daniel went down on his haunches and peered at the old Indian more closely, something deep inside him immediately recognizing that this was not a chance meeting. He slipped easily, almost happily, into his father's language. "Why are you here, Grandfather?" he asked again, then winced, knowing from his conversations with Lokwelend that the slowest way to the end of any journey was the path an impatient man took before first preparing himself for the trip. "Forgive me, Grandfather," he added, inclining his head in a sign of respect. "I am Tasukamend, and I welcome you to this place, which is a holy place of our people. I offer you what is mine and ask only that you honor me with your words, your wisdom, your company at my fire." He reached into the pocket of his deerskin jacket and pulled out a plug of tobacco he had brought along to lay on Lokweland's grave. "For you, Grandfather," he said, holding out his gift.

The Indian grinned around the drumstick, which was

once again lifted to his mouth. "I accept your gift, Tasukamend, that you, in your wisdom, in your respect, have offered to me. I will please you by accepting the seat at your fire. I will eat from your bowl and sleep on your blankets. I will be your guest. And the stronger you make me, the more you will see. For you have spoken with your lips only, not from the heart, the heart that burns with questions it is still afraid to ask. Soon you will learn what is in your heart, learn the answers to all the questions that burn there, and then we will speak of the future. You see the many gray hairs on my head, know I have had many winters, have gained much wisdom. I will be your teacher."

Daniel looked toward the place where Lokwelend's body had been buried beneath the soil his son had died to protect. "I had another teacher once, long ago."

"Lokwelend," the Indian said, wiping his greasy mouth with a filthy sleeve. "A good man with a good sight. He had many dreams, Tasukamend. Many of them were of you."

Daniel's mouth had gone dry. "You knew Lokwelend?"

The Indian tossed the remains of the drumstick over his shoulder into the trees, muttering something about feeding the little creatures that foraged under the moon, then held out his hand to Daniel as he slowly straightened out his legs, his bones creaking loudly in protest. "Help your grandfather to his feet, boy, for the ground is damp and his bones are old. I was once called Taquachi, which means the Frozen One, because my body does not move well, but I have taken a new name these past years. Gunitakan, which means Long in the Woods. Too long in the woods, Tasukamend. Too long frozen, waiting. Waiting for you and your strong body and fine mind. Now you are here, and we can begin. Why do you hesitate? Bend down, Tasukamend, and pick up my tobacco."

Reverence for the wisdom of one of the last Lenape in the area was one thing. Respect for his elders, long ingrained in Daniel by both Lokwelend and his adoptive parents, was another. But common sense was still common sense, and Taquachi, or Gunitakan, or whatever name he gave, was a far cry from the man and mentor Lokwelend had been, and Daniel was not about to blindly believe every word that came out of the man's mouth. Not until he had taken more of a measure of the man.

And not that he'd need a long yardstick. Gunitakan was of an unimpressive height, as if he had been the runt of the litter and never strong enough to feed well in his youth. Or, perhaps, he had been stuffed into a small barrel just as his limbs had begun to grow and then left there until they had turned crooked and misshapen. The man was bent and twisted and leaned heavily on the stout stick he had employed to boost himself up after Daniel had taken hold of his forearm to give him leverage. For all his thick, iron gray, shoulder-length hair, his black berry eyes that twinkled with secrets, and his straight white teeth, the overwhelming impression he gave was one of someone life had pushed down more times than it had ever lifted him up.

And like all of those to whom life has been ungenerous, he had most probably found alternative ways of surviving. One of them, Daniel believed, was the stench of rum that surrounded Gunitakan, a smell so strong a man could hang his hat on it.

Gunitakan shook free of Daniel's grasp and scurried to the center of the grassy slope that made up the area between the tree line and the edge of Lenape Cliff. He moved quickly, in a sideways sort of scamper, like a crab outracing a gull, then turned to confront Daniel, his dark eyes as animated and dancing as his deerskin shirt was probably alive with fleas.

"Such a narrow strip of land is left to the Lenape, Tasukamend," he said, striking the ground with the tip of his rude cane. "Just this, and no more. I have not room to spread my blanket. I hear sighing and sobbing in yonder direction," he said importantly, pointing to the west. "Too many white men, too few wise leaders left to help us. Look hard, Tasukamend, and see the black clouds drawing toward each other. There! There! And there!" he all but shouted, jabbing his arm westward, to the northwest, the southwest, then holding it outstretched, as if Daniel could not be trusted to know that he was talking about the growing tension beyond Fort Pitt, up and down the Ohio, where white settlers were impatiently pressing the new America for land, always more land.

Daniel smiled to himself as he added cunning and a nimble tongue to Gunitakan's compensating accomplishments. Combined with the Indian's undoubtedly agile brain, these compensations more than made up for the man's lack of physical perfection. And Daniel felt reasonably sure he was about to be treated to a small demonstration of just how the Indian's mind worked. He shoved his hands into his pockets, a part of him enjoying Gunitakan's little show, another part of him wondering just where this tale was leading and how it might end, he felt sure, with an appeal for a few coins leaving those pockets and ending up in Gunitakan's pouch. Ah, well. He had always been happy to pay for his entertainments.

"There is peace now, Grandfather," Daniel said reasonably, knowing he was expected to register a protest to Gunitakan's dark prophecy. "The dark clouds of war are not visible from Enolowin."

"Geptschat!" the old Indian spluttered, calling Daniel a fool—one of the Lenape epithets he himself had employed more than once during his growing-up years to describe some of his classmates and not a few of his teachers.

Gunitakan, bent and twisted, looked sideways at Daniel, as if measuring him for a suit of clothes he planned to make for him, then sell him at some exorbitant price. "If a man is blind and cannot see it, does that mean the sun does not rise? Does he not still feel the warmth on his skin? I have come here, waited all these years here, to tell you this, Tasukamend. There is another war coming. The last war. And it will not go well for the Lenape unless you fulfill Lokwelend's dream, Lokwelend's hope. *You* must be our leader, Tasukamend. You are white, so you think like the whites. You are Lenape, so you are wise like the Lenape. With you we cannot lose. Without you we cannot hope to survive. But first, Tasukamend, you must sit at my feet and learn from me. Learn all that I know while remembering all that Lokwelend has taught you, all the white man has taught you. Now, take me to your fine house, and we will begin. After you feed me."

So, it wasn't going to be as easy as the simple exchange of a few coins. Gunitakan, it seemed, was an optimistic man and had planned not a single payment but a much richer reward for his entertaining recitations, his outlandish dreams, his outright fibs. Had he even known Lokwelend? Or had he merely been repeating what he'd heard in New Eden, where tongues were undoubtedly wagging about the half-breed who had come to Enolowin, and then guessed at the rest? After all, it was common knowledge that Lokwelend had been able to see in his dreams. . . .

Daniel decided he did not wish either to insult Lokwelend's memory by turning his back on one of his grandfather's comrades-in-arms or deal shabbily with someone who might just be his only link to the Lenape heritage he longed to explore. Besides, the man amused him. "Very well. I will take you to my house, Grandfather. I will feed you," Daniel said, shaking his head as the old Indian began to dance about, as if someone had lit an invisible fire under his feet. "But as for the rest of it, this business about my having anything to do with warfare—"

Gunitakan held up a hand, effectively cutting off Daniel's objections. "You think you owe your father nothing?" he asked, his eyes narrowed accusingly. "We must change your name. You are not the Blameless One. You are the greedy one. Taking, taking. What do you have that you have not been given? What sacrifices have you made, Tasukamend? What sorrows have you known? *Kau!* No, I say!" he warned, holding out his cane as if Daniel were about to interrupt him, which he wasn't. Daniel Crown was too occupied in balling his hands into impotent fists, knowing the old Lenape was now speaking nothing less than the truth—though how he had come to know his history this well was beyond him. Unless it was true that he *had* known Lokwelend.

And if Gunitakan had known Lokwelend well enough to know Daniel's history, then it was possible that he had known him well enough to also know some of his beloved grandfather's dreams and visions, even those that Lokwelend had not committed to his journal. Daniel had to listen to everything the old Indian had to say, sift through the self-serving demands, look past the man's unimpressive exterior, go beyond the sure knowledge that Gunitakan's first love might well be rum, not war, and filter the truth from the fanciful.

After all, what could he lose by listening to the old man? And what did he have, if not time?

"You are good to remain silent when in the presence of unhappy truths," Gunitakan said as Daniel inclined his head respectfully, urging the man to speak once more. "When the white woman who bore you breathed her last, she died with her heart full of love for you. When your father's blood spilled on the land he would hold, he died for you. We Lenape, as a nation, died for the freedom of the Americans in their war and were thanked by being lied to yet again, by the loss of more of our land, by the massacre of more of our women and children. And where was Tasukamend? He was in the land of the *Yankwis,* eating fine food and wearing fine clothes. Dancing, singing, prancing. While we stayed here and bled for you. Think, Tasukamend. Do you not owe something back? Is that not why you are here? To learn your place in life? I *know* that place, my son. I know your destiny."

"I was a child when my adoptive parents returned to England," Daniel said, feeling that he had been badgered enough. "It was not possible for me to stay here and help my people, old one. If you know anything, you know that."

Gunitakan spat on the ground. "Pematalli had only eighteen summers before he came to rest on this hillside, having died a warrior's death. What were you about in your eighteenth summer, Tasukamend, while your people were being herded westward like cattle?"

Daniel looked toward the west, unable to meet Gunitakan's eyes, knowing that during his eighteenth summer—on his birthday, to be exact—he had won his first sailing race, gotten himself falling-down drunk, and collapsed into sleep with his head resting on the plump, bare breasts of Lady Miranda Gaithers, the wife of the man who'd lost the race and a small fortune to the upstart half-breed.

Shame swept over Daniel, and he forgot that Gunitakan was cunning. For the man had unwittingly gone to the heart of his uncertainty about the world and his place in it. "I have no apology to offer, Grandfather," he said at last, his humble tone very much at odds with the confidence he was always so careful to show the world. "I remained a child longer than Pematalli lived. A willful, reckless, feckless child."

Gunitakan's homely face crumpled, and he began to cry. "You are no worse than me, Tasukamend. No worse." He reached inside his ragged jacket and brought out a dark brown bottle, pulling out its cork with his fine white teeth. While Daniel watched, the old Indian lifted the bottle to his lips and drank deeply, then wiped his sleeve over his wet mouth. "This!" he said, holding out the bottle to Daniel. "This is where I was when Pematalli was dying, when your father was fighting to rid the land of the white man, when Lokwelend was dreaming his dreams. Here, Tasukamend, inside this bottle. In this bottle is where I fought my wars, and I have triumphed in none of them." He took another long drink.

"Grandfather—" Daniel began, embarrassed by the man's tears, embarrassed for the man whose physical shortcomings would not have allowed him to be a warrior, even if his lips had never touched the white man's liquor.

"Kau! No! Do not speak! You are Tasukamend, the Blameless One. I am Taquachi, the Frozen One. Gunitakan, Long in the Woods. Frozen in my shame, hiding from it. While I was frozen, while I hid in the woods, hid inside this bottle, in the space of my lifetime, Tasukamend, the Great Nations were all but destroyed. Smallpox, this thing called measles, too many wars to be counted—all have helped to defeat the Lenape. But *this!"* he held out the bottle once more, then took another drink, staggering as he lifted his head in order to drain the bottle's contents. "This has killed more of us than all the others put together. Lokwelend was a great warrior, as was his son. But Lokwelend is no more, Pematalli is no more. Their kind is no more, gone in the space of one lifetime. See what the white man has done to us. There are no warriors anymore. Not here. Not in New Eden. Not wherever the white man has walked and brought death as his companion."

Daniel rubbed at his forehead, searching for something to say that might ease the old man's pain, the old man's shame. For, whatever rig the man had meant to run on him, he had obviously gone beyond it and was now in real pain. "Lokwelend told me, Grandfather, many times, that the Lenape can lose all else, but we will still have pride. Because we are descended from a long line of heroes."

"Dead heroes," Gunitakan grumbled. "Leaving me and my bottle. This is what we have come to. All of tomorrow's heroes are gone west to fight the last fight, to die the last hero's death." He swayed where he stood, the rum he had drunk obviously loosening his balance if not his frozen, twisted limbs.

He looked at Daniel owlishly, and giggled. "Have you been to *Manahachtanienk,* boy? It is the place your mother's people now call Manhattan, and the place where first the Lenape met the white man. No? Well, then I will tell you a story. *Manahachtanienk.* You know the meaning of the name we gave this land? It means the place where we all became intoxicated. The white man came across the big water in their great ships, and they gave us strong drink, and we took it. And the dying began. They gave us baubles and trinkets to pay us for *Manahachtanienk,* and we took them also, although we could not sell them what belonged to everyone. But it would have been rude to refuse their gifts. Baubles and trinkets in exchange for our freedom, Tasukamend, and the white man thought they had made a shrewd bargain while we laughed and thought them to be stupid children. What did we need with their baubles and trinkets? We had better ones."

Gunitakan shook his head, his entire posture one of defeat, of deep, unremitting sorrow. "Man-hat-tan," he said, spitting the word. "Do not go there, Tasukamend. It will never be a good place for the Lenape."

The empty bottle slipped from the old man's hand, falling into the long grass, and he looked at Daniel, confusion as well as drink clouding his eyes. "I forget. Did I remember to ask for coins to buy more rum? I wanted to end with that, I believe, but I got lost somewhere along the path. Don't need a bed. Need another bottle."

The old man shook his head, nearly toppling over from his exertion. "Never mix too much truth with the lies, Gunitakan," he scolded, speaking aloud, but to himself. "You never remember that, just as you can never forget your sad, stupid dreams where you are straight and strong and a great chief. No, *he* was to be the chief this time, remember? Ah, well. It is no matter. You're tired. You should go to sleep now."

Gunitakan began to crumple in front of Daniel, his twisted body slowly aiming itself toward the ground. Daniel stepped forward, catching the man as he fell. "Not here, Grandfather," he said kindly as the Indian snored against his shoulder. "Here there is not enough room to spread your blanket, remember? You'll come with me to Enolowin, where you may very definitely consider yourself my guest. I, however, believe your presence will be more in the nature of penance on my part. Not for winning the race or even for bedding my opponent's wife. But for ever being falling-down drunk. In that I've dishonored my father's people, who have suffered enough at the hands of the white man's rum. As for the rest of it? Well," he hesitated as he slung Gunitakan over his shoulder and turned to retrace his steps down the hillside, "that will have to wait until we're both sober enough to see clearly."

Brianna ran her fingers over the harp strings a last time, allowing the notes to play out slowly, then just as slowly die away, leaving the music room silent, yet still alive with the memory of sound.

"That was beautiful, Brianna, and sad at the same time, as it makes me remember how seldom you play."

Brianna looked up to see her mother standing just inside the doorway and she blinked, feeling as if she had been brought back to Pleasant Hill too abruptly after spending the past hour lost somewhere in her dreams, her hands plucking the harp strings from memory while her mind danced through the rooms at Enolowin, seeking Daniel. Always Daniel.

"Have you settled the war in the kitchens, Mama?" she asked as she set the harp upright once more and stood, brushing down her skirts.

Bryna nodded as she sat down on the small settee, then patted the space next to her, encouraging her daughter to come sit beside her. "There are times I miss Lucretia's steady hand in the kitchens even more than I miss her as my dear friend. Why your father should have thought a French cook would please me remains a wonder. I keep longing to remind the foul-tempered fellow that he left France to escape tyranny, not to transplant it to our American soil."

Brianna grinned as she sat down, remembering the clang of thrown pots she had heard earlier. "Jules has taken umbrage with Lotte's paring yet again?"

Her mother nodded. "The vege-table," she said, dropping into a fine imitation of Jules's broken, heavily accented English, "she is to be sliced just so—on ze angle. This girl, this *groseille à maquereau,* she butchers ze carr-ots, makes ugly of them! This I do not abide, madam!"

"Poor Lotte," Brianna said, tongue in cheek, knowing the young kitchen servant lived in delicious dread of Jules's twice-weekly tantrums. "You told her, of course, that being called a gooseberry is the epitome of French flattery?"

"I pulled her out from behind the bread cabinet, dried her tears, and sent her off to wring a few chicken necks," Bryna corrected. "She promised to pretend that each one of them was Jules's scrawny throat. I believe they'll be married before Christmas, don't you?"

"Definitely," Brianna agreed, then lapsed into silence, her hands twisting in her lap, her mind full of questions that had been plaguing her for two weeks, and longer. Not that she wanted to confide in her mother. Oh, she might feel the *need,* but she wasn't sure she knew how to put her confused feelings into words. So she latched onto another, yet related, subject. "If we are to speak about the sad mismatching of people, Mama, do you suppose Corliss and her Englishman will also wed?"

Bryna patted her daughter's hand. "You don't believe them to be well suited, do you? Or is it just that Addison Bainbridge seems so very mundane when put up against our own Daniel? That, and the fact that it is quite obvious to anyone who looks that Daniel considers Mr. Bainbridge to be beneath his contempt. Don't shake your head and look surprised, pet. You're not the only one who notices things others don't bother to see. Or did you think your insights into Daniel's mind meant that the two of you were especially fashioned for each other?"

Brianna looked toward the windows, where the afternoon sun slanted in through the sheer draperies, reproducing the pattern of the windowpanes on the carpet. "We were speaking about Corliss, Mama," she said, doggedly sticking to the subject at hand. "She's such a sweet, innocent person. Addison Bainbridge may be handsome and worldly, but he seems a cold fish." She turned to look at her mother. "Why, if I didn't know better, I'd say Corliss has more affection for the man's slave than she does the man. I'd think she was encouraging Bainbridge's suit only so that she could see Marcus—if I didn't know that Corliss doesn't have a devious or adventurous bone in her whole body."

"Unlike her friend Brianna, who comes to deviousness and adventure with an enthusiasm that takes her mother back to her own girlhood and makes her spend an extra hour fingering her holy beads at least twice a week," Bryna responded, leaning over to give her daughter a kiss on the cheek.

Bryna pressed her head on her mother's shoulder, only for an instant, then sat up, smiling, a twinkle lighting her eyes. "Papa says you know me so well because we're so alike, you and I. I thought he was simply being kind. In truth, he was warning me, wasn't he? No matter how I try, I can never keep a secret from you."

"If you're referring to your treatment of Daniel these past weeks, yes, pet, you are as clear as a pane of glass. To me. And to Daniel as well, I believe. Although Winifred Bing must be delighted with your company. Poor Daniel. He must turn each corner in his house, seeing you everywhere and yet not seeing you. Have you decided how long you'll tease him this way? Or are you waiting for him to come to you on bended knee, begging you to speak to him?"

Brianna shook her head, sighing. "I don't know, Mama," she said honestly. "I don't know what I want anymore. I-I have these *dreams—"* She broke off, feeling the betraying heat run into her cheeks. What was she thinking? She couldn't tell her mother about her dreams! About the way Daniel figured in those dreams . . . holding her . . . loving her . . .

Bryna squeezed her daughter's hand yet again. "You're growing up, pet," she said quietly. Sadly. "But Daniel grew up a long time ago, while you were still playing with dolls such as the one your Aunt Brighid sent you. Seven years is a long time in anyone's life when they're still young, but the years mean less once we're grown. A year ago, two, I would have read you a lecture on wishing for things you'd have no notion of what to do with were you to get them. But you'll be eighteen in a few days, and Daniel is a young man of five and twenty. The years between you matter less now. It's the *relationship* between you that must frighten him. I think he is finding it difficult not to see you as his young cousin, the baby sister of his childhood friends."

"Exactly!" Brianna all but bounced up and down on the settee cushions, excitement filling her, loosening the lock she had put on her tongue as she spoke to her mother woman to woman. "I truly believe the man is *afraid* of me! Why, he as much as admitted it when he kissed me—" Too late, Brianna pressed her hands against her mouth, cutting off her own words. She wrinkled her nose, grimacing, as she then let her hands drop into her lap. "I suppose Papa and I will be facing each other in his study soon, having another one of our little chats," she said, sighing theatrically.

"What? And give the poor darling man an apoplexy?" Bryna responded, smiling conspiratorially. "Your father still believes you are his little muffin, who will spend her life worshiping her dearest papa. It was difficult enough for him to come to grips with the idea that your sister was old enough to marry. You, pet, are his baby. I don't think he's ready for you to be having babies of your own."

"But you are, Mama?" Brianna asked, eyeing her mother suspiciously, yet with hope blossoming in her chest, for having her mother on her side would greatly improve her chances of bringing Daniel Crown to his senses. "Are you ready for me to be having babies of my own?"

"As none of your brothers seem ready to oblige me, and Felicia lives so far away, I suppose the thought of having another grandchild does have some certain appeal. However," she added, just as Brianna reached for her, ready to give her a hug, "I am not all that certain Daniel is the man for you, pet, no matter how much he might be intrigued by you and, yes, no matter that he has kissed you—an action that must have frightened the pair of you down to your toes. Daniel needs a woman by his side, a strong woman, a woman who will help him find his way, then be willing to walk that way with him, whether he remains here, returns to England, or takes another path entirely."

"I know that, Mama."

"Do you? Do you really? You're treating Daniel like some sort of prize you have set yourself to win, which tells me that you're still, in many ways, the child he believes you to be. I gave my childhood to your father, gave him my dreams, my hopes, even my anger and my fears. It took a strong man to make me happy, Brianna, to teach me to be a woman, to help me understand what it means to share not only kisses but also trust and responsibility and compassion—and even heartache. Not all of those lessons were easy. If we had shared only passion, only kisses, we would never have been able to survive. Do you know what I'm saying? Are you prepared to be a woman, Brianna? Because once you cross that threshold, your childhood will be forever behind you."

"And the rest of my life will be before me, Mama," Brianna said quietly, blinking back tears that stung her eyes; for her mother was at last speaking to her as an equal, and she was as honored as she was frightened. "The rest of my life, with Daniel. I have made up my mind to have him and, much as I love you and Papa, there is nothing that will change that. I love Daniel. I really, truly love him. And, once he stops being so blessed stubborn and figures out that *I* am what he is looking for, I believe he'll love me, too."

She lifted her chin, speaking from her heart, from the depths of the determination that had been her hallmark, her blessing, her curse, since she had been in leading strings. "No matter what it takes, Mama, no matter what I have to do, I'm going to prove to Daniel that I'm not some easily dismissed infant, not his cousin but a *woman.* A woman who loves him."

"And to think that your poor deluded father still believes you to be a child." Bryna took a deep breath, letting it out slowly. "All right, pet. You do what you feel you must do—although I would hope you'd spare your old mother most of the details, as I already have this lamentably fertile imagination of mine and the memory of my own fairly headstrong youth to frighten me. You have my blessing if you want it. And may God help us all," she said, gathering her youngest daughter into her loving arms.

Much malice mingled with a little wit.

JOHN DRYDEN

chapter eight

Gunitakan slept the clock around, his loud snores prompting Finn to remark to the ceiling above his bed that he was giving considerable thought to smothering the Indian in his sleep. Instead, believing his employer might frown on such drastic measures, and not entirely sure Daniel Crown wasn't in some way related to the rum-soaked old savage, Finn had risen early from his bed in the servant wing and dragged himself out to the side porch, where he found his employer and Otto Bing already sitting on their spines in a matched set of rocking chairs, their feet propped up on the railing, each contemplating the sunrise over Lenape Cliff.

"Dressed yourself in those heathen animal skins again, I see," Finn groused as he leaned against the porch railing and scratched at an old itch. "Soon you'll be needin' me less than I need this stiff leg and be shippin' me back to Ireland, which is a nice enough place if you like rain, but not one I want to be seein' anytime soon, you know. Will Mrs. Bing be servin' soon, do you think?"

As if she had heard him, Winifred Bing appeared on the porch, wiping her hands on her huge white apron, a wide smile splitting her apple-cheeked face. "Ei-yi-yi!" she exclaimed, giving Otto Bing's booted feet a push, knocking his legs down from their resting place on the porch railing. "First you step in it, then you drag it with you from place to place. Now go scrape those boots like you're supposed to do before you climb onto my nice scrubbed porch."

Otto stood, hiked up his trousers, and sniffed, his long nose twisting as he pursed and unpursed his lips. "There's no manure on my boots, woman," he protested. "I've been no nearer than I had to be, just throwing the chickens over the fence some feed. But I could eat some breakfast," he continued as he obediently stepped off the porch and scraped one boot sole after the other over the thin edge of a small cast-iron ornament that was fashioned in the shape of a long, low hound. "I'll wager that fine hash you made up yesterday is all, and I didn't have none of it."

"Um, hash!" Finn exclaimed, looking to Daniel, who was still sitting quietly, very much awake, but not moving so much as an eyelash.

Winifred stuck her fists on her ample hips and glared at her husband. "Of course it's all, Otto, what with this hollow-legged Irisher sticking his feet under my table every time I turn around. Why didn't you eat some when I had it?"

Otto turned his head and winked at Finn and Daniel before turning back to his wife, saying patiently, "Well now, wife, why would I do that? You know I don't like hash. But you could make two eggs for my breakfast if you had a mind to."

As Mrs. Bing flounced off—and she was of a fine body for flouncing—Finn leaned down to Daniel and whispered in his ear, "Make him two eggs? What do you think, sir—does he expect her to *lay* them? And aren't I the one what keeps tellin' you these people talk funny? Not at all well-spoken like the Irish."

"Shhh, Finn," Daniel warned, slowly recrossing his legs as they rested against the porch railing, still pretending to be half asleep, and enjoying himself very much. "Our friend Bing is in a fine mood this morning, and I don't want to miss a word. It shames me, but I am finding myself easily amused these days."

"Glory be to God, but if it's a tickle to your funny bone you want, then you should go apologize and get that sweet girl to come back over here without first checkin' to be sure you're nowheres about," Finn said, sniffing. "Then maybe you'd throw that old Indian back where you found him. He won't be any great help to you in searchin' up your past," he continued with the cheerful confidence of a man who believes that no plan will ever succeed. "And I won't bathe him once he wakes, neither. Not if it costs me my position. And I think it only fair to tell you that he'll find himself another spot to snore in before tonight, or I could prove myself to be a violent man."

Daniel ignored his valet's comments about Brianna, knowing it would only encourage the man to take greater liberties if he seemed the least put out by his warnings. "Stubble it, Finn. Bing's done scraping his boots like a good husband and is bound to have a few choice words to say about his loving wife."

Bing climbed back up onto the porch once more, shaking his head and clucking his tongue. "Ei-yi-yi! What a woman! She's all about herself, powerful cross, and taking all her meanness out on me. Her bread cracked while baking last week, so she's sure there'll be a death in New Eden anytime soon. Been counting the days ever since, waiting for the church bell to toll, itching to make her funeral pie."

"She's superstitious?" Daniel asked, then waited for Bing's answer, knowing the man had one coming, for he seemed entirely too pleased with himself.

"That she is, sir. Superstitious. What nonsense th woman talks. Now, if I hadn't run outside right quic yesterday, when I thought to sneeze at breakfast—*the* we'd be having us a fine funeral."

Daniel made a small sound in his throat, which h hoped Bing wouldn't recognize as a suppressed laugh.

"A funeral is it, Bing?" Finn remarked, soundin suddenly hopeful. "We Irish truly love a good funera Why, it's our favorite way to pass the time, don't yo know, death being such a happy release and worthy o celebration. Will there be enough to drink, do yo think?"

"You Irishers. Always looking for any excuse to drin yourselves for dumb," Bing said, and sat himself dow once more, lifting his feet onto the porch railing an looking like he planned to take up residence in the rocke for the remainder of the morning. "Ah, this is good sitting here."

"Laziness is a great burden to you, isn't it, Bing? Finn bit out, obviously smarting from the other man' remark. "But you live well on your wife's work, I'd say Maybe I should get me a little ace of spades and settl down myself."

"Ace of spades?" Bing repeated, frowning at Daniel who told him that the term referred to a widow woman—why, he himself had no idea.

"Yes," Finn ruminated, winking at Daniel, "I coul get me a fine broth of a woman, like dear Mrs. Bing She's like a Mullingar heifer, you know, beef to the heels Fine, fine doorful of a woman. You not planning o turnin' up your toes anytime soon, are you, Bing? No that I'm thinkin' of marriage all that quick, bein' only eight and forty—still a little young for a bachelor bo like me to be gettin' himself bracketed. But the loaf di crack, didn't it, Bing?"

Bing stood up, hitching up his pants, sniffing. I seemed a ritual with him, this hitching and sniffing Daniel wondered idly if Finn ever saw anything o himself in the spindly-shanked Bing, but he doubted it—as his valet thought of himself as one who had been made in a perfect mold the good Lord had then quickly broken.

The caretaker scowled at Finn, saying accusingly, "You're trying to make fun with me, aren't you, Irisher?"

Finn pushed himself away from the railing, gave a pull at his own waistband, then sniffed loudly. "Would a duck swim?" he countered cheekily.

The two men turned and squared, both with their hands still holding up their pants, and Daniel reluctantly rose to step between them. "Finn. Apologize."

"Me?" The Irishman exploded, even while standing in place. "It wasn't me what started it! A man spends his whole night awake, tossing and turning while the thunder booms inside the house, shaking the very walls, and then he's supposed to take lip from some lazy, egg-sucking layabout? Why, I—"

"I'll move the Indian," Daniel said, knowing that this was the price his valet had decided upon to maintain peace at Enolowin and his reason for inciting Bing to forget his laziness enough to seriously consider entering into a brawl with the Irishman.

Finn sliced his employer a quick look, never really taking his eyes off Bing—who just might be the sort to put a punch in while nobody was looking—and pressed his advantage. "And you'll go to dinner at Pleasant Hill? Or ask the folks there to dinner here? Or just go see the girl and get it over with? I need you out of those animal skins and back in some decent duds. I truly do, or else there's nothing for me to do here save split this man's lip, so itching to do something I am."

"Finn, I'm warning you," Daniel said, feeling his own lips tightening.

"See the girl?" Bing interrupted, looking from Finn to Daniel and back again, and then grinning, proving that, although he might be a lazy sort, he wasn't exactly dull-witted. "Ei-yi-yi! So the wife is right, then? She says she smells some April and May-ing there, and she ought t know, for she's always been a quick one for that sort o thing. And that Miss Crown is a good girl. I've know her long already, and a man could do worse. Goo thinking, Irisher."

"Thank you, Otto," Finn said, nearly forgetting him self to the point of taking a bow.

"How wonderful," Daniel said to no one in particula "They've both cried friends, while leaving me wonderin if maybe I should be the one contemplating mayhem." Daniel glared at Finn, who was now busily and pru dently inspecting the tops of his shoes. "Why, the wa I'm feeling at the moment, within a few hours I imagin all of New Eden could be busy making funeral pie for a certain big-mouthed Irishman." He then turned to skew er his estate manager with a dark look. "And how man peals of the church bell would be needed to call out you years, Bing?"

Bing coughed twice, then hit his stomach with hi fisted hand, forcing a last gush of trapped air out of hi lungs as he took a sudden deep interest in peering out a the clear morning sky. "It's going to make rain soon, say, a few long days of it. Good. If it rains Monday an the wife can't wash, it will bother her terrible, troubl her all the week as she tries to catch up. Best I go see i the roof wants patching at the chicken house if rain i coming."

"Otto Bing, where are you going?" Winifred asked having come back onto the porch while the three me were otherwise engaged. "And you, too, Mr. Finn," sh added as Bing shuffled off the porch and the valet bega slinking toward the front of the house. "Doesn't anyon want breakfast this morning?"

Finn, never down for long and rarely ever out, turne smartly on his good leg and beamed a smile at th housekeeper. "I wouldn't be sorry to get some tea, Mrs Bing," he said cheerily, slipping past Daniel, wh growled at him, because he knew Finn wouldn't feel happy or forgiven without that growl. "But you shouldn't be doing so much for me, sweet lady. How about I make up some conny wabble for us all this fine morning? It takes just a jot or two of brandy in those eggs your fine husband was asking for. Here—I'll show you how. Bing? You coming along? Or are you going to stand there in the dirt, even now, while Miss Crown bears down on you on that great beastie of hers?"

Daniel's indulgent smile at his servant's antics disappeared as he turned to look out over the scythed lawns to see Freedom's Lady trotting up the drive, Brianna sitting tall and straight on the mare's back, riding astride, and clad in the same breeches and white shirt he'd first seen her in the day he had arrived at Enolowin.

"So," he breathed quietly, "she's back. With each of us two weeks older, and neither of us probably so much as a day wiser." Without a word to the others, who were all standing to one side, smiling as if they had been personally responsible for Brianna's presence on Enolowin land while the master was to home, Daniel walked the length of the wraparound porch and descended the front steps to the gravel drive, waiting for Brianna to rein in her mount.

She couldn't quite seem to hide her pleasure at the sight of Daniel, although her first words, uttered as she lifted her leg over the mare's neck and gracefully slipped to the ground did little to encourage him. "So, you're here," she said, allowing him to loop Lady's reins through the ring on the nearest hitching post. "I would have thought you'd be long gone, as you usually are when I arrive. Does this mean you've become more fearless, or did you merely play slugabed this morning?"

"It's your shy, retiring ways that I believe I've missed most, infant," he commented, taking her arm and walking her away from the house—and the three interested parties who were all but hanging off the porch railings, the better to see the pair of them. But he avoided her eyes, because he knew he had been deliberately lingering on the porch this morning, hoping she'd arrive.

Brianna's quick, unaffected laugh pleased him, as did her next words. "I hadn't thought to see you, to tell you the truth, as you're usually gone by now, out hunting up your ancestors in the woods or whatever it is Mrs. Bing says you're doing that you invariably come home smelling all woodsy and bringing her a brace of rabbits more often than not. She'd greatly appreciate a pheasant one of these fine days, although she'd never be bold enough to say so."

"There is nothing Mrs. Bing isn't bold enough to say to me," Daniel offered, mentally setting his sights on procuring the housekeeper her very own fat pheasant. "And little you wouldn't say to me," he added. "Bearing that in mind—may I ask why you're here today? I don't believe Mrs. Bing plans to change the bedsheets again until next week."

Brianna looked up at him, blinking innocently. "Sheets? What have I to do with the sheets at Enolowin?" she asked, sliding her arm through his. God, it felt so good to have her this close again, touching him, teasing him with both her presence and her wit. "No, in truth, I came here today to sew up some salt and bread crumbs in the lining of your best coat."

"Of course you did," Daniel said, wondering if he was meant to feel dizzy and slightly off balance every time he was with Brianna.

She nodded, her expression serious. "Mrs. Bing swears that salt and bread crumbs sewn into a man's jacket or a woman's hem will keep that person from homesickness. Just in case you've been pining for England, you understand. I mean to be certain that you don't leave me—right up until the moment you realize that you never can."

"Dominick must be getting old and tired," Daniel said, looking down at Brianna's smiling face in amazement. "Otherwise, he would have sat on you twice a day until you learned how to behave. But, tell me—if you only mean to hold me until, as you say, I realize that I could never leave you—what will you do then?"

Her smile wavered, then disappeared, and she occupied herself in dragging a few wayward strands of her living-fire hair away from her cheek. "I don't know," she said quietly, honestly. "I would have imagined that you would know what came next."

Daniel closed his eyes, his senses swimming as a vision of what he would do, what he wanted so desperately to do, flashed before his eyes. Brianna, lying beneath him, her fiery hair fanned out on his pillow. Her bare arms raised, pulling him down. Their bodies meeting, joining, becoming one.

"You're not the least bit afraid of me, are you, Brianna?" he asked at last. "Most women are."

"I'm not most women, Daniel," she answered, her smile, her tone, completely devoid of pretense. "Or is all of England populated by brainless, giggling twits?"

"You're such a child, Brianna," he ground out, turning her around, walking purposefully back toward her waiting mount—for, otherwise, he'd have to kiss her. "Willful, headstrong, stubborn—and I'd be a fool to allow myself within ten feet of you, let alone listen to your nonsense."

"But you'll come to my birthday party on Saturday night, won't you?" she asked, smiling again, as if his cutting words had no power to hurt her. And of course, they couldn't—for she had seen his reaction, and the female in her gloried in it, damn it! "Mama has invited the Paytons, as well, and even the odious Mr. Bainbridge. We won't have dancing, but Papa has promised some sort of entertainment."

Knowing he couldn't refuse Bryna Crown's invitation and not be considered rude, Daniel barked out his agreement to the arrangement, then untied Brianna's mount, signaling that he wanted her gone—now.

But she walked straight past him, smiling up at the old Indian who had appeared on the porch, rubbing at his eyes as if trying to grind the sleep, and the ravages of rum, out of them. "Joe!" she exclaimed happily, lightly bounding up the few steps and carefully depositing a kiss on the single spot on the man's face that appeared to be reasonably free of grime. *"Itah!* How good it is to see you again. I had thought you were still visiting in Easton jail."

Gunitakan grinned like a small boy who has just been offered a peppermint stick. *"Itah,* Wapa-Kwelik! My old eyes are young, seeing you again. Tasukamend, look—it is the Dawn Sky, come to warm me." He leaned closer to Brianna. "You will give me a coin, yes, for me to spend on bread?"

"Bread now comes in a small brown bottle, Joe?" Brianna asked, her tone clearly teasing, clearly loving. "I will cook for you, yes. I will find you a new shirt to wear. But I will never give you a coin."

"Yiiii! Wapa-Kwelik sees too clearly. But she looks with her heart, so that I am happy. But I need no rum, Wapa-Kwelik. Now I can fill my head and belly with dreams, for Tasukamend has come. And Tasukamend will make me whole again. He will make all the Lenape whole and chase out all the bloody *Yankwis."* He patted Brianna's arm reassuringly. "We will leave you your hair, Wapa-Kwelik, because you are kind."

Brianna looked at Daniel, who was still struggling with the realization that there was nobody—nobody—in all of New Eden who Brianna did not know, who did not love Brianna. "What's Joe talking about, Daniel? Have you decided on your purpose here? Are you going to smear on war paint and go looking for scalps? Should I be afraid?"

"You should be spanked," Daniel muttered under his breath, cringing inwardly as she grinned at him, her emerald eyes dancing. "I met Gunitakan yesterday afternoon on Lenape Cliff, and he convinced me that I should bring him home with me. Declaring war on America was solely his idea, and one I'd hoped he would have forgotten by this morning," he ended, looking sternly at the old Indian, who was smacking his lips together as if trying to summon up some spit in his drink-dry mouth.

"Sometimes the drink talks for me and says too much," Gunitakan said at last, lifting his nose to sniff at the air. "There is food nearby. I shall go in search of it. You did promise to feed me, did you not, Tasukamend? Or did I dream everything?"

"I said I would feed you, old man," Daniel agreed gruffly, trying not to look into Brianna's sweetly smiling face. *Good God,* he thought, *she looks ready to melt, as if I've done some great good deed that has impressed her all hollow.* "I also agreed to house you in return for your wisdom and counsel. I did not, however, agree to make war with you. Now go and eat, Grandfather, and don't be surprised if Mrs. Bing threatens you with her broom and makes you take your food out-of-doors until we can dunk you in lye soap and water a time or two."

Gunitakan scrambled away in his sideways, crablike scamper and left Daniel alone to face Brianna's approval.

"I can't believe it!" she said as soon as the Indian was gone. "Crazy Joe, living here at Enolowin. So your trips into the woods have borne fruit, I imagine, or so you must believe. Goodness, Daniel, the whole of New Eden soon will be whispering about the madman at Enolowin. Don't you know Crazy Joe is a thief? A drunkard? And none too well furnished in his upper rooms, as my Mama would say—which is her polite way of explaining what everyone else says, which is that the poor old darling is brain-addled into the bargain."

"He knew Lokwelend," Daniel said by way of explanation, wondering why he was bothering to justify what he did on his own land, in his own house. He also wondered where the urbane, sophisticated London gentleman he had been had disappeared to, for he was uncomfortable with this unusual feeling of being unsure of himself, his motives, his reasons. And he most certainly was unaccustomed to *explaining* himself to anyone, especially a laughing young girl who should be at home, sewing samplers or some such thing.

Brianna threw back her head and laughed aloud, the sound a musical tinkling that sent a shiver running down Daniel's spine. "He knew Lokwelend? *That's* what this is all about? You look at Crazy Joe and see Lokwelend? Why, that's like looking at an anthill and seeing a mountain."

She sobered, shaking her head. "Poor Daniel, still trying to see to the past, aren't you? But Lokwelend is gone and has been for many years. His way of life, your father's way of life, are also gone in just these few short years. The Lenape, what's left of them, are living on the other side of the mountains, on the edge of the White River. Crazy Joe may talk a good story, dream a fine dream, but he will never leave New Eden to join them. He couldn't stand to be so far from his beloved rum."

"He means well," Daniel said, feeling foolish, more than foolish. Like a dreamer, his own dreams as far-fetched as those of Gunitakan, of the sad shell of a man the world knew as Crazy Joe. And each word Brianna spoke made him angrier and feeling more foolish, more hopeless.

She walked down the few steps to the gravel drive and laid a hand on his arm. "Daniel, you can't change anything. Papa explained it all to me years ago and it's sad, terribly sad. We took a proud race and destroyed them with our guns, our diseases, our thirst for land—our rum. Lokwelend saw it coming more than thirty years ago and told my father all about it. And still there was nothing anyone could do to stop the bloodshed. The Lenape are doomed."

"Gunitakan spoke to me of a great war that is coming." Daniel shook his head, sighing. He wished he could have held back that betraying sigh, knowing he shouldn't even be considering what he was considering—which was to mount his horse and ride to the West, to see his father's people while they still existed, to speak with them, possibly to join them just for a while. "Is he right, Brianna? It's difficult for me to believe the Lenape will give up the last of their lands without a fight."

"Joe must be talking about the wars waged on the frontier by the Lenape and the Miamis in the past few years since they've joined forces. They've banded together beyond the mountains, thirty-five tribes in all, I believe Papa has said, in an effort to rid the land of the white man. They've already beaten back armies under General Harmer and those who fought with Governor St. Clair in the past few years. But the end will still be the same, Daniel, because America wants more land for its settlers. Why, just last night at the dinner table, Papa told us that he heard we soon will be forming another army under someone named General Wayne—Mad Anthony Wayne, he's called—and the next war will be the last. By this time next year, it will be over. The Lenape who survive will have to move westward again until they disappear, and all that will be left will be the few we cannot defeat, like you, and the sad, broken ones, like Crazy Joe."

"His name is Gunitakan," Daniel said, the muscles in his jaw paining him.

Brianna dropped her hand to her side. "I've made you angry," she said sadly. "You've called me a child, Daniel, more than once. But who is the child now? Of both of our dreams, which is the most unrealistic? Or are you going to tell me that you haven't dreamed of your father's people? Of living with them? Of seeing them the way Lokwelend described them—proud, strong, free? I wonder. Does Marcus have the same dreams about himself, about his people?"

She shook her head, her curls sweeping against her shoulders, then reached up to kiss Daniel's cheek, startling him with her simple, artless show of affection, of compassion. "Thank you for taking care of Joe, Daniel. You've a good heart. But, then, I already knew that. I'll see you Saturday night."

She had taken the reins from his hand and had already sprung lightly into the saddle before Daniel could find his voice. "I thought you were going to sew salt and bread crumbs into the hem of my coat," he said, trying for a lighter tone, a more teasing tone—wanting to put their relationship back on a less intense level. Because he wanted to see her as little more than a child, *needed* to see her as little more than a child, and not the intelligent young woman who had just seen straight inside him, clear through to his confused heart.

Her smile nearly destroyed him. "There's no need for that. You're not going anywhere, Daniel Crown. I know that now, even if you don't. And don't forget to bring me a present on Saturday. I really do so love presents."

And then she was off, having turned Freedom's Lady and urged her into an instant gallop, leaving him alone once more, waving away the dust the mare's hooves had kicked up and reminding him that for as much as she swore she wanted him to stay, *she* seemed to be the one who was forever riding out of his life.

Crazy Joe—no, no, Gunitakan!—appeared on the porch, looking in the direction of Brianna's departing figure. "Wapa-Kwelik," he said, sighing deeply. "Ah, Tasukamend, if only I were a young chief. Tall and straight and strong. There would be no war that could take me from her. There would be no other destiny than to be by her side, no greater battle than to win her."

Daniel rubbed his hand across his eyes, fragments of a saying learned in his youth flitting, unwanted, through his mind: "True speaks the child; and through the fool speaks the wise man . . ."

He told himself he was riding into New Eden, Finn by his side, Gunitakan sprawled inelegantly in the back of the wagon, to buy the Indian some new clothes, but

Daniel knew he was really heading there to shop for a present for Brianna.

"Did we have to bring him along?" Finn asked, indicating Gunitakan with a sharp inclination of his head. "He gives me the fidgets, and no mistake. And I'm not much likin' the way he keeps caressin' that there knife of his while lookin' at my hair. It's some terrible stories I've heard, listenin' to Bing."

Finn all but jumped off the wagon seat as Gunitakan spoke from directly behind him, having crawled to the front of the wagon as the Irishman grumbled. "Many may think they know me, but do not listen to the singing of the birds which fly by," he intoned heavily as Daniel did his best not to laugh.

"Devil mend the man, he about scared me out of ten years' growth!" Finn exclaimed nervously, clutching one hand against his heart, the other lifted to protect what was left of his lanky brown hair. "And what is it you're findin' so funny, sir? Is it after making a fool of me you'd both be?" he asked Daniel accusingly as the horses slowed, then stopped in front of Dominick Crown's Inn and Stores.

"I'd never think to do for you what you do so well yourself," Daniel said as he jumped down from the wagon and went to tie up the horses. "Now, come on. We've got some shopping to do. And don't forget to pick up that jar of dark molasses for Mrs. Bing, as she's promised us a treat."

Finn scrambled down after him, still with one eye fixed on Gunitakan. "Better have a stout cork in the bottle, then, or else the old fleabag will drink it all before we get home, thinkin' it's rum. Well then," he then demanded of the Indian, "are you comin' with us or not?"

"My own clothes suit me," Gunitakan said stubbornly, remaining where he was. "With my own hands did I slay the deer, giving thanks for his sacrifice. With my own teeth did I chew the hide, making it soft. With the quill of the porcupine did I sew the pieces, did I place the beads. I do not want the white man's clothes."

"Gunitakan," Daniel said, sighing. "We have already discussed this. Mrs. Bing refuses to allow you back into the house until you have a new suit of clothes. And a bath," he ended under his breath.

"Having a problem with one of your, um, *domestics,* Crown? I would have thought you could teach the animal to heel."

Daniel turned around to see Addison Bainbridge standing on the raised wooden flagway in front of Dominick's building, what looked to be a London Exquisite beside him—a handsome man of about forty years who wore his sophisticated sneer with the ease of long use. Bainbridge was impeccably dressed in well-tailored riding clothes and looked to be enjoying the sight of Daniel in his deerskins. Daniel returned his look for a long moment while ignoring the unknown man, his expression unreadable, then turned back to Gunitakan, having given both men the cut direct—if either of them were bright enough to recognize the insult. "I ask you this, Grandfather, do not shame those who belong to Enolowin in front of fools," he said in guttural Lenape, then held out his hand to assist the Indian down from the wagon bed.

"I'll take Joe inside, sir," Finn volunteered, eyeing the two men who still stood on the flagway, exchanging smiles. "Unless you'd be wantin' me here to watch your back? Those two look as cute as pet foxes, and no mistake."

"You have spoken good words, Chitanitis," Gunitakan said as he scampered down from the wagon, nodding sagely. "I see two men, but no friends."

Finn looked at Gunitakan owlishly. "What did you call me? Chi-ta-*what?*"

"Chitanitis," Daniel repeated. "It means strong ally. Feel honored, Finn. The Lenape give names that fit the person. I'd say Gunitakan has looked at you and seen a friend."

Finn's grin all but split his face. "Chitanitis! Well, and if that don't make me feel as proud as a whitewashed pig!" He slung an arm around the old Indian's shoulder, obviously forgetting the family of fleas that resided inside the man's clothing. "Come with me, Joe, my fine boyo, and we'll get you outfitted all right and tight. Might even go on over to the inn side and split us a bottle, once we're done. You'd like that, Joe?"

Daniel watched the two new friends climb the steps to the flagway and enter the building, heading right, into the trading area, then turned to head across the hard-packed dirt street, to take a look in the shops that lined the area, wondering if a bonnet would be too personal a gift for Brianna.

"Wait a moment, Crown," Bainbridge called after him, and Daniel stopped and turned, a little surprised that he had all but forgotten the man's presence. "Although you must have left your manners at home with your civilized clothing, I'd still very much like to introduce you to your dear uncle's new houseguest. Monsieur le comte, may I present to you Daniel Crown, your host's adopted nephew—part savage Indian, part unknown. Crown, I give you the Comte Hugh De Sauville."

"Comte," Daniel said, bowing slightly, taking in the man's tall, slightly beefy body, his faintly fleshy yet handsome face, his tightly tied-back blond hair, the long gray eyes that flashed colder than a February morning.

The comte allowed the quizzing glass that had been stuck to his right eye to fall against his chest and dangle at the end of a black riband as he made Daniel an elegant leg, flourishing a snow-white, lace-edged handkerchief as he waved his hand across his body in greeting. "Charmed, I am most assured, Mr. Crown," he said, his English clearly understandable, if a bit accented. "If you are half so welcoming as my good friend Dominick and my new friend Mr. Bainbridge, I will be most delighted to beg your company inside, where I have been promised a well-chilled bottle of wine."

"Dominick's inside?" Daniel asked Bainbridge, who smiled and nodded. "He and Mr. Payton have their heads together in the taproom, speaking of millstones and waterwheels and the like. A most delightful topic, I'm sure, but perhaps we might still join them and convince them to speak of other things. Like the dear Brianna's birthday celebration tomorrow night? You *are* invited, aren't you?"

Daniel ignored Bainbridge's jibe as he climbed up to the flagway, bypassing the steps to his left, and motioned for the comte to precede him into the taproom, leaving Bainbridge to follow as best he could. He spoke to the comte in flawlessly accented French. "My uncle did not speak of your arrival when I saw him yesterday. My aunt must be delighted to have company, however."

The comte smiled, clearly pleased to be able to converse in his own language. "And Bainbridge told me you were nothing more than a savage, monsieur! How very wonderful to find him wrong. You have either spent time in Paris or had a very good tutor. We shall speak of this later, yes? And, yes, I have come to this lovely place, quite uninvited, to throw myself on the mercy of your good uncle. I came first to take refuge in this place called the Sun Inn in Bethlehem, and then remembered the dear Lord Dominick lived close by. Thankfully, he has offered to be my savior. There is talk of fever in Philadelphia, where I first met Lord Dominick, you understand, and I have hoped to escape the city until the fall by prevailing on his generosity. I am in this country on orders from what is left of us poor beleaguered Royalists, I will tell you before you ask, to help convince you Americans to remain neutral in my country's struggle to put down this terrible rebellion. But now, with all of your government scurrying into the countryside to escape the threat of fever, I ask only for a safe haven."

"From the fever, Monsieur le comte, or from the revolutionists?" Daniel asked as Dominick looked up from a table across the room and motioned for the newcomers to join him and Payton. "I imagine it is equally as *warm* in Paris for the nobility right now as it is in Philadelphia. Or are rumors of the guillotine that has been brought into that city not to be believed?"

The comte slapped Dominick's back heartily as he gave out a bark of appreciative laughter. "You are as sharp as Madame Guillotine's blade, *mon cher,"* he said, speaking in English once more. "Addison, my new friend, you err when you say this man is a savage. He is utterly delightful, and I wish to buy him a bottle. I will buy us all a bottle, *oui?"* He turned and walked up to the small bar, calling loudly: *"Garçon!* Wine, if you please, for myself and *mes bon amies!"*

"You're smiling now, Crown," Bainbridge said in a near whisper, his head close to Daniel's. "But I accompanied the comte here from Pleasant Hill, leaving a thoroughly dazzled Miss Brianna Crown behind, waving us on our way. You've competition now, my friend. These innocent colonial women—so easily tempted by a chance of a taste of exotic French pastry."

"You've always been an ass, haven't you, Bainbridge?" Daniel remarked blandly, turning to face the other man. "I had almost forgotten that about you. But, then, why would I think of you at all? Although I must say I'm beginning to regret that you hadn't the backbone to show up for our meeting that long-ago morning."

Bainbridge's blue eyes narrowed into slits, turning frigid with undisguised hatred. "As if you wouldn't have shot me in the back as I turned to walk off the paces! I wasn't about to serve myself up to be murdered by a savage. If it weren't for you, you bloody half-breed, I'd be in London right now, planning a remove to a country house party at the end of another Season. Do I wish you unhappiness? With all my heart, Crown. With all my heart! As will our new friend, the comte, once he learns to know you as a rival for the fair Brianna's hand. He has only been here for a few hours, but I've already discovered that the man says whatever comes into his mind. His mind and his empty pockets are now all centered on the beautiful Brianna. The beautiful *rich* Brianna. The man might be a posturing idiot, but he wishes to hedge his bets. If the revolutionists succeed, he has lost his lands, his title. Brianna's dowry would go a long way to ease his pain."

"Suddenly I feel as if I have never left London," Daniel drawled, looking past Bainbridge's head and through the window, longing to be outside, where he could breath. "However, as we are both here, and you've brought up that most uncomfortable subject of money and the ends one will go to supply himself with a new supply, I should like to make you an offer, Bainbridge. Five hundred pounds for your slave. A thousand if you'll depart New Eden—and Miss Payton—on the next stagecoach leaving the Sun Inn."

"Go to hell, Crown," Bainbridge growled, his cheeks going red, then icy pale. "You can just go to hell!" He then turned on his heel and went to help the comte carry bottles and glasses over to the table in the corner.

"Yes," Daniel said under his breath, "I had rather expected that would be his answer." He walked across the room to join his uncle and Mr. Payton and listen to their advice on the subject of falling grain prices, a topic that successfully excluded both the scowling Bainbridge and the affable comte from the conversation—until it turned to the possibility of Daniel perhaps allowing his stallion to be mated with one of Mr. Payton's mares.

At that point Bainbridge leaned both elbows on the table, saying, "Strange that you should mention horse breeding, sir. I was reading one of your books last night in your study, as I could not sleep. William Penn, the man who founded this colony originally, was quoted in it as saying—let me see if I can recite from memory—yes, I have it!—'Men are generally more careful of the breed of their horses and dogs than of their children.'" He turned to smile at Daniel. "I can think of so many who prove that point, can't you?"

Dominick's presence at the table was the only thing that kept Daniel from leaning across its surface and pulling Bainbridge out of his seat by his neckcloth, then tossing the smirking man through the window and out into the street. Instead, he only lifted his glass to within an inch of his lips, smiled, and said, "Looking in mirrors again, Bainbridge?"

"*Zut alors!* What have we here? A rivalry?" The comte deftly shifted forward in his chair, putting his body between the two men. "Lord Dominick, I thought you had promised me that I should be bored into *ennui* within a week here in New Eden. Now I see that I shall be enjoying myself very much."

Daniel mumbled an apology and then quit the table, but not before seeing the calculated gleam in the comte's gray eyes. Bainbridge could be looking for trouble, but nothing Daniel didn't feel he could handle, as he had handled the man before in London.

But the comte was a lover of mischief. Daniel didn't like the idea that he'd be spending the rest of the summer under the same roof as the impressionable Brianna.

"That Frenchie walks like a hen in stubbles," Finn said as he sat up beside Daniel on their way back to Enolowin. And did you see all that lace?" The Irishman shook his head. "You have the man beat all hollow, you do, when you let me have the dressin' of you. *If* you'd let me have the dressin' of you. Shames m'mother no end the way you had to stand there, drippin' fringes of deerskin while the Froggie dripped lace." He put his head in his hands. "Forgive me. I've been ridin' the water wagon too long, sir, and have fallen off with a mighty splash. Too much ale, much too much much ale. Oh, my head!"

Gunitakan, still clutching the tied-up brown paper

holding his new shirt and suit of deerskins, leaned in between the two men. "Where did the frog come from? I have never seen his like before. And why does Chitanitis call him this? He does not look like a frog. Does he sit by the water at night and croak? It seems a silly thing to do."

"Chitanitis is being vulgar, Grandfather. Just ignore him. And the comte is French and comes from across the Big Water," Daniel answered, his mind still back at the inn. "From there, and lately, from Philadelphia. He has come a long way."

"I have been to Kúeqiemàku—this place the whites call Philadelphia. I have traveled in my time. It is not so far. Not so far that a frog cannot hop it, if he goes slowly."

Finn began to giggle, as he definitely had downed his share of rum, and was now easily amused by his new, good friend. But then he became deadly serious, as only the fairly inebriated can. "I don't like that Bainbridge fellow one bit, and bad manners to him says I. He smiles too much. You should cut a wide berth around that scalpeen, sir, a wide berth. I don't think he much would mind watchin' while you took a fall."

Daniel wanted a change of subject, as Bainbridge and the man's veiled insults were both topics that did not interest him. "I settled him once in London, Finn, if you remember, when he fled from our duel all the way to America. The fellow is basically a coward. He wouldn't be so foolhardy as to come back for a second defeat."

"Foolish boy," Gunitakan muttered, shaking his head. "I see your grandfather has much to teach you. It is good I allowed you to take me into your house."

Daniel chuckled at the old Indian's agile twisting of their relationship. "I am honored indeed, Grandfather," he said, turning the horses onto the lane that led to Enolowin.

Gunitakan hiccuped, proving that he had drunk his share of the ale Daniel's money had provided. "You know what we Lenape do when a man such as this enemy of yours would come into our gatherings?"

"Bainbridge is *not* my enemy," Daniel corrected calmly.

"Yes, Tasukamend, he is. You shamed him, made him see himself for the coward he is, made everyone see him for the coward he is, and he will never forget that or cease to hate you. Now, be quiet while I will tell you of the Lenape way. When the undesirable one comes, one by one, those already in the gathering place will steal off, leaving the man at last alone where so many had been before he came, so that he can suffer the dishonor he should feel for being such a bad man."

"That's a good idea, sir," Finn agreed. "If you think yourself too honorable to warn your uncle or that Mr. Payton fellow, then just walk away from this Bainbridge person. But don't go turnin' your back to him. Or to the Froggie, either. Never had much to say for Froggies. And they looked too friendly to suit me, like they're peas from the same pod who just found one another. But, then, one cockroach always knows another, I say." He leaned back on the plank seat to peer intently at the old Indian, nearly succeeding in tumbling into the wagon bed. "Gunitakan—what was it that you called the two of them? *Machi*-somethin'?"

The old Indian pushed Finn upright on the seat, using the bundle of clothes as a lever. "The frog I called Machtitsu. The smiling one, Machtesinsu. You drink too much, Chitanitis."

"And you both talk too much," Daniel said as he steered the horses around to the stableyard. "And now, you two good friends, we are home, and you can get about the business of bathing the one of you—while you both soak your heads under a cool pump."

He helped the two grumbling men on their way, watching as Finn limped alongside Gunitakan, keeping up with the man's crablike scamper, and shook his head. He'd rather have the Irishman and the Indian beside him than a roomful of London dandies or French aristocrats sharing his table.

Machtitsu. *Mean.* And Machtesinsu. *Ugly.*

Through the fool speaks the wise man?

Daniel lifted his own packages out of the wagon, passed the horses over to Skelton and Toby, then turned toward the house, wondering if perhaps he should be listening more closely to what his good friends said.

These poor half-kisses kill me quite.

MICHAEL DRAYTON

chapter nine

Brianna sat on the small back porch of the summer kitchen—or on the *stoop,* as Mrs. Bing called it—her chin in her hands, and looked out over the gardens of Enolowin.

Such a beautiful place. Different from Pleasant Hill, but wonderfully so, with all its seemingly randomly placed outbuildings; the summer kitchen, the bake oven, the curved roof that covered the root cellar, the wash-house beside the spring, and all of them mingled in with the flat slate paths and sprawling gardens that were so much less formal than those at her own home. Ivy clung to the stone walls of the springhouse, and wild roses climbed the split-rail fences that marked the boundary between the kitchen garden and the lush, faintly overgrown flower gardens her own mother had helped plant so many years ago.

Over the years, Mrs. Bing had added to the blooms, planting roots and bulbs that had been carefully nurtured on their journey down the Rhine and across the sea until the gardens, begun with such careful planning, now sprawled informally in several directions, wandering and meandering here and there, with hollyhocks growing beside lemon lilies, sweet rockets, and forget-me-nots jumbled in with peonies and tulips, a well-shaped boxwood sharing space with the more homely sweet williams.

The sunny, cloudless sky above Brianna's head was so blue it hurt her eyes, and the very air was alive with the mingled scents of showy blooms and fresh mint, the tantalizing smell of hickory smoke and curing ham from the smokehouse, the friendly buzz of bees as they flitted from flower to flower. And in the center of all this appealing jumble was a huge black cherry tree, giving shade to the wooden, weathered bench that encircled the trunk, a clever seating place that the marquess of Playden had built for his wife with his own hands so many years ago.

To Brianna's left, and wrapping almost clearly around the estate, lay the rolling fields of Enolowin, most of them lying fallow these many years, all of them cleared for planting and edged by rows of oak and maple and locust and lovely berry bushes meant to lure the birds away from seeds when they were planted in the fields.

To her right, barely visible from this vantage point, stood the huge barn and the adjoining stables where Daniel housed his fine purchases that had been shipped to New Eden from Philadelphia—and still leaving ample room for Brianna's beloved horses, she thought, thinking that to be a most wonderful coincidence.

And beyond the barn, the stables? There stood Lenape Cliff, and Pematalli's all-seeing eyes, watching over Enolowin, guarding those who lived at Enolowin.

"Was there ever such a beautiful place?" she asked aloud of the flowers, the bees, and the cloudless blue sky above, her heart swelling with love for the house, the land, and the man who lived there.

But it was Finn who answered. "Can only be lovelier when you are here, Miss Crown," he said, stepping out of the summer kitchen to stand before her, grinning as he licked his sticky fingers. "It would only be you, I'm bettin', who could talk dear Mrs. Bing into bendin' her rules and bakin' on the Saturday. It's a grand love I have for molasses, and that's a fact. What did she do with that great mess of the sweet stuff anyways, do you know? I only got a lick or three from the bowl before she yanked it away and dunked it in the dry sink, saying I was worse to have under her feet than a whole gaggle of kiddies."

Brianna smiled, and patted the sun-warmed expanse of slate beside her, encouraging the valet to sit down. "Shame on you, Finn, for pestering the dear woman. We are just now done with making up some shoofly pies for my party tonight, and they're baking in the oven over there right now. You'll smell them soon and weep with joy over the fine smell. Mrs. Bing shooed me outside while she cleans up the kitchen, saying that she works best alone when it comes to sprucing up. You will be coming along to Pleasant Hill tonight, won't you? We always have a kitchen full of food for everyone, you know. It's Mama's rule, and a good one."

Finn was shaking his head. "Was it *shoofly* pies you said, Miss Crown—and I'll be proud to be in the Pleasant Hill kitchens this evenin', thank you and your dear mama."

Brianna nodded. "Yes, shoofly pies. We made a full half-dozen of them, as a matter of fact. Lovely crust, which is why Mrs. Bing calls it a pie, although I truly believe it is more of a cake, made simply of flour and brown sugar, butter and some lard. And molasses, of course. Not a light molasses, or one that is too dark, but just the *right* molasses. This is most important, you understand, Finn. Add one amount of the perfect molasses, and you have a lovely cake inside the pie crust. Leave out some of the flour, and the molasses settles to the bottom, making it wet. Then—just for fancy, as Mrs. Bing says—she adds flaky bits of sweet crust crumbled in your fingers and arranged on top before baking. I prefer my pies wet, and I'm confident you will, too, when you take your first bite and think you have died and been lifted up to heaven."

She wrapped her hands around her knees and leaned back, closing her eyes and sniffing the air. "Ah, smell them, Finn, as they bake. Isn't that wonderful?"

Finn looked skeptical. "And you call this bit of heaven *shoofly* pie?"

"Of course, Finn," Brianna answered, giving him a pat on the cheek. "Because it's so sweet and wonderful and smells so good that you have to keep *shooing* the flies away from it!"

Finn threw back his head and let loose a peal of laughter, then wiped at his eyes with a huge white handkerchief he pulled from the depths of his pocket. "What a wild tale you've told me, Miss Crown, reelin' me in like a fish and then landin' me with a mighty thump. And is it sure you are you haven't taken a lick of the Blarney Stone?"

"I'm Irish, Finn," Brianna reminded him. "Or at least, so Mama says the better half of me is." She sighed, tipping her head as she looked at the valet inquiringly. "Mama also says there is nothing like Ireland, and there are times she still misses those soft green hills terribly. We're to travel there on our way to England this fall, stopping off to see my cousin Mary Catherine in her convent. How did you come to leave, Finn?"

He shrugged, getting a far-off look in his eyes. "Wasn't any reason to stay, Missy, although I miss my ma, who would be singin' with the saints now, I suppose," he said quietly, then grinned at her. "Sent me on my way with a boot to my bottom, she did, as I was a great sorrow to the dear lady. I was ridin' the horses then, you understand, and maybe known to take a flutter or two on the bangtails while I was about it. One flutter too many, a few coins too little in my pocket, and many more coins owin', and these very big, very angry gentlemen came scratchin' at my dear ma's door, asking to take me out and very kindly make it so my knees bent both ways, if you take my meanin'. Well, and there is no use in talkin'—my ma pushed me out the back door while they were waitin' on me in the front garden, and I took the first ship headin' out of port, which landed me in England, as chance would have it."

"Gambling," Brianna said, nodding. "It's a particular curse on the Irish, Mama says. I believe her father took a flutter or two on the bangtails himself, along with having a fondness for a deck of cards—not that Mama has ever said as much. So," she asked quickly, believing herself to be clever, "Did you meet Daniel when you first got to England?"

Finn's smile told her he knew what she was about, and he began to speak again quite freely, but not quite as directly as Brianna had hoped. "So, your grandfather was a gamblin' man, was he? Better than my dear da, who went off with the fall of the leaf, for horse stealin', it was. Ah, the devil's own rogue, my da was. Hanged by his thievin' neck and laid under the dirt, which he would have jumped up from to steal another horse, Ma always said, if anyone was to lay down a halter on his headstone. The poor, poor Finns. Always in the field when luck was on the road. Now, what was it you were sayin', lass?"

Brianna smiled broadly, gave Finn a hug, then deliberately dropped into the broad brogue her own mother still took out and dusted off when she was in a particularly festive mood. "Never mind. Truly. I could listen to you for hours, I could, with your lovely Irish drippin' from your tongue like pearls. And it'll be tellin' me more about you and your fine family you'll be, if you please."

"Oh, you're a rare handful, you are, aren't you, missy?" Finn took a last lick of his index finger, savoring the lingering taste of molasses, and obliged her. "Let's see. The Finns. Well, Ma was a saint, of course—you'd know that. Then there was Da, the horse thief, and m'grandmother Rose, a real pisser—um, that is, a right fine one, who once shot herself an Englishman and buried him in the back garden. I have an uncle who, last I heard, had got himself made a bishop, and my older brother who is the mayor of our small town, while my younger brother takes considerable pride in being the village drunk. Then there's my sister the holy sister, and me, who rode the ponies for rich men, and—"

"Oh, stop, stop! Now I know you're bamming me, Finn. Tell me, how did you meet Daniel?"

Finn reached up and scratched at the back of his neck, as if prodding himself into memory. "Was it ridin' one of his horses I was? Yes, that's it. No. It was tumblin' off one of his fine racin' horses I was. Tumblin' off and breakin' this leg of mine in more pieces than you can find in a sack of rock candy."

"He took care of you," Brianna interjected, casting her beloved in the role of hero, because it suited her that he would always do the heroic thing.

"He gave me a purse and didn't kick me for killin' his fine horse," Finn responded, his eyes twinkling. "It wasn't until some long, lean months had passed, when I was fairly well down in my heels, that I saw him again. The dear man saw me actin' barker for a bowwow shop, hobblin' up and down in front of this mean little secondhand clothes shop, leanin' on m'crutch—I was still not walkin' as well as I do now, you understand. Anyways, there I was, cryin' out 'Clothes, coats, or gowns, what d'ye want, gemmen, what d'ye buy?'—I had sunk that low—so that he took me up with him and brought me to Playden Court. Which is where I've been ever since—by his side. He's a good man, lass, no matter that his head is all muddled right now. A good, fair man."

"Yes," Brianna said quietly. "He is that. A true gentleman."

Finn gave her a nudge in the ribs with his elbow. "But get him mad and he can curse the bladder out of a goat," he confided, then pushed himself to his feet. "And he's in that field out there," he added, pointing to his right, "probably hot and dry and wishin' for a cool drink as he digs great holes in the ground like he's no more than a poor farmer who has to put up his own fences. Yes, yes," he continued, winking down at her, "it's wantin' a cool drink the man must be. Wonder who'd be kind enough to take him one?"

Brianna jumped up and grabbed Finn's face between her hands, pressing a quick kiss on his cheek. "Hold on here, lass," he protested, although his smile betrayed his pleasure. "Don't go runnin' off without hearin' my story, for it's a sad Irishman I'd be if I didn't give you a story in exchange for the one you told me about that shoofly pie."

"Help me with the pump and I'll listen," Brianna said, in a hurry to go to Daniel. She picked up a jug that sat beside the pump outside the summer kitchen and held it under the stream of water as Finn manned the pump handle.

"Did your dear mother ever tell you about the fairies, lass?" he asked, pushing down on the wooden handle with both hands.

"The fairies?" Brianna balanced the full jug on her hip as she picked up the ladle, planning to take it with her into the fields. "Why, what sort of mother would she be if she hadn't? Fairies are lovely people. At night, during the summer most especially, you can hear them in the breeze as they travel from one of their fairy forts to another. You must say a short prayer each time you hear the breeze, because you never can be certain if the little people are bent on doing good or evil as they fly by. I know it's silly, but I still whisper a quick 'Glory Be to God' when the breeze kicks up on a summer evening. And now, Finn, I'll be on my way. Thank you so much for your help. For *all* your help."

Finn shook his head, his expression so suddenly solemn that Brianna hesitated, looking at him curiously. "What? Do I remember the story incorrectly?"

"She didn't tell you of the *other* fairies, lass? Of the leprechauns?"

Brianna relaxed, only then realizing that she had been holding the ladle so tightly that her palm hurt. "You mean the fairies who hold the pots of gold? The little fellows who wear green coats and knee breeches and have red caps on their heads and bright silver buckles on their shoes?"

"Those would be the ones," Finn agreed, looking at her intently. "Very tricky fellows they are. They hide in the shades of evenin' but can be seen in the moonlight, going about the business of being themselves. Happy enough they are, but they'd give the world for a taste of poteen—their thirst for the fire and heat so strong that if you dare to catch him, he'll offer to show you where his treasure is hid or gift you with a purse of gold, just for some poteen."

He leaned toward her, his eyes narrowed and intensely staring. "But take your eyes off him even once and—poof!—he's gone, takin' your poteen and disappearin', so clever he is in thinkin' up tricks to make you look around while he's makin' good his escape, keepin' his freedom. That's the leprechaun, lass. Happy enough on his own, or so he thinks, but with that burnin' thirst for the fire and the passion. Hard to catch, he is, and even harder to hold. Do you take my meanin'?"

Brianna wet her dry lips with the tip of her tongue. "I think I do, even if I don't much care for what you're inferring. But surely you're not comparing Daniel to a leprechaun? I don't think he'd appreciate that, Finn."

"To tell God's truth, I suppose he'd skin me alive," the valet agreed, smiling again. "Just remember that he thinks he's happy enough on his own, sittin' out there in those woods, no matter how he longs for the fire and the passion. And that's the lesson. Don't give more than you get, lass, and you'll end up gettin' it all."

"Why, Finn, now you sound just like Mrs. Bing!" Brianna exclaimed, feeling her cheeks betraying her by turning a fiery pink—although she could not, hard as she tried, find it in herself to be angry with the man. "The whole time she was rolling out the crusts she was making sounds about a man never buying himself a cow for his own as long as he could get milk without spending a bent penny—as if I didn't know what she was talking about. The two of you are incorrigible, that's what you are. And I think you have a mighty low opinion of your employer if you believe he'd not always behave like a gentleman."

"There are temptations and temptations, lass," Finn said, bowing his head to her. "Just like for some the thing what cannot be had is always just what suits. Better it is that you first both be sure of what the one wants and what the other needs."

"But you're sending me into the fields with this water, Finn," Brianna reminded him, still mightily embarrassed, but refusing to drop the jug and run home to Pleasant Hill.

His wink was broad, and friendly. "That I am, lass. I'm, at the heart of it, a bad, bad man, even if I've enough of a conscience to give you fair warnin'. You see, when you get right down to it, I already know what *I* want."

Brianna shook her head, grinning at the crafty Irishman. "Shame on you, Finn, shame on you. And bless you!" she ended, hiking up her skirts with one hand and turning about to begin her brisk walk into the fields in search of Daniel.

Time is a burden, Tasukamend. Think of accomplishments, of dreams, of where you are going and where you have been. Then, Tasukamend, time is as nothing.

Daniel read the passage a second time, a third, then closed Lokwelend's journal, rubbing his hand across the worn leather binding before placing the book on the grass.

He sat in the middle of the sunlit field he was in the process of dividing into separate enclosed pastures for his horses, taking a respite from his labors, stripped to his waist because of the heat, leaning against one of the newly placed posts that soon would hold the split-rail fence in place.

He had been doing as he had since the first, opening the journal at random, reading the page that appeared, and still denying the urge to begin at the beginning of the book and read straight through. And, to his continuing surprise, each time he had opened the journal, the page that presented itself had seemed so right, so correct for his mood and his questions that he was reluctant to change his methods. With each reading, he had marveled at Lokwelend's clear sight, even from beyond the grave.

Until now.

"Time is a burden. Time is as nothing. Think of your accomplishments, Daniel," he said as he gazed up at the brilliant blue sky. "Think of your plans, your dreams, where you are going, and where you have been."

He pulled the thin strip of deerskin out of his thick black hair, running a hand through the shoulder-length tangle that was damp with sweat. "Your dreams are impossible, your plans nonexistent, and time is something that has already passed beyond you or will never come." He threw the leather strip at the ground, unsatisfied with the gesture. *"That's* where you are, Daniel Crown. Tasukamend. Whoever in bloody hell you are."

He had come to America, to New Eden, to Enolowin, with one dream in his mind. To discover who he was.

Now he had two new dreams, neither of them resembling the first. To travel to the west, to find the Lenape, to live with them, work with them, struggle with them, or, secondly but just as compelling, to gather Brianna Crown close to him and, with that closeness, block out the entire world and all his questions. All his possible responsibilities. All his shame for having stayed so long in London playing the rich white man's son. All his hopelessness because—having studied well at school, and knowing what he did about the nature of man, about the certain outcome when the strong decided to vanquish the weak—he knew that the Lenape would die whether he was with them or not to watch their inevitable passing from the pages of history.

It had taken Gunitakan, that dear, sad shell of a man, to show Daniel how foolish his dreams of living with the Lenape were when stacked alongside the realities of life. Daniel had nothing in common with the Lenape. Nothing save his blood. They were not his people and hadn't been since the day Brighid Cassidy Crown had brought him with her to Fort Pitt to be returned to the world of the white man.

Yes, he had roamed the woods as a young child, these very woods, with Lokwelend by his side to guide him. He had learned many of the Lenape ways and forgotten half of them within a year of going to live at Playden Court. His memories that remained had been only the golden ones, untainted by the reality of life here in America, both before the Colonies had rebelled and since. To him, the Lenape way of life had always seemed a glorious dream, his unknown father's struggle a valiant one, his death a hero's sacrifice.

But Gunitakan was the reality. A few thousand trapped, desperate Indians huddled along the banks of the White River, preparing for victory, resigned to inevitable defeat and destruction. *That* was reality.

Leaving him—where? Ready to take ship back to England, back to the parents who loved him, the brothers and sister who loved him? Back to the overheated salons, the insipid conversations, the never-ending round of social silliness? Should he stay here, just for a year, until he could go back to Philip Crown, having fulfilled their bargain, and accept his adopted father's gift of land he could call his own?

Or was he ready to make a commitment to this land, to Enolowin? To Brianna Crown, the half-child, half-woman who would not stay out of his mind, his dreams, his every waking and sleeping moment?

Brianna. The beautiful daughter of Lord Dominick

Crown, destined to travel to England at the end of summer, to be fitted into ball gowns and paraded about for the delectation of those vapid young men who had so bored him during his own time in London, but whose blood was as blue as it was unmixed, and whose fortunes and holdings would make a small estate like Enolowin seem like a poor hovel on the edge of the earth. He could barely imagine Brianna in English society as she was now, although he could easily picture her being the center of everyone's attention and adoration the following spring, after Brighid had the handling of her for a few months, her come-out causing a minor sensation throughout all of London.

He had to give her time, give himself time—to know what she wanted, what he needed. He couldn't go to her while he was so conflicted, and she shouldn't come to him until she had seen more of the world than New Eden could show her. Because he was the older if not the wiser and because he had been raised to be a gentleman, he could not kiss her again—shouldn't have kissed her at all. He couldn't hold her, bury his face in her warm, inviting hair, accept the gift of her body when she had no notion of all he would want to take. Already wanted to take.

An unexpected breeze danced across the open field, cooling his sun- and work-heated body and ruffling the pages of Lokwelend's journal. Daniel reached for the book, ready to close it and tuck it away in the pocket of his jacket before going back to work, then hesitated, deciding to read the page where the book had opened.

Did you ever wonder, Tasukamend, about the other half of you? About your mother, Johanna, the one our people called Wingenund, the Willing One? Think of her, my son, and learn. Your history does not begin and end with your father, Tasukamend. Your limits are not bounded by blood but given unlimited space by your dreams. Wingenund chose to bend, to change, to fit herself into life as it changed around her, and she was happy because she had found love. It matters not where you are, who you think you may be, if there is love.

Daniel closed the journal once more and looked out across the field and saw Brianna coming toward him, her skirts dragging in the long grass, a jug balanced on her hip, her free hand waving a greeting, her flaming hair, her entire body, lit by sunlight.

And, suddenly, time was as nothing.

Daniel scrambled to his feet and reached for his shirt, slipping his arms into it as Brianna came closer, the twinkle in her laughing green eyes doing definite damage to his image of himself as a gentleman.

Buttoning his buttons, and amazed at the way his fingers had all turned to thumbs, he walked toward her and took the jug even as she pulled the ladle from its confinement under the sash of her simple blue gown. "Shouldn't you be at home, preparing for your party tonight?" he asked, pulling the stopper and, ignoring the ladle he could have used as a cup, lifted the earthenware container and drank deeply, straight from the mouth of the jug. "Ahh," he said, wiping his mouth with the back of his hand, "that tastes better than the finest wine. Thank you, Brianna."

She watched as he tipped the jug once more, pouring some of the cool well water into his cupped hand and then rubbing it against the front of his neck, behind his head, on his upper chest, where his collar lay open. "If you took off that jacket, you could pour some of that water directly over your head and cool yourself better," she pointed out reasonably. "I have four brothers, Daniel, remember? I have seen a man's chest before this."

"I'm quite sure you have, Brianna," he said, putting down the jug. "Although I should warn you not to say the word chest once you're in polite company in London.

The gentle ladies' sensibilities easily become overpowered by such plain language, and we gentlemen can get mightily bored with propping up swooning females."

She sat down on the grass, her feet straight out in front of her on the ground, spreading her full skirts around her as she looked up at him. "You make England sound positively stifling, Daniel," she complained, pouting. "And I did so want to go." Her pout turned to a blindingly bright smile. "Well, that settles it. I'll simply have to stay here in New Eden, where I can say chest and leg and maybe even rump with impunity and even pursue moody young men into their own fields, unchaperoned, to make sure they are going to make good on their promise to come to my party tonight. Monsieur le comte will be wearing most lovely satins, or so he told me, and will be at my side all of the evening, for I must surely know he cannot ze breathe, he cannot ze live, when he is gone from me, *n'est-ce pas?"*

Daniel felt the muscles in his jaw tightening. He didn't like the comte just on general principle, because of his too-astute insights, for his politics, in response to his baldly stated mission in America. Or so he thought. Or was it that he was merely jealous of the sophisticated, urbane older man who happened to be residing under Dominick Crown's roof at the moment; of his freedom to pursue Brianna with his flattery; of his undoubtedly intriguing tales of life at court in Paris, of his damned exotic accent that turned a simple request for accompaniment during a walk in the gardens after dinner into an invitation to romance?

Either way, he decided not to rise to the bait Brianna was dangling in front of him, for if she knew he was upset by the attention the Frenchman was paying her, she'd make his life a living hell.

He dropped to the grass beside her and slanted a look at her from beneath carefully hooded eyes. "You're incorrigible, you know, little one," he told her, realizing yet again that Brianna Crown was everything that he was not—open, trusting, friendly, and always so outwardly affectionate.

He was so damnably attracted to her, even as he felt repelled by her threat to his own more solitary, guarded way of looking at life, at other people. She had already gotten deeper inside him, closer to his usually well-hidden insecurities, than anyone had ever done before, and that meant she held more power over him than he had ever previously given to another human being. That he had trusted her with his revealing confidences, however grudgingly given, and that he still trusted her with them retained the power to amaze him.

He also remembered something he could only seem to forget for brief moments at a time: how much he wanted her. He looked at her now, knowing he was devouring her with his eyes and knowing that she knew how he felt, that she gloried in his unaccustomed unease.

"Incorrigible?" Brianna repeated, picking a long blade of seed-topped grass and twirling it between her thumb and forefinger before drawing its soft top down the length of her cheek, looking more provocative than any sophisticated society beauty employing a painted fan to its best advantage. "I think I'll take that as a compliment." Then she threw back her head and laughed aloud, breaking the growing tension between them.

"What's so damnably funny?" he asked in rare embarrassment, taken off balance once more by the quick shift in her mood, from the blatantly seductive to the genuinely amused.

"Nothing," she said, pressing a hand to her mouth to stifle her giggles. "Nothing at all, really. It's just—it's just that I was trying to picture you in a green coat and knee breeches, with a bright red cap on your head and silver buckles on your shoes and . . . and . . . well . . . you looked so *silly!*" She waved away his questioning look as she collapsed onto her back in the grass, giggling once more. "And I can't imagine *anyone* gifting you with her poteen with you all dressed up like that!" She hugged herself, rocking side to side on the grass as she laughed, her long fiery curls spread, fanlike, in the grass and flowering clover. "Daniel Crown, his so serious head stuck in a silly red cap! Oh! I have to stop this! My sides hurt!"

Red cap? Silver buckles? Poteen? "Finn!" he exclaimed, sure he knew the source of Brianna's humor, if not the reason behind it. Without really thinking about what he was doing, he leaned over Brianna, pinning her to the ground by placing his hands on her shoulders. "What did that miserable, interfering Irishman say to you?"

Brianna lifted a hand to his face, pushing the hair out of his eyes, tucking it behind his ears as she said, quite calmly, "Why, Daniel Crown, I believe you're upset." Then she giggled again, adding, "I can't imagine your reaction if you were ever to learn what Mrs. Bing had to say on the subject."

"On what subject?" Daniel gritted out from between clenched teeth, suddenly aware that their hips were pressed tightly together, and knowing he was damning himself, damning the both of them, because he wasn't about to move away from her. Couldn't move away from her. From the sweet softness of her, the fresh clean smell of her, the joy and the life and the freedom and, yes, the passion, that she so innocently offered.

Her tongue came out, moistening her full lips, giving them a gleam that invited, enticed, even as her nervous action betrayed her confusion. She had wanted to gain his interest, to gauge the depth of his desire. He was sure of that. But now that she had both, it was equally as apparent that she hadn't the faintest idea what to do with either. Such a child, yet with a woman's body, a woman's wiles.

"They were both warning you away from me, weren't they?" he persisted, pinning her to the ground with not just his hands and his lower body but with his eyes—looking at her intensely, all but devouring her with his hot gaze. "Just the way *I* have been warning you against me. But you're as stubborn as you're irresistible and have always been the sort who touches the stove after someone tells you it is hot just because you have to experience everything for yourself."

Her emerald eyes returned his gaze for long moments, then she shifted her head away as she mumbled, "Not really. Well, yes, I suppose they were warning me, but not precisely warning me *away.*" Her voice trailed off as she sighed deeply. "Oh, I don't know what you mean, or what I mean, or what *anybody* means! Please, Daniel, let me up now. I have to go home and get ready for my party."

"Oh, yes," he ground out, speaking to her deliberately turned head, not easing up on his grip on her shoulders. "Your party. Where you'll be surrounded by everyone who loves you—and everyone does love you, don't they, Brianna? You could charm the birds out of the trees with your smile, and you know it. They all fall at your feet, adoring you. Your parents, everyone at Pleasant Hill, the townspeople in New Eden, my own bloody servants—even rum-soaked Crazy Joe. You've got a titled Frenchman drooling over you, and Bainbridge would leave Miss Payton and her father's money in a quick second for one smile from you. No one can do enough for you, say enough good things about you. Nobody can resist you. Except for me, Brianna Crown." He gave her shoulders a single shake. "Except for me. And it's killing you, isn't it?"

She grabbed at his wrists, trying to push him away. "You've been in the sun too long, Daniel Crown," she shot at him, "and you're talking out of your head. I couldn't care less what you think about me."

"Liar," he countered, his voice low and rasping as he eased his grip on her shoulders even as he bent his arms slightly, leaning closer to her, knowing his breath was hot against the side of her throat. "You've been throwing yourself at my head since the day I arrived at Enolowin. Why, I might even think you fancy yourself in love with me. God knows you've hinted at it often enough. What's wrong, little one? Wasn't one kiss, one taste of what a man wants—what a half savage like me needs—enough to scare you away? What will it take to get me out of your dreams, to get you out of mine? Do I have to take you? Here? Now? Giving you a birthday lesson on hot stoves, and how badly they can burn?"

Her eyes opened wide as she turned her head to look up at him once more. "You wouldn't dare. Papa would skin you with a dull knife! He'd do it anyway if I told him what you've said to me today."

Daniel didn't know where his quick rage had come from, but he certainly knew the reason behind his passion. He wanted her. He wanted her badly. And he couldn't have her. It wouldn't be fair to her. It probably wouldn't be fair to him, as well, for she was still a long way from the woman he knew she could be, and he was still equally distant from knowing who he was or where he belonged—if he belonged.

A mighty war was being raged inside his head, his heart, his gut, and he was about to fling himself away from Brianna when she moved beneath him, probably in the hope he would release her, and innocently unaware that her effort had exactly the opposite effect on his intentions. His rapidly crumbling will.

"May as well be hanged for a sheep as a lamb," he muttered under his breath, sliding his hands under her back and lowering his mouth against hers, grinding his lips into hers, moving his body so that he rested more fully against her, letting her know just how fully she had aroused him.

Her lips opened beneath his assault, whether in welcome or to curse him for what he was doing, and he took advantage of her vulnerability, sliding his tongue inside her mouth, rimming the edges of her straight, white teeth, rasping over the roof of her mouth, dueling with her own tongue, which had begun an untutored assault of its own.

Fire flashed through him, searing him from the base of his throat to the swelling manhood straining against the laced crotch of his deerskin leggings. His eyes closed, brilliant flashes of light exploding behind his eyelids like rockets bursting in a night sky, he still felt Brianna's arms slide up and around his chest, her fingers fluttering against his back as if not sure if she should form them into fists and beat on him or spread them wide against his back, pulling him closer, closer.

He made her decision for her, wrenching himself backward and sideways until he lay on his back in the grass, a forearm across his closed eyes, his chest heaving as he struggled to regain his breath. "Go away, Brianna. Go away, *now!*"

The world was silent for long moments, so that he heard only his own rapid breathing and the pounding of his own blood in his ears. He didn't dare take his arm from his eyes, open those eyes to see the hurt in hers—or worse, the disappointment.

"We both still have a lot to learn about each other and maybe even about ourselves. Don't we, Daniel?" she said from somewhere above his head, and he could feel the slight coolness as her shadow moved across his body. "But I do know one thing," she continued, sounding as breathless as he did himself, "and that is that you most definitely need *this!*"

Daniel just lay there, holding his breath, as she emptied the jug of cold water over his head, then he chuckled low in his throat as she ran away from him after throwing the empty jug to the ground.

God, what a minx the girl is! he thought ruefully as he sat up and dragged his hands over his face, pushing the water out of his eyes. *And damn me for an idiot and a fool—I probably am in love with her!*

Had laws not been, we never had been blam'd:
For not to know we sinn'd is innocence.

Sir William Davenant

chapter ten

"Ei-yi-yi, sir, and don't you look all flashy-dashy!" Winifred Bing said as she stood in the foyer pretending to polish the large mahogany table that stood at its center, while she really had been lingering there in order to get a good close look at her employer as he went off to Pleasant Hill for dear Miss Brianna Crown's birthday celebration.

"Why, thank you, Mrs. Bing," Daniel said as he descended the staircase, Finn right behind him, still flicking imaginary bits of lint from the shoulders of his master's dark blue frock coat. "I must admit that this is an almost welcome change from the deerskins I've been living in lately."

"Oh?" Finn chirped, pushing past Daniel so that he could be at the bottom of the staircase, looking up at him as he descended the last few steps, just making one last check on his employer's appearance. "And where would my needle and thread be at a time like this, I'm askin', when I should be stitchin' those very words onto a pillow so that I can cushion my poor knees with it the next time

I find myself dropped to the ground, beggin' for you to make me proud again?"

"You're like a dog with a bone, aren't you, Finn?" Daniel commented as he stepped to the large mirror at the side of the front door, checking the position of his neckcloth.

Finn jumped up at the taller man like a jack-in-the-box just sprung free, slapping Daniel's hands away. "Arrrgh now, don't you be touchin' that, you hear!" he exclaimed, moving deftly, rearranging the foaming fall of lace that looked so startlingly white against Daniel's sun-darkened skin. "And it's a good thing we'll all be travelin' over to Pleasant Hill after you've gone, for the kitchen party, don't you know. You sneak away as the clock strikes nine, and I'll meet you out by the herb garden—just to give you another quick look-see and shake a bit of the wilt out of you after the worst is over."

"I could have you in Philadelphia and on a ship back to England inside a week," Daniel threatened without heat, feeling another knot tightening in his stomach. He was not looking forward to the first few minutes of the approaching evening.

Finn sniffed and gave a twist to his mouth, so that his long, thin nose twitched. "You couldn't manage without me," he said confidently, then tipped his head to one side and peered up at Daniel. "Could you?"

"Never," Daniel assured him as he looked into the mirror again to see that Gunitakan had entered the foyer behind him, dressed in his fine new deerskins and smelling much more pleasant than was his custom. "*Itah,* Grandfather. Dominick Crown's family will be honored tonight by your presence."

"Sure they will," Finn whispered out of the corner of his mouth, "even while their servants are busy tuckin' all the silver out of sight. Found another salt cellar under his bed, I did, just this mornin'."

"You would not have found it had I wanted to keep it hidden from your eyes, Chitanitis," said the old Indian, whose hearing was much superior to his skill at petty thievery, as he made his usual crablike advance across the tiled floor. "I only do what is expected of me, and nobody expects much. Besides, I may be spreading my blanket somewhere else if Tasukamend dies in honorable battle, and must keep in practice with the skills which feed me."

"And here I thought you'd be heading west and dying with me, Grandfather," Daniel said, barely suppressing a smile as Finn handed him his hat and gloves after dusting the brim of the one with the fingers of the other, then tsk-tsking loudly over the result.

"Ei-yi-yi, all this talk of war once again," Mrs. Bing lamented, fanning her flushed face with the hem of her large white apron. "Fidgety it makes me now, you know. Just stop it once, I say."

Finn sent the old Indian a damning look. "The devil bless you, Gunitakan, you old sot, now you've got poor Winifred all aflutter with your nonsense. If she isn't up to makin' me my corn fritters in the mornin', I'll know who to blame." He turned back to Daniel. "The man deals in the wonderful, don't you know, never thinkin' to tell the truth when a lie will do good enough. The two of you headin' west to run around as near to naked as the day you was born, paintin' your faces and runnin' screaming through the trees? I don't know if I should be shakin' my head and laughin' or blackin' both his rheumy little eyes for him."

Feeling like a nanny pushed into disciplining an unruly clutch of nursery brats, Daniel stepped between his valet and a glaring Gunitakan, saying, "Who has my present for Miss Crown? Finn? Didn't I give you the wrapping of it?"

Looking immediately shamefaced, Finn muttered, "I'm a jockey turned valet, sir. Haven't the skills for pretty ribbons and bows, you know."

Daniel looked hopefully toward his housekeeper. "Mrs. Bing?"

"I gave it over to the husband, the lazy *dumpfkopf,* seeing as how he had nothing better to do all day than to be down on the porch sitting, keeping it from flying away to the sky."

"Bing has the package?" Daniel closed his eyes, even as his eyebrows climbed high on his forehead. "No," he said after a moment. "I'm sorry. I can't even imagine that."

Gunitakan grumbled something unintelligible as he advanced on Daniel while reaching inside his deerskin jacket and pulling out a small package—a most gloriously constructed affair of bits of white paper encased nearly completely by strings of tiny colored beads and then decorated with feathers and even a few very small bells that jingled merrily as the Indian shook the box. "Here. I told you, Tasukamend. We Lenape never needed trinkets from anybody. Ours are better. We are better."

Taking the package, Daniel held it up in front of him, twisting it this way and that, listening for the sound of the bells. "You never cease to amaze me, Grandfather," he said sincerely. "I am honored by your labor, as will be Wapa-Kwelik when I tell her of your kindness. Thank you. Thank you very much."

Gunitakan snapped his fingers in Finn's face as he walked past him and out the opened front door, as if to say, "You see how superior I am to you, white man, and to your pressing irons and your silly blacking polish?"

"It's a wonder to me that the man can make it through a doorway, so big his head is," Finn said grumpily, then smiled. "Now, it's been puttin' it off long enough you have, sir. Time to go to your party, and not with your fingers in your mouth, neither. There's time enough to bid the devil good-morrow when you meet him, and not go seein' trouble that may never come."

Daniel was instantly sorry for having had those two

glasses of wine this afternoon, and then sharing a bit of his misery over his damning interlude with Brianna with his trusted valet while sitting in a hot bath. "I full well know what has to be done, Finn, and I will do it—no thanks to you and your stories of leprechauns."

"And a better man you'll be for it, sir, I promise you!" Finn called out brightly as Daniel walked through the open doorway and down the stairs to where young Toby held Lenape Traveler's reins.

Daniel would have answered his valet, but he'd be damned if he could think of a thing to say. He was feeling most inarticulate at the moment as he mounted his stallion and rode off toward Pleasant Hill and his coming interview with Dominick Crown.

"I think I like you better rutsching," Wanda said as she combed through Brianna's long curls, watching her mistress's wan expression as it was reflected in the dressing table mirror. "You're looking more like a klook than a sweet little peep, and you're only just going eighteen."

"I'm neither an old broody hen nor a baby chick, Wanda," Brianna answered dully, fingering the pale green ribbons that decorated the bodice of her new gown. "I'm just not in the mood for a party, I suppose."

"Not in the mood for—ach! Now you're talking crazy, missy. Or maybe you're sickening for something? I could get the powwow man up here from Reading town iffen your pa would send a wagon. Better yet, a dose of castor oil. Nothing a dram of castor oil won't fix."

Brianna rolled her eyes. "You bring any of that vile stuff anywhere near me, Wanda, and I'll have to think up something suitably terrible to do to you. And I don't need the hex doctor, either. He'd just have me rubbing myself with roasted chicken feet."

"Only iffen you have warts," Wanda countered, offended. "And it worked for me, too."

"Yes, I suppose it did, although I don't think Papa has

forgiven you yet for then burying those smelly feet under the house eaves because the powwow man told you to. I think he meant the ground under the eaves, you know, Wanda, and not the rafters in the attics."

Wanda bent down low, her stays creaking, and whispered into Brianna's ear. "Laugh if you will, missy, but I know more than you think I do. I know the powwow way to make your sweetheart your very own."

"How?" Brianna whispered, her heart pounding even though she knew it silly to react this way to the maid's superstitions. But after this afternoon and the way it had ended—? She turned on the padded bench, wincing only slightly as Wanda's hold on her hair made the movement a painful one. "Tell me, Wanda."

"There are two ways, neither the better or the worse," Wanda whispered, her eyes darting about as if the entire world might want to know what she was about to say and was standing at the ready, with paper and quill pen, ready to write down every word. "You pluck a few feathers from a rooster's tail and press them into the loved one's palm. Or, if you like, you can take the tongue of a turtledove into your mouth, then kiss your young man. After that, he can never love another."

Brianna grinned, turning back to the mirror, which earned her another inadvertent tug on her hair. "That's just silly, Wanda. I don't know why I listen to you, truly I don't."

"Because I made you smile, missy," Wanda countered matter-of-factly, "and a smile is what you'll need before you go downstairs, or else your mama will be all over you, wanting to know what's wrong. Now, here, take this," she said, reaching into the pocket of her apron and pulling out a flat package wrapped in brown paper and tied with rough string.

"What is it?" Brianna asked, still feeling wary about chicken feet and turtledove tongues.

"Your birthday present," Wanda said, already busy

again with the brush, then twisting Brianna's hair near the top of her head and tying it with a fine ribbon, allowing the warm, fiery curls to then tumble freely down her back. "Or did you think I would be so *geitzich* as to let this day pass without giving you a small gift?"

Brianna blinked back sudden tears as she looked at the package in her lap, then turned and buried her head against the maid's ample midsection. "You're never stingy, Wanda," she protested, giving the woman a quick squeeze. "I don't deserve you, really I don't."

"No, you don't," Wanda agreed amicably, stepping back from Brianna's embrace in order to raise a corner of her apron to wipe at her own eyes. "Now open it at once, and stop this fussing."

Tearing into the package with more excitement than she had felt since leaving Daniel to drown in his own field this afternoon, Brianna was soon rewarded by the sight of a square of bleached linen into which Wanda had worked a colorful sampler decorated with a cross-stitched flower border.

"The flowers are just for fancy," the maid explained, plucking at a corner of the sampler.

"Why, Wanda," Brianna said, holding up the square. "You told me you never sew, not for anyone. And it's lovely, just lovely!"

"Not for any *man,*" Wanda corrected, openly preening now. "Can you read the words?"

"I can," Brianna said, nodding, because she was feeling tearful again, knowing how religious Wanda was, how much her adopted religion meant to her. " 'Not from Jerusalem, but from Bethlehem, there cometh that Which blesseth me.' " You told me the story about this old song just last Christmas, didn't you, Wanda? About how Count Zinzendorf, on a long-ago Christmas Eve, sang it on the Moravians' first Christmas Eve here in America."

Wanda nodded, her tears falling freely now. "The poor

Moravians, so cruelly told to pack themselves up and move out of their dwellings in nearby Nazareth just as Christmas was coming on," she said, telling the story again, and thrilling Brianna with it again, just as she had been the first time she'd heard the tale. "So there they were on Christmas Eve, all of them living close together in one big log house, their animals just on the other side of the wall, so near they could hear them, and their sheep out on the hills with their very own Moravian shepherds watching over them."

"And that's when Count Zinzendorf lit his candle and led all of his people outside and into the stable side of the building, singing the old song—" Brianna said, then broke off, knowing Wanda would sing the song for her.

"In memory of the dear Savior's birth, yes. They went into the stable and sang until their hearts melted. *Nicht Jerusalem, Sondern Bethlehem,"* Wanda sang in her high, clear voice. *"Aus der kommt Was mir frommet."*

"And then they named their new settlement Bethlehem," Brianna said, sighing as she ran her fingertips over Wanda's neat rows of stitching. "Wanda, I will treasure this forever and ever."

"Ach, now, don't go making more of it than there is. It's a simple sampler only, that's all." Wanda sniffled a last time, then motioned for Brianna to stand up so that she could inspect the results of all her efforts at turning what had been the pale-cheeked, hollow-eyed, fairly frantic looking creature who had cried into her pillow for most of the afternoon into the breathtakingly beautiful young lady who stood before her now. "There now, would you look at you? Many a heart will break tonight. Don't run off now yet, because your papa sent up the stairs a box with a lovely present inside it. I know because I peeked," she ended, winking at her charge.

Brianna stood very still, holding her breath, as Wanda stepped behind her and fastened a necklace behind her head, then raced to the dressing table mirror to see the double string of perfect pearls that now hung just to the beginning swell of her bosom. "Oh, Wanda! Aren't they just the most beautiful things you've ever seen? What a lovely present! Even Papa must now believe I'm all grown up."

"There's earbobs to go along with them," Wanda said, holding out the earrings that were fashioned of a single pearl that rested against the earlobe, with a fall of smaller pearls attached to them. "Not that I can think of a thing you've done lately to deserve anything so fine," the maid ended, clucking her tongue at Brianna teasingly, then instantly frowning when Brianna's bottom lip began to quiver.

"Oh, Wanda, I'm such a trial to them! You just can't know what I've done!" Brianna wailed, plunking herself down on the padded bench, looking like a lovely flower on the verge of wilting before it could fully bloom.

"Here, now, I didn't mean that none," Wanda protested, putting an arm around Brianna's shoulders and giving her a shake. "You're young, that's all, and you're your own mother's sweet loving daughter, sure as spit. Now take yourself off downstairs and have the best birthday ever you had. The rest will work itself out by and by."

Brianna nodded, biting her bottom lip between her teeth. Then she stood up, her emerald eyes brilliant with unshed tears, fitted the earrings into her ears, took a deep breath, squared her slim shoulders, and went off to see Daniel Crown, wondering if he would say anything to her.

And worrying even more that he wouldn't even be there when she descended the staircase.

Dominick Crown had his back to Daniel as the older man poured them each a glass of wine. "I'm glad you arrived first, Daniel," he said as he turned and handed over a glass, then lifted his own and took a long drink. "Ah, I needed that! Although I doubt Bryna will allow us to hide out here in my study once the guests begin arriving."

"Thank you for not including me in their number, sir," Daniel said, waiting until Dominick sat down behind his desk before carefully splitting his coattails and taking his own seat. Even if he'd rather remain standing. Actually, he wished he didn't have to be here at all, but he had left himself with no other option.

"You're not company, Daniel," Dominick said with a smile. "You're family. Which most likely means that Bryna will find some small chore for you to do before the night is over. Have you much experience in sitting beside very old ladies with very poor hearing? If so, don't tell my wife, or she'll have you stuck to dear Letitia Carruthers for most of the evening. Lovely woman, but deaf as a post—not that anyone has been successful in dissuading her from keeping her place in the church choir, God help us. She's always a note ahead or a note behind everyone else. My wife, of course, finds this to be wonderfully amusing, while everyone else in the church is audibly grinding their teeth in frustration, myself included."

Daniel smiled, wishing he could spend the next quarter hour in such light conversation or find a comfortable way to ease into what he had to say, but as time was passing and he had to get this over with, he only uncrossed his legs, sat forward to put his glass on the desktop, and announced baldly, "I'm here to beg your forgiveness and to offer for Brianna's hand in marriage. You see, sir, I—I have compromised her."

His adopted father had told him many things about Dominick Crown, one in particular that he had never forgotten. Dominick Crown was a quiet man, greatly intelligent, wonderfully loyal, and remarkably slow to anger. But, when pushed too far, his retaliation was swift and terrible. In short, Daniel was fully prepared to find himself being horsewhipped within the next ten seconds.

"Have you now? Compromised her, you say?" Dominick said quietly after a long silence that had sent the very air around Daniel's head to crackling with tension. "How?"

Daniel gave a slight shake of his head. "I beg your pardon, sir?"

"It's a simple enough question, son, and one the father of one's youngest daughter is entitled to ask. *How* did you compromise her?"

A quick picture of how he had lain across Brianna's body that afternoon, eager to introduce her to delights that would astound them both, flashed behind Daniel's eyes. He rubbed a hand across his forehead, trying to banish the image, desperately attempting to collect his wits. He had been prepared for anger. For physical violence. He had expected both, perhaps had desired them, to help ease his aching conscience. But this was beyond his comprehension. "You expect me to provide you with *details,* sir?" He shook his head. "You'd make me twice the cad?"

He watched, astounded at the older man's composure, as Dominick picked up a letter opener and balanced it, tip to tip, between the index fingers of both hands. "Let me make this simple for you, son, all right? Would it be possible that my daughter could be presenting me with my newest grandchild after the new year?"

Daniel leaped to his feet, then placed his hands, palms down, on the desktop. "Give me *some* credit, sir! I kissed your daughter. Not once, but twice. No more than that, but that is more than enough. God knows I wanted more, still want more." He sank back into his chair, his legs gone suddenly weak. "You have no idea, sir, what a temptation that girl is to a man," he ended, momentarily forgetting he was speaking to Brianna's father.

"Don't I?" Dominick remarked, chuckling deep in his throat. "I've been married to her mother for thirty years—and quite happily, I'll add. Felicia is a good child, a sweet child, and I adore her. But from the moment she was born, I knew that Brianna would be a rare handful. Beautiful as her mother, headstrong as her mother—*daring* as her mother. Why, Daniel, from the instant Brianna looked at you, took aim at you, you didn't stand a chance. I did try to warn you, if you'll remember? But that doesn't mean I'll be party to a marriage born in your fairly innocent compromise of a willful young girl who has chased you from one end of Enolowin to the other and probably goaded you into both those kisses and a whole lot more."

"Sir?" Daniel's head was spinning. "I don't understand. In England—"

"We're not in England, Daniel," Dominick reminded him quietly.

"If it's my Lenape blood—" Daniel said, beginning to anger, only to be cut off again as the heavy brass letter opener hit the desktop with a loud crash.

Dominick stood up, glaring at Daniel. "Now who isn't giving the other man credit?" he growled, and Daniel quickly remembered his adopted father's warning about Dominick Crown's rare but famed temper.

"I'm sorry, sir," Daniel apologized sincerely, feeling stupid, more than stupid. Dominick had already told him he didn't care about his Lenape blood. Obviously he was a man accustomed to being taken at his word and not being made to repeat himself. "I think it might be best if I just shut my mouth and let you explain what it is you are trying to tell me."

Dominick stepped out from behind his desk and began to pace, his limp only faintly apparent. He walked up and down the length of the carpet once, twice, then turned to look down at Daniel. "Are you in love with my daughter?"

This was neither the time nor the place for uncertainties, for anything less than the complete truth, and Daniel knew it. "Yes sir, I am. Not that I want to be."

There was a slight twitch at the corners of Dominick's mouth. "I sympathize completely. And although I know you will never fully understand her, even if you were to live with her for thirty years, I believe you do know her well enough to be sure of at least this much—Brianna would never, never *ever,* consent to marry you if she thought you had been forced into asking for her. Do you agree?"

Daniel bowed his head, letting his pent-up breath out in a low *whoosh.* "Most definitely, sir. She'd want me if I came to her on bended knee or crawling over hot coals, telling her I couldn't live without her—and I'm no longer sure I could. But if she thought I had come to her because I was honor bound to do so—well, sir, I believe she just might have me pickled."

"Precisely!" Dominick slapped a hand down on Daniel's shoulder. "And I think the child does love you, son. I know she is fully old enough to be wed, although I would have wished she'd first been to England, to give her mother the delight of seeing her being whisked off in a country dance by her share of lovestruck young bucks."

"I had thought of that," Daniel agreed. "I've had my share of time in society, and I know what a rare jewel Brianna is. But she's still so young, so inexperienced. She hasn't seen enough of the world to be sure that I'm really the one she wants. She already must be getting a taste of what society is like for a beautiful, well-dowered young miss, what with the comte dangling at her shoetops. And if you want to know how I learned that, it's because she made a point of telling me about it. But still she comes to me, seems to want only me. And, sir—" he said, turning in the chair, looking up at Dominick, his voice trailing off, for he was unable to put into words the fact that with each new meeting with Brianna, the need to make her his own in every way was becoming more impossible to deny.

"And you want her," Dominick finished for him. "Desperately. And as long as my far-from-shy daughter keeps throwing herself at your head day after day, you don't know how much longer you can fend her off? That is what you wanted to say, isn't it?"

"Not to her father, I didn't," Daniel admitted honestly, shaking his head in wry humor directed at himself as he stood up to face Dominick Crown. He took a deep breath, then said solemnly, "I will see to it that we're never alone again, sir. I will, with your permission, begin to court her as a gentleman should, and I fully understand that she should be made to travel to England for a season in London before committing herself to me if by the end of the summer you and her mother still insist upon it. I won't like it, but I will understand it."

"Make no promises you cannot keep, son. I am confident that you will do the best you can and follow your heart. I will ease your mind, I hope, by telling you that I have every confidence that the eventual outcome of your little dance with Brianna will be far from dishonorable to either of you, no matter what route you eventually take to arrive there. I only wish Philip and Brighid could be here to enjoy watching my daughter tying you up in knots as much as I will."

Dominick gave Daniel's shoulder another pat, then turned him toward the door, his arm slung companionably across Daniel's shoulder, for they could both hear the sound of arriving carriages and knew it was time to join the party. "You know the stream that runs next to Lokwelend's cabin?" he asked conversationally as they stepped out into the hallway.

"Yes, sir," Daniel answered, feeling some of the tension he had felt all day finally beginning to drain out of his body.

Dominick smiled as his wife came floating down the hallway toward the two of them, looking flushed and lovely in a deep emerald green satin gown, diamonds twinkling at her throat, in her ears. "God's teeth, but she's a beautiful woman, isn't she, son?" he said quietly. "Thirty years, and I still can't believe my luck in winning her love. Anyway, Daniel, about Lokwelend's stream. I spent a lot of time there in the first few weeks after meeting Bryna. Found myself desperately plunging into its cold waters fully clothed a time or two, as a matter of fact. It's just a suggestion."

"Yes sir," Daniel answered, wondering if he could possibly be blushing. Then Bryna Crown joined them, turning so that she could take each of their arms as they walked back down the hallway just as one of the servants opened the wide front door, letting in the first of their guests.

"I think Daniel Crown is developing a tendre for you, as Mama would say after listening to all those Philadelphia society ladies speak," Corliss Payton told Brianna when the two of them could at last sneak away into the gardens for a private coze. "I've been watching him these past hours, especially when the gypsies were performing for us—wasn't it wonderful of your papa to find them?—and he couldn't seem to take his eyes off you." She shook her head, sending her blond ringlets dancing. "Although it must be rather unnerving that he doesn't smile the whole time he's about it."

Brianna lifted a hand to tangle her fingers in her pearls. "I think he's planning ways to murder me and dispose of the body with no one the wiser," she said, trying to smile, although she believed that tonight had to be the most trying of her life. She had been afraid Daniel wouldn't come to her party, then nearly ran from the drawing room when he did arrive. She was a bundle of nerves, and she was beginning to believe either she had overreacted this afternoon or that Daniel had not reacted enough. Either way, she was not happy.

Brianna turned on the wooden bench the two friends had been sitting on and impulsively squeezed Corliss's forearm. "I've disgraced myself terribly, Corliss," she admitted quickly. "And now I think Daniel may believe he has compromised me and must tell Papa. I mean, if we were being absolutely strict about the thing, he compromised me once before, but that was more out of anger, so I really don't think it counts. This time—well, this time was different."

Corliss swallowed hard a time or two, obviously struggling to find her voice. "Compromised you?" she got out at last, her blue eyes wide, her voice a soft, fairly unladylike squeak. "Dear God—how?"

Brianna sat back on the bench and rolled her eyes in frustration at her friend's question. "Surely, Corliss, you know *how*. I rather thought you'd ask *why*."

Every time Brianna was sure that Corliss was a sweet but timid mouse, the girl surprised her. As she did now by saying airily, "Oh, piffle, Brianna. I know *why*. You undoubtedly *drove* him to it. Why, you have every young man in New Eden drooling over you, and you don't even try to engage their affections. If you were ever to deliberately set out to capture someone—which I believe is what you did with Mr. Crown—well, the poor man shouldn't be blamed for accepting what you offered. But Mama says that men never buy the cow—"

"Oh, please, Corliss," Brianna interrupted, laughing with real humor for the first time that evening. "Not you, too! I'm surprised Wanda didn't think to work *that* little saying into her sampler. And stop thinking thoughts that would get you tossed straight out of heaven. Daniel compromised me, yes, but only with a few kisses—and yes, I probably did ask for those. No, I *definitely* asked for those. Not that no one kisses each other, of course, but in English society it is much different from here, where courting couples are allowed much more freedom. Or so I've heard."

"Oh. How, um, well, how *depressing*, actually. I had hoped you could explain some of the more confusing points to me—Mama gets so flustered that I really have only a vague idea of what she's talking about when she speaks of such things as marital duty—but if he only kissed you?" Corliss frowned. "Brianna, you're not making any sense," she pointed out reasonably. "And did you say something about a sampler? What sampler? Oh, never mind, as I'd probably only be more confused if you explained. Now, do you really think Daniel Crown is going to be offering for your hand because he compromised you? And if he does—will you accept?"

Brianna stiffened her spine, her chin lifted at an angle that would, hopefully, keep any leftover tears from spilling down her cheeks. She had made up her mind to the answer of that particular question earlier in the afternoon, when she had asked it of herself. "I will not," she said firmly. "I won't be the object of any man's pity, Corliss. Surely you know that?"

The other girl bobbed her head in agreement with Brianna's words. "Yes, I can understand that. But you're too proud, Brianna. I mean, if the man loves you—"

"Does he?" Brianna began fingering the dainty gold and pearl pin at her bodice, the pin Daniel had given her for her birthday, the pin she would wear on her nightgown later tonight and on her gown tomorrow and never ever take off as long as she lived.

"Of course he—" Corliss stopped speaking and shook her head. "I don't know, Brianna. How could I know? How can either of us really *know?* I *think* I know what love is, what real love is." She put her hand in Brianna's lap, lacing her fingers through Brianna's long slim ones. "Love is wanting what is best for the other person, no matter how much it might hurt us. Love is watching from a distance while longing to come up close to him and talk . . . and touch . . . and—" She squeezed Brianna's hand, then attempted to rise. "Well, enough of this! We should be getting back to the party."

Corliss landed on the bench with an audible *"Oof!"* of air being forced out of her lungs by the force of Brianna's sharp tug on her hand. "Corliss Payton, you're in love! Why, you sneak! And you said you didn't know how you felt about Mr. Bainbridge. Why didn't you tell me?"

Corliss pulled her hand free, not without a small

struggle, and stood up once more, her posture rigidly erect, her shoulders squared as if ready to do battle. "I think Addison Bainbridge is an odious slug, Brianna Crown, and I cannot believe you could conceive of me ever having such poor judgment!" Then, before Brianna could even realize that her jaw had dropped to half-mast, let alone formulate an answer to her friend's unexpected show of temper, Corliss was gone, leaving her quite alone in the gardens. Alone and thoroughly confused.

"It is always most amusing, is it not, *ma cherie,* to see a spine suddenly appear in the jellyfish?"

Brianna looked up to see the Comte de Sauville standing a short distance away, obviously having overheard at least some of her conversation with Corliss. "You eavesdrop often then, sir?" she asked, exceedingly angry with the man she had formerly believed charming if a bit old to be so devotedly romantic.

His shrug was purely Gallic, and his broad shoulders and exquisite suit of pale blue satin did nothing to take away from the gesture's attractiveness. "At court it is an all-consuming activity. A sport, I shall say, as well as sometimes necessary to one's survival. Listen, and look, and learn, *ma cherie.* One never knows when some small piece of information may be of use. If you were to look and listen more closely you would know, as I do, that our dear Mademoiselle Corliss is quite hopelessly infatuated with Monsieur Bainbridge's quadroon. It is amusing, *oui?* And rather romantically tragic, I suppose. Do you think her papa gives her enough pin money that she can eventually buy him and send him to his freedom while she remains behind to wither away and die in the name of lost love?"

Brianna's eyes sliced to her left in the direction in which Corliss had disappeared, then she looked back at the comte. "Corliss? And Marcus? I had thought, but—I don't believe it."

"You disapprove?" de Sauville asked, his handsome smile showing off his white teeth in the moonlight. "How very droll. Especially when one considers how you, *ma cherie,* are so eager to tip yourself over for a half breed savage. *Zut alors!* I imagine if I were to recount your little conversation with Mademoiselle Payton to your dear papa that he would be most eager to have you married to someone more, shall we say, *acceptable,* and as quickly as possible. For instance, someone like myself—rather than for you to be presenting him with the evidence of your hot blood in the form of another bastard savage Crown. Or do you truly believe a man who would so willingly compromise you is then going to save your honor by entering into a marriage with a child like yourself when there is no need to do so?"

Brianna could barely hear over the thrumming of her own blood in her ears. "You seem willing enough, sir," she said, fighting through her anger, her shock, her disbelief that any of this was happening to her. Had she led so sheltered a life here at Pleasant Hill that she hadn't known people such as the comte existed? No wonder Daniel had come to New Eden, if this was what London was like!

The comte smiled again, looking very handsome, faintly dissipated, and strangely kind, for all that his blunt words cut straight to her heart. "But, then, *ma cherie,* I am a man of exquisite taste. A taste for my own continued comfort, you understand. It would be a fair trade. My very creditable title in exchange for your honor, and a generous share of your papa's money of course. If the Revolutionaries kill off enough of the Royals before they are vanquished, why, think of it—I could be in line for the throne. The little half-breed bastard could end up as a son of the Empire, no?"

"There *is* no little half-breed bastard!" Brianna leaped to her feet, all confusion gone now, anger propelling her into speech. "And, furthermore, sir, my father will personally toss you off Pleasant Hill property before the sun comes up!"

"Such heat! But I think not, *ma cherie.* Because, you

see, you'd then have to tell him what you have done—or do you seriously wish for me to believe you have not been lying with Daniel Crown? I am not the silly Mademoiselle Payton, to be so easily lied to, to be fobbed off with this business of innocent kisses. I have looked at Daniel Crown, taken my measure of the man, and he isn't the sort to be long content with mere kisses."

Brianna turned her head away as she bit at her top lip. The comte was right. Daniel had said as much to her—warning her that she was not old enough for the games grown men played.

"So silent? Very well, I will talk. I am here to offer my help, *cherie,* I promise you. It is obvious to me that your beloved savage has not done, shall we say, the *honorable* thing, or else we would have heard word of your engagement by this time—or your lover would be dead. Either one, *ma cherie,* but not neither. So," he shrugged once more, the mannerism Brianna had thought charming now only serving to curl her upper lip with disgust, "being a good and generous man, and with only your best interests at heart—no, *our* best interests at heart—I shall bide my time, waiting for your little *liaison* to bear fruit, and then I will step in and make my offer if the savage does not. He may surprise me and step forward, but if he does not, I, the Comte de Sauville, will be there for you. Enjoy yourself this summer, *cherie.* I am content to wait. If you're half so fertile as your dear mother, and half the hot-blooded wanton I hopefully believe you to be, I would imagine I won't be waiting long. Besides, I've never been like so many others, wanting an untutored virgin in my bed. He is, I sincerely hope, a reasonably talented lover?"

Brianna only heard half of the comte's last statements, her mind concentrating on a single fact. Daniel had compromised her, but he had *not,* as she had feared, gone to her father with a full confession of his actions and an offer of marriage. She hadn't wanted him to, had wanted his love, not his obedience to some ridiculous code of honor that would have her wondering, always wondering, if he had married her out of love or because he had felt the deed necessary.

But now? Now, she discovered, she found herself crushed by the thought that Daniel hadn't cared enough for her or for her honor to approach her father with the truth.

Because he didn't really want her. He didn't love her. He didn't, at the bottom of it, even respect her enough to consider what they had done—and what they had almost done—that afternoon to be reason enough to marry. "Go away," he had told her, and she foolishly had believed that he needed her gone because he couldn't trust himself alone with her. What he had meant was "Go away—I can't stand to look at you!"

She had sickened him. Chased him, tormented him, goaded him, enticed him—and left him disgusted with both himself and with her.

"Ma cherie? You are curiously silent," the comte remarked kindly. "I amaze myself, truly, by feeling most wretchedly sorry for you, for your youth and lost innocence. Does it hurt so much then, being used? Don't worry. I shall be here to save you from yourself. Why, it may just be my destiny, *oui?"*

Brianna's bottom lip began to tremble, and without another word she ran toward the house, passing by Wanda in the kitchens and telling her to inform everyone that she had a headache and was going to bed, where she did not wish to be disturbed by anybody.

"Ach, missy, but it's your birthday!" Wanda called out as she put down the half-eaten apple tart she had been enjoying, and tripped off after her mistress.

Brianna didn't answer the maid, nor did she lift her head from her pillow when her mother, undoubtedly summoned by Wanda, knocked on her locked bedchamber door a few minutes later. She didn't respond at all until Bryna Crown used her own key to open the door and came to sit down on the bed beside her daughter, rubbing Brianna's back.

"Are you crying because Daniel had to leave, pet?" she asked quietly. "Surely you understand that he had to, what with word coming to him that one of his mares has gone down in her stall. Brianna, you're too much the horsewoman not to understand that. Now, come on. I'll just wet a cloth with some cool water from the jug, and you can bathe your face and come back downstairs. Wilhelm has brought along his fiddle, and he has told me he insists the two of you play a duet. You wouldn't want to disappoint your guests, now would you?"

"No, Mama," Brianna said, sitting up, but with her back turned to the older woman, grateful both for Daniel's convenient absence and the dim light in the room. "You're right, I'm being silly. You go on along. I'll be there in a minute."

Bryna gave her daughter's back a last loving rub and then a final bracing pat. "True love never did run smoothly, I've heard. Tomorrow is another day, pet. And he's weakening. I could see it tonight in his eyes."

Brianna hiccuped a small laugh. "You and Corliss, Mama," she said, dabbing at her eyes with the handkerchief she had pulled from the bodice of her gown. Wanda always made sure she had a handkerchief handy, as all finely bred ladies should. "The two of you are such sad romantics." She turned on the bed. "Mama, what would happen if Corliss were to fall in love with someone her parents believed to be unsuitable?"

"Corliss?" Bryna frowned. "Why, I can't picture that sweet little girl saying boo to a goose, let alone disobeying her parents—so I imagine she'd simply agree to have her heart broken, poor child. Not at all like you, pet, who would move heaven and hell together to get what you wanted, and damn the consequences."

"Yes," Brianna agreed dully, trying her best to summon up a smile. "And damn the consequences."

[illegible]

book three

the revelation

Love comes from blindness,
friendship from knowledge.

COMTE DE BUSSY-RABUTIN

Perhaps it was right to dissemble your love,
But—why did you kick me downstairs?

ISAAC BICKERSTAFFE

chapter eleven

If Brianna thought to punish Daniel by staying clear of Enolowin, he thought, she had certainly concluded correctly. Not only did he miss her, miss her terribly, miss her more than he could believe it possible to miss someone, but his servants were making his life a living hell, very vocally blaming him for their loss of her company.

Mrs. Bing missed Brianna's presence in the kitchens, the way she hoisted herself up onto the thick oaken table and told silly stories while the housekeeper rolled out pie crusts and slapped fat loaves into shape.

Otto Bing missed her visits with him on the porch, when she would more than likely listen, bright-eyed, to his same old well-embroidered tales about his younger days, when he had driven Conestoga wagons—"Invented right here by us Dutchmen, you know. It's only the horses what come from that there Conestoga Valley"—to Philadelphia and even Fort Pitt.

Finn, never lacking for something to say, an opinion to give on most any subject, swore that the light had gone out of Enolowin, it had, and he sorely missed the sunshine, "if you take my meanin', sir."

Even Skelton, who had helped Daniel through a long three days and nights at the stables, when one horse after another had gone down with some strange ailment, only to eventually rise again as if nothing had happened, had mentioned that Toby was pining for one of those lovely peppermint sticks Miss Brianna never failed to bring him, and now Toby's dear ma was thinking that Skelton wasn't being a good master to her boy.

Only Gunitakan, seemingly bored now that he didn't have to scramble for each bite he put in his mouth, had not mentioned Brianna. Instead, after his careful observation from the gardens of Pleasant Hill the night of Brianna's party, he had been telling Daniel almost daily, "You have two enemies now, Tasukamend, not one, and stubbornly will not know it. Come away with me to the Ohio, to where you can know your enemy."

But Daniel didn't need to travel to the White River to find his *real* enemy, because he saw him each morning when he peered into his mirror, shaving himself while Finn lamented that there was nothing more for him to do than spit in his shoe when his master wouldn't even sit still for a decent shave.

Why—he asked himself while he was shaving, while he was eating, during the hours he spent in his bed, trying to sleep—had he been so stupid, so careless, as to have kissed her again? Hadn't their first kiss shown him that he had no restraint, no gentlemanly instincts, when it came to Brianna Crown? A man who had always prided himself on his ability to hide his emotions, he was like a raw youth whenever he was within sight of the woman, and he knew it. *She* knew it in the way women have always been able to sense when a man is attracted to her.

But Brianna was still very much the child. *He* was the one who was older, hopefully more mature. *He* was the one who should have put a stop to her flirtation long since, knowing that he was still unsure of what his future held, where it would find him, how it would find him.

He knew now that he could not leave Enolowin in Bing's hands for a few months and travel to the White River to meet with the Lenape who gathered there. They wouldn't accept him, had no reason to accept him and, other than the interest he had in seeing them, watching them, he had nothing in common with them except for his blood. He didn't share their dreams, he hadn't been made to suffer their hardships. He could not fight their war.

And, with each day that passed, he was more and more certain that he would only see England again during visits to his adopted family because he could not live there while his heart belonged to Enolowin. He hadn't thought it possible to love a piece of land, but he did. His land. The land he would work for a year, then own.

While Brianna went off to Playden Court with her family this fall, and then on to London for the season.

Would she come back? Or would she be dazzled by the flash and dance of English society, and find her own place in it? His adopted mother had left America for England and been very happy. Of course, she had Philip with her, and Brighid would be happy anywhere as long as her husband was by her side.

Daniel knew himself to be different from Brighid. Even with Brianna beside him, he could not be happy in England. Not after standing on his own porch as dawn broke over the low blue mountains, watching as the sun lit the craggy outcrop of limestone that formed Pematalli's face.

This was home. This was where he belonged. In his heart, in his hopes, he longed to believe that Brianna belonged here as well, by his side. Could he wait for her, wait as she traveled to London and sampled the excitement she would find there? If he went to her now, told her he loved her, would she forgo her trip, that trip that meant so much to Dominick and Bryna, and stay with him? And if she did, would she always wonder . . . wonder . . . what had she missed?

Daniel turned to go back into the house after spending the past hour or more looking up at Lenape Cliff—determined to find himself something more profitable to do than continue this endless round of questions he kept asking himself, never to find a single answer that suited—when the sound of his name being called brought him up short.

He looked to his left and saw that Bryna Crown was riding up the drive in a small cart, her gloved hands handling the reins with the ease of long practice. "Good morning, ma'am," he said as he went to the horse's head, waiting until she had set the brake before going to her and offering his assistance as she stepped lightly to the drive.

"Good morning yourself, Daniel," she said, lifting her cheek for his kiss. "My, what a fearsome scowl! Ah, well, it's a fine day for sulking, isn't it?" she asked lightly, then left him standing where he was, trying to believe he'd heard her correctly, and walked up onto the porch to sit herself down in Otto Bing's favorite chair.

"Ma'am?" Daniel prompted as he pulled up the other rocker and sat down.

Her smile was dazzling because she was a beautiful woman, and because her smile reminded him of Brianna's—so much so that his heart squeezed in his chest. He was hopeless, totally hopeless, and it was time he faced that fact!

"Well?" Bryna questioned after a moment. "Aren't you sulking because you and Brianna are quarreling about something or other? Heaven knows she's looking downpin lately for one reason or another, although, being the sunny child she is, she seems to be finding it difficult to remember that she shouldn't smile so brightly when Jules brings her special delicacies he has made in the hope of cheering her or say thank you quite so politely when dear Lotte comes to collect the empty dishes. Do you believe I should tell her that one shouldn't exhibit such a healthy appetite if one plans on going into a sad decline?"

Daniel smiled and shook his head, considering both mother and daughter. "No guile," he said, speaking to himself. "None at all. Neither one of them." Brianna wasn't staying away to punish him for kissing her; she was angry with him for not having lingered long at Pleasant Hill the night of her birthday and kissing her again! Just in case he was suffering from much too high an opinion of himself, he asked, "She's angry because I had to leave the party early?"

"I'm sure I wouldn't know, my dear. I've never been the sort to meddle, you understand." The fact that a wide, mischievous smile accompanied those words served to give Daniel his first cheer in three long days and nights.

"Yes," he answered, tongue in cheek. "My mother said that about you all the time."

Bryna laughed out loud, her eyes merry, then looked out over the scythed grounds and sighed. "I do love it here," she said, gesturing toward Lenape Cliff. "Philip couldn't have picked a better spot to build his house. It nearly broke Brighid's heart to leave, even as she knew they had no choice. I don't know if they ever spoke of it to you, but being loyal to the king had become a very dangerous indulgence once we got word of the first incidents in Boston. Very dangerous."

"They would have had to leave eventually, even if the colonies hadn't rebelled," Daniel pointed out reasonably. "My father had duties at Playden Court that couldn't be denied once his father died and he assumed the title. And, frankly, I think he did the right thing. They're very happy, ma'am, and I imagine their only sorrow is that they can't see you more often."

"I suppose," Bryna said, then turned to look at him, her intelligent eyes measuring him. "But we'll be traveling to Playden Court at the end of summer. Will you consider going with us?"

Daniel had thought about it. Surely, his father wouldn't hold him to his promise of a year at Enolowin if he understood the reason for the interruption. A few months at Enolowin, a few months at Playden Court, a long six weeks spent watching Brianna charm all of London, and then he would claim her as his own and bring her back to Enolowin. If she still wanted him.

"I have an agreement with my father, ma'am, and cannot in all good conscience break it," he said at last, pleased to hear the steadiness in his voice. "But I will not deny you your dream, if that is what you're asking."

"Is that what I'm asking, Daniel?" She returned her gaze to Lenape Cliff. "Am I so selfish? To want to see Brianna being presented at court? To stand by proudly as her uncle, the marquess, hosts a fine ball in her honor? To take her to all the lovely shops and watch the sparkle in her eyes upon her first visit to the theater?" She shook her head, sighed. "My dreams aren't necessarily hers, Daniel. Not anymore. Not since you came to Enolowin. And, above anything else, my dear boy, I love my daughter."

Daniel didn't know what to say, where to look. "Dominick tells me that my father already believes he has found a suitable match for Brianna," he informed her, sure that she already knew this, had heard it from her husband.

Bryna looked at him curiously. "Dominick has told you this?" She shook her head. "Thirty years, and the man still finds ways to surprise me. I had no idea he was so devious. Either that or he has been watching me and learning. I must remember to compliment him when I get home. So, Daniel," she continued brightly, just as if her last words hadn't been meant to confuse him, confound him, "as we plan to leave from Philadelphia approximately the middle of August, don't you think you've wasted enough precious time?"

"I think, ma'am," Daniel admitted honestly for he felt sure that, like her husband, Bryna Crown would settle for nothing less than complete honesty, "that I have already sufficiently rushed my fences where Brianna is concerned."

Bryna looked at him for a long time, as if reading his mind, rooting out all his secrets. "Felicia was a shy child," she said at last, "staying with her dolls longer than I would have supposed, finding her enjoyment in needlepoint and tending the gardens I set aside for her. Her courtship was slow, and tender, and Geoffrey won her heart with gentle words and long walks after Sunday services. She is the perfect wife for him as he tends his estate and serves in the Virginia government. A perfect wife, a perfect hostess, a wonderful, loving mother. But Brianna is not her sister and, much as I love her, she's far from perfect. She comes complete with bumps and angles, Daniel, with so many sides to her that to be around her, trying to understand all of her, can sometimes be dizzying. She's full of life and fire and excitement and, yes, even danger. I cannot see her in a tame courtship, a proper courtship. Not if she follows her heart, and I've never known her not to, to be truthful."

"You can't be telling me . . . giving me permission to . . . ."

"I am telling you nothing at all, except to follow your heart, Daniel," Bryna said, saving him as his words died away, just as they had when he'd had a similar conversation with Dominick. "You'll never hurt her, I know that. Now!" she continued, reaching over to touch his forearm—just like her daughter, so free with her affection. "Would you like to hear a story about one of Brianna's childhood exploits? Not that she acted alone, for her four brothers were certainly not innocent in the matter . . ."

* * *

Brianna felt Daniel's presence even before she saw him, and quickly slid the sketch she had been working on back in the case she had carried with her to Lokwelend's cabin. Then, to test her new theory that Daniel was still waging a losing battle against his love for her—and the devil take the comte's outrageous insinuations—she deliberately pulled her skirts a little higher on her shins, almost to her knees, and continued to dangle her bare legs in the cool water of the stream.

She raised her hands to the back of her head, lifting the long, heavy mass of her hair and slowly letting it drift through her fingers, then continued into a languorous stretch, her arms reaching toward the sky as she arched her back.

"Should I be fetching you a bowl of cream, little cat? You'll be purring in a minute," Daniel said from just behind her, and Brianna considered giving out with a maidenly shriek of surprise, but opted instead for simply tilting her head back to smile up at him.

She didn't know what pleased her more, soothed her hurt feelings more—the soft growl in his voice or the sight of the frustrated scowl that made him appear so much more the elemental savage than the polished English gentleman. For it was the elemental savage she wanted here with her today. And—because her heart was still feeling somewhat battered by all that had happened in the past few days—she wanted him on his knees.

She fluttered her lashes the way she had seen Lotte shyly beat hers at Jules. "Why, it's Daniel Crown, isn't it? Heavens, I didn't see you there! My, hasn't it been an age?"

His upper lip curled high on one side. "Don't push me, Brianna," he warned, his voice tight.

"I haven't the faintest notion what you mean, Daniel." She fluttered her lashes again, just for good measure. "The last time we spoke—for I refuse to count those few moments of conversation we had together when you attended my party and we were simply *surrounded* by other people—was to have you say 'Go away, Brianna.' Being an obedient sort, I went."

"You? An obedient sort?" Daniel repeated, pushing her packet of sketches out of the way and lowering himself beside her on the grassy bank. "My God, I'd better sit down before I fall down."

"Yes, you do seem to fall down quite a lot, don't you? I seem to vaguely recall that you might even have toppled over onto me." She wrinkled up her nose. "But we won't talk about that, will we?"

He picked up the packet of sketches and began playing with the untied laces. "You're dying to talk about it, Brianna, and, frankly, so am I. I was too abrupt," he said, avoiding her eyes. "I should have explained . . . apologized—"

"Apologized?" she interrupted, finding that there was definite enjoyment to be gained in making the love of her life uncomfortable. Hadn't she been uncomfortable? More than uncomfortable. Because of Daniel she had cried for most of her birthday. She still wept into her pillow every night, even after time and distance had made her rethink her conclusions of that fateful afternoon and evening, perhaps even feel some small pity for what had to be his very confused emotions concerning her. "You shouldn't have done anything you had to apologize for, Daniel."

His head shot up and he looked at her inquiringly. "It wasn't the first time I'd kissed you, imp," he pointed out, smiling, suddenly seeming more at ease, as if he could see through her pose of outraged young miss. "Aren't you a little late with all this righteous indignation?"

Brianna kicked out her right leg, sending a splashing spray of water toward the center of the stream. She had already anticipated this question, when she had imagined this meeting in her mind, and had her answer at the ready. "Perhaps I was simply being magnanimous. Once. After all, I know little of the customs in England. Why, for all I know, young men and women there could be constantly mauling each other in back gardens. But twice?" She shook her head. "The only explanation I can find is that you must be entirely undisciplined or—" she hesitated for several seconds, then ended, "or that you're just simply quite mad with love for me and lost your head for a few moments."

Then she delivered what she hoped would be the coup de grâce, the words that would bring him to his knees, maybe even to his senses. "Either way, I'm afraid, I have decided that your behavior is decidedly fatiguing."

"Fatiguing?" Daniel stuck out his bottom lip as he nodded his head sagely, as if considering her words. "I see. My attentions, which you succeeded in attracting after weeks of pursuing me even into my bedchamber at Enolowin—lest we forget your small trick with the bed sheets—are *fatiguing* to you? I had no idea."

Why was he still talking? Teasing her? Why wasn't he kissing her? Didn't he know that he should be kissing her, proving to her that she was not indifferent to him? Honestly, the man had no imagination! Had he never read a novel? Brianna lifted her chin, turning her head from him and looking downstream at the willow branches trailing in the water. "I-I didn't wish to hurt you," she improvised wildly. "I had no idea your affections were so easily engaged. I was such a child, with a childish infatuation. But now—now that I'm older—"

His crack of laughter had her whipping her head around to look at him just in time to see him falling back on the bank, collapsed in mirth. "God, yes," he choked out in his mirth, "you're positively *ancient* now, aren't you, imp? All of eighteen." He grinned up at her as she contemplated how his head would look stuffed and mounted on her father's study wall. "Christ, Brianna, I hope you didn't stay up too many nights thinking up this drivel."

As she had lain awake nights planning this moment, just to have him ruin everything by laughing at her,

Brianna immediately bristled. "Of course not! You overestimate yourself and your charms, Daniel Crown, if you think I have given even one second of my time to thoughts of you since you . . . since you . . ."

"Since I kissed you last Saturday?" he asked, pushing himself up on one elbow. "Since you came into my fields, that damn jug on your swaying hips, waving me hello and then doing everything but inviting me to put my mouth on you, put my hands on you? Are you angry because I kissed you, Brianna, because I dared to press my body against yours, give you a small education in what it means to rouse a man's passions? Or are you spouting all this ridiculous gibberish because I sent you away?"

Tears stung at Brianna's eyes. This wasn't going anything like she'd planned. She had meant to entice him, possibly even enrage him. Make him hurt, as she did. Make him suffer. Make him believe, if just for a while, that she held him in disgust—if she thought about him at all. But he was laughing. Laughing at her silly, childish posturing. Laughing at *her*.

"Stop it!" she shouted, leaning over to push at his elbow, so that his head went crashing back down against the grass. "Just stop it! You compromised me, you miserable bastard, and you weren't even man enough to go to my father and tell him as much! Not that I would have had you in any case."

He sobered, unexpected sorrow visible in his night black eyes, even if she might possibly be the only person in the world who would notice that quick flash of vulnerability she was confident he never allowed anyone else to see. "No, you wouldn't have, would you? You want me on my knees, Brianna, but you don't want to think it was anybody but you who got me down there."

She frowned, her head tipped as she considered his dully spoken words, his darkened expression, and came to an earthshaking conclusion. "You—you *did* go to my father. Didn't you, Daniel?" Her mouth went dry, even as her heart began to beat painfully fast in her chest. "You played the gentleman and confessed what you'd done. When? That same night? The night of my party? You told him you compromised me and offered to marry me. Of course you did. Why didn't I figure that out sooner? And then you left, not even saying good-bye to me. Did he turn you down? Of course, he did. He turned you down! Why would Papa have said no? *Tell* me."

Daniel sat up once more, picked up the packet of sketches again, idly played with the strings again, his dark eyes hooded now, an invisible shutter drawn down over his emotions. "Perhaps he felt sorry for me and believed that such a dire punishment could prove to be worse than the crime?" he offered, smiling. But his smile didn't reach his eyes.

"Bastard!" Brianna pulled the packet out of his hands and hit him over the head with it. Once. Twice. She would have hit him a third time but the packet, never secured, opened, sending a spray of sketches onto the grass.

"What's this?" Daniel asked, picking up one of her sketches with one hand even as he easily held her away from him with the other.

Brianna sliced a quick look at the sketch, still more intent on beating the love of her life into a jelly, then, her eyes wide, made a quick grab for the paper. "Give me that! You aren't supposed to see that!"

He shouldn't have seen any of her sketches, but he was looking at them now, one by one, still holding her away from him, even as she knew he would probably sit on her to keep her stationary if she continued to struggle.

The first sketch he had picked up was the one she'd done of him sitting rump down in a mud puddle, his expression one of frustration, his horse only slightly visible in the distance, and Brianna standing over him, laughing at his predicament.

From there, it only got worse. And Brianna knew it.

There was a sketch of Daniel as he would look with a

stunned pigeon clamped in his jaws, like a dog returned from the hunt.

Daniel with pointed ears and the body of a horse.

Daniel dressed in his fine English clothes—but with the addition of heeled shoes and a large beauty patch on his chin, his stance one of foppish, and laughable, elegance. Beside him, his head stuck on a miniature, bandy-legged leprechaun, was Finn, busily employing a hot iron to press the dripping lace on one of Daniel's cuffs.

Then there was the hauntingly eerie one of Daniel's face, rather than Pematalli's, mounted on Lenape Cliff.

And the sketches she had made of him in his deerskins, with Lokwelend's cabin in the background.

And lastly, she knew with dread invading her, curling her insides, there was the sketch she had finished only that morning. The one that showed him stripped to his waist, his legs spread wide as he took up his stance in the long grass, a jug of water raised to his mouth as his head was flung back, his unbound hair ruffled by an unseen breeze.

She turned away, all the fight having gone out of her, and sat with her back to him as she heard the papers being shuffled as he looked through them one by one.

Daniel paged through the sketches a second time, examining them, saying nothing, while Brianna dried her feet with the hem of her gown and wondered why she was still alive when she wanted to be dead. Dead with shame for having displayed her love for him so openly. Yes, there were the silly sketches, the ones she had done in a fit of childish temper or just for the thrill of it. But those last ones—well, those had been done from her heart.

And he'd have to know that.

"You're very good," he said at last, replacing the sketches in the packet, then tying it shut. "Very good. I've seen less talent exhibited in London. Is there anything you can't do, Brianna?"

I can't get you to say you're in love with me. That you couldn't bear to live without me. "They're only scribbles," she said instead, taking the packet from him as he offered it and laying it down as far away from him as possible. "You're not going to answer me, are you? Did you go to my father?"

He shook his head, but not to deny her question, because he then said, "You're young, Brianna. Young and isolated here in New Eden. You need to see more of the world. You deserve it."

"That's what Papa said? Even after you told him you had compromised me?"

"A few kisses, Brianna, that's all. Hardly enough to ruin your reputation, especially since you'll soon be in London."

"I see," she said quietly. "And you want me to go to London? While you stay here?"

"Yes, Brianna," he answered just as quietly. "Yes, I do."

She looked out over the stream, her eyes hurting as the sunlight reflected off the ripples caused by the strong current at its center. "Mama believes I will be something of a sensation."

"Your mama is probably underestimating your impact on the gentlemen of London."

She tilted up her chin. "And that doesn't bother you, Daniel?"

He made to get to his feet, but had only half risen before, one knee still on the grass, he said, "We shouldn't be having this conversation."

"What conversation should we be having, Daniel?" Brianna asked, suddenly feeling stronger, older, wiser than he. "We can't talk about what happened last Saturday. We can't talk about the fact that you asked my father for my hand, confessed that you had compromised me. We can't talk about London. Would you care to discuss the weather?"

He continued to his feet, then looked down at her. "If I

had any sense at all, I'd tell Gunitakan I'll head west with him, join up with the Lenape, and offer my services as a warrior. It would be safer."

She knew her smile affected him from the way that he seemed to flinch as she grinned up at him, the way he watched her as she got to her feet, moving close to him, moving against him. She put her hands on his chest, coming closer so that he backed up, backed up until he stood very close to the elevated bank of the stream. "You love me madly, don't you?"

He closed his eyes, sighing. "Brianna, don't start something I've promised not to finish."

Her hands stilled against his deerskin-clad chest. "Promised? Promised my father? You promised him you wouldn't touch me?" She opened her mouth to say more and found that she simply could not speak. It was unbelievable. That Daniel and her father could have such a conversation, make those decisions for her. How dare they!

"Your mother wants you to go to London, and I agree," he continued as he simply stood there, not touching her.

"My mother? You spoke with her, as well? Oh, this is getting better and better. And what did Wanda have to say on the subject? Or Jules? Perhaps if you inquired of Fortune's Lady, she could strike her front hoof against the ground in answer—once for 'Send the silly girl away to learn about *real* life,' twice if she thinks you ought to just throw me down on this bank and *teach* me about real life!"

She had gone too far, and she knew it the moment Daniel's dark eyes flashed in anger. "Brianna, this isn't getting us anywhere. If anything, I'm beginning to feel as if the last thing I need in my life right now is the complication of having to deal with a stubborn, willful, *spoiled* infant who can't see when everyone around her is trying to act in her best interests."

She bent her head, looking down at the ground, waves

of self-contempt washing over her. "Oh, God, Daniel, you're right," she whispered, feeling ashamed, heartsick. "I tell you I'm not a child, and then my actions make lies of my words. It's just—" she looked up at him, barely able to see him through her tears. "It's just that I need to know one thing."

He caught an escaping tear with his fingertip, then brushed a hand lightly over her cheek. "What do you need to know, imp?" he asked gently, healing her in all the places she felt so broken. "Do you want to know if I want to kiss you? Want to hold you? Want to love you? I think you already know the answers to those questions."

"I won't change my mind, you know," she told him honestly. "Everyone is always saying that I want what I want until I get it, and then I don't want it anymore. They still see me as if I'm a complete child, playing at drawing or the harp. I imagine they expect me to go to London and forget you in a fortnight. Maybe you think that, too. I can't believe I'm asking this, but—are you afraid I'm going to hurt you, Daniel?"

"No one has ever gotten close enough to me to hurt me, Brianna. I've talked more to you, said more to you, than I've ever said to anyone, even my parents. And you've seen deeper inside me than I've ever before allowed anyone to look. Yes, Brianna, you could hurt me. I just don't want to hurt you."

She allowed her tears to flow freely, not caring that her nose would probably soon start to run and her eyes were already most probably turning red. "I would never hurt you, Daniel. But perhaps Mama and Papa are right. I am still a child, or else I wouldn't do half the silly things I do, tease you the way I tried to tease you today."

"I probably shouldn't say this, imp, but I rather like the way you tease me, how unpredictable you are. No matter what else happens between us this summer before you leave for London, I'd only ask that you don't try to behave around me, don't try to be anyone you're not."

Brianna felt a smile threatening behind her tears.

"You're going to court me, aren't you, Daniel? Will you bring me flowers from the gardens at Enolowin? Will you write long, impassioned poems to my eyes?"

"No, imp. But I will teach you how to fish, if you want," he told her, his smile returning and, this time, reaching his eyes.

"Hah! I'll have you know, Daniel Crown, that I am the best fisherman in all of New Eden. Why, I once tickled a trout the size of a—" She broke off, blushing furiously, realizing that she was doing it again, once more putting herself in competition, even when there was no reason to compete. "I'm sorry. I don't know why I keep finding this need to make you proud of me."

"You wouldn't be Brianna if you weren't headstrong and boastful and impulsive—and more than a little incorrigible," he told her. "Don't try to change for me, imp, or for anybody. There won't be a gentleman in London who will be able to resist you."

"You're a good man, Daniel Crown, and very wise. I probably should listen to you," she said sincerely, reaching up to kiss his cheek. She was most likely going to regret what she did next, but she was suddenly willing to take the chance.

Daniel reached forward, moving until he was slightly off balance, clearly intent upon returning her kiss. He was really being most cooperative, although he certainly couldn't know that, the poor, wonderful man. "Oh, Daniel," she breathed, looking as soulfully as she could into his dark eyes. Then she gave him a mighty shove in his midsection, sending him reeling backward, arms flailing, into the stream. He gave a surprised shout, then landed with a mighty splash.

Giving in to this particular impulse was wonderful—cleansing—and had taken a large weight off her heart. Because now they were back to being who they had been before her birthday—two people who were attracted to each other—and the devil with rules and conventions!

"You're right, Daniel," she yelled to him as he struggled to his knees in the water, "I feel *much* more like myself again. Thank you!" And then, as he shook himself like a spaniel, she picked up her packet of sketches and, giggling, ran for the safety of Pleasant Hill.

Daniel stayed at Lokwelend's cabin, wading hip-deep in the stream, trying and failing to tickle a trout, and waiting for his deerskins to dry after he had laid them out over some tree branches. After the first hour he had pulled on his still damp trousers and sat down on the bank, content to enjoy the sound of the gaily running water, listen to the song of the birds in the trees above him, breathe in the utter peace and tranquiltity that reigned here—and savor the memory of his recent interlude with Brianna.

He still smiled every time he thought back to his conversation with her, how it had begun, and how it had ended. When he had thought of marriage, which hadn't been often, he had always believed that he would marry a woman much like his adopted mother. Strong, steadfast, a lady in every way, but with banked fires of passion and the occasional flash of mischief in her eyes.

He hadn't expected to fall in love with a total hoyden, an artless, impetuous, imaginative, recklessly innocent woman-child who seemed always to be ripe for any adventure. Unlike himself, Brianna was wonderfully spontaneous, openly affectionate. She genuinely enjoyed other people—even while displaying a rather endearing tendency to be boastful and an equally stubborn determination to dominate. Her considerable riding skills, and everything else from the similarities they shared to the differences he privately celebrated, all seemed to be seen by Brianna as confrontations to be "won."

Brianna loved fun and frolic, which made her a joy to be around—even when that impulsive fun and frolic ended with him rump down in the stream, shaking water from his hair as she had stood above him, laughing, then run away before he could retaliate. There was such an aura of excitement always about her, rather like anticipating that moment when something wonderful happens—or waiting for the other shoe to drop.

But there was more than lighthearted fun and impressive determination to Brianna Crown. She was highly intelligent, wonderfully talented, and had a way of looking at the world, at life, that was at once simple and remarkably astute. She had certainly taken his measure quickly, seeing his struggle over his conflicting loyalties, his confusion over who he was and where he belonged, and then putting all his convoluted wonderings into a simple, straightforward context, telling him that his answers lay inside himself. And she'd been right.

No wonder that everyone in New Eden loved her. No wonder that he loved her.

And how he was going to keep his hands off her, keep his promise to Dominick Crown, to Bryna Crown, and still retain some slim hold on his own sanity was a question he had no way of answering. Especially since Brianna had guessed that he meant to court her, even while he was determined that she should have her season in London before committing herself to him. Most especially because he knew full well that she now would do everything within her power to make him break those promises to himself and to her parents by teasing him into hungers he wanted to satisfy but, being a gentleman, must somehow refrain from indulging.

Because Dominick Crown had been wrong. Even an unplanned dip in a cool stream had done nothing to cool his ardor.

In my conscience I believe the baggage loves me,
for she never speaks well of me her self,
nor suffers any body else to rail at me.

WILLIAM CONGREVE

chapter twelve

Daniel sat on the porch as twilight slowly won its battle over the warm summer sun, wondering why he was at Enolowin when Brianna was at Pleasant Hill. He'd have to host a dinner party soon if Mrs. Bing was willing, which she probably was, although the thought of having the comte under his roof had little appeal. The man bothered him. He didn't know why, as the Frenchman was always unfailingly friendly, but there was just something about him that sent off warning flares in Daniel's brain. Something oily in his genial smile. Perhaps something even desperate.

And then there was Addison Bainbridge, another pair of highly polished boots Daniel didn't much care to see sliding under his table. The man was a fortune hunter, plain and simple, and it would take a blind man not to see that his interest in poor, timid Corliss Payton was purely monetary. He'd as soon switch Corliss for Brianna, or any young woman whose father had sufficiently deep pockets.

And these men were only two examples of the sort of

"gentlemen" Brianna would be exposed to in London. She'd have Dominick and Bryna to watch over her, Philip and Brighid to sort out the hangers-on and miscreants, but Brianna was still a fairly impressionable young woman, and her head might be turned by some dashing young buck who looked at her youth, her beauty, her fire and wit—and saw only her father's fortune.

Why didn't he simply marry the girl and have done with it? She certainly was willing enough. He certainly loved her enough. He could just get up, saddle Lenape Traveler, ride over to Pleasant Hill, and state his intentions. Explain to Dominick how he would always strive to do his best to make his youngest daughter happy, how he'd keep her here at Enolowin where they would raise children and horses and begin a dynasty as Dominick and his wife had done thirty years ago.

They'd be so happy to know that their daughter would always be close by, able to bring their grandchildren to them. The marriage would unite the family in yet another way, even if he was a Crown only through Philip's largesse. Brianna would never be poor, never be hungry, never be lonely.

And she'd never have the thrill of going down the dance with the adoring son of a duke or ride through the park beside a handsome young Hussar or be the belle of her very own coming-out ball . . .

"You're looking terrible enough," Otto Bing said genially as he walked up the steps to Daniel's right and sat himself down in the chair next to him. "The wife will be bringing out the tonic if you don't be watching yourself." He reached into his pocket and pulled out two long, thin cigars, handing one over to Daniel. "Here. Smoke on this stogie. Might not help you, but it'll keep the wife away."

Daniel eyed the cigar warily, for he had been around Bing and his stogies before and knew that its aroma was not exactly of the finest. "Why is it called a stogie,

Otto?" he asked as Bing struggled to light his own poor wrapped cigar, sucking in his thin cheeks until Dani thought the man would turn himself inside out.

Bing blew out a stream of blue smoke, sighed i seeming ecstasy, and began to rock back and forth in h chair, clearly settling in for a story. "It's because of t wagons, of course. Used to drive the Conestogas I di long years ago since. Most of 'em was built down near Lancaster, where they raise a good, strong tobacc Smoke kept the bugs away as we drove, and at four for penny, it was heaven on earth to have them. Then drove a Blutz-wagon, but it hurt my rump somethi terrible—not half the wagon the Conestoga is—so I ga it all up and found me a good plump woman."

He took another pull on the long cigar and winked Daniel. "Much more comfortable to sit in, she is, if y take my meaning. Ach!" he then exclaimed, sinki lower on the chair as he changed the subject. "What day I've had, walking the orchard, checking the hors shoes on all the trees. Must have had to hang a doze more shoes. And all the wife says is that I'd best h myself to the churn first thing tomorrow early, or else t butter won't reach for lunch. Sometimes the Conestog call me, no lie."

Daniel slid the stogie into his pocket and, to keep Bi talking, asked him about the horseshoes and what th had to do with fruit trees.

Bing's pained expression told Daniel that he had on again displayed himself to be a know-nothing—who w soon to be educated. "It's simple enough," the caretak explained. "Always hang old horseshoes on fruit trees that they feel the weight, feel on themselves a burden bear. Won't get no fruit without them." He turned Daniel, looking skeptical. "You didn't know this no Ai-yi-yi! How do you keep from starving over to E gland?"

Daniel's amusement built slowly as he thought of t

ɔgic behind giving a tree a burden to "bear" fruit, rowing from a smile, to a chuckle, to an outright laugh. Bing, I swear it—there are times you truly frighten ne."

Bing twisted up his nose, sniffed. "Don't see why. Only common sense, you know. Ei-yi-yi! Would you look ow who's coming up the drive from over to the stables? nd the two of them looking like they've nothing better ɔ do than the whole day in New Eden spend, showing veryone how lazy they are. A good thing you have me, I ell you, so that people can know you're not such a silly *'umpfkopft* as to have all lazybones around you."

"Yes," Daniel answered, thinking he'd probably hurt imself if he kept his laughter inside him at Bing's boast f his own industry. And if Brianna were here to hear Otto Bing's boasts, well, the two of them would probably ave both collapsed in mirth. "I can't imagine how I'd ver get on without you, Otto. Truly." Then he stood, ishing he hadn't thought of Brianna, walked over to the teps, and waved a hello to Finn and Gunitakan, who ere both weaving their way toward the porch.

"There was a letter waiting for you in New Eden when Gunitakan and I went there to find me some proper hread to sew a button on that shirt that hasn't hit your ack since you started in on sportin' those heathen nimal skins," Finn said as he climbed up onto the orch, the old Indian behind him, a happy glow of ngested ale about him.

"A letter?" Daniel was surprised, as he hadn't thought letter from England could reach him so quickly. "Did ou bring it with you?"

Finn rolled his eyes heavenward. "No, sir, I left it ittin'," he said cheekily, reaching into his waistband nd pulling out a crumpled sheet of folded paper. "O'course I brought it. Couldn't read it and tell you what t says, now could I?" Then he shook his head, looking urprised at himself. "Did I say that? Got to climb back on the water wagon, that's what. Gettin' too cheeky half. Comes from havin' nothin' to do, that's what," continued as he walked past Daniel—staggered pa Daniel—slipped an arm around Gunitakan's shoulde and entered the house.

"I have to start treating that man more like n employee or else he'll drink himself to death," Dani remarked as he rejoined Bing on the rockers. "Maybe I let him shave me tomorrow."

Bing sniffed. "He can shave me," he offered as pushed himself upright, probably intent on finding h wife and getting her to "make him" some thick slices bread slathered with apple butter. "Got enough to do my own and could use a little help around here."

"You're a saint, Otto," Daniel agreed as solemnly he could, sliding his thumb under the thick wax seal the letter, opening it, and quickly scanning the page see Lady Lilith Crown's flamboyant signature scrawl at the bottom. "Maybe we can even get Finn to chew f you," he added absently, "leaving you more time to n horseshoes on pear trees."

Bing coughed, a nervous, choking sound that broug a smile to Daniel's lips. "I'll be off to see the wife no sir," he said, and quickly made his escape—movi faster than he had done since the unforgettable morni Daniel had watched his caretaker being chased arou the chicken yard by an angry rooster.

Brianna would have enjoyed Bing's hasty departure well, and Daniel knew it, even as he wondered if would ever again be able to so much as sit on his ov porch, in his own rocking chair, and not think abo what it would be like to have Brianna sitting there wi him. Sharing the twilight with him. Laughing with hi And then, as the moon climbed in the sky, and the sta twinkled in the darkness, he would take her hand as s smiled at him and they would go inside, climbing t stairs to the huge bedchamber arm in arm . . .

He shook his head, clearing the vision from his mind, and concentrated on Lilith's letter:

My Dearest, Already Missed Little Savage,

We have just said our good-byes at the docks, and I have returned to Half Moon Street and the house that is one of my many ill-gotten gains. I stumbled inside, feeling the weight of my years, the burden of my loneliness, and have spent the past hour weeping over my wasted life. It was, I must tell you, a most fatiguing exercise, and not the sort of indulgence one of my advanced years can partake of with impunity.

So—and dear Philip would be aghast to know it—I am now happily "well liquored," as one of my less erudite paramours was wont to say, and taking pen in hand to gift you with one last lesson learned with difficulty.

We, you and I, are people who do not love easily. We raise our hackles, see demons where there are none, problems where they do not exist. We protect ourselves because we are mongrels, Little Savage, always waiting for the sting of the boot. And, in protecting ourselves, we lose so much.

I had a love, once, so many years ago. So young, Little Savage, so young! A good man, a simple man for all that he was a peer of the realm. He bought my favors and won my heart. But we could not marry. I could not hurt him with my mixed blood, my less than sterling reputation. I laughed at his proposal and broke his heart. Broke my own heart. I sent him away to marry someone better suited to his happiness. And, Little Savage, I ruined three lives.

His wife is dead now, probably after cursing me with her last breath, and I am still alone—with even my Little Savage, the child of my heart, gone away. And I have done a terrible thing. I have had my maid take a note round to my dearest Cholly, asking him come to me if he is still of the same mind as he was more than two decades past.

Am I scribbling, Little Savage? Can you read the words my tears fall on? Can you hear the ragged beating of my heart as I wait for his answer?

Little Savage, Little Savage, if you ever look at love, don't look away. That is my last lesson to you, my best gift to you, and one I pray you learn.

With love and anguished tears,
Lilith

Daniel took a deep breath, whispered a silent prayer, then turned the paper sideways so that he could decipher the nearly illegible scrawl in the margin.

My love! My love! We leave tonight to honeymoon in Scotland! Dear God, I have another chance!

Daniel folded the paper carefully, slid it into his pocket, then wiped a hand across his eyes, unsurprised to find them wet—and saw Corliss Payton standing on the drive, twisting her gloved hands together as she waited for him to notice her.

Brianna found the comte in the music room, paging through a magazine and looking elegantly bored. She had purposely stayed a careful distance away from him until she felt she could face him without longing to twist off his aristocratic nose. But, now convinced she had Daniel's love—if not his ring on her finger—she felt new confidence in seeking a spot of revenge against the meddling Frenchman who had done his best to make her life miserable.

She had decided to seek her retaliation through some well-placed mischief rather than a full frontal assault that could only end in another trip to her father's study and another "small discussion." And here her quarry was, sitting like a chicken ready to be plucked. She smiled, already feeling satisfied with herself.

She walked into the music room, knowing she looked her best this morning in her new peach gown that flattered her tumbling curls and added new depths to her green eyes. She then stopped halfway across the room and posed and waited for him to notice her.

The comte did not disappoint. He looked up from his magazine, shut it with a snap, and flung it onto the table in front of him, then hopped to his feet like the eager frog he was, walking toward her, saying: "*Tres magnifique!* My dear child, you are *ravissant* this morning—truly breathtaking!"

As well she ought to be, having all but reduced Wanda to tears, fussing over her appearance! "Why, thank you, sir," Brianna gushed, holding out her hand so that he might raise it to his lips. "Thank you—*Hugh.* How wonderful that a gentleman of your sophistication, your wider view of the world, should even notice this poor provincial. Lord knows no one else in this benighted backwater would think to even look at me, let alone compliment me."

The comte's left eyebrow climbed ridiculously high on his forehead as he took her hand and led her over to the carved-back settee, waiting until she had spread her skirts around her before sitting down himself. Puffin, who had followed her into the room, her tail held high, hopped up on the settee, placing her fat, furry body between her mistress and the French interloper.

"What a lovely animal," the comte said, reaching out to stroke Puffin, who rewarded him by taking a claws-bared swipe at his hand, drawing blood before hopping down to the floor and sitting there, licking her paw, obviously content at having made her "statement" concerning her opinion of the man. "It is not working out then, this hoped-for liaison between you and the savage?" the comte asked, calmly taking out his handkerchief and dabbing at the three bright red drops of blood that had appeared on his skin. "Is he brick stupid or has he reached inside himself and—horror of horrors!—discovered a modicum of scruples? How very fatiguing for you, *ma cherie.*"

Brianna feigned outrage—which wasn't difficult, although hiding her joy at Puffin's sterling performance had been only made possible by biting down on the tender flesh of her inner cheeks. "How cruel of you, Hugh, to believe that the man has spurned me! Can it not be possible that *I* have simply weighed my options and seen the strength of *your* arguments? After all, I could be a comtesse. Live in Paris—away from all this provincial squalor, never to see a pig again unless it was served up to me with an apple in its mouth. I have thought of little else since last we spoke."

His puzzled look said little for his confidence in his own appeal, but he swiftly rallied, taking her hand in his again and raising it to his lips. *"Ma cherie!"* As he kissed her fingertips, one after the other, Brianna felt sure he was mentally estimating: "She is worth—what? Ten thousand? Twenty thousand? *Fifty* thousand?"

Brianna withdrew her hand before she gave in to the urge to gag, pretending a maidenly modesty. "Please, Hugh, do not make my heart flutter so. Surely we have things to discuss?"

He was suddenly all business, very pragmatic, and nearly drooling with avarice. "Very well, we will not waste time. You have the face of a goddess, *ma cherie,* but the soul of a shopkeeper. We are about to make a trade, *n'est-ce pas?* Your dear papa's money for my title. I cannot yet give you Paris, but that will come in time."

"Yes, I am aware that the gift of Paris is beyond you at the moment, Hugh," Brianna replied, feeling powerful, more than powerful. Honestly, the man was swallowing the bait so rapidly it was a marvel he wasn't choking on it. "Therefore, I have decided to ask another gift of you, one that will prove to me that you are serious about wishing this alliance. After all, I have already been walked down one dark garden path, with nothing to show for it save a wider experience and a determination to never allow my heart to be touched again."

"I'll have to thank Daniel Crown for his clumsiness, next I see him," the comte murmured, stroking Brianna's forearm, his mind already undoubtedly figuring out ways to contact his tailor and order up an entire new wardrobe. "All right, little shopkeeper, we will bargain. You have taken the first step, so that I must take the second. Give you a demonstration of my ability to please you, to live up to my end of our bargain, *oui?* What do you want? Diamonds? This would be difficult, what with the problems in Paris, but not impossible, I promise you. Perhaps something simpler, *cherie,* until I am home again, yes?"

Brianna frowned, pushing out her bottom lip even as she withdrew her arm from his touch, as if diamonds had been precisely what she had coveted and she was now rethinking their entire bargain. "This is disheartening, Hugh," she warned, and then lowered her eyes, hiding her glee as the man looked ready to weep.

She took a deep breath, exhaling it slowly, watching him squirm as he sensed his golden opportunity slipping away from him. It was time for her to reel in her fish or cut her line—either way, she had to be quick, and then remove herself from his vicinity before his anger and frustration got out of hand. So, having led the gratifyingly willing comte to hunger after her bait, take it into his mouth, she would now let him feel the sharp bite of the hook. After all, as she had told Daniel, she was quite the best fisherman in all of New Eden.

There was no satisfaction to be had if her request was not wholeheartedly earnest and yet woefully flimsy, so that even a fool selling his chickens while they were still just eggs could not help but see what this silly little girl was about, what this entire conversation had been about from the very beginning. She forced her eyes open wide, as if suddenly struck by inspiration. "I have it! It's something I've wanted since I first saw it, but I haven't enough pin money for the purchase, and Mama and Papa will have none of it. Hugh, I want you to buy Bainbridge's slave for me. If he lends that insufferable dolt cachet, just imagine what he can do for me on the streets of Paris! You'll get him for me, *oui?*"

The comte's long gray eyes narrowed to calculating slits that glittered like chips of February ice—dark, dirty, and bitingly cold. He got to his feet, a tall, elegant, deadly dangerous creature, his menace only slightly lowered by his misstep that had caught Puffin's tail, so that the cat howled, spat, then escaped under the settee. "You silly, transparent child! You believe yourself to be very clever, *non?* Use my gullible self to your own ends and then disavow me, *oui?* You have not the finesse for Paris, *ma cherie.* And you will pay for this insult, I promise you!"

Brianna stood also, looking intently into the Comte's eyes, her expression equally fierce, her heart pounding as she claimed victory. It was time to put an end to pretense and cut her line, letting him know he had been royally tricked—that her object was not to get Marcus at all but to "get" the comte himself.

"Oh, dear, now I've disappointed you, Hugh, haven't I?" she asked, her voice dripping sarcasm. "And after all your high hopes? Let me think—there must be something I can say to ease your pain. Oh yes, I've got it, and out of your own mouth! I should say that *I amaze myself,* truly, by feeling most *wretchedly sorry* for you, for your advancing years, your pathetic desperation," she said, turning his own words on him, twisting them only slightly for her own benefit. "Does it hurt so much then, *being used?* Don't worry. I shall be here to watch as you leave Pleasant Hill as penniless as you arrived. Why, Hugh, *it may just be my destiny, oui?*"

He glared at her, so that she lifted her chin, refusing to flinch as she believed—if only for a moment—that he might actually strike her, and was still returning his stare as Whittle announced that she had a guest.

"Good morning, everyone," Daniel said as he strolled into the room, looking young and fit and more the aristocrat in his deerskins than did the comte in his fine French fashions. It was, Brianna concluded with a smile as she turned to greet Daniel, probably the grayish tinge to the comte's cheeks that put him at such a disadvantage. That and the fact that she loved Daniel Crown.

The comte smiled and bowed, recovering himself with an aplomb that would have brought Brianna's admiration—if she didn't already feel certain that he'd undoubtedly had endless experience in covering his real thoughts with a polite expression. "How good to see you again, sir," he said, holding out his hand to Daniel. "Have your horses quite recovered? Dominick has told me that they all seem to have taken ill, one following the other. How unfortunate, when your success in this venture is all that stands between you and your ignominious return to England, to once more be an unwanted burden on the good family that rescued you from a life spent speaking gibberish and dancing naked around open campfires, *n'est-ce pas?"*

Daniel sliced a quick look toward Brianna—who was doing her best to look oblivious to anything that had been said—then smiled at the comte. "Toss any rocks my way that you wish, sir. It's the only satisfaction you'll have." Then he turned to Brianna, shaking his head. "That innocent look speaks volumes, imp, as does the smell of tension in the air I sensed the moment I entered the room. Have you been naughty again?"

"Oh! How unfair you are, Daniel, to accuse me!" Brianna answered, wondering if there was anything about her that this wonderful man didn't already know and—thankfully—appear willing to view with indulgent amusement, even love. "I've simply been practicing what the good comte has been so good as to teach me. "Isn't that right, my dear comte?"

The comte looked at the pair of them, from one to the other, and spat out a low, Gallic curse. Then, unbelievably, he smiled. "Shall I choose to be amused? Perhaps it would be prudent. And you probably deserve each other, *oui?* However," he said, already striding toward the door, "I do believe I shall have to seek my own pallid revenge—as I'm convinced Addison Bainbridge will be most grateful to know the new worth of his slave." He stopped at the door, turned, and executed an elegant leg. "Amateurs," he said, his smile little more than a most elegant sneer. "Yes. I have chosen to be amused. *Au revoir!"*

Brianna, who had been feeling fairly pleased with herself, sank back onto the settee, all the joy gone out of her—except that remaining smidgen of womanly satisfaction that was crushed as Daniel demanded to know: "What's he talking about, Brianna? What in bloody hell did you do now?"

She looked up at him helplessly, immediately—and yet so horribly belatedly—realizing what she had done and the consequences involved. "The comte overheard me in the gardens on the night of my party, crying over you and confiding in Corliss, and he told me he'd be happy to marry me once you'd ruined me and then refused to do the honorable thing," she explained quickly, her words tumbling over themselves as she fought through her terrible confession.

Daniel's eyes flashed black fury. "He said *what?* Christ, Brianna, why didn't you come to me?"

Brianna pulled a face at him, then pointed out that, at the time, she had been fairly certain that the comte was right, and that Daniel's actions on her birthday could be interpreted as those of a first class rotter. "Besides, when you get right down to it he grossly insulted you and if anybody was going to say anything nasty about you that night, Daniel, it should have been me!"

"I suppose that makes sense, if I remember it's you saying it. But this is all my fault, Brianna. I should have come to you myself that night—" Daniel grumbled, only to have Brianna put up her hands to stop him.

"No! It wouldn't have made any difference, Daniel, because the damage was already done, and I probably wouldn't have listened to you." Her eyes narrowed as she remembered again all the comte had said to her in the gardens. "He was so smug, Daniel, so arrogant—so insufferable! I couldn't go to Papa, demand he toss the man out of the house, because then Papa would know that . . . that—"

"He would have known what I had already told him," Daniel bit out, interrupting her again. She really wished he wouldn't do that. It was difficult enough to say what she had to say, admit what she had to admit, without his interruptions. She winced as he ran a hand through his hair, clearly distracted. "But we've already talked about this, Brianna. I thought, foolishly I suppose, that we had come to some sort of an understanding. Why would you persist in hiding anything from me?"

Brianna looked down and wondered, realizing she wasn't being exactly rational to worry about such things at the moment, if he noticed that Puffin had come out from her hiding place beneath the settee and was now busily rubbing herself against his pants leg.

She spread her hands helplessly and tried to answer Daniel's question. "Why did I do it? Because I'm an idiot child? Because he hurt me, insulted you, and I wanted to hurt him back? Because if I told you instead of Papa, you might just go knock him down and demand a duel, and I didn't want to have that happen? I don't know, Daniel, I just don't know. I just thought he deserved to be taken down a peg or two, sent on his way back to Philadelphia, and that I could handle the job on my own and nobody else would ever have to know."

Daniel sighed deeply, then bent low, took her hand in his and raised it to his mouth, pressing his lips against her burning skin for all too short a moment. "I'm sorry, imp. I shouldn't ask questions when I already know the answers. You look very lovely today, by the way—although I begin to think I miss your shirts and breeches. But tell me, how does Marcus figure in any of this?"

She couldn't smile, not when he forgave her, not when he complimented her appearance. The enormity of what she, in her stubborn unwillingness to let anyone best her, had done, was coming home to roost in her head, making it ache with humiliation and frustration. And fear. "That's the worst, Daniel, and I didn't even see it! How could I have been so blind?"

Brianna blinked back tears, longing to collapse against Daniel and sob. She tried to explain, but her breath was suddenly ragged, her tears forcing her into disjointed speech. "The comte told me that same night that Corliss was in love with Marcus . . . which I had already begun to believe . . . and I thought I'd use that very information to give the wretched hound some of his own back."

"I'm still confused," Daniel admitted, earning himself a glare from Brianna, who was trying to get through her explanation as quickly as possible, for not a word she had to say would come easily. "Have pity on me, imp, and go through this slowly, leaving nothing out."

"I wanted to get him—the comte—on his knees, thinking I had agreed to marry him. I needed him to believe that he had found his way straight to Papa's money . . . even to begin spending it in his head. And then I'd ask him to buy Marcus for me, to prove he was serious and to give me cachet . . . which would prove that I really *didn't* mean to marry him because he'd know I'd certainly never want a slave and would only have been using him to buy Marcus so that Corliss could be happy. After all, it was the comte who told me Corliss loved Marcus, so he'd have to see what I was doing and why."

She took several deep breaths before she could go on. "And he did, Daniel. He saw straight through me, just as I'd wanted him to . . . but not until his greedy head was spinning, already planning ways to spend Papa's money. I really thought then that he might hit me, but then you walked in and . . ." She put her head in her hands, now crying in earnest. "Oh, God, Daniel, I've ruined everything! It simply never occurred to me! The comte will go straight to Bainbridge and tell him about Marcus, and then he'll never sell him. *Never!* How could I have been so *stupid!*"

"Sweet Jesus," Daniel breathed, sitting down beside her at last, taking her hand in his. "Before we put our heads together on this—and there is no way you'll make a move from here on in without my being a part of it, understand?—I should tell you something. One of the reasons you scare me, imp—and you *do* scare me—is that you're very different from me. Another is that in some ways we're too alike. I rarely admit it, although my very wise parents would agree with this statement, but there are times I can be very stubborn, going on with something even after I know it's wrong. Which is probably what you just did with the dear comte? There, does that make you feel better?"

Brianna made use of the handkerchief Daniel had handed her, then nodded, giving him a watery smile as Puffin hopped up onto his lap, kneading his soft deerskins before seeming to settle herself down for a nap. "A little better," she said, then frowned again. "Bainbridge won't sell Marcus now, though, will he? Not that he would agree when Papa asked to buy him." She shot Daniel a look from under her eyelashes. "Mama told me that he'd approached Bainbridge that first night at her request and because he is totally against slavery, which I should have known."

"Yes, we both should have known that your parents would be outraged about Marcus," Daniel agreed, grinning and shaking his head when she offered to return his ruined handkerchief. He rubbed at Puffin's furry throat, sending the cat into ecstasies that should, by rights, have embarrassed the usually aloof animal. "But Bainbridge turned me down flat as well when I approached him. Which is what I tried to explain to Corliss last evening."

Brianna nodded her head thoughtfully. "So, perhaps my blunder isn't quite so dreadful. After all, the comte won't exactly be telling Bainbridge anything he doesn't already—" Her head shot up. "*What* did you say?"

Daniel's smile made Brianna long to hit him—although she wouldn't want to hurt him, of course. "Miss Payton paid me a visit last night, hoping to convince me of the wrongfulness of slavery. She believes, because of my Lenape ancestry, that I should have some special affinity for understanding the plight of someone who has little or no control over the circumstances of his life. I tried to tell her that I most certainly could understand the feeling of being locked inside a life that isn't quite real, but I had a difficult time slipping a word in edgewise. She had an entire speech prepared, you understand, and it didn't seem fair to interrupt her."

Brianna bit on her bottom lip, sorting everything out in her mind. "Just when you believe you know someone through and through . . . she must love him very much, mustn't she?"

"She'll totally perish without him, would leave her parents' home and travel to the ends of the earth to be with him, would gladly lie down in a ditch and die if they can't be wed," Daniel told her, adding with a smile, "I'm simply repeating what she said, you understand."

"That doesn't sound at all like the Corliss I know, but then she didn't sound at all like Corliss last Saturday night at my party. What did the comte say? Something about it always being such a shock to see a jellyfish develop a spine? I've never seen a jellyfish, but I think Corliss is showing signs of being a genuine heroine. I'm so proud of her!" She turned to Daniel, laying both hands on his forearm. "What can I do to help?"

Daniel winced and shifted the sleeping Puffin onto the cushion beside him as he turned to Brianna. "I was afraid you were going to ask that, imp," he said, rising as they both heard a slight noise outside in the hallway. "I'll talk to you later, all right? We can meet at Lokwelend's cabin at about three," he whispered quickly as the very English, very proper Whittle entered the room, excused himself, and told Daniel that Mr. Dominick Crown had seen his horse outside and wished to speak to him about the recent sad problem in Mr. Daniel Crown's stables.

"I'll be right there, Whittle, thank you," Daniel answered, then looked down at Brianna as the butler bowed and withdrew from the room. "Go on, imp. Ask your question," he said, sighing in much the way her father did when she dared to nudge her nose into a matter her father felt to be none of her business. Those sighs hadn't stopped her when they came from her father, and they didn't stop her now.

"I don't think I like that you're beginning to know me so well," Brianna admitted, allowing him to assist her to her feet. "But I'll ask anyway. Daniel, didn't you find it odd that the comte knew so much about the problem with your horses and that he seemed so very happy to bring up the subject?"

He leaned down, kissing her cheek, making her wish that the rest of the world could simply conveniently disappear until she could convince him that a season in London—two seasons in London—weren't worth five minutes spent in his arms. "Make that four o'clock, imp. I believe I'm going to need time to arm myself against your quick mind and your too intelligent questions."

"Then you think that the comte . . . that he . . . but, Daniel, why would—?"

His mouth covered hers, cutting off her questions about the Frenchman, making her head swim with other questions that had little to do with Marcus or the comte or sick horses, until she was once more sitting on the settee, feeling faintly breathless as she watched Daniel stride out of the room on his long, deerskin-clad legs.

Puffin crawled onto her lap, butting her head against

Brianna's breast, purring loudly. "Yes, my love, I know. You were utterly shameless. But you're forgiven. The man's entirely irresistible, damn him, which I, apparently, am not. But I do believe I have him on the run," she ended hopefully, dropping a kiss on the cat's shiny black nose even as she decided that it was time to take her brother's outgrown breeches out for another airing.

For God's sake hold your tongue,
and let me love.

JOHN DONNE

chapter thirteen

Daniel spent two long hours trying to run Addison Bainbridge to ground, which shouldn't have been difficult in a hamlet the size of New Eden, but had no luck in finding the man. With nothing to show for his efforts, and knowing he would face endless questions from Brianna when they met at Lokwelend's cabin, he made a detour to the Enolowin stables to check on the condition of his recovering horses.

Only Lenape Traveler had not gone down in his stall, felled by the strange malady that Gunitakan's vile-smelling remedy seemed to have cured—much to the consternation of Skelton, who had fought long and hard against any "heathen remedies." But they had already lost one animal, a very promising-looking mare, and Daniel would have employed snake charmers and fire walkers if he had thought there would be any chance to save the rest of the horses. Living with Gunitakan's preening over the success of his native medicines might be Skelton's problem, but it surely wasn't giving Daniel sleepless nights.

"How's the roan?" Daniel asked, dismounting from Lenape Traveler's back and walking over to confer with Skelton, who was grooming the bay that had arrived only two days earlier. "She looked better to me this morning."

Skelton slid his employer a look that somehow managed to be both satisfied and chagrined. "Eating her damn fool head off, that's how she is. That's how they all are. And that damn savage won't tell me what he gave them. For all I know, they'll soon be dropping like flies again and I won't have the smallest notion as to what to do with them."

"I'll see if I can flatter Gunitakan into sharing his secret with me." Daniel smiled. "We . . . um . . . we speak the same language, you understand, so he might be willing to teach me, share his wisdom, so to speak."

"He's probably the one who poisoned them in the first place," Skelton grumbled. "Just so he could save 'em and get in close with you. Or maybe not," he ended, looking up at Daniel sheepishly. "Sorry, sir."

"No need to apologize, Skelton," Daniel said, leaning down to pick up the bay's foreleg, checking the mare's shoes. "Tell me—do you really think someone poisoned the horses? How would they do that? Put something in their feed?"

"That's how I see it," Skelton said, nodding. "I was wondering when you'd ask. That there stallion of yours never took sick, but he was with you up to Pleasant Hill, and first thing I did was clean out all the feed and hay and put out fresh, thinking it may have gone moldy or buggy—some such thing. O'course, I put out fresh water, too. Could have been in the water. I asked Toby if anyone was near to the stables while I was off to the house for m'dinner, but the lad says he didn't see nobody. And I've been sleeping here in the stables every night since."

The trainer rested the currycomb on the mare's back and tipped his head in Daniel's direction. "I didn't say nothing because I don't know nothing, you know, but is there someone around here you've got mad at you, sir? Someone who wouldn't mind overmuch if all your horses died and every last penny you've sunk into them was lost and gone?"

Daniel was careful to keep his expression blank. "I'll admit to having made up a short list in my head," he said, already walking back toward Lenape Traveler. "I appreciate your dedication, Skelton. It can't be comfortable, sleeping in the stables."

The trainer hustled after him. "No, sir, it's not. Which makes me bold enough to ask you, sir—would it bother you overmuch if I was to go off with Toby and his ma this Sunday? Bing would be here to keep watch, and it'll only be for a couple of hours, you know, and I don't think anything will happen now anymore, and it's just a silly church thing the woman has stuck in her craw that she has to have my company for and all, thinking to show me off is what I have a feeling she wants. But if you think I should be here—" he trailed off hopefully.

"Don't turn me into the ogre who upsets Toby's mama, Skelton. Take the entire afternoon," Daniel said, grinning down at the red-faced man from atop Lenape Traveler. "Having trouble swallowing, Skelton? Maybe it's that marital noose you feel tightening around your neck?"

"Yes, sir," the trainer said, running his index finger around his collar. "But it ain't so bad, I don't think. And she's a wonderful cook, sir, and no lie—almost as good as Mrs. Bing."

"I can think of no higher compliment," Daniel said sincerely. "When the time comes, Skelton, I'll be happy to arrange for a small house to be built here at Enolowin for you and your new family."

Skelton's thanks followed Daniel out of the stable yard as he turned Lenape Traveler toward the main road and the short trip to Lokwelend's cabin, his mind fully occupied with questions about both the comte and

Addison Bainbridge. Both disliked him, each for his own reasons, and either one of them could have put something in the horse's feed or their water, although his money was on Bainbridge. The opportunistic comte had only wanted him out of the way in order to clear the field with Brianna, and poisoning horses seemed a very roundabout way to that end. Yes, it was Bainbridge who seemed more the sort for petty, backhanded revenge.

Either way, it was time they were gone. Both of them.

By the time Daniel had dismounted, leading Lenape Traveler through the woods to the stream, his mind was less involved with his two possible enemies and more fully engaged in conjuring up some way to tell Brianna he had not yet succeeded in purchasing Marcus—and keeping her from instigating what was bound to be some bizarre plan of her own.

Daniel shrugged as he considered this, wondering if occupying Brianna's fertile mind with Corliss's problem might not be preferable to having to fend off his beloved's continuing efforts to convince him to abandon his plan to see her settled in Playden Court in time to prepare for a season in London.

Which, he realized the moment he saw her, was about as ridiculous a hope as wishing for Otto Bing to suddenly take it into his head on his own to paint the barn.

Other women dressed for seduction by donning satins and lace and elaborate jewels. They sat themselves down in overheated ballrooms, employing ivory-sticked fans to their best advantage, or strolled through the park, smiling and flirting and casting out their lures.

But Brianna Crown wasn't like any other woman. She was very singular, unique, and seemed to instinctively know that the way to her victim's senses lay not in powder and patch but in a careless simplicity, an artless casualness, a maddeningly naive and seductive presence consisting of a wide, unaffected smile, a deliciously sun-kissed complexion, sweet-smelling unbound hair, and a pair of cast-off breeches that had never been displayed to better advantage.

"Have you had any luck?" she asked as she saw him step into the clearing and immediately rose from her seat on a flat rock near the stream and began walking toward him as he tied up Lenape Traveler—her long, burnished curls falling down over her back, bouncing against the enticing swell of her young breasts that strained against the starkly white lawn shirt she wore open at the collar. "I've been so worried."

Unlike Bing and Skelton, I find I don't give a tinker's damn if she can cook, he thought wildly, then shook his head, trying to clear it. "Bainbridge was nowhere to be found," he told her, taking her hand and walking her back toward the stream bank, sitting down beside her, watching as she drew up her legs to her chin and wrapped her arms around her knees, all her attention focused on his words—while all his attention centered on her long, clean sweep of thigh. "For that matter, the good comte was likewise invisible. You know what that means, don't you?"

She lowered her forehead against her knees, nodding. "They're together, and it's all my fault. I've spent the whole afternoon here, calling myself every sort of fool I can imagine, and it isn't enough. Mama says I'm growing up, and growing up is invariably painful." She turned her head, her cheek resting against her knees as she looked at Daniel through tear-wet eyes. "It just doesn't seem fair that Corliss should be the one feeling most of the pain."

Daniel looked at her quizzically. "You spoke to Bryna about this? Told her about the trick you played on the comte this morning?"

Brianna's smile was beautifully sad and slightly colored by her usual good spirits. "There is no priest close by for my confession, Daniel. Besides, Mama is very wise, which she tells me was not always so. She's shed her share of tears over past mistakes and lessons learned with difficulty." She sighed, sitting back and wiping at her eyes. "Papa always said I was my mother's daughter."

"I can think of worse failings than being fiercely loyal, Brianna," Daniel said, reaching out to touch her hand. "At the heart of it, you took on the comte to avenge my good name, and because you wanted to protect both your father and myself from knocking the bastard down and possibly ending up on the dueling ground."

"And because I wanted to get some of my own back, Daniel," she answered, bringing out her own personal sun once more with her wide smile. "Let's not forget that. And it was a delicious moment, watching as he realized what I had done to him, how I had led him on, only to turn the tables on him. I think I'm a mean person, Daniel, at the heart of it." She shook her head, making her curls dance around her shoulders, then looked at him intently. "So—what do we do now?"

I press you back against this soft, warm grass and introduce you to delights that will make both our heads swim, Daniel thought, then quickly banished the words, and the images they conjured up, from his mind. "*We* don't do anything next, imp. I will simply wait until Bainbridge surfaces again—probably in time to stick his legs under Mr. Payton's dinner table this evening—and then ask again to buy Marcus from him. And this time I'm willing to double my price. Treble it, if necessary. The man may be mean-spirited, but I don't think he can afford the luxury of turning down that sort of money."

"And then you'll free him, of course, and he and Corliss will marry and live happily ever after," Brianna said, sighing. "Except that I wonder if Mr. and Mrs. Payton will allow a marriage between their only daughter and a former slave, a man of color, which is the term I've heard my father use. Do you suppose Corliss would really run off with Marcus? Or will she watch him as he walks away, then spend the remainder of her life as the sad little thing who talked to me so soulfully about the meaning of love the night of my party?"

"There are those who would consider me a man of color, Brianna," Daniel pointed out quietly. "And as a savage as well. No matter if Corliss's parents accept Marcus or not, there will always be those who will stare and point, criticize and condemn. Or haven't you thought about that?"

Brianna rolled her eyes. "Well, that's just plain silly, Daniel! As if anyone of any sense would care a fig what such shallow, bigoted creatures might think." Then she frowned. "Daniel? Have you been thinking that about *us?* Because if you have—"

"I won't lie and say it hadn't occurred to me," he said, cutting her off as hot color flew into her cheeks, a clear indication that she was about to deliver him a lecture on how "just plain silly" he was as well. "But both your mother and father quickly disabused me of the notion as it concerns them."

"And you believed them?" Brianna shot back, showing once more that she, above anyone in his life, understood him, understood everything about him.

"No, imp, I didn't. Not wholly, not at first. But I believe them now. Probably because I'm beginning to believe in myself now, believe in who I am, what I am, and feeling more comfortable in my own skin. Tell me, have your parents ever spoken to you about your father's half-niece, Lilith? She's a most wonderfully intelligent lady, and I most particularly want you to meet her while you're in London. I'm convinced you'll be great friends, imp, even if that friendship shocks all our mingled Crown relations."

"Lady Lilith?" Brianna nodded. "She would be your father's sister? Philip's sister? Mama says she's outrageous, but she smiles when she says it. I imagine it must be great fun to be outrageous."

Daniel chuckled low in his throat. "You're sitting on a stream bank, entirely unchaperoned, dressed in your brother's clothes, openly flirting with a man who has twice so forgotten himself as to kiss you, to touch you—and nearly driving that same poor man out of his mind *again.* Other than that, I don't think I'm even going to comment on that statement, imp," he said, once more remembering that he had seen a slight resemblance to his adored Lilith in Brianna's mischievous smile, in the liveliness of her bright eyes.

"You didn't think I'd play fairly, did you, Daniel?" she asked after a moment, still looking at him directly, unflinchingly. "I mean, this season in London is purely your idea and my parents' idea. No one has consulted me, asked me what I want. That's because you all still see me as a child, isn't it? You look at me and see the baby you watched being born, the little sister of the cousins you played with before you left for England. And I know that I'm still young. I still do impetuous things. But I'm eighteen—and half the girls in New Eden who are my age have been married forever and already have their own babies. I'm not too young to know that I'm in love with you, Daniel, that I'll always be in love with you. I don't care that you're not really a Crown. I go down on my knees nightly, thanking God that you're not. I wouldn't care if you were rich as a king or poor as a church mouse. I wouldn't care if you owned Enolowin or only those deerskins on your back. I don't care if you're English or American or Lenape—or a Chinaman. I wouldn't care if you were bloody *purple!* I love *you,* Daniel Crown, and you love me. And I think it's time you tell me as much. It's time you *show* me as much."

Daniel sat very still for a long time, trying to remember why he had ever believed that he could allow Brianna to take ship for London, leaving him behind, going out of his life even for a little while. Did he believe himself to be some sort of saint? Some sort of martyr? He had passed beyond believing himself to be inferior to Brianna, made an outcast by his blood, his confused heritage. He had come to America and known, almost from the first, that this was where he belonged. This place was his home, would always be his home. As long as Brianna was there to share it with him. Without her, Enolowin was simply a place. With her, it was every dream he had ever dreamed, every hope he'd ever hoped.

He closed his eyes for a moment and heard the words Lilith had written to him. *Little Savage, Little Savage, if you ever look at love, don't look away.* And he opened his eyes once more, seeing clearly, more clearly than he ever had, and saw Brianna still sitting there, looking into his face, searching his expression, hoping to see the words he had yet to speak.

Reaching into his pocket, he withdrew the heavy metal key that fit into the lock on Lokwelend's cabin door. He had carried the key with him as a talisman ever since Brianna had first flung it at him, keeping it as a constant reminder of the day he had unlocked that first door to who he was, who Lokwelend, in his wisdom, had always known him to be.

Without saying a word, for he couldn't trust his voice, Daniel put out his hand to Brianna, helping her rise with him, then lifted her high in his arms as he walked toward the log house. She laid her head against his chest, curling her slight body against him, putting all her trust in him, offering him all of her love.

Once inside, with only the dusty light coming in the open door to guide him, he reached out and pulled the old blanket from the wall, tossing it to the floor before going to his knees and slowly, gently, lowering Brianna onto it. Still on his knees, he looked down at her, saw her hair spread out on the patterned blanket, saw the love and trust in her eyes, and nearly lost his courage.

"Do you know what you're giving up, Brianna?" he asked, his voice husky, his hands shaking, fearful of hurting her, more afraid she would change her mind and leave him.

"I know where my heart lies, Daniel," she answered, raising her arms to him. "And it lies here, with you."

He released his breath on a sigh, and lay down beside her, taking her into his arms, looking deeply into her eyes and realizing that his twenty-five-year journey was over. He was home. He knew now that his home wasn't a country or a house or to be found in either of his parental heritages. His life, his love, his very existence, were all centered in this young woman's warm and giving heart, and he would gladly reside there for the rest of his life, and beyond. "I love you, Brianna Crown. I will love you forever."

His kiss was gentle, careful, as he was aware of her innocence and no longer wanted to frighten her away or punish her for having entered his mind and confused him beyond all endurance. For all the passion he felt for her, his overriding emotion was one of caring, of cherishing, of forging a union that would know its share of passion but would form its foundation on the trust she showed him, the confidence she entrusted in him, the gift she was about to give him.

Her mouth was soft and yielding beneath his, and he worshipped it with his own, even as he stroked her soft cheek, slid his fingers through the warm living flame of her hair. Her untutored hands mimicked his moves, which nearly unmanned him, and when he at last dared to slide her buttons free of their moorings, and she raised a hand to the front of his shirt, her fingertips grazing his bare skin, he had to tear his mouth from hers and take several deep, ragged breaths in order to keep his passions from exploding.

She pressed her lips against the side of his throat, whispering softly, telling him she wasn't afraid, telling him that she loved him, would always love him.

So perfect. Her breasts were so perfect. Her skin was so white, so creamy, her curves more exquisite than his most damning dreams. The swell of her breast fit his hand, lured his mouth. The sweep of her bared hip began a tight aching in his loins.

Her soft, shallow breaths inflamed him. Her hands, working inexpertly at the front closing of his deerskin trousers, burned his skin like hot irons, so that his muscles clenched, rippling convulsively beneath his heated skin.

She was moist, warm, and only shy until his hand found her, his fingers found her. And then she became silken in his arms, her long legs relaxing even as she raised her hips to him, opened herself to him.

Neither spoke a single word. There was only the dark cabin, the single spill of dusty light, the cot where Lokwelend had slept, where his beloved grandfather had dreamed and died, the lingering relics of a long-ago time, a long-ago heritage. Lokwelend had died here, and a great love was now being born here. To begin again. To live again.

Brianna held on to him tightly, her body growing more taut as he suckled at her breast, as his long strokes between her thighs raised her higher, higher. She was afraid, and he knew it. She had to be afraid of the hunger she felt inside her, the sensations that her virgin body welcomed and her mind told her were impossible. But she was brave, and he also knew that. Brave and only a little foolhardy. And she loved him. God, Brianna loved him! Loving him, she allowed him to continue touching her; allowed his mouth and tongue and teeth to caress her breasts, allowed his fingers to seek and find the very heart of her, to stroke and gently tease and finally torment her hot, wet flesh, until her mind at last gave permission to her senses and her body exploded in its first experience of ecstasy.

He didn't wait for her to lose the spiraling edge of that ecstasy, refused to indulge himself as she held on to him tightly, raining kisses on his cheeks, his throat, fiercely whispering her love, wetting his skin with her hot tears. Rising slightly, he repositioned himself between her legs and entered her, moving slowly, carefully, until she became aware of the pressure between her thighs, until she stilled in his arms and looked up at him questioningly.

"Finish it, my darling," she breathed quietly, then rewarded him with a watery smile. "You know I've always been interested in learning new things."

Her courage, her passion, her indomitable lighthearted spirit, combined to send him over the edge. He lowered his mouth, his kiss no longer gentle, and broke the last barrier between them. If she felt pain, she didn't show it, so that the only pain he could know was in his heart as he promised to never hurt her again as long as they both lived.

And then he felt her legs go up and around him, urging him to move, to take, to possess—and he was lost. He began the rhythm that also seemed natural to her as she raised herself to meet him, plunging his tongue into her mouth with every new thrust of his hips, the two of them moving as one, becoming one.

Never to be separated again.

Brianna sat on the bank of the stream, floating somewhere between total bliss and a niggling concern that the Almighty must have indulged a most odd conception of humor when he'd planned out the details of lovemaking between humans.

"Are you all right, imp?" Daniel asked, coming up behind her and dropping a kiss on her nape before sitting down beside her. He had walked several dozen yards downstream, to the other side of the trees, allowing them both privacy to bathe themselves—a consideration that endeared him to her even more—and his long black hair was still wet. He looked so elemental, so handsome, and her immediate physical reaction to the sight of him, the sound of his voice, would have shocked her if it had happened a week ago, a day ago, an hour ago.

She knew her smile was probably too wide, perhaps even silly. "I suppose I should be having a fit of the vapors or swooning or even weeping for my lost virtue. Isn't that what one of your fine London ladies would be doing right now? If so, I imagine this confirms the suspicions held by all of my many governesses, Daniel. I am a hopeless provincial and glad of it. But I am polite. Could you make love to me again, please? After all, I want to master this new skill."

"You're politely incorrigible," Daniel said, lifting her hand to his lips, turning it over at the last moment, and pressing a kiss in her palm.

"I love you, too," she shot back as she playfully pulled her hand away, feeling so alive and so very comfortable. She turned her head, looking out across the bubbling stream. "Have you noticed, Daniel? The trees are greener, the water bluer, the air sweeter. I'm looking at an entirely new world, and it's lovely, simply beautiful! And so much more exciting than any of my daydreams."

He ran his fingertips down the side of her throat, along the exposed skin above the open collar of her shirt, their easy intimacy pleasuring her. "Tell me about your daydreams, Brianna. Not that I have much hope of ever understanding all that goes on inside that inventive head of yours. Did you dream of princes and castles? My sister Johanna once confided that she had dreams of a great king riding up to Playden Court on his charger, claiming her as his long-lost princess daughter, and taking her away from her wretched prison. Of course, she was quite young when she told me this, and it was after she had been sent to her rooms for nearly setting fire to the home woods as she pretended to be an Indian maid." He chuckled aloud, the sound of his easy laughter warming Brianna's heart. "You two are going to enjoy each other, I think."

"I've often played at Indian maid," she admitted, idly picking a few small wildflowers that grew in a patch near her feet. "I've also pretended I was a white captive, like Cousin Brighid, stolen in a raid and carried off into the wilderness. I'd hide in these woods for long hours and hunt berries and weep copious tears for my lost family as I—stop laughing at me!" She gave him a cuff on his shoulder, then threw the wildflowers at him for good measure. "You did ask, remember?"

"I'm sorry, imp. We'll change the subject. Tell me instead about the day you and your brothers decided to stage a fox hunt."

Brianna shot him a quizzical look from beneath her lashes as she felt her cheeks coloring hotly. "Mama told you about that, didn't she? And blamed me for the whole of it, I suppose?"

"Perhaps you'd better tell me your version of what happened?" he suggested, still grinning. "Let's see. You'd heard about fox hunts in England and decided to have one of your own, although you were momentarily stymied by the sad lack of a fox to chase. Is that right so far?"

Brianna's lips twitched as her mind whirled back to the day of Brianna's faux-fox pas, as her father had dubbed the incident. "It was all perfectly innocent, Daniel," she began, then settled in to tell the story. "The boys, all four of them, were more than happy to go along with my idea, although Felicia considered herself too much the lady to even consider such a thing. I was about eight, I believe, which would have made Sean and Damon thirteen and Roarke and Nicholas close to nineteen—certainly old enough to have talked me out of such mischief, which they did not! You see, I felt I had to keep inventing new entertainments for my brothers so that they would include me in their adventures, Felicia being such a dull thing, always looking into mirrors and worrying over her freckles."

"It must have been a sad trial, imp, being the youngest," Daniel interjected, laughter still evident in his voice.

Brianna rolled her eyes. "You have no idea! But I'll tell you about the fox hunt anyway, just to be sure Mama didn't have it wrong. It was all very innocent, as I've already told you, or would have been if Roarke's hounds hadn't been so poorly trained."

She settled herself on the ground, her legs crossed Indian-style in front of her, and told her story. "We had no fox, as you also already know, but a hound will follow most any trail if it's laid well enough. I took that job upon myself, considering that it was my idea, and because I could run very fast. We tied a freshly plucked chicken—I, um, *appropriated* it from the kitchens when the cook's back was turned—smeared it with bacon grease, tied it to the end of a rope, and gave the dogs a sniff. Then I took off running, dragging the chicken behind me, to lay the trail."

Brianna looked at Daniel, who seemed to be having some difficulty keeping his expression suitably solemn. "The boys had promised to give me a good ten minutes' worth of head start, but they couldn't hold the dogs, who came barking and chasing not five minutes after I'd set off across the field." She shook her head. "Terrible dogs, every one of them, and brick stupid. I was terrified and too panicked to simply drop the rope—or maybe too angry. I'll never know for sure. But the trees were too far away for me to reach them before the dogs were on me—the boys whooping and hollering silly things like "Yoicks! Away!" behind me—so I did the only thing I could."

"You headed for the front door of Pleasant Hill," Daniel supplied, helping her tell her own story, "and the small luncheon your mother was hosting for a dignitary and his wife visiting from Philadelphia."

"And the starchiest man with the most *strident* wife you could imagine!" Brianna added, then began to giggle. "It was terrible, just terrible. Lucas—he was our butler then—grabbed hold of my arm as I ran through the foyer, dragging me back toward the door and opening it again after I'd slammed it shut on my way to safety, telling me he would show me, once and for all, the way *proper* young ladies closed a door. Before I could stop him, he'd opened the door, the dogs had rushed in, I had shoved the rope into Lucas's hands—and the chase was on once more."

"Ah, so that's how it happened," Daniel said, his shoulders jiggling with mirth. "Your mother said she's never been quite clear on precisely *how* the rope got from your possession into Lucas's."

"Poor man. He was so used to collecting our things as we came through the door that I suppose it simply seemed natural for him to take the rope when I offered it. Well, the dogs were going wild, barking and leaping as Lucas held the dirty, one-legged chicken above his head, and the boys were in the foyer now, too, still crying 'Tally ho,' whatever that means. Lucas shrieked and went sort of wild-eyed, you know? He took off running lickety-split, as Mrs. Bing would say, still holding the chicken high above his head, and ran straight into the drawing room. He hadn't gone more than ten feet before he tripped over one of the dogs—and the chicken flew through the air and landed in the strident wife's lap. She stood up, screeched along with Lucas, who was properly mortified, then straightaway fainted into the poor man's arms."

She had to stop a moment, to contain her giggles as her words brought back vivid memories of the scene, then continued. "Poor Lucas, who is not a large man, and the strident wife, who most certainly was, tumbled backward into the visiting starchy man's lap. Did Mama tell you that the fellow had been stuffing his face with a lovely lemon and meringue creme at the time? Well he was, and the small chair he was sitting on slowly, oh, so slowly, buckled under the added weight and . . . well, you can imagine what happened next!"

"According to your mama—who said the afternoon had been proving to be a deadly bore—as she had been pouring the gentleman tea at the time anyway, she simply looked down at the tangle of arms and legs and lemon and meringue creme the dogs were licking from the man's face and waistcoat and very politely asked if he preferred sugar."

"She did! She did!" Brianna exploded, nodding fiercely and wiping at her streaming eyes with the sleeve of her shirt at the same time. "She was wonderful and never turned a hair as she summoned other servants to help sort out the mess while she soothed everyone's ruffled feathers." She sobered then, but only with difficulty. "And then she ordered another small *conference* with Papa in his study. Not the first one and certainly not the last. But at least this time I had my brothers with me for company."

Brianna's heart did a small nervous flip in her chest as Daniel's expression also sobered. "What's wrong? You're thinking about having your own small conference in Papa's study. Aren't you, Daniel?"

"It can't wait," he told her, reaching for the hand she held out to him. "I've broken my promise to your parents, my promises to myself."

"We—we could tell him that I led you on shamelessly, lured you to disgrace by dragging a freshly plucked chicken across your path?" she suggested weakly, hoping to see his smile again.

"*We* won't be telling your parents anything," Daniel told her. "*I* will be telling them that I love you too much to wait for you to have your London season and that you have agreed that I should accompany you and your parents this fall as your husband."

"You—you'd go back to England with me? Leave Enolowin? But I overheard you that first night, telling Papa—that is, I *thought*—Daniel! Didn't you tell Papa that you'd agreed to stay at Enolowin for a year so that your father would deed the land to you? If you leave, if you go back? Oh, Daniel, after all your dreams? I can't let you do that! I won't! I don't care a fig about seeing London."

"Your parents do, and you're going—we're going—no matter what happens to Enolowin. So we'll simply have to face that particular fence when we come to it, imp," he told her as she moved close, leaning herself against his strength. "But I promise you, I knew all of this before we ever took one step toward Lokwelend's log house. I love you, Brianna. It's as simple and as complex as that."

She wrapped her arms around him, her head pressed tight against his chest. "And I love you, Daniel. More and more each moment I know you." Then she lifted her mouth for his kiss.

The passion came more quickly this time, heating her blood, melting her bones. And, although he returned her kiss with satisfying passion, Daniel did not lay her down on the grass or run his hands over her body until she went mad. He only kissed her firmly, embraced her for a long moment, and then grasped her shoulders and held her at arm's length from him.

"Not until I've spoken to Dominick," he told her, and she laughed, believing him to be joking. After all, they had already made love. What harm could it do to make love again?

"But you won't tell him we've made love? Why?"

"If I don't have to, no, I won't," Daniel answered, looking suddenly weary, so that her heart broke for him. "I don't want to involve you in that way if I can avoid it."

"And if he turns you down, thinking that Mama still wants this season for me? Will you still go to London with us if my father won't agree to our marriage?"

"It won't come to that, Brianna, I promise you. I love you and I'm going to marry you. Now."

She wanted to see a smile on his face again, needed to banish the look of concern he couldn't quite hide. So thinking, she tipped her head to one side and smiled up at him cheekily. "Yes, but what if I'm terrible to you? I can be terrible, you know. Will you still want to marry me if I'm terrible?"

"I'd want you if you were wearing a freshly plucked chicken around your neck, imp. You'll never be rid of me. But that doesn't mean that I can trust myself with you for another five minutes."

A younger Brianna—the Brianna of just a few short hours ago—would have pouted prettily at his answer, teased him again, reminded him that she had never been known for her patience. But she was not that Brianna anymore. "I understand, Daniel," she said quietly, and leaned forward for one last, lingering kiss before watching as he got to his feet. "Lenape Traveler is over there, Daniel," she said, pointing toward the tree line. "Where are you going?"

"Downstream, to throw myself into the deepest water I can find, hoping it's very, very cold," he answered shortly, already discarding his deerskin jacket and opening the buttons on his shirt. "I'm determined to keep at least part of my promise to your father."

"Oh," Brianna said softly, smiling as she watched him walk away. Then she lay back on the grass, her crossed arms cushioning her head, and smiled up at the bluer than blue sky . . .

Our disputants put me in mind
of the skuttle fish, that when he is unable
to extricate himself, blackens all the
water about him, till he becomes invisible.

JOSEPH ADDISON

chapter fourteen

Daniel rode home slowly, his mind still occupied with thoughts of Brianna. Brianna, laughing, teasing, lifting his heart to new heights. Brianna, warm and willing and eager, lying in his arms, teaching him that he had never before known the joy of true love. Brianna, sitting beside the stream after their loving, that ever-present aura of excitement hovering around her even as she sat still, as if she was waiting for something wonderful to happen.

He would never get enough of her. Never have enough time to be with her.

There were still barriers between them, but they were few and slight. He'd find Bainbridge tonight, purchase and free Marcus.

He'd go to Dominick Crown and ask him—no, *tell* him—that Brianna had agreed to become his wife. Now. Next week. Soon. Very soon.

He'd write to Philip Crown to explain that he would soon be at Playden Court with his wife, to discuss the disposition of Enolowin. A bargain was a bargain, and Daniel was ready to give up Enolowin if it came to that, to take the horses, which were his only real assets, and start over again if he had to—although he didn't really believe it would come to that. Philip Crown was a fair man, and he knew how easy it was to go to any length, dare any loss, for a great love.

And lastly, he'd learn the identity of the fine English gentleman Philip had told Dominick he'd "had in mind" for Brianna's husband. That should prove to be interesting, especially if the fellow, who was soon to be disappointed, had already been installed at Playden Court to await Brianna's arrival.

Daniel felt good, more than good. He drew Lenape Traveler to a halt on the slight rise that looked down over Enolowin from the west and watched as the late afternoon sun glinted against the side windows, warming the gray stone and sparkling white paint of the window embrasures. He could see the always busy Winifred Bing exiting the summer kitchen to dump a bucket of sudsy water into the small patch of bare dirt beside the buttery, and watched as Otto Bing lazily pulled himself along the drive, heading for the porch and his rocker after yet another long day spent avoiding as much real work as possible.

Finn was doubtless upstairs, bustling about in the master bedchamber, laying out clothing he prayed his employer would, just this one time, agree to don for dinner. And Daniel would, as his plans for the evening included not only a visit to John Payton's household but to Dominick Crown's private study. He would dress himself in fine linen for both encounters, the first for the air of sophistication it would set, the second out of respect for the man he would soon ask to give him his youngest daughter.

Daniel dismounted, having decided to walk the last quarter mile to the house, taking his time as he shifted his gaze toward the stables, seeing Skelton busy at his chores and remembering that he still had to consider the possibility that either the comte or Bainbridge had tried to destroy his horses.

But did it matter? Once their engagement was announced, and after Brianna's "trick" of this morning, the comte would probably find it prudent to move on to hopefully greener pastures. And Bainbridge? Well, if Marcus and Corliss had a chance of being together, Bainbridge would soon find himself facing a host who had tired of his presence.

Daniel really didn't care which of them had crept into his stables if, indeed, the horses had been poisoned. As long as they both left New Eden he'd be satisfied and forget them both as if neither had ever existed. As he had forgotten Addison Bainbridge before, after the man's ignominious departure from England after their near encounter in a field outside London. Philip Crown had told him more than a single time that this was a dangerous failing, this ability to cut people out of his life, out of his memory, without a backward glance, a second thought.

But Lokwelend had taught Daniel that it was wasteful to exert himself in hatred or to spend his time plotting revenge. A man of character and judgment dealt out justice when he could and forgave where he could—then moved on. This kept the heart pure, as the Great Spirit wished, and the mind open to new experience. Old grudges, Lokwelend had said, can become like old shoes, comfortable to wear, but unsightly for the rest of the world to look upon.

Daniel raised his eyes to Lenape Cliff, to the face of Pematalli, to the last resting place of his beloved grandfather. Tonight he'd read from Lokwelend's journal again, this time starting from the beginning and reading every word. Because he felt sure of himself now and ready to learn all that Lokwelend wished for him to know.

Passing by the fence that lined the small pasture

outside the stables, Daniel saw Gunitakan sitting on his haunches against a post, his small, misshapen body barely visible in the deepening shade. *"Itah,* Grandfather, good be to you. Why do you sit here? Won't Mrs. Bing feed you until you take another bath?"

The old Indian looked up at him, tears filling his rheumy eyes. "Word has come to me today from beyond the mountains. Our people move closer to *Wapahani,* to the White River, not eager to join with the Miami who would have us attack the Yankwis again. Westward, ever westward we go, soon to be lost to those who remain behind. Even Little Turtle, the great chief of the Miami, would now speak of peace. But hotter blood rules, Tasukamend. One year from now or less, and Makhiakho, the Black Snake, will have killed us all."

"Makhiakho? You mean General Wayne, don't you, Gunitakan?" Daniel asked, crouching down beside the old man. "I've heard of him before this and asked Dominick Crown about him. He's a great war chief, Grandfather. You are right to feel fear."

"I cannot go, Tasukamend," the old Indian said sorrowfully, hanging his head. "I am old and weak. I cannot go to our people. I have no sons to offer for the fight." He looked up at Daniel once more. "I thought I could make you go in my place to give me honor. But I only think that way when I drink, when I muddle my mind. I cannot drink now, Tasukamend. My heavy heart will not allow me any such peace. The path to the west has closed and I cannot travel it again."

Daniel didn't know what to say to the man. Had no comforting words for him. He laid a hand on Gunitakan's shoulder. "You will stay here, Grandfather, and teach me as Lokwelend has taught me. In my turn, I will teach my children, pass on your wisdom, your stories, the proud history of our people, as it has been passed on since the first. This is how the Lenape will live on, how you, Grandfather, will live on. In those who are still to come. Remember, Grandfather, *N'dellennówi! Lennápe n'hackey!* I am Lenni Lenape. I am of the Original People."

Gunitakan sniffed, wiped at his eyes, and visibly brightened. *"Halas!* I can do this. I know the words. I have sat at the campfire, at the feet of the elders, learning them. *Sayewitalli wemiquna wokgetaki. Hackung-kwelik owanaku wak yutali kitanitowit-essop.* At the beginning, the sea everywhere covered the earth. Above extended a swirling cloud, and within it, the Great Spirit moved. These are the first words of the Wallam Olum, Tasukamend, the words of our ancestors, telling of our creation, our travels, our greatest chiefs. I will do this. I will teach them to you."

"I will be honored to be your student, Grandfather," Daniel said, helping the old man to his feet. "Now come with me. Mrs. Bing is probably worried about you."

Gunitakan flashed Daniel a wide, gap-toothed smile as Toby ran up to lead Lenape Traveler to the stables. "She fancies me, Tasukamend," he said brightly, shuffling along beside Daniel. "Finn says she favors him, but it was I who got the second slice of cake last night. Finn is a stupid man. He does not know to give the woman pretty beads and will never get a second slice of cake. Shall I teach you about women as well, Tasukamend?"

Daniel smiled, shaking his head. "I think I'll just try to muddle through on my own, Grandfather, thank you anyway." He stopped in front of the house, intending to go inside and have himself a glass of wine before dinner, while Gunitakan joined the others in the kitchens. "Please tell Mrs. Bing there's no need to have her fussing in the dining room, as I want to be on my way to a meeting within the hour. And I'd appreciate it if you'd tell Finn to have hot water and his razor waiting upstairs in about fifteen minutes."

Gunitakan stopped, cocked his head to one side, and looked up at Daniel. "I hear the sharp snap of the bow in your voice, Tasukamend. This meeting, you do not wish it?"

Daniel smiled. "There are two of them, and I simply want them both over," he told the man, then sent him on his way and entered the house, heading for the drinks table in the drawing room. He didn't precisely *need* to seek courage in a bottle, but he wanted some time alone. To think. To find the right words that would induce Bainbridge to sell Marcus, that would convince Dominick Crown that his daughter's future was safe in Daniel Crown's hands.

He poured himself a glass and walked over to the glass doors that looked out over the gardens, mentally preparing and rehearsing the conversations he would have that evening before losing himself in a smile and memories of his afternoon spent with Brianna. It was difficult to concentrate on anything else, think about anything other than the next time he would see her . . . be with her . . . hold her . . .

He heard the front door open, turned in surprise as it then slammed shut, and saw Corliss Payton rushing toward him, her face contorted by her tears, her limbs shaky, as if she would fall to the carpet before she could reach him. He moved across the room quickly, instinctively catching her to him as she toppled forward into his arms in a dead faint.

Sliding his arms around her back, beneath her knees, he lifted her, carrying her over to the settee and laying her down, then knelt beside her, calling for Mrs. Bing even as he opened the top three buttons of Corliss's gown, trying to give her air.

He was still leaning over her when Addison Bainbridge dramatically burst into the room, followed more leisurely by the Comte de Sauville, who was daintily patting beads of perspiration from his upper lip.

"Cad!" Bainbridge called out loudly, pointing at Daniel even as the Bings, Finn, and Gunitakan gathered in the doorway, Finn still holding the chicken leg he had doubtless been gnawing on in the kitchens. "Take your filthy savage hands off my betrothed!"

The two men had followed Corliss Payton to Enolowin, of course. After doing something that was sure to send the young woman here to him. Daniel shook his head, wondering how he could have been so thick as to believe Bainbridge would go away without one last roll of the dice, one last-ditch attempt to gain his objective. John Payton must have more money than Daniel believed, or else Bainbridge was more seriously bankrupt, more desperate, than he had imagined. "Your betrothed, you say?" he asked calmly, placing a hand on Corliss's shoulder as she began to stir and tried to sit up against the cushions. "It may be crass of me to point this out, but the lady appears less than overjoyed with the arrangement."

"A most clumsy insult, Addison, but one you must doubtless seek satisfaction for, *oui?*" the Comte murmured, eying the drinks table.

Corliss reached up and tugged at Daniel's sleeve. "He—he has *sold* Marcus! And then . . . and then he went to Papa, saying I had agreed to a marriage between us. Mama—Mama is so happy. She came to me not an hour ago, telling me her plans for my wedding, and I didn't know how to tell her, what to say! Oh, please help me, Mr. Crown! You *promised* to help me!"

Daniel squeezed her hand, then slowly rose to his feet, looking toward the comte. "You now own Addison's slave?"

The comte flourished his handkerchief. "Hardly, Crown, although the notion has some merit. I believe our good friend Addison has sold the creature to some passing—what were they, Addison?—*mule* drivers? Yes, that's it. That, Crown, or something equally quaint. I believe they are already moving westward to sell munitions to those who would wish all savages like you underground."

"Want me to knock the froggie down for you, sir?" Finn asked, taking two steps into the room, flourishing his chicken leg. "It would pleasure me no end, and that's the God's honest truth."

"Thank you, Finn, but it will be enough if you go ask Skelton to saddle Lenape Traveler and a second horse and have them ready for me in five minutes." Daniel said, then turned back to Corliss, who was now sitting up, nervously rebuttoning her gown. "I'll leave immediately," he told her, adding, "this makes it simpler, Miss Payton, in the long run. I'll have Marcus here at Enolowin by morning, I promise you."

"As long as you're back by dawn, Crown," Addison Bainbridge warned, stepping up to him and smartly slapping him across the cheek, once, twice, with his riding gloves. "You have compromised my affianced bride, ripped open her clothes, and pawed her for everyone to see, and I demand satisfaction. At dawn, Crown. Atop that cliff I've heard so much about. Might as well drop where they'll bury you—with the rest of the heathens."

"Oh, well done, Addison, well done! *Tres magnifique!*" the Comte exclaimed, applauding. "I will be honored to be your second, *n'est-ce pas.*"

Daniel refused to rub at his stinging cheeks but only smiled at his adversary. "You've been longing to do that ever since I knocked you down at White's, haven't you, Bainbridge? My presence here in New Eden simply served to take the scabs off a few old wounds you would have been better to allow to heal undisturbed. Very well, since you seem to wish it so badly, I'll be happy to oblige you."

Bainbridge colored hotly, obviously incensed past any hint of prudence, and goaded on, emboldened by the comte's presence. "You have no choice, you half-breed bastard son of a whore—if you've any pretensions to being any sort of gentleman!"

"Yes, Bainbridge, there is that. We're supposed to be

gentlemen, aren't we? Tell me, have you told the comte here that he'll probably be alone tomorrow when it comes time for our meeting? And I wonder—do you have another friend here in New Eden, one who will agree to shoot at me from the trees? Or haven't you told him that this small chore might be included in his services?"

"Liar!" Bainbridge shouted, backing up a pace. "I refused to meet you because you were no gentleman—you *are* no gentleman. You're nothing but a dark-skinned, bloody savage!"

"No, Bainbridge. I'm more than that," Daniel told him. "I'm also a much better shot than the man you hired to shoot me in the back as I stood waiting for you. Before he died, he gave me your name. Both our seconds heard him. The doctor heard him. And *that's* why you were forced to leave England—not through my fault but your own. A wise man once told me never to blame others for my own failings, and I blame myself for not settling you when I had the chance. That said, I believe I owe you something, Bainbridge."

The feel of his fist as it connected squarely and solidly with Bainbridge's jaw was more than a little satisfying to Daniel. Watching the man hit the floor, sprawled on his back, proved to be equally enjoyable. "We'll choose pistols again, I imagine?" he asked as he stood over the fallen man, then looked to the comte. "See that he appears on the cliff tomorrow morning, at sunrise. No later, I warn you now, or I'll come after you instead. Do you understand?"

The comte was still smiling. Was there nothing that did not serve to amuse the man? "But who is to be your second, Crown? The rules have it that we must confer, attempt to settle the argument without bloodshed."

Daniel looked to the doorway and saw Gunitakan standing there, a sad look on his weathered face—as if he had just witnessed another feat for which his frail body had not been built, another adventure his infirmities had never allowed him. "I would be honored if my grandfather would stand with me," Daniel said shortly, and the old Indian seemed to rise up taller and straighter than he ever had before, a grin splitting his wrinkled cheeks.

Daniel wanted nothing more than to be on his way, knowing that he had to go after Marcus now, and forgo his visit to Dominick Crown's study—a thought that doubled and redoubled his anger toward Addison Bainbridge and the conniving Frenchman. Finn had already raced upstairs and returned carrying a pouch filled with coins, and Daniel tucked it in his pocket as he headed for the front door.

He hesitated only long enough to tell Mrs. Bing that she and her husband were to accompany Miss Payton back to her parents' home before he slammed out of the house, leaping onto Lenape Traveler's back from the porch steps and taking the reins of the second horse from young Toby.

Finn stepped onto the porch. "Gunitakan told me you'd be wantin' your fine clothing for this evening, sir," he called to him. "Was it someplace special you were goin'? Like up ta Pleasant Hill, sir, for a little April and May-in'? Should I be goin' there instead, to say where you're off to? Miss Brianna will be wondering, sir, if that's where you were supposed to be tonight. I could be puttin' her mind to rest, don't you know."

It didn't take more than a moment for Daniel to decide on an answer. "Tell Brianna what's happening? For God's sake, man, that's the last thing I need! I'd rather she thought I was a bastard than to have her know the truth about where I'm heading. And if you breathe a word about tomorrow morning to her, Finn, I swear I'm going to have Gunitakan scalp you with a dull spoon!"

"Brianna, would you please be kind enough to come over here and sit down? Your incessant pacing is making me dizzy," Bryna Crown complained as the click of her rapidly moving knitting needles nearly goaded her daughter into lunging across the room, ripping the knitting from her mother's hands, then tossing it to the floor and stomping on it.

But "Yes, Mama," was all Brianna said as she walked to the settee and sat down, careful not to wrinkle her favorite blue gown, the gown she had dressed in so carefully before dinner, believing she should look her best when her parents finally called her into the room to give her their blessing on her upcoming marriage.

Which she was sure they would have done if Daniel had only shown up to *ask* for her hand in marriage.

Which was an experience she was sure she would have most thoroughly enjoyed if she didn't long to throttle Daniel Crown even more than she wanted to marry him. Because he had *not* come riding up to the door of Pleasant Hill dressed in his fine London clothes, and he had not gone into her father's study to ask for her. He had not so much as sent a note saying that he had broken his leg in a fall off his horse—which would be the only reason Brianna could think of that would serve to bring her forgiveness.

And now, just to make matters even worse, her father had gone out—summoned to John Payton's farm to look for a mule or some such thing. What did her father know about finding missing mules?

It was after ten o'clock, and she was still waiting, knowing that the evening was getting away from her, the hour growing too late. Even if her father could tear himself away from the hunt for John Payton's mule. Even if Daniel at last screwed his courage up to the sticking point.

And that was another thing! Daniel wasn't a coward. Far from it. He had told her he'd be at Pleasant Hill this evening, and he would have been there if he could. Which might mean that he was sick, or dying, or . . . or . . . or that he was over at John Payton's farm, riding about in the dark with the other men, all of them enjoying themselves most mightily as they hunted for some stupid mule who probably knew its own way home but was also probably just being too stubborn to do so!

Brianna sat on the settee, her toes tapping under the hem of her gown, her fingers drumming out a nervous rhythm against her kneecaps, her angry gaze going to the clock on the mantel every few seconds, her bottom lip caught between her teeth as she bit back a frustrated scream. He wasn't coming. He wasn't coming.

Why wasn't he coming?

"What's wrong, pet?" Bryna asked, laying her knitting in her lap. "You were down to dinner an hour before the bell, yet you barely ate a thing. You stood outside until it was fully dark, as if waiting for someone to come up the drive, and now you're fidgeting like a child expecting a birthday present—or some dire punishment. Does all of this have anything to do with Daniel?"

Brianna shot her mother a startled look. "Daniel? How could you—that is, no! No, it has nothing to do with Daniel. But Papa's going over to the Paytons reminded me. I—I simply thought Corliss might visit this evening, as it has been an age since we saw her," she said, knowing she was speaking too rapidly, knowing she was close to babbling—knowing she had never been able to successfully lie to her mother. "I mean, we were the very best of friends as we grew up, and now she has been in Philadelphia this age, and then home again—but always in the company of that Bainbridge person—so that, I vow, I cannot remember the last time we were together, just the two of us."

Bryna continued to look at her assessingly. "As this is Friday, I would say it is approximately one week since you last saw Corliss at your birthday celebration. Hardly an interminable amount of time."

Brianna began toying with the ribbons on the front of her gown. "No, I suppose not," she said weakly, then stood up once more, unable to remain still. "I think I'll go to bed now, Mama, if you don't mind. Will you be waiting up for Papa? And where is the comte, not that I can say I missed him at the dinner table tonight. You'd think he'd have the good grace to find someone else to visit for a few weeks until he goes back to Philadelphia, wouldn't you?"

"Yes, pet, and your father pointed that out to him just this afternoon, as a matter of fact," Bryna told her, picking up her knitting once more. "If you could bring yourself to remain at home from time to time, you would have seen the footmen carrying out his trunks just before six to be delivered to our inn until the fellow can arrange transportation back to the city or wherever he plans to land. Whittle was most pleased to pack him up and to shut the door behind the dear comte on his way out of our lives—but, then, you'd understand that, wouldn't you?"

"Whittle?" Brianna repeated, remembering that it was the butler who had come into the room to announce Daniel's arrival just that morning, while she was playing out her mischief on the comte. Was that only this morning? It seemed so long ago! Her eyes narrowed, and she looked at her mother intently. "What did he say to Papa? What did he tell him?"

"Much more than you've told either of us, pet, obviously," Bryna answered, frowning down at a dropped stitch. "Oh, dear, I *never* do that!"

Bryna sat down at her mother's feet, then shook her head as she looked up at this woman she loved dearly. Her mother had to be bursting with questions and more than ready to fly to the aid of her last little chick, yet she had said nothing, waiting for that chick to come to her. Would she ever understand that sort of undoubtedly hard-learned patience? Perhaps when she had children of her own? No, probably not. Because Daniel wasn't coming to talk to her father, who wasn't there anyway, and she was going to die alone, a sad spinster who played the harp and painted watercolors and raised five generations of cats. "Did Whittle tell you how reckless I was and how I nearly got myself slapped for my efforts?"

"He did mention something about the comte looking daggers at you while you looked daggers back at him, yes," Bryna said, "but I don't know *why* you two had come to that point. It was enough for your father and me that you had. Whittle did, however, tell us that Daniel seemed to rout the man smartly enough when he came upon him, and your papa simply finished the job. Besides, the dear comte's dinner conversation had become more than a little repetitive on the subject of your father's supposed influence with our government, so it was much better that he leave." She smiled at her daughter. "You'll find some discreet way to thank Whittle, of course."

"I have a watercolor I painted last year that he's quite fond of," Brianna answered absently, then laid her cheek against her mother's knee and asked the first question that popped into her head—then found its way out her mouth before she could sort out why the thought had occurred to her in the first place. "Is the missing mule Papa is hunting for named Addison Bainbridge and is Mr. Payton only *wishing* he's gone missing? Are we ridding New Eden of more than one visitor today?"

The clock struck out the half hour before Bryna answered. "I've always said you were more my child than your father's. And I should have known you'd settle for nothing less than total honesty from me. So, yes, pet, your father has gone to assist the very nice but very timid John Payton in ousting Mr. Bainbridge from the cozy nest he has built himself in that gullible man's household."

"Why?" Brianna asked, rising quickly to her feet and already making another great leap of logic, believing that Daniel, as well as her father, was probably lending John Payton his support this evening. "Does this have anything to do with Marcus?"

"Marcus? You mean Mr. Bainbridge's slave?" Bryna

looked confused for a moment, then shook her head. "No, pet. I don't think so. All your father told me before he rushed off was that Corliss has unexpectedly taken Mr. Bainbridge in complete dislike, and she refuses to set a single foot outside her room until the man is removed from the house. She has locked her door, your father also told me and won't to speak to anyone. I did tell you that the child could prove stubborn, as the quiet ones often do. I'd planned for the two of us to drive over tomorrow morning to lend Susanna our support if Corliss hasn't come to her senses by then, as the poor woman must be fairly distracted. Why, she must feel as if her little lamb has suddenly turned into a tiger. I didn't say anything to you tonight because I didn't want you haring off into the night, to see Corliss."

Brianna looked down at her mother, her eyes narrowed, her heart pounding furiously. "Mama?" she asked carefully. "Does Papa ever lie to you?"

Bryna laid her knitting on the pillow beside her. "Never," she said immediately, then added thoughtfully, "but he has been known to occasionally omit a few truths that he feels would upset me . . . cause me to possibly *interfere* where he thinks I should not. Brianna, what do you know?"

"I know that Corliss is desperately in love with Marcus, for one thing, and that's why she asked her parents to allow Addison Bainbridge to visit them in the first place—so that she could continue to see Marcus," Brianna said, striding into the hallway, quickly asking Whittle if he would please have her mother's carriage brought around immediately. She walked back into the drawing room, where her mother was already standing, pulling her shawl around her shoulders. "I know that Mr. Bainbridge has refused to sell Marcus to either Papa or Daniel, who have both asked him. And I know—please don't ask why—that the comte has gone to Mr. Bainbridge just today to warn him not to sell Marcus to

Daniel when he asked today, for a second time, to buy him and free him because Corliss begged him to do so. Now I ask you, Mama, why would Corliss suddenly want Mr. Bainbridge out of the house and still be so unhappy as to have locked herself in her room? And worse—where is Marcus?"

"Run upstairs and get your gloves, pet," Bryna ordered from between clenched teeth. "It's better that you drive the horses, as you've got younger eyes to see through the dark. Thank goodness there's a full moon."

"So you agree that there might be trouble at the Payton farm?"

"I can guarantee it, pet," Bryna said tightly, brushing past her on her way outside. "And it will begin the very moment I lay eyes on that father of yours."

It was only two hours before dawn when Daniel, Marcus exhausted and silent beside him, rode up the stone lane to John Payton's sprawling wooden farmhouse, the two horses being allowed to set their own pace after a long night of riding.

"There is a lamp burning in Corliss's room," Marcus said, seeming to rally from the doldrums he had resided in for most of their journey, sure that John and Susanna Payton would turn him out of the house, out of their daughter's life. "You have freed me as best you can, Daniel, and I thank you again, but I will never be free of her. She is kindness itself, with the heart of an angel. I will go to my grave loving her."

"For quiet people, you and Corliss Payton are the most dramatic souls I've ever met," Daniel said, trying for some levity for, between Marcus's protestations of love for Corliss Payton and his repeated promises to someday repay Daniel for his generosity, their conversations until this point had been entirely too solemn. "And if you really love the woman, my friend, don't be so willing to give in to defeat. John Payton seems a fair man. At least he'll hear you out. Although I would find some way to quickly apologize for having foisted Addison Bainbridge on him all this time."

Then Daniel frowned as the drive took them past the stables and he thought he recognized Dominick Crown's horse in the small paddock, Bryna Crown's carriage pulled up in front of the fence, its horses gone. If Bryna was there, if Dominick was there, could Brianna be anywhere else?

He looked up at the sky, judging how much time he had before the sun rose, how much time he had to ride back to Enolowin, change out of his deerskins, and still meet Addison Bainbridge at the top of Lenape Cliff at sunrise. He clenched his teeth, the muscles in his jaw working as he considered what would happen if Bainbridge was inside, sitting with the Paytons and the Crowns and possibly telling them about the coming duel.

"I'll face John Payton for you, Marcus, if you face Miss Crown for me," he offered only partly in jest as they came to a halt outside the door and dismounted.

Marcus looked at him in confusion. "I don't understand. Miss Crown is a good friend. Corliss told me so. And I do not think to presume that Mr. Payton has anything to say to me or I to him. I have come back only to return your horse and to say my last good-byes to Corliss."

"Then you're a fool, my friend," Daniel said wearily, motioning for the other man to join him on the porch before he raised his hand to the knocker, "and I've wasted my time going after you. You're a free man now, Marcus, by law, but you've always been a man. And a man doesn't give in to defeat without first putting up one hell of a battle. Now—are you ready?"

Marcus lifted his chin even though he remained on the drive, his hands drawing up into fists at his side. "I'm ready, my friend. For Corliss, I am ready!"

Which was a good thing, Daniel thought a moment

later, for just as Marcus finished speaking the door flew open and there was a blur of pink-and-white striped skirts as Corliss Payton, crying and calling out her beloved's name, hurled past him and launched herself off the porch and into Marcus's arms.

Daniel stepped to one side and watched as the Paytons and the Crowns—Brianna included—followed Corliss onto the porch. They all watched in silence as the young couple knelt in the drive, holding each other close, heads buried against each other's shoulder, the two of them crying now, rocking back and forth, clearly overcome by the moment of reunion.

"Mama and I explained everything, and Mr. Payton says they may marry," Brianna told Daniel quietly as she sidled up beside him, slipping her hand into his. "She's their only child, you understand, and they would do anything not to lose her. Marcus is to take their name, if he agrees, and the Payton name will continue through him and Corliss. Why didn't you send me a note, telling me you had to go after Marcus? Do you know what I've been through tonight?"

"You and Corliss have talked, I take it," Daniel asked carefully, guiding her down the length of the porch, away from the others.

"Corliss has cried, and I've listened to her cry. Incessantly," Brianna corrected, sighing. "And now, much as I long to tear a strip off your hide, the way Mama did when she found out the whole truth from my father, I think I'm going to go home and go to bed to sleep until noon. Other people's hysterics can be fatiguing." She went up on tiptoe and kissed his cheek. "I do love you, you know. But if you aren't in Papa's study by one o'clock, I may have to do you a small injury."

Daniel couldn't believe his luck! Corliss must have been too overwrought to remember hearing about the coming duel between him and Bainbridge, much less tell Brianna about it. "Perhaps I've changed my mind, imp," he teased, giving her hand a last squeeze as he saw Dominick begin making his way toward them, his right hand outstretched in greeting, and perhaps even in admiration of a good night's work.

"It's too late for that," Brianna whispered. "You've ruined me utterly, remember?"

"You seduced me," he whispered back, still smiling at Dominick, who had been momentarily waylaid by John Payton, who was now shaking his hand and clapping him on the back, obviously well satisfied with the way things had worked out for his daughter.

"I did," Brianna admitted rather happily. "Would you like to sneak off into the trees with me when no one is looking so I can do it again? I doubt we'll be missed."

Daniel chuckled low in his throat, wondering if Dominick and Bryna would agree to a wedding this very Sunday, because there was no way he was going to be able to keep his hands off Brianna if she was going to torment him so effectively. "I've been in the saddle since suppertime, imp. But rest assured we'll discuss your idea in some depth later today, *after* I've spoken to your parents."

Dominick reached them then, and Bryna soon joined in with her husband, congratulating Daniel for a job well done and one Philip and Brighid would have been proud to witness. Daniel was then dragged inside for a half hour, where he was hugged by Susanna Payton, had his hand pumped and his back slapped by John Payton, and had his deerskins wept on by a still tearful Corliss, before he at last escaped to his horse, pleading fatigue and turning down an invitation to an early breakfast.

With the others still inside, and with a last look at Brianna, who was smothering a yawn as she leaned against the porch railing and listened to Corliss tell her, yet again, what a wonderful man Marcus was, Daniel turned Lenape Traveler toward the drive and rode off, believing he'd had a narrow escape and would be able to settle Addison Bainbridge without any interference from the love of his life, who was still blissfully innocent of the upcoming duel.

He did not look back when he reached the end of the drive, so that he didn't see Brianna looking suddenly wide awake as she gave Corliss a quick kiss on the cheek, then lifted her skirts high above her ankles as she ran toward the stables.

He who digs a ditch for others
falls in himself.

PENNSYLVANIA DUTCH SAYING

chapter fifteen

It was nearly dawn by the time Brianna tied up Freedom's Lady beside the other horses grazing at the base of the mist-shrouded hill that led up to Lenape Cliff. She had raced home on her father's mount, which she had ridden bareback, her skirts bunched up beneath her, and quickly dressed in her shirt and breeches before pushing her long auburn hair up under an old wide-brimmed hat, taking up one of Dominick's Pennsylvania long rifles, and heading out once more.

Behind her she had left a startled, sleepy-eyed groom and a weeping Wanda, who had made her promise not to do anything too reckless before wailing "Would you look at who I'm asking?" and collapsing onto the bed.

Lenape Traveler was nowhere to be seen, which didn't surprise Brianna, who knew the stallion had already been pushed to his limit last night, but there were two Enolowin horses there that she recognized. Daniel was already waiting at the top of the cliff and, as there were two rented nags also tied to the tree branches, so were Addison Bainbridge and the comte.

She had to hurry.

She looked up the grassy hill, then turned to her right, having already decided to make her way up to the cliff through the trees, where she and her rifle could take up position out of sight, but not so far away that she couldn't keep the weapon trained on the comte, who she didn't trust not to shoot Daniel in the back.

It amazed her that she was not worried that Daniel would be hurt in the duel—if it were to be an honest fight, with no tricks by either Bainbridge or the Frenchman. Her confidence in Daniel was so complete, her belief that this coming meeting was an inevitable outcome to what had been begun in England years ago so strong, that she was only angry that Daniel had chosen not to tell her about it.

Not that she didn't know *why* he hadn't told her. And it hadn't been because she'd try to argue him out of it or weep on his neck, saying she was afraid he'd be killed, but because he must have known that she'd want to be there, to be a part of the justice Addison Bainbridge had eluded for much too long.

Daniel wouldn't kill the man unless he was left with no other choice. She was positive of that. He wouldn't want the man on his conscience, for one thing, and he wasn't the sort who went out of his way to search out trouble. But Corliss had told her how Bainbridge and the comte had followed her to Enolowin after gloating to her that Marcus had been sold. Corliss also had told her about Bainbridge's absurd allegation—that ridiculously transparent, trumped-up business about Daniel having "compromised" Corliss. What utter nonsense, what a crudely heavy-handed conspiracy. Why, he may as well have called Daniel out because he didn't like the cut of his deerskins!

Yes, it was Bainbridge who had wanted this meeting, had engineered this duel, and Daniel had only obliged him. After knocking him down with a well-placed punch, of course, a thought that still brought a smile to Brianna's lips.

But to have chosen Gunitakan as his second? Truly a romantic gesture, but one so foolhardy as to be ridiculous. Gunitakan knew nothing of duels, knew little of firearms. And he could be falling-down drunk into the bargain.

So Brianna was here, where she wasn't wanted. She was here, where she might be needed. Did Daniel actually believe it could be otherwise?

Obviously not, or he might have told her what was happening this morning.

She climbed through the trees, careful not to stumble over any fallen tree limbs, turning sideways at times to avoid brushing up against any branches or disturbing any small creatures who might chatter or fly up into the trees and give away her presence. She kept her body low, as her brothers had taught her when they had played at Indian war parties in the woods, and held the rifle beside her, its barrel aimed slightly toward the ground.

Her heart was beginning to pound more rapidly than she liked, and her breathing was becoming shallow and more frequent, but she continued to tell herself that she wasn't the least bit afraid. The duel would go off as planned, Bainbridge—most probably with a hole in his shoulder—would be carried off to the doctor by his nefarious second, and Brianna would be home and in bed before her parents returned from the Paytons.

And Daniel would never even know that she had been within a mile of Lenape Cliff.

She heard voices coming to her through the mist and crouched even lower, her advance slowing, her mouth going disturbingly dry. And then, through a small break in the trees, she saw them.

Her gaze flew first to Daniel, who was standing furthermost from her, conferring with Gunitakan as the two of them stood near the graves of Lokwelend and Lapawin. He wore tight-fitting dark trousers and the footwear he had worn early in their acquaintance—the boots that held a long, sharp knife concealed inside the right boot.

"Good," Brianna breathed quietly, complimenting her beloved on his choice. She swallowed hard as she took in the rest of his appearance: the snowy white, full-sleeved shirt he wore open at the collar, his long dark hair tied back at his nape, the small beaded headband—most probably a gift from Gunitakan—that encircled his forehead. He looked tall and dark and definitely menacing. If she were Bainbridge, she would already be on her horse and on her way to Philadelphia!

Gunitakan stood beside Daniel, dressed all in deerskins and with two eagle feathers stuck into his gray hair, his expression solemn and, thankfully, sober, although the slashes of paint he'd marked across his cheeks seemed somehow sad rather than fearsome. The two of them were conferring, speaking quietly and in the language of the Lenape, with Daniel using his hands to point to the spot Gunitakan would be required to take up before the duel could commence.

Brianna sliced her eyes to her left, to where the grassy hillside began its long, sloping descent toward the horses. Her upper lip curled as she watched Bainbridge take out a large handkerchief and wipe perspiration from his forehead this cool morning, and then she smiled as she noticed the purplish bruise on his jaw, the small cut beside his mouth. Corliss had been right, Daniel had definitely knocked the man down with a fine, fine punch.

Bainbridge was dressed much like Daniel, although his appearance seemed more studied, more theatrical, his shirt of silk, his trousers less revealing of strong thigh muscles, his tall boots gaping behind his calves. This was a man who felt most comfortable in drawing rooms. What on earth had possessed him to challenge Daniel to another duel?

Then Brianna looked to the comte and saw her answer. The man's gray eyes were fairly dancing with mischief, his smiling mouth proving that he was enjoying the proceedings immensely—and would probably be just as happy if both Daniel and Bainbridge fell to the ground, mortally wounded. Is this what passed for entertainment in Paris? If so, Brianna could only hope the comte returned to France in time to see this Madame Guillotine invention she'd heard her father speak of, and she hoped the man might see it from the tumbrel as he was driven into the square to face the madame's sharp blade!

As she watched, the comte left Bainbridge's side and walked halfway toward Daniel, then stopped. "Mr. Bainbridge has suggested, sir, that you carry a knife in your right boot, for he has heard of this while you were both still in London. While I find this no end of amusing, I believe we shall have to beg for you to dispense with the naughty piece, *oui?*"

Brianna's eyes flew to Daniel. "Don't do it, don't do it!" she breathed quietly even as she moved the rifle more fully into position, wishing Bainbridge and the comte were standing closer together, cursing her position that left her able to shoot one of them but not see both of them at the same time.

Daniel gave a slight nod of his head, walked forward, and bent to withdraw the knife from his boot, handing it to the comte with a smile. "My apologies. I dressed in haste and forgot to remove the blade. May I inspect the pistols?"

"Of course," the comte agreed, and Brianna shifted on the balls of her feet once more, watching as the Frenchman retrieved a long wooden case from the ground not ten feet from where she had hidden herself. She was barely breathing at all now and feeling suddenly less certain of the outcome of this early morning meeting. "They are my own," the comte told Daniel as he stood before him and opened the velvet-lined case, exposing two long-barreled, silver-handled dueling pistols. "One never knows, does one, when such tools will be necessary in this violent age in which we live."

"Tools," Daniel repeated, picking up both pistols one after the other and hefting them, checking the barrels. "Interesting choice of words. I'll take this one if there are no objections?" he said, keeping the pistol he held in his right hand and replacing the other. "I'll load my own, from the same shot and powder Bainbridge uses, of course. You'll call out the count?"

The comte's shrug was eloquent, his voice amused as he raised it so that all could hear. "I should be speaking with your second, Crown, to see if we might avoid this distasteful business in some way. Does he understand me?"

Daniel turned to look at Gunitakan, and Brianna did as well, just in time to see the Indian spit on the ground at his feet. "I believe that was fairly eloquent," Daniel said with a similar amusement evident in his own tone, then looked past the Frenchman to where Bainbridge was still fidgeting—now running his hands down the length of his thighs as if trying to dry his palms. "Bainbridge?" he called out, his voice now devoid of humor. "I'm hungry for my breakfast. Let's get on with this. Unless you'd be willing to answer a few questions in exchange for a more peaceful settlement of our differences?"

"I see no benefit to be found in talking to a dead man," Bainbridge replied tersely, watching as the comte loaded the remaining pistol for him once Daniel was done. "Once I've dispatched you, fairly and cleanly blowing a hole straight through your heart, the comte will accompany me back to England and inform my father as to my honorable behavior. He'll welcome his prodigal, resume my allowance, and I will be free to return to London to take up the life you stole from me."

Brianna narrowed her eyes as she digested Bainbridge's words. Was all of this to gain the comte another soft landing in a gravy boat deep enough for him to swim in until the revolution was put down and he could return to France? Was all of this done for money? For a devious man's self-serving ambitions? The comte's pursuit of her, his use of Marcus, his dislike for Daniel, his manipulation of the disgraced Bainbridge—was all of it done out of pure selfishness, pure greed?

She looked to the comte, who was casually taking snuff. Yes. Yes, it was. All of it. Done for the comfort and ease of the Comte de Sauville!

Bainbridge took a deep breath, then continued, speaking quickly, almost as if he couldn't help himself. "It's all so perfect, so simple. You'll be lying here, you bloody savage, molding in the dirt, while I make my triumphant return to society. The comte promises to be most dramatic in his telling of his understanding as to how you had purposely misled me that morning. He'll tell them how you admitted to having one of your hired men calling on me early that morning with a summons that sent me off to quite another place where you had asked me to meet with you privately to talk out our differences—which left my seconds to come for me and find me gone, then be forced to apologize for my supposed cowardice. I left England, yes, but not because of any cowardice. I left because you had destroyed my good name and my father demanded it of me. My own *father* believed me to be a coward—all because of you!"

"A rather far-fetched tale, but with some merit, I agree. And your father will believe the comte where he couldn't believe you? The good ladies and gentlemen of society will believe him?" Daniel inquired politely, and Brianna saw a side of him she'd not witnessed before—a part of him that was pure English gentleman, no matter what his blood, his heritage. She felt a sudden longing to see him in London, wearing lace and jewels and commanding all the respect and attention he deserved. "You're right, Bainbridge, he must be a most convincing liar."

"Shut up! The herd will believe him because you were never one of them, not really. But you were a Crown, so they had to accept you. I watched, half-breed, and I *know*. It's one of the reasons I've always hated you."

"How strange," Daniel said quietly. "While I never really noticed you at all until you dared to speak badly of my family. I had no idea I'd so disturbed you just by being alive, Bainbridge. My apologies, I'm sure."

Bainbridge sneered. "So pure, so *honorable*. So bloody sickening! How I have always loathed you. Did you know that my mother's brother was killed by one of you? Right here, Crown, in this pathetic backwater! A good soldier, a good officer—butchered like an animal, and then scalped! You're heathens—all of you! To see you in London, peacocking in society? It made me *sick!* I bought that damn slave just to avenge myself. I gloried in owning a man, reveled in making him serve me the way all those of inferior blood should serve."

Gunitakan growled, taking two steps forward before Daniel stopped him with a slight wave of his hand. "You've yet to answer the question I had thought to propose, but your intolerance interests me greatly, Bainbridge. Please, continue. Tell me more of your plan, for surely this isn't all of it. What about the assassin who tried to shoot me down from the trees?"

Bainbridge's smile soured Brianna's stomach, as did his hateful words. "Why shouldn't I tell you the whole of it? After all, you won't be there to contradict me, will you? Before you die here today you will have confessed within the good comte's hearing that *you* had hired the assassin who shot from the trees, that you'd hired him only to dishonor me. Hired him, made him believe he was working for me, and then you shot him like the coldhearted bastard you are. Who will society believe, half-breed—a French nobleman or their memories of a man most of London accepted only on sufferance because of his relationship to the marquess of Playden? As the comte pointed out to me yesterday—with you dead, Crown, I can go *home!* I don't need that missish Payton bitch. I don't need *any* of you!"

"And my second? Obviously you couldn't afford to let him live if I were to die in our duel, not if you're going to tell such a mad story. How will you explain his death?"

"You couldn't have picked a better man to help us, Crown." Bainbridge sniffed derisively. "He's only a drunken heathen. Nobody will believe him or even ask him what happened. Besides, I wouldn't waste my time explaining anything to these pathetic colonials, these traitors. We'll be leaving for London as quickly as we can find a ship."

Daniel turned and bowed to the comte. "My compliments, sir. Your actions, however, say little for your confidence in your countrymen overcoming the revolutionaries in Paris. But, then, I've never seen you as the sort who would martyr himself to any cause save his own. You will, I assume, collect the lion's share of Bainbridge's quarterly allowance in order to assure your continued cooperation with the story you've made up for him? I'd advise you to keep him from the gambling tables, however, and I would most certainly never turn my back on the man."

"I could have liked you, Crown," the comte said, returning Daniel's bow. "But, alas, you are worth more to me dead. It's a pity I shan't be here to console your little *chérie amie.* If she had been more willing, you would not be dying now, *oui?"*

Brianna allowed the rifle to silently droop against the soft grass, her mind totally involved in the small melodrama unfolding in front of her. How could she have been so young, so naive, as to believe she could take on a mind as inventive, as deadly devious as that of the comte? She had been a little girl, playing at childish games. The comte played at more grown-up games, and they were deadly serious.

As serious as this "duel" would be unfair. And Daniel

had to know that now. Bainbridge didn't have the starch to stand across a dueling field from him. He wouldn't be here at all if he could have seen any other way to get himself back to England, back into his father's good graces—and his pocketbook. *You know all you need to know, Daniel,* her mind screamed silently. *Now just shoot Bainbridge and I'll take care of the comte!*

So thinking, she began to rise, to let him know she was here, ready to help him.

"Just one small question of my own before we begin, if you don't mind," Daniel said as Bainbridge moved forward, prepared to begin the duel—or to move closer as to greater guarantee a better shot. Brianna knelt down once more, grinding her teeth in frustration. "Which one of you poisoned my horses? It's a trifling thing, but I confess to a certain niggling curiosity, you understand. You won't allow me to go to my grave without an answer, *oui?*"

Brianna's attention was caught by Gunitakan, who had begun shuffling toward the trio of men, his crablike walk slow and quiet, his mouth busy as he chewed on something that made his cheeks bulge. As she watched, a bit of foam began to show itself at the corners of his mouth and he wiped it away, then pushed something green—a leaf?—into his already crowded mouth. She didn't know what he was doing, what he was planning—if, indeed, he was planning anything—but she felt sure that he, like she, knew there was to be no fair "duel" here this morning. They were here to see a murder, and Gunitakan certainly wasn't going to be left alive as a witness.

"You poisoned his horses?" Bainbridge asked the comte, drawing Brianna's eyes back to the other men. "Why in bloody hell would you do that?"

"It was nothing," the Frenchman said, shrugging dismissively. "At the time, I had thought the hot-blooded little chit to be interested in me and wished to eliminate any competition from our savage. I was wrong." He looked to Daniel. "The horses all should have died, you know. You're a lucky man. Or you were—up until this moment. Addison," he said, hefting Daniel's knife in his hand, "shall we drop this uncomfortable pretense and be on with it? The old man, I believe, is mine, *non?* Oh, and Crown? I wouldn't bother trying to fire that pistol. Something to do with the powder, Addison *comme il faut?*"

"Right you are, my friend," Bainbridge said, looking odiously triumphant as he dropped his own useless weapon and reached into the back of his too large boot to pull out a small, evil-looking pistol, pointing it directly at Daniel's heart. "But we made plans to cover that, I believe."

Brianna cursed under her breath and raised her rifle in Bainbridge's direction, ready to squeeze the trigger, but the comte stepped into her line of fire—to get out of the way of Gunitakan, as it happened.

For the Indian had hopped and danced into the middle of the three men, howling as if in great pain, his eyes wild, his mouth now heavily foamed, his body moving jerkily as if he had taken a fit.

"He's gone mad! Rabid!" the comte screamed, quickly dodging out of Gunitakan's way as the Indian flung out his arms and launched himself toward the Frenchman. "For God's sake, Bainbridge—shoot him!"

Bainbridge moved his aim from Daniel to Gunitakan and back to Daniel, who was standing with legs bent, his arms out on either side of him, poised to move either right or left depending on what Bainbridge did next. "I only have one shot!" he yelled to the comte. "Use the knife! Use the bloody knife!"

"Nobody moves another inch!" Brianna called out loudly, leaping to her feet and stumbling into the clearing as Daniel crouched lower and moved forward, the barrel of the long rifle all but pulling her off balance as she dragged it back and forth in front of her, aiming from Bainbridge to the comte. Her hat had fallen off and her hair hung in her face, making it difficult to see. "Everybody stands very, very still! And don't think this pathetic colonial doesn't know how to use this rifle!"

"I'd believe her, gentlemen," Daniel said as she backed toward him, wishing he'd take the weapon from her before she fell down. He reached over her shoulders and placed his hands on top of hers, then removed the rifle from her grasp. "Remind me never to go anywhere I don't want you to be, imp, unless I first tie you to a chair," he said quietly before stepping away from her, the rifle leveled at Bainbridge, who still held the small pistol in front of him, looking panicked and more than ready to use the weapon. "Bainbridge, put down the pistol. It's over."

He whispered in Brianna's ear. "It would have been over much more simply if you had stayed hidden in the trees, as I'd hoped, imp, but I'll forgive you."

"You needed me," Brianna shot back, forgetting how much she loved this man who didn't have the decency to thank her for rescuing him.

"No, I didn't, and I was none too happy to have smelled your perfume a few minutes ago. Lovely scent, by the way. But you see, Gunitakan had already muddied the waters nicely, as planned, and would have had my knife back by now while Addison and I would have been rolling in the grass, fighting over his toy of a weapon. Very clean, very simple. Isn't that right, my good comte? My honored grandfather had you quaking in your fine French hose."

"*Au contraire,*" the comte replied silkily, and Brianna turned toward him, seeing that he now held Gunitakan in front of him, Daniel's knife pressed to the old Indian's throat. "Timing is all, as you had supposed, and Miss Crown threw yours off badly, long enough for me to recover. And now it is your turn to put down your weapon. Addison, aim your pistol just between Miss

Crown's lovely breasts, if you please. There's a good fellow. What a sad muddle you've made of a ridiculously elementary plan."

Nobody moved. Addison disobeyed the comte and doggedly continued to point his pistol at Daniel, who kept Brianna's rifle leveled at him. Gunitakan, still most prodigiously foaming at the mouth, even as he spat out a mess of dark green, well-chewed leaves, mumbled something in his native tongue and Daniel grunted a rapid response. The comte pressed the knife a little closer against the Lenape's throat, warning him to be quiet and drawing a small droplet of bright red blood while he was about it.

And Brianna stood in the middle of it all, her hands drawn up into fists, counting enemies and weapons, and realizing that those numbers simply did not add up correctly unless the comte was more agile with a blade than she was ready to give him credit for being. "They need us all dead now, Daniel," she said, squaring her shoulders, a small part of her mind wondering why she wasn't screaming. "Don't give them the weapon they need to do it."

He ignored her, as she supposed he had a right to do under the circumstances. "Let Miss Crown leave here unharmed, and I'll hand over the rifle," he said, which brought a shout of laughter from the comte.

"You—you'd kill her?" Bainbridge asked, his face now pouring perspiration, the small pistol beginning to shake visibly in his hand as he directed it toward Brianna. "I don't think we can kill her."

"You don't think at all, Addison," the comte fairly purred. "That's what I find so enjoyable about you. Very well. We'll let her go. We'll let them *all* go. Then the pair of us, both near penniless, can stumble off and starve in these very woods unless they catch us and hang us before the bears eat us. Is this what you want, Addison? Is it?"

"No!" Bainbridge shouted, lifting his arm before Brianna could blink.

Brianna screamed as Daniel wasted precious moments pushing her down onto her back, then nearly flew out of her skin as the deafening sounds of the pistol and the rifle exploded around her, sending the birds above them screeching into the morning sky.

The echo of gunfire bombarded her ears, the smoke and smell of gunpowder choked her nose and throat as she lay there, her breath having been knocked out of her for only the second time in her life. She struggled to raise her head, looked down the length of her body, and saw Addison Bainbridge lying stretched out on his back, his arms and legs spread wide, a gaping hole in his chest. She would have screamed again, but she still couldn't breathe.

Gunitakan was also on the ground, having been thrown there by the comte, who was still smiling as he came toward her, the knife in his right hand, his left extended and ready to pull her up to her feet, obviously preferring to use her as his new shield—or simply to kill her, slice her throat. She began backing away from him on all fours, her limbs stiff and unwilling to move.

"Daniel. Daniel!" she shouted, still trying to gulp fresh air into her uncooperative lungs. She twisted her head around to see him, to make sure he hadn't been killed by Bainbridge's shot, and saw him rolling toward the edge of the cliff, his right pants leg already soaked a deep, wet red. *"Daniel!"*

And then, after everything in the world had seemed to happen at twice its normal speed, the world slowed down, nearly stopped.

Gunitakan rose groggily to his knees, holding his head, a look of horror coming over his face as he saw what the comte was about to do.

The comte smiled as he dropped to his knees and grabbed onto Brianna's hair, raising her slightly, exposing her neck to the knife even as she strained her head sideways to watch Daniel's agonizingly slow, end-over-end progress toward the cliff.

They were going to die. Both of them. The comte would use Daniel's knife on her, and Daniel would tumble over the cliff, unable to stop his fatal roll down the slope because of his injured leg. It was over. Before it had begun, her life was over.

She looked up at the comte, looked into his amused gray eyes. His deadly gray eyes. She barely registered the solid, sickening *thunk* of a knife burying itself nearly to the hilt in his chest. She saw it there, a solid black stem that had started a small, bloodred rose blooming on his white shirt, but couldn't comprehend how it had gotten there.

Neither, it seemed, could the comte. He still held her tightly by the hair as he looked down dumbly at the knife, then toward the cliff, before returning his gaze to her face. "How?" he asked quietly, his question echoing the one inside her head, and she watched the confusion enter his eyes even as the glow of life slipped out of them, leaving them glazed over with a milky shadow that sent a new scream building in her throat.

Brianna raised her hands against the comte's weight, pushing him away from her with all of her strength as his body went slack and heavy against hers, crawling out from beneath him, her entire body shaking in a nervous palsy.

"How?" she gasped, repeating the comte's last question as Daniel helped her to her feet. She pressed herself against him, holding on to him convulsively, gulping for air, her eyes closed tightly against the memory of the Frenchman's dying eyes.

"When I first came here, I gave a gift to an old friend," Daniel said tiredly, easing her to the ground a few feet away from the comte's body as he sat down himself, his right leg held straight out in front of him. "Today he was kind enough to give it back. Gunitakan!" he called out as Brianna tried to ask him to explain his answer. "Are you all right, Grandfather?"

"At last I am a warrior!" the old Indian shouted, doing

an impromptu dance around the comte's fallen body, Daniel's knife in his hand. "I will take this one's scalp."

"No!" Brianna cried out, burying her head against Daniel's chest. "Oh, sweet Lord, don't let him do that. Please!"

"Grandfather, leave him where he lies. He was worthless, his scalp would bring you no honor. We'll have someone gather up the bodies later. Besides, I am bleeding, Grandfather, and think I might require some assistance, if you don't mind."

Brianna had forgotten about the blood she had seen on Daniel's trousers. How could she have forgotten? And how could she help him, when she was still trembling all over like some silly, missish female who should be at home, tending to her knitting? "Here," she said, pushing away from him so that she could look down at his leg, "let me help you. Does it hurt very much?"

"It is but a bee's sting, Tasukamend," Gunitakan said from above them. "See—the bullet only ripped the cloth and flesh as it went by. Bloody, but not deadly." And then, to Brianna's surprise and consternation, he laughed. "Had the bee stung on the other side of your leg, Tasukamend, there would be no little ones for me to teach the ways of the Lenape."

Brianna, her cheeks burning, pulled her shirt free of her breeches and ripped off a long strip of cloth around the hem, wrapping its length around Daniel's thigh then pulling it taut, which earned her a grunt from her beloved—which served him right, for he had laughed right along with Gunitakan. Really! Did men have no shame at all!

"Are you able to walk down to your horse?" she asked as she helped him to his feet, keeping her eyes averted so that she wouldn't have to look at the two bodies sprawled on the grass. "Mrs. Bing is very good with wounds, you know. Roarke once tripped over a log while carrying his rifle and ended by shooting Nicholas in his—um—can we go home now?"

"Got him in the backside, did he?" Daniel asked, still chuckling, but Brianna noticed that he was looking rather pinched and pale, so that she knew the wound hurt him more than he'd let her know. "We're going to have to talk about this, you know," he went on as the three of them slowly made their way back down the sloping hillside to the horses.

"Talk about Nicholas's rump?" Brianna offered in confusion. But she knew what he was doing, bless him. Daniel was trying to turn her mind from what had happened on the cliff. Eager to oblige, she then went on quickly. "Well, he was in bed for nearly three weeks, stuck flat on his stomach with pillows stuffed under him. And Roarke had a *long* discussion in Papa's study about the—"

"I'm talking about the fact that you showed up here this morning," Daniel said, and Brianna winced, much more willing to discuss Nicholas than she was her rash actions.

"Oh. That," she answered weakly as they neared the bottom of the hill. And then she lifted her chin, deciding that she was actually more angry than she was feeling guilty about chasing after him when he clearly hadn't wanted her within five miles of Lenape Cliff that morning. "You're going to say I shouldn't have come, aren't you? Would that be before or after you apologize for lying to me?"

Daniel leaned against the side of his mount, looking down at her, his expression stern. More than stern. *Angry.* And with good reason, although he'd never hear that admission from her! "You could have been killed, you know," he told her as she offered him the reins, noticing that her hands were still shaking badly. "You could have gotten us all killed."

Brianna turned her head away, remembering those long moments of terror after she had stupidly run into the midst of four angry men, but it didn't take her long to rally. "What else was I supposed to do?" she asked, glaring up at him, her fists pressed against her hips. "I thought you were going to be shot. I'm not Corliss, Daniel. If I had loved Marcus, I would have gone after him myself—not waited for someone else to rescue him for me. And I certainly was not going to go home to my bed like a good little girl, waiting for someone to bring me word that the only man I will ever love had been shot down in a duel—and most likely shot in the *back!* I still can't believe you even consented to *meet* Addison Bainbridge, after the way he tried to have you killed the last time. And I wasn't there to *stop* the duel. Not precisely. I was there to make certain it was a fair fight. And it wasn't. Now, what's wrong with that?"

Daniel reached up a hand and rubbed at his forehead. "You knew about our first duel? Oh, yes—you'd already got that information out of me, hadn't you? I'd forgotten. Christ, Brianna, if you knew what I was going through up there, trying to get Bainbridge to talk, trying to keep the comte occupied, knowing he was standing close enough to you to smell your perfume if the wind changed even a little bit—"

She laid a hand against his chest, her eyes stinging with unshed tears. "Oh, Daniel, I'm so sorry! I'm everything everyone has ever said about me. Incorrigible. Impulsive. Childish. And so bloody sure of myself. I went up that hill today fully believing I could save you from those two monsters. *Me!* Just me and my rifle! And look at me now. I'm still shaking all over and will probably have nightmares for weeks, seeing the comte hovering over me, ready to kill me. I couldn't move, Daniel! I just lay there, waiting for the knife. Gunitakan's got a bump the size of one of Mrs. Bing's best layer's eggs on his head, and you've been shot! How *stupid* can one person be? If you were very, very smart, you'd stay as far away from my father's study as you can—and twice as far away from me!"

"You're probably right," Daniel said solemnly, nodding. "What could I possibly want with a woman who loved me so much she was ready to kill for me, was willing to die for me? I can't imagine."

Brianna cocked her head to one side, looking up at him, seeing that his mouth had begun to twitch at the edges, and her heart gave a small leap in her chest. "You're going to forgive me, aren't you, Daniel?"

"That depends. Will you forgive me for not telling you I was going after Marcus last night? Will you forgive me for not being honest about where I was going this morning? Because I know now that I never should have tried to keep secrets from you. It isn't fair, for one thing. And," he added, running a hand over her hair, drawing his fingertips down the side of her cheek, "you'll find me out anyway and make my life a living hell. Isn't that right?"

She didn't bother giving him an answer he already knew. "I've won the shooting contest at the New Eden Fair three years in a row," she told him instead, turning her face into his palm, pressing a kiss against his flesh. "I'm bragging again, I'll admit, but I wanted you to know that I didn't go up onto that cliff with only a wild idea and no way to really help you." She looked up at him, her eyes dancing, amazed that her body was no longer trembling. "That's also probably a warning, just in case you may have decided not to offer for me again after all."

He looked down into her face, his gaze intense enough to curl her toes inside her boots. "How long will it take to get a priest to New Eden, imp?"

Brianna smiled, biting down on her bottom lip. "About as long as it will take for Mrs. Bing to have you up and around on that leg, I imagine. A week?"

"No more than that," Daniel warned, wincing only slightly as he swung his injured leg up and over the saddle, then waited as Brianna and Gunitakan mounted as well. "Not a day more."

"My, you mean that, don't you, Daniel?" she teased,

moving Freedom's Lady forward so that they could ride side by side.

He urged his horse toward the roadway that led back to Enolowin. "I don't like being shot at, I've discovered, and if I haven't made an honest woman out of you within a week, your father will be taking aim at me. More than a week, and I'd have to worry that you'd be the one coming after me with a rifle. You did say you're handy with a weapon, didn't you?"

"Three years in a row," she agreed happily, amazed at how bright the sun looked this morning now that it had burned off most of the mist and turned the dew-wet grass to sparkling diamonds.

"But not a fourth," Daniel warned, urging his horse forward into a fast trot. "I'm certain I'm the better shot."

Brianna dug her knees into Freedom's Lady's sides, riding after him, her heart light, her whole world colored with hope and love and just a little bit of mischief.

"Not so fast, Daniel Crown," she called out to him. "Perhaps we ought to have a small contest . . ."

moving Freedom's Lady forward so that they could ride side by side.

He urged his horse toward the roadway that led back to Innsbrook. "I don't like being cheated. I've discovered and if I haven't made an honest woman out of you within a week, your father will be taking aim at me [illegible] a week, and I'd have to worry that you'd be the one coming after me with a rifle. You did say you're handy with a weapon, didn't you?"

"Three weeks in a row," she agreed happily, amazed at how bright the [illegible] looked this morning now that it had [illegible] in the dust and turned the dew-wet grass to sparkling diamonds.

"But not a fourth," Daniel warned, urging his horse forward into a fast trot. "I'm certain I'm the better shot."

Brianna dug her knees into Freedom's Lady's sides, riding after him, her heart light, her whole world colored with hope and love and just a little bit of mischief.

"Not so fast, Daniel Crown," she called out to him. "Perhaps we ought to have a small contest . . ."

epilogue

the vow

Come live with me, and be my love,
and we will some new pleasures prove . . .

JOHN DONNE

Slow but sure moves the might of the gods.

EURIPIDES

epilogue

Brianna laughed as she listened to Joseph and Michael Crown arguing over which one of them she had promised the next Scottish reel as she stood alone at the edge of the ballroom floor, fanning herself while trying to locate Daniel's tall frame in the small crowd of tall Crown men huddled together on the far side of the room.

He looked so handsome in his fine London clothes, just as she had known he would, and she had already decided that she was the envy of every woman in attendance this evening because *she* would be going home with him when the ball was over. Once they were back in their suite of rooms at the marquess's London mansion, Daniel would dismiss Wanda and then help her off with her lovely pearl necklace and ease her out of her gown as he moved her slowly toward the bed, whispering to her in French, in English, in the curiously seductive words of the Lenni Lenape. Oh, yes! If these fine London ladies only knew how very much they should be envying her!

And how wonderful it was to be in London at last,

although she hadn't minded the postponement of their trip until the early spring so that her four brothers could accompany them. She had been much too happily occupied in settling in at Enolowin, learning the joys of being a wife.

But Daniel had been right. She *adored* London. It was gay and happy and full of wonderful things to see, interesting people to meet. Most intriguing of all had been Philip and Brighid Crown, the marquess and marchioness of Playden and, of course, Lilith and her dear Cholly. She found Daniel grinning at his beloved Lilith from time to time, shaking his head as if still unable to believe that she was now tolerated—if not yet precisely *welcomed*—into society as the countess of Bexford.

Brianna and Daniel had yet to travel to Sussex and Playden Court, as they had come straight to London three days ago, but there would be time for that. There would be time for everything now, long, lovely years stretching out ahead of her with Daniel by her side. There would even be another wedding ceremony at Playden Court so that Philip and Brighid could be there to hear their vows. The Lenni Lenape, Daniel had explained, had no wedding ceremonies, and husbands and wives stayed together only as long as it pleased them. But Daniel wanted all sorts of ceremonies, and Brianna was more than happy to agree.

She looked his way again as Joseph—grinning widely, obviously having won out over his brother—took her hand and fairly dragged her out onto the dance floor as the musicians began sawing on their violins. Daniel was placing a long, flat packet inside his waistcoat, and his expression seemed to hover somewhere between bewilderment and joy even as Dominick and Philip Crown threw back their heads, their hearty laughter coming to her across the room.

"I think I should go to Daniel," she told Joseph even

as they lined up to begin the dance. "It appears that something has happened."

"My brother can wait his turn," Joseph told her, also looking toward the small group of men. "I know what it's about, and everything is fine, I promise you. Besides, I've already pledged Michael the loan of my new carriage for a week in order to have this dance, so you can't leave me standing here, now can you?"

A new bubble of laughter escaped Brianna, who then agreed that she most certainly couldn't disappoint Joseph now, and she threw herself into a full enjoyment of the dance.

"Did you enjoy yourself, imp?" Daniel asked as he watched the door close behind a muttering Wanda, then turned to help his wife with the clasp on her necklace. "I imagine so, as you and my mother were whispering and giggling together in the carriage all the way back here."

Brianna turned in his arms, raising her hands to begin loosening his neckcloth for him and he smiled, knowing how their already pleasant evening was bound to end. "I adore your mother, darling. And she tells the most delicious stories about the days she and my mother were young together in Ireland."

And then, before he could know what she was about, Brianna had snatched the packet from his waistcoat and run across the room to the bed, launching herself onto it as she held the folded pages in front of her, demanding to know what they were.

Daniel pulled off his neckcloth, sliding the material over the back of his neck, then tossing it in the general direction of a chair he'd remembered seeing in the room as he walked over to the bed, already stripping off his snugly fitting evening coat. "My father has been full of surprises, it seems," he began explaining as he joined her on the satin coverlet. "You'll remember our wedding present, I suppose?"

Brianna nodded, still holding the packet out of his reach, as if he might snatch it back from her. "The deed to Enolowin, made out in your name when you were little more than a baby. It's one of the reasons I adore the man. He never told you about it, wanting you to have the freedom to make up your own mind as to where you wanted to live, where you belonged. I can't believe Papa knew about the deed all along and never told me. Of course, this is also the same man who, when you finally had that meeting in his study and demanded we be allowed to marry, greeted you with the words 'I'm only surprised it took you so long, son.' Honestly, Daniel, I never knew men were so devious or so closemouthed about secrets."

"Neither of them told us about Lokwelend's dream, either, imp," Daniel said, lightly tugging on her legs, moving them forward so that he could ease off her dancing slippers. He'd leave her hose alone, for he liked the feel of the sleek silk as she wrapped her legs around his back. "Wouldn't you be more comfortable out of that gown?"

"Lokwelend's dream?"

Daniel busied himself unbuttoning his waistcoat, shrugging it off his shoulders. "If you'll remember, your father told me that mine already had a suitor in mind for you. I asked my father the man's name this evening, on the off chance he might be at the ball. He was."

"Who?" Brianna asked, and he could see her mentally considering all of the gentlemen she had encountered that evening and dismissing them one by one.

"Me," Daniel answered as the waistcoat hit the floor beside his already discarded jacket, both probably to be wrinkled messes by morning. Ah, well, Finn was always after him to give him something to keep him busy. The least he could do was oblige the man. "My father had written that particular letter to yours when he found out you were coming to London and before I told him I was leaving for Enolowin. Open the packet, Brianna, and you'll understand. It contains a letter from Lokwelend, his last letter to me. He'd made my father promise to give it to me after you and I were married."

"After you and I—?" Brianna opened the packet with trembling fingers, still looking at Daniel, then carefully unfolded the dry, wrinkled pages. She read the words aloud:

"'*Tasukamend, my Son,*

Itah! Good be to you! Good be to Wapa-Kwelik, who is your own Dawn Sky!

Long ago you came to me, a gift from the Great Spirit and the Nipawi Gischuch, your mother, the one who is the Night Fire. You were the comfort of my old years, the promise of a thousand tomorrows. And then the Great Spirit further honored me with the gift of a great dream. I saw Wapa-Kwelik in that dream, saw her walking toward you out of a rising sun, straight and strong, filled with courage, with love. I told my friend Crown of this dream long ago, told Tauwún, your good father, Philip, of this dream, even as Bryna Crown still carried her first daughter under her heart.

I well remember the dream, the words. The Bright Fire, I told my friend Crown, will be mother to a girl child before the first snow. I will bounce this new little one on my knee, as I did your sons, as I will the sons and the daughter yet to come. I will see that last child before I go. I will look down at the comfort and torment of your old age, my friend, and she will be the Bright Fire born again. I told Tauwún what I had seen, that you, Tasukamend, had much to look forward to and much to fear.

Because you are reading this while I sleep, I know that you have conquered your fears. You have destroyed those born of the dark past who would harm you. And you have the Wapa-Kwelik by your side, with her courage and her great love. The Great Spirit has promised.

I have given Crown a gift you will have now, the pretty face the Bright Fire gave me so long ago, which I have worn all these years. It is right that you now give that face to Wapa-Kwelik. It is good these things stay in the family.'"

Daniel reached into his trouser pocket and pulled ou a small, perfect cameo that hung from a long gold chain "I knew this the moment I saw it again. Lokwelen always wore it around his neck," he told Brianna clearing his husky throat, for hearing Lokwelend's word from beyond the grave had stirred his emotions. "Domi-nick gave it to me tonight, when my father handed ove the packet."

"It's beautiful," Brianna whispered, taking the came of a young woman's face from him and pressing i against her breast as a single tear rolled down her cheek "Please—read the rest of Lokwelend's letter for me. I-I'm having trouble seeing the words."

Daniel took the pages from her and began to read although he already knew the letter by heart, havin gone off by himself during the ball to read it over an over again.

"'Have you read the books I left for you, Tasukamend? The great chief Euripides said many wise things. I tell you one of them now. Who knows, the great chief said, but life be that which men call death, and death what men call life? We none of us know until we are sleeping, Tasukamend, but I have thought about the wise chief's words and would ask of you one last gift. Take the markers from my sleeping place, my son, and from that of Lapawin, the old one you called grandmother. We are free now, as you are, to live. With Pematalli, we are Always There, Tasukamend. Through you and others like you, we will always be there. Again, my good son, itah!'"

Daniel heard the rustle of silk as Brianna leaned forward, sliding her arms around his shoulders. "You were very lucky to have had Lokwelend, darling, if even for so short a time. I wish I could remember him, although it seems he had always known everything about me. About all of us." She pressed her head against his, so that the perfume in her hair teased at his senses. "I love you, Daniel Crown. *K'dahólel,* Tasukamend. I love you very much."

Daniel folded the pages carefully and placed them on the chest that stood at the bottom of the bed. There were still things Daniel had learned tonight that he had not shared with Brianna. He had heard the history of Addison Bainbridge's uncle—the man Lokwelend had referred to when he had written of those "born of the dark past" who had come to New Eden thirty years earlier, for one. He had learned of the violent fate of that same dangerous, ambitious man, Lieutenant Renton Frey, at the hands of Brianna's own father, Dominick. But it was a story that was not his to tell, and probably best forgotten. The circle was complete now, all the demons of the past banished, all the gods satisfied. It was time to put that past away, for him, for all of the Crown family, and get on with what promised to be a bright future.

He took one last, deep breath, clearing his head, and turned to Brianna, pushing her down onto her back on the bed. "There's still one thing that troubles me, imp," he said, using his lips to nudge her gown from her left shoulder.

"What's that, Daniel?" she asked, raising her body slightly so that he could reach behind her and undo her laces.

He raised his head, smiling into her face. "Lokwelend knew we'd marry," he told her. "Your father knew. *My* father knew. And, if they knew, so did our mothers. Wouldn't you have thought one of them would have been merciful enough to have told *me?* Think of the time and trouble it would have saved us."

Brianna's smile lured him closer as his concentration began to center on her full, lush lips. "*I* told you, Daniel," she said, running her hands beneath the fine fabric of his shirt. "In every way I knew how. I yelled, I teased, I plunked myself down at Enolowin so that you couldn't move two paces in any direction without tripping over me! I chased you. Why, according to you, I even *seduced* you!"

He nipped her bottom lip with his teeth, beginning what was sure to be a long night of loving. "You're right, imp, you did. And you know," he admitted happily as she tried to bite him back, "I do believe I like this last way best of all."

afterword . . .

There exists in North Whitehall Township, Pennsylvania, looking west over Ranger Lake, a rugged limestone cliff face that partially washed away during heavy storms in the autumn of 1993, leaving a hauntingly striking outcropping resembling the face of a Lenape chief. I saw a photograph of that strong, proud face in the September 23, 1993, edition of Allentown's newspaper, *The Morning Call,* and the image haunted me.

I gave this image a name, Pematalli, which means Always There. I kept the photograph beside me as I researched and wrote *The Homecoming* (Dominick and Bryna Crown's story), *The Untamed* (Philip and Brighid Crown's story), and *The Promise,* the book you have just read. I tell you this, dear reader, in the hope it may give you just a little insight as to how dreamers dream and why writers write.

Also: In the year following this fictional story, 1794, General "Mad" Anthony Wayne, known as Makhiakho (Black Snake) by the Lenape, advanced into the area we know now as Indiana, bent on clearing the land of

Indians and opening it to settlement. The great Miami war chief, Little Turtle, did indeed try to open peace negotiations and prevent a war, but his proposal was defeated and he was deposed.

Wayne set out after the outnumbered, badly supplied Lenape and other combined tribes and found them in a forest that had been destroyed by a tornado. The engagement that followed has become known as the Battle of Fallen Timbers and ended in the last great defeat of the Lenape and the entire Delaware Nation.

From that time on, the Lenape were pushed ever westward to the far side of the Mississippi, to Texas, to Kansas, to Oklahoma. A once great nation of proud people nearly disappeared, forbidden to own the fields and meadows they had claimed for untold centuries, denied by law to hunt the deer and other animals they needed to survive. By the mid 1840s, the United States had made good its boastful claim of Manifest Destiny, extending its power from one coast to the other, and the Lenape became strangers in their own land.

But the Lenape are not gone. They live on in Oklahoma, in Kansas, in Wisconsin, New York, and Canada. And in Pennsylvania a few Lenape remain, living their lives, celebrating and teaching their proud heritage.

As Lokwelend had seen in his dreams . . . and as Pematalli watches.

Itah!

POCKET BOOKS
PROUDLY PRESENTS

ESCAPADE

KASEY MICHAELS

Coming Soon
from Pocket Books

The following is a preview of
Escapade. . . .

After a night of deep drink and gambling, Simon Roxbury, Viscount Brockton, was weary and more than eager to return to his London mansion and his bed.

He waited patiently as his servant opened the door of his coach, gave his friends a smart salute as they stood back on the flagway, telling him to have a safe ride home, then pulled himself forward into the coach . . . to find himself face to face with a loaded pistol.

"Sit down, sir, and tell your coachman to drive on," the dark shape behind the pistol ordered in a gruff but unmistakably female whisper.

Simon turned his head, looking back out the door to where his footman and his two friends still stood not five feet away, oblivious to his predicament.

"Don't do it, I warn you, or I'll blow a hole straight through your head and laugh as your brains splatter all over this coach."

"How unpalatable," Simon said quietly, his mind already dismissing the thought of being shot in order to concentrate on *not* being shot.

He could probably let go of his two-handed grip on either side of the doorway to the coach, propelling himself backward onto the flagway as the bullet went whizzing harmlessly over his head and straight into the door of the gaming hall he had so recently vacated. Probably. But, as the pistol was rather heavy, and its holder noticeably nervous as she struggled to hold it with both hands, he could also end up being shot dead before he hit the ground.

"Very well," he said quietly, so that his friend Armand Gauthier, who was just then listening to Bartholomew Booth telling him that tardiness was a deplorable practice he could not condone, would not hear him and investigate. "I'll sit down now, if you'll withdraw that evil-looking toy a bit, madam?"

"It's not a toy, and I would prefer you did not call me madam, for I am no woman, sir," his captor responded as he levered himself into his seat across from her and the door closed behind him, locking them together in the darkness. "Now, order your coachman to drive on."

"Of course you're not a woman," Simon agreed as affably as possible. It was always best, he believed, to humor lunatics—at least until they were disarmed. "How could I be so blind? You're a regular brute of a fellow, aren't you? Pity that you've been cursed with the voice of a young girl not yet out of her teens. It must prove no end of sorrow to you. With that thought in mind—isn't it time all incorrigible young children were home and tucked up in their cots?"

"Your death would give me no sorrow at all," she said, even as he noticed that his assailant's clog-clad feet did not quite touch the floor of the coach.

Cheeky little brat! he thought, longing to reach across the space dividing them, snatch up the pistol, and then tan the infant's backside with it. He could disarm her in an instant . . . less than an instant. All he had to do was remain passive, keep his smile intact, and then . . . His smile never wavered, even as his plan did the moment he heard the pistol being cocked.

"I said," his captor repeated, "order your coachman to drive on. And wipe that odious, condescending grin off your face, if you please. This is a serious business."

"Oh, yes, quite. I can certainly see that," Simon agreed, even as his brain registered the sound of Armand's coach being drawn around his and heading off along the street. He weighed the possibility that he was about to have a rather large hole blown in him by a perfect stranger against the curiosity he felt concerning the reason behind this ludicrous assault. Curiosity, which had been leading from the moment this little adventure had left the gate, won by several lengths. "Very well, my fine young brigand, I'll do as you ask. But only because I am amused—for the moment."

He leaned forward, causing the "young brigand" to quickly shift to the corner of her seat—the pistol still cocked and pointing in his direction—and opened the small door giving access to the coaching box. "Hardwick," he called out sharply, "you and I will be having words on the morrow concerning the depth of the devotion in which you hold your esteemed employer. I believe, you must understand, that a certain lack of vigilance on your part may have served to land that employer in an exceedingly undesirable position."

"Beggin' yer pardon, m'lord?" Hardwick asked, his florid face appearing in the small boxy opening in the roof of the coach. "Oi don't know as ta wot yer talkin' about, m'lord, by the 'oly, I don't."

"That's reassuring, Hardwick," his lordship responded genially, slanting a look toward his captor, who was now no more than three almost effortlessly breached feet away from him; the pistol, a mere two. And it could be easily grabbed—if he were still so inclined. He was not. The pistol was cocked, and the chances of one of the pair of them being shot quite dead were high. Daring was one thing, red-brick stupid was quite another. "Otherwise, Hardwick, my good man," he continued, "I might be forced to believe you to be disloyal."

"Would you stop prosing on like some vacant-headed ninny and just *tell* him!" the intruder whispered fiercely, waving her pistol, rather wildly, Simon decided, beginning to feel some genuine concern for his anxious captor's obviously volatile nerves.

He again mentally measured the distance between himself and the barrel of the pistol. No. It really was too much of a gamble. He was a man who chose his odds carefully, and in this case they were decidedly against him. "Patience, my sweet kidnapper. We shall be on our way anon. Do you have a particular destination in mind, or will I be forced to bother dear, obtuse Hardwick a second time?"

"Order him to drive toward Hampstead Heath. There's an inn there, the Green Man. Do you know it?"

"That I do. And green I would be, indeed, to venture anywhere near that den of thieves after dark. Can't you think of some place closer to town, and with some semblance of safety?" Simon sighed theatrically. "Ah—there you go, waving that pistol again. It's prodigiously distracting, you know. Oh, very well. Hardwick," he called out, "to the Green Man, my good fellow. And make haste. I've a sudden urge to be relieved of any worldly possessions I might have upon my person."

He then sat back against the squabs once more, crossed one leg over the other and both hands across his chest as the coach moved off over the cobblestones.

"Happy now, my dear?"

"Immensely so, my lord, if you must know," his kidnapper replied in a rather appealingly husky voice—much more interesting than her purposely gruff whisper—then said nothing more for a long time—until Hardwick had driven them free of the city, as a matter of fact.

Simon also kept his own counsel, although his mind

was far from quiet. He was wondering, as it happened, how on earth he would ever live down being robbed by a mere girl if the news were ever to become public knowledge. A gentleman did, after all, have his reputation to consider.

Besides, it was late, and he was mightily fatigued, and possibly even bored. No, he was most definitely bored. This realization of his rather incomprehensible reaction to the grave danger he might be in was enough to keep him awake for a little while but, after a bit, surprised at himself as he was, the gentle movement of his well-sprung coach actually lulled him into a light slumber.

He might even have snored.

"Aren't you in the least interested in why I have abducted you?" she asked at last, chagrin evident in her tone, anger more than evident in the force behind her hard kick to his shin.

"Truth be told, not particularly," the earl answered honestly, yawning as he fought to come fully awake. He had been gambling and drinking rather deeply for several hours, and yearned more for his bed, frankly, than he did for information. "But I rest easy in the knowledge that you will tell me everything I need to know in your own good time. That will be soon, won't it? I long for my bed, you understand, scintillating as your company has been this past quarter-hour or more."

"God, but you're insufferable!" She directed another kick at him. "I could shoot you now, just on general principles."

Simon resisted the impulse to rub at his now twice-insulted shin, for clogs were a considerable weapon. "I'd be more comfortable if yours was a unique statement. However, since it is not, I suppose I should spend the next few days in deep reflection, considering how I have so abused my fellow man—and woman—as to have been termed insufferable so often, by so many. Is there perhaps an organized group of you? Do you hold meetings? Keep minutes? I could peruse them, learn to pinpoint my more gross failings—if I am not shot dead before sunrise, of course."

"Oh, just shut up!"

"So sorry," he said, wondering how much longer the young woman could hold on to the cocked pistol without it going off. "Consider me a monk, sworn to a vow of silence."

The whole time he spoke and, indeed, for much of the time he'd spent in the coach, Simon had been cursing the darkness that kept his captor's face and form hidden from him. He had, however, been able to deduce that she was not at all tall, fairly slim—and that she smelled of lavender water and horse. Not an entirely unpleasant combination, but one he hadn't expected. Her accent was cultured, educated, with only a hint of the country miss—one blessed with any number of brothers who had taught her manners, words and expressions she should not know—which was also confusing to him. Not being in the habit of seducing innocent country maids, he could think of no woman who would wish him injury or death.

Which left him with the notion, not too odd, that he was being driven into the countryside to be handed over to yet more kidnappers who would then solicit a ransom from his sure-to-be-appalled mother, the Viscountess Brockton. His mother would be horrified, frightened, and as scatterbrained as was her custom, which would probably also mean that he would be at the mercy of his captors for at least a week before the Viscountess recalled the location of the Roxbury family solicitors and gained access to the funds required to free him.

Of course, that also meant he would miss Lady Bessingham's bound-to-be crushingly boring rout, which couldn't be considered entirely a bad thing. . . .

His captor pushed aside a corner of the coach's leather curtain and peeked out into the countryside, just then beginning to grow light with the coming of yet another damp English dawn. *Rain's a curse,* he remembered

Bartholomew saying. When was that? An hour ago? A lifetime ago?

She let the curtain fall back into place. "We're nearly at our destination, so I suppose it is time I got on with this."

"Got on with this?" Simon repeated, a small part of him at last beginning to take the evening's adventure seriously. "Would that mean that you are going to hand me over to more kidnappers, or that you are simply going to shoot me and run off with my coach? Be gentle with Hardwick and the footman, I beg you. They may put up a slight protest in concern for their master, and I wouldn't wish them injured in any way."

"Kidnappers?" The girl's tone was incredulous, and Simon exercised his jaw muscles, wishing he had exercised them less a moment earlier. Clearly the girl had not considered kidnapping, or ransom. Had he now put that idea into her head? And was that idea better or worse than the one that had instigated his abduction? "Good God, man, I wouldn't want you in my company above another ten minutes. Why on earth would I want to hold you for ransom?"

"Then you do plan to shoot me," Simon said, his relaxed pose belying the fact that he was fully prepared to launch himself across the space separating them and wrench the pistol from her bound-to-be tired grasp. "But you hadn't planned to do that just on general principles, if I remember correctly. Which means you have a definite reason for this small travesty. Would it be too much if I were to ask you to explain yourself?"

The pistol remained steadily pointed at his chest, perhaps even a bit more steadily than it had the past thirty minutes or more. "At last you're interested? I had begun to think you hadn't a brain in your handsome skull for anything more than how best to fuzz a card!"

Simon grinned, relaxing once more. Clearly the chit wanted to talk much more than she wished to shoot. "My handsome skull? Oh, you do flatter me, madam.

Please go on. But first, what's this about fuzzing cards? I assure you, madam, that Viscount Brockton is known for many vices, but cheating at cards is not amongst them. Why, I do believe I may choose to feel insulted—although that mention of my handsome skull has dulled the pain somewhat."

He watched as the pistol drooped slightly, then was righted. "Viscount Brockton? What the devil are you talking about? Who is Viscount Brockton?"

"Well," Simon said, smiling as the dawn broke over his predicament, if not the world at large—and definitely not over his companion's confused head. "Do I detect a small problem here, young lady? A trifling complication, perhaps? Yes, I believe so. And, in that case, please allow me to introduce myself." He held out his hand, not for a moment believing he was about to have the pistol placed in it. "I am Simon Roxbury, Viscount Brockton, of Sussex and Portland Place—and various other places in between, which I will not bore you with at the moment. Now, your turn. Whom did you think I was?"

But his captor didn't appear to be listening. Instead, she was muttering something that sounded much like, "Of all the cork-brained, numbskulled, *idiotic* . . . how could I have been so wrong? The crest was his, I could have sworn it!"

"The crest?" Simon interrupted, preferring to keep the young lady more focused on the moment at hand and not the pistol that she held. One never knew what could happen to an untended firearm, after all. "Are you referring to the crest on the doors of my coach, by any chance?"

"I—I—*what?*"

"Force yourself to concentrate, my dear brigand, if you can," Simon said affably. "Or, as I believe I understand what has transpired here this night, allow me to explain. You came to Curzon Street this evening in search of someone—some awful, terrible person who has done you or one you love a considerable injury, possibly pertaining to card-playing—and then crawled into entirely the wrong coach. Do I have the series of events correct so far? Although I still believe I'll be having a small talk with Hardwick, who has proven to be a weak link in the impenetrable defense I incorrectly assumed I had built against being brought face to face with a loaded pistol. And just think of the wear and tear on my horses! Why, I do believe I should be much angrier than I am."

"Would you *stop!* You're making my head ache!" The pistol sagged again, now being supported by just a single small hand, as the other was involved in rubbing at the young woman's temples. "I planned, and planned, and screwed up my courage to the sticking point—and for what? To end up talked to death by this idiot? Oh, *now* what do I do?"

Simon leaned forward, only slightly, just enough to be faintly intimate, not enough to be threatening. "If I could brook a suggestion," he said kindly, "I would say you might begin by lowering your weapon?"

The pistol was once more held between both hands, once more directed at his heart. "I think not, my lord," the young woman said cuttingly—and still in that so strangely appealing husky voice that hinted of darkened bedrooms and earthly delights, even while speaking of blood and mayhem. "I've no great desire to end this night hauled away to the gaolhouse and clapped up in irons."

"Clapped in irons? Oh, foul, foul! As if a gentleman would do such a thing!" Moving very carefully, Simon reached to his right and dropped the curtain, letting in the first light of dawn so that it could reveal the earnestness of his expression. "There has been no crime committed, I assure you. Why, I often end my evenings by ordering my coachman to take me for a relaxing drive in the countryside. Truly."

"Don't be nice to me!" his captor shot back angrily. "I

don't like you even a little bit, and I certainly don't trust you. You're too jolly by half, and besides, I think you're making fun of me."

Simon's chuckle was deep, coming from low in his throat. "Making fun of you, my dear? Why, of course I am. Bloody hell, madam, what else is there for me to do—except this!"

The pistol was in his hand a moment later, probably before his former captor could even register his movement—a happy surprise of concentration and calculated movement that doubtless would give Simon reason to compliment himself later, once he was shed of the girl.

"Now," he said, as the young woman cowered against the squabs, doubtless in fear for her life, so that he considerately pocketed the pistol, "perhaps you'll allow me to have a slight verbal exchange with Hardwick concerning our destination. Yes? . . . I thought so."

He leaned forward and opened the small door, all the while keeping his interested gaze on the young woman's face. As he ordered Hardwick to turn the coach around, he conducted a cursory inventory. Figure, small and slim beneath a too-large cape and atrocious leggings and crude clogs. Face, unidentifiable beneath the slouch hat and dramatic black-silk cloth tied around the mouth and nose. Eyes—the only part truly visible—a lovely, wide, rather frightened green. He'd always had a weakness for green eyes.

"Ah, that's better," Simon said, once he had done speaking with his coachman, who had muttered a few none-too-inspiring words about lordships who drink too deeply before calling the horses to a halt, then beginning to turn the coach. "Now, to pass the time on our ride back to London, perhaps you'll be so kind as to tell me a small story?"

She pulled the silk scarf higher on her face, clearly wishing to hide her eyes, and yet unable to do so and still see him, or to keep him from noticing that her brows, although dark, hinted of a hair color no deeper than chestnut—which went quite well with her remarkably clear, milky skin. "There's nothing to tell, my lord," she said, her tone grudging, and not a little angry. "I thought you were someone else. Either let me go or turn me over to the watch when we get back to the city. I owe you no explanations."

"I hesitate to bring this to your attention, but anyone would think you were still holding the pistol, love," Simon remarked, opening a small door at the side of the coach and thus revealing a space that held a silver decanter and a half dozen small glasses. "Would you care for some brandy? There's always an unwelcome chill at dawn, don't you agree?"

She remained stubbornly silent as Simon shrugged, uncapped the decanter, and poured three fingers of brandy into one of the glasses, then threw it back, allowing his eyes to close for a moment as the liquid heat ran down his throat, warming his belly. "Ah, superb. A name, fair lady," he then said quickly, skewering her with his eyes. "Just give me a name, and we'll call quits to this entire affair. No watch, no magistrates, no gaol. Just a name—and your freedom. Whisper it, if you wish."

The small figure grew a full inch as her back went stiff and straight against the squabs. "I would die before I gave you my name, sir!"

"Good God, girl, what would I do with *your* name?" Simon asked, enjoying the young woman's daring high dudgeon in the face of total ruin. It would be easy enough to ferret out that information later—as he didn't plan on allowing her to disappear from his life quite yet. But, for the moment, another name interested him more. "I want the identity of the man for whom you planned a murder most foul this evening. After all, I might wish to warn him. Then again, if he really is a card sharp, I might just wish to stand back and enjoy the show. I'm a well-loved man, and with a reasonably good heart, or so I'm told, but I am not without my small vices."

She spread her hands as if in surrender, saying, "If it will shut you up, I'll be more than happy to tell you. His name is Noel Kinsey, the Earl of Filton, and a more odious, horrible, heartless—"

"Vile, despicable, *dangerous* man would be difficult to find," Simon interrupted, shocked to his toes, although he would not allow this young girl to know it. "Are you out of your mind? I could have had your weapon any time I wanted. Filton would have not only had it, he would have used it on you in a heartbeat. I begin to think you'd be safer if I turned you over to the watch, truly I do. Or I could order Hardwick to drive us past Bethlehem Hospital and we could have you fitted with your very own straitwaistcoat. Are you mad, child?"

"Your opinion means less than nothing to me, my lord," the infuriating girl announced, even as she pulled a second pistol from beneath that damned cape. The small sound that followed told him that the pistol had been cocked. "And now, if you'll consider my apology already rendered, I believe it is time we said good-night."

And then she kicked out both legs, sharp and hard, sending those damnable heavy clogs winging straight at his head.

Simon, acting more from a sudden anger than any attack of common sense, caught the clogs before they could do any harm and made a move toward the girl as she reached over to open the off-door of the coach. The pistol went off, nearly taking his left ear as the ball whizzed past him and plowed into the rear of the coach. Hardwick gave a shout and yanked on the reins, causing the tired, already slow-moving team to halt even as the young woman threw open the door and launched herself out of the coach.

Simon, his ears ringing from the report of the pistol, his throat clogged with blue smoke and the stench of gunpowder, reacted a full second slower than usual, bounding out of the coach in time to observe the young woman vaulting onto a saddleless horse that had been following close behind the coach and yelling to the companion holding its reins to "follow me!"

As exits went, that one was fairly dramatic, even if Simon did not consider the fact that the damned, stocking-clad female had mounted the horse from behind, landing astride on its back, and all with a fluid grace many of his male acquaintances would envy. As it was, all he could do was watch as the two horses wheeled and sped away, then approach his footman, who was still wiping sleep from his eyes as he cowered in the boot, and ask him if he hadn't thought it bloody odd that a man riding one bloody horse and leading another had been bloody following the bloody coach *ever since they'd left bloody London?*

The clogs, which had somehow ended up in Simon's hands, had gone winging into the trees lining the roadway, one following closely after the other during the course of his questioning of the footman, both shoes flung away in some heat, and with impressive force.

"Milord?" the footman explained rapidly, visibly wilting under Simon's rare verbal attack, his seldom-seen anger. "Oi thought they wuz yours, milord."

"Mine? Mine. Oh, I see now. *Mine.* Of course you did. Forgive me for not realizing that," Simon said, recovering his usual sarcastic calm as he turned back to the coach. "Take me home, Hardwick, if you please," he ordered wearily, knowing that he had probably seen the last of the young woman who had abducted him, then intrigued him with her mention of Noel Kinsey.

It was only the discovery of a small, crumpled white handkerchief on the floor of the coach that served to cheer the Viscount Brockton at all. A small white handkerchief embroidered—fairly clumsily—with the letter "C." He raised it to his nostrils to find that it smelt of lavender, and horse—and bread and butter.

Still holding the handkerchief as he drew down all the curtains and continued his search as the coach lurched its way back to Portland Place, Simon soon espied a stale crust of buttered bread wedged into a fold of the velvet squabs. He picked it up, gingerly holding it between thumb and index finger, eyeing it owlishly.

And then he smiled. He even, much to the surprise and consternation of both Hardwick and the groom, who could hear him, laughed aloud. Aloud, and long, and hard.

"What cheek! I've *got* to find her," he said at last, talking to himself. "She spent the time waiting to shoot me by having herself a bloody picnic." He shook his head even as he smiled, then stretched out his long legs on the facing seat and crossed them at the ankles, a gentleman once more feeling fully at his ease.

"God," he mused aloud, chuckling low in his throat as he drew the handkerchief beneath his fine, aristocratic nose once more, "Armand will positively adore the chit!"